OCRACOKE BETWEEN THE STORMS

EDWARD P. NORVELL

OCRACOKE
between
THE STORMS

A Story of Love and Healing on the Outer Banks

Cover photograph by Ann Ehringhaus

Library of Congress Cataloging-in-Publication Data

Norvell, Edward P.
  Ocracoke between the storms : a story of love and healing on the Outer Banks / by Edward P. Norvell.
    pages cm
  ISBN 978-0-89587-610-2 (alk. paper) — ISBN 0-89587-610-8 (alk. paper) 1. Bereavement—Fiction. 2. Communities—North Carolina—Outer Banks—Fiction. 3. Ocracoke Island (N.C.)—Fiction. I. Title.
  PS3614.O78275O28 2013
  813'.6—dc23
                        2013004708

10 9 8 7 6 5 4 3 2 1

To Susan, Mary Linn, and Philip
and to the people of Ocracoke Island, our beloved second home

⚬ACKNOWLEDGMENTS⚬

Ocracoke Between the Storms is a story told with fictional characters in the real-life setting of Ocracoke Island, North Carolina, during the period of 2010-2012, complete with actual storms and real activities that occurred on the island at that time.

I want to thank the very special people of this magical island—my second home. They have a wonderful spirit of volunteerism and an enduring spirit and faith that gives them the strength to survive and thrive against great odds in a place that is both hostile and idyllic.

The forces of nature have a direct effect on the daily lives of the residents of Ocracoke on a scale that is hard for outsiders to understand. This in turn gives them a genuine humility, a tolerance for others, a special joie de vivre, and a deep understanding of their place in the universe in the face of the awesome power of nature.

2010

≈CHAPTER ONE≈

Luke Harrison was drawn to the angry, boiling surf in the inlet at the southern end of Ocracoke Island. He was ready to surrender to the waves, let them have their way with him. He had come to the Outer Banks because he had fond memories of going fishing, as a boy, with his foster father. So he outfitted his white Jeep Cherokee with rod holders and bought new fishing rods, bait, and tackle before he left Kannapolis. He drove as far as he could drive, and it had taken him here.

He wore rubber waders that smart fishermen wear in April on the Outer Banks because the water was cold. As he looked out over the churning water of the inlet, the pain was too great. The water impelled him forward.

He put down his fishing rod and began to walk into the water.

The angry, whitecapped waves hit him again and again.

When the water came to his chest, ice-cold water rushed into his waders. He had read about drowning and hypothermia, that it can be almost peaceful once you surrender to it and no longer struggle. So he continued to walk forward as the water became suddenly deeper. As it filled his waders, it began to drag him under.

Just as his head went under the shockingly cold water, he felt a sudden jolt. Something was grabbing him by the waders. It was pulling him back to shore.

When Luke's head broke the surface, he gasped, then shouted, "What are you doing?" He tried to fight the hands that had him in such a firm grip. "Leave me alone."

His savior did not listen. Instead, he continued dragging Luke out of the water by the neck of the wader. Again Luke tried to fight him, but the man was too strong. He towed Luke through the water like a lead weight, until it was shallow enough that he could pull Luke up and make him stand. He then walked Luke onto the beach and helped him out of the waders. By this time, Luke had stopped resisting. Although he was in his mid-twenties, Luke didn't have the energy to fight off this man, who appeared to be in his fifties, yet was as stout and strong as an ox. The man fetched a blanket from his pickup truck and wrapped it around Luke.

"What's your name?" the man asked, pouring a cup of hot coffee from a thermos in his truck and handing it to Luke.

"Luke," he said through shivering, purple lips.

"My name's Hank Kilgo," the man said, shaking Luke's hand; it was ice cold. Reaching into his truck for his coat, Hank asked, "Where are you from?"

"Kannapolis."

"I'm from Ocracoke, retired from the United States Coast Guard. I guess you're lucky that it was me that drove by when you went under, someone else wouldn't have known what to do."

"Yeah, lucky," Luke said, staring out over the waves, dazed and disoriented.

"What brings you here?" Hank asked.

"Fishing. I drove until the road ended."

"Where are you staying?" Hank asked.

The question seemed to confuse Luke. "Uh, the Park Service campground, I guess."

"My wife and I have plenty of room at our house since our boy left and moved to the other side of the country."

"I don't have much money," Luke said, turning to look at Hank.

"Don't worry about that," Hank said, slapping Luke on the back. "Let's get some dry clothes on you, then you can follow me to my place. Cora will fix us one of the best fried fish dinners you have ever eaten."

"That would be nice, but I don't want to be any trouble," Luke said, his hands clasped around the cup of coffee. He started to shiver again.

"No trouble," Hank said, pulling out his spare set of clothes from a metal box in the back of the truck. "With our boy gone, Cora doesn't know what to do with herself. She loves to cook for hungry young guys."

Hank handed Luke a dry flannel shirt and some old chino pants.

After Luke dried off, warmed up, and changed into the dry clothes, he climbed into his Jeep and followed Hank to his house in Widgeon Woods.

≈

The large A-frame house, built in the 1970s, stood on pilings. It had gray board-and-batting siding, a deck that ran around it on three sides, and a screen porch in back that overlooked the marshes. As they pulled up in front of the house, Hank's wife came to the door.

As Hank got out of his truck, he said, "Cora, I met this man on the beach and asked him to join us for dinner. I didn't think you would mind."

Cora looked at Hank real hard. "Hank Kilgo, when are going to stop bringing home people for dinner without calling me first. I think I have enough," she said. "I went to the fish house this afternoon and picked up some fresh flounder. I can always make some more slaw, and we have plenty of potatoes."

"I don't want to be any trouble, ma'am," Luke said, sheepishly.

"You are no trouble. It is not you. It is this crazy husband of mine that I have a complaint with."

Luke looked askance at Hank as Hank said, "Cora, Luke nearly drowned on the beach. I brought him home to warm him up and feed him. Back off, okay?"

"Oh, my goodness. I am so sorry," she said, her whole demeanor changing. She took hold of Luke's shoulder and led him into the house.

"Here, I'll fix you a hot cup of coffee."

"Thank you, ma'am, but if it's too much trouble I can leave," Luke said.

"No, it's no trouble at all. I'm sorry I was so unwelcoming, son. I have a son about your age who I haven't seen in a long time," she said with a kind smile.

"I'll be happy to help you in the kitchen, ma'am. I can even cook."

"Be careful, boy. Don't show me up with Cora. Before long, she'll be asking me to help her cook, too," Hank said, as they entered the house.

"That'll be the day," Cora said, leading the way into the kitchen. She was tall and thin with short, dark, salt-and-pepper hair. Luke could tell right away that she was a bundle of energy. She looked to be in her mid-fifties.

Luke went to the bathroom and came out in the hallway where he heard, Hank whisper to Cora, "I asked him to spend the night. When I found him on the beach, I had to pull him out of the water. He got in over his waders, and the waves pulled him down. He was disoriented, and I didn't want to leave him by himself."

"That's fine, but he can't stay here forever," she said.

When Luke stepped out of the hall into the kitchen, Cora instantly put him to work. He helped her cut cabbage and make slaw, then he buttered the potatoes and put them in the oven.

Soon they sat down to eat. As they passed dishes around the table, Cora noticed the gold wedding ring on Luke's hand and asked him, "Are you married, Luke?"

"I was married," he said, looking down and taking a bite of fried fish.

This piqued Cora's curiosity.

"You were married?"

"My wife died in an automobile accident in January."

"Oh, my God! I'm so sorry," Cora said, her face reddening. She turned to Hank. "Did you know this?"

"No," Hank said.

"I see," Cora said, and immediately changed the subject. "Do you want some ketchup for your fish, Luke? My boy, Hank Junior, always puts ketchup on his fish."

"No, ma'am, but thank you for asking."

"Hank told me that he invited you to stay with us tonight. After supper, I'll show you your room."

"Thank you, ma'am. I don't think I have ever tasted fried flounder as good as this in my life. Back home in Kannapolis, the only flounder we get is frozen."

"This is fresh, just off the boat. I bought it this morning at the fish house. Nothing better than fresh fish. I don't think I would ever eat frozen fish after eating fresh."

"I can see why," Luke said with a big smile.

After dinner, Cora took Luke upstairs to her son's room.

"Hank Junior stuck around Ocracoke for several years after graduating from college," Cora told Luke as she picked up a picture of his college graduation on the dresser. "He worked in restaurants and did odd jobs, but then he fell in love with an island girl and decided that he needed to make a living and raise a family. That is when he joined the Coast Guard like his father. He is stationed in Oregon, and we rarely see him. I left his room just like he had left it so he would know he always had a place to come back to."

Luke brought his things in from the Jeep and got settled. He took off his clothes to take a shower and looked in the mirror on the back of the bathroom door. He hadn't looked at himself in a full-length mirror in a long time. He had been an athlete in high school, the quarterback for his football team. Since then, doing construction work outdoors kept him in good shape. He was six feet two inches tall and still had an athletic build with broad shoulders tapering down to a slim waist and hips. He had lost twenty pounds since he lost his wife, so he was even leaner than normal. Ripped and shredded, that was what he and his buddies wanted to be back in the days when they worked out in the gym. They would be jealous to see him now, his body was stripped of what little body fat he had gained since he married, every detail of his musculature stood out. His sandy brown hair was cut short, and his eyes were blue. His wife had often told him how handsome he was, but so what, he thought, little good all that did now. Handsome couldn't keep the pain away. Handsome couldn't bring Karen back. His image mocked him. Outwardly, he was the picture of health. Inwardly, he felt sick, weak, and powerless.

Luke dreaded the night. He hated to sleep because in sleep he couldn't escape the dreams.

≈

It was Saturday, January 16, and Karen was going shopping at Concord Mills Mall.

"Don't you want to go, honey?" Karen asked him.

"No, I need to stay here and get some work done. Thanks, though. You go on and have fun."

"Okay. I'll be back in a few hours." That was the last time he saw her alive.

He had stayed home to work on some cabinets in the shop for a customer. Karen had a good job as a personal banker at First Bank in Concord, and Luke worked for a contractor building houses. For the past few years, with all the building going on in the Charlotte area, there was plenty of work to go around, and Luke was a good carpenter. Some even called him an artisan. He never found a cabinetry challenge that he couldn't meet. After a while, people began to call him to do custom cabinetwork, which he could do in his shop in the backyard. He and Karen had just bought an old Cannon Mills house that he was renovating. Her father had loaned them the money for the down payment. Karen's father, Samuel Coltraine, used to work in management at Cannon Mills before it went out of business, then he got a job with the telephone company.

Luke was still amazed that Karen had chosen him. He never thought someone as beautiful and smart as Karen would even give him a second look, but she did. And they fell in love when he was a senior and she was a junior in high school. They married after Karen got out of college. They were ready to start a family. They were so happy.

Luke had grown up in a series of foster homes. He was taken from his mother when he was six. She had worked at the mill before being arrested for possession of cocaine and going to prison. He had little contact with her after that. He never knew his father, who died when Luke was a baby.

Some of his foster parents were good to him, like the Andersons who had seen him through high school. Gary Anderson took him on fishing trips to the Outer Banks with his other boys. It was then that Luke learned to fish and first saw the Outer Banks. Other foster parents were not so good.

When the woman from the highway patrol called and asked for Luke, he honestly had no idea what she was calling about. "There has been an accident. You need to go to the hospital emergency room."

If he had only gone with Karen, he thought, he could have done something. He could have driven. He could have avoided that truck. If not, he would have been killed with her. He would rather have died than live without her.

He woke up in a cold sweat and began to sob quietly.

≈

That morning Hank and Cora got up at 7:00. Cora called up to Luke. "Luke, you want some breakfast? Scrambled eggs and homemade fish cakes?"

"Yes, ma'am," Luke said, walking out of his bedroom and looking over the railing down to the kitchen below. He wore blue jeans and was pulling on a white T-shirt.

"Want to go scalloping?" Hank asked. "Saturday and Sunday anybody can harvest a bushel per person; that is two five-gallon buckets. During the week, the commercial guys do it with a license. This season the sound is full of scallops. Better get them before the birds do."

"Sure," Luke said, entering the kitchen. "I've never been scalloping. What do you do?"

"Well, because it's cold, you need to wear waders," Hank said. "Basically, we walk through the shallow water in the sound, look for birds diving, and pick the scallops off the sandy bottom. They look like dark rocks and mostly hide in shallow grasses. Sometimes they even scoot off when you approach. I use a rake to stir them up. It's great fun, and if we're lucky, we can have ourselves a fine meal tonight."

Hank turned to his wife. "Cora, you gonna come?"

9

"Naw, I'll let you men do that. I'll stay here and clean up."

"Aw, come on. It's a warm sunny day, a great day to get outside. You can clean anytime."

Luke saw Cora look out the kitchen window across the salt marsh that bordered their property. The sky was cloudless and there was little wind; the sun glistened in the slick brown marsh grass. "Okay. It is a pretty day, but I'm not staying out all day. When I get tired, I want to come in." She looked at Luke. "Hank doesn't know when to stop. When he gets caught up in something, he loses track of time and forgets that other people are with him. I'll go along to keep him from wearing you out."

Luke's waders were still wet from the day before, so he borrowed some from Hank. They were tighter than his and hard to pull on. He wore only socks and underwear in them, because they were too snug if he wore his pants. He also wore a white T-shirt and a tan Columbia quick-dry nylon shirt. He strapped sandals over the feet of his waders. Cora had her own waders that were perfectly suited for her. Hank wore some older ones that were a little small for him, but after much effort, he tugged them on.

They loaded a ten-foot aluminum boat plus oars and six five-gallon buckets into the back of Hank's truck. They also took bottled water.

Cora packed some pimento cheese sandwiches wrapped in plastic sandwich bags.

"I know that if we get into the scallops, Hank won't want to come home to eat lunch. I always think about the next meal. Hank doesn't until it's time to eat."

It was April, cool and sunny, as they drove out the long, sandy Park Service road that led to the south point. The long road ran through the middle of the salt marsh. Fields of shimmering marsh grass fanned out on either side of them. The road was bordered on both sides with tidal trenches filled with brown brackish water. The marshes were filled with colonial waterfowl. A delicate white ibis stepped gently in the narrow trenches, looking for food. In the distance, a clump of cedar was filled with white herons. Waterfowl flew in a broken V-formation above them. About halfway out the road, Hank turned right onto a side road that led to a sand berm and a tidal creek that wound its way through the marshes out to the sound. They pulled the little boat out of the truck and hauled it over the berm and into the water where Hank pulled it to the sound. Cora and Luke walked along a sandy path that ran beside the marsh creek.

The path ended at the sound near Teach's Hole. The water was only a few inches deep.

"I brought the boat to hold our gear, and when the water gets too deep we can climb in it. When it is six or more inches deep, the boat will float," Hank said, dragging the boat out of the creek and onto the sandy flat that opened into the sound. Luke took one corner, and they both lifted the front and pulled the boat through the dark wet sand toward the water.

Hank pointed in the distance. "That's Springer's Point, where the pirate Blackbeard and his men camped before he was killed on November 22, 1718, at the hands of Lieutenant Robert Maynard and his crew from Virginia."

A bank of dark green live oak trees jutted into the sound before the village. Behind the village stood the squat whitewashed Ocracoke Lighthouse. Beyond Springer's Point were houses scattered along the shore of the sound facing southwest.

"Is the lighthouse still working?" Luke asked.

"Yep, built in 1823 and still in operation," Hank said. "Seventy-five feet tall, brick, the oldest continuously operating lighthouse in North Carolina. It still has its original Fresnel lens, which shines a constant beam of light. It can be seen for fifteen miles out to sea."

They stopped dragging the boat when the water got deep enough to float it. Hank immediately took off trudging through the shin-deep water toward a dark area of the clear water, where he knew the seagrass grew and where the scallops could be found. The boat was tied with a rope to his waist.

"What are we looking for?" Luke asked Cora, as they followed Hank through the water.

She reached down into the clear water, scooped up an open scallop shell, and held it in her hand. "This is one that has been opened, but in the water they look like rocks."

"Do you have to dig them up, or do they lie on top of the sand?" Luke asked.

"They mostly lie on the top of the sand, but they like to hide in the grass—like this!" she said, reaching down in the water and plucking an unopened scallop.

Luke bent down and picked up what looked like a dark round rock covered with green growth, "Is this one?"

"Yes, that's it," Cora said, bending to pick up another one. Soon they were surrounded by scallops, picking them up and dropping them into their buckets, which floated on top of the water. The buckets were held up by oval net floats that Hank had attached to them with a rope. Then, suddenly, there were no more scallops. White seagulls swooped overhead diving into the water and dropping shells on exposed sand.

"What are they doing?" Luke asked.

"The birds see the scallops more easily than we do," Hank said. "They pick them up and drop them on the sand to open the shells, then they swoop down and eat the meat. Haven't you seen the shells on the road and in parking lots in town and near the ferry?"

"Yeah, I wondered how they got there."

"Birds. The birds are having a regular feast," Hank said, watching them lift into the air, drop the shells, then swoop down to peck open the shells and swallow the tender meat inside.

"Hank always says follow the birds. They will show you where the scallops are," Cora said, reaching into the water for a shell, picking it up. Seeing that it was already opened, she dropped it back in the water.

With the sun reflecting on the water, Luke had to shield his eyes to see inside Hank's bucket; it was about half full. His was a quarter full.

"How do you open them?" Luke asked, picking up a tightly closed bi-valve.

"Best way is to take them home and lay them out in the sun until they open up themselves," Cora said. "When that happens, you insert a flat knife and twist it open."

"Do you eat everything inside, like an oyster?"

"No, the only thing you eat is the thick muscle that holds the two shells together. It looks like a plug of white meat. You wash it and throw out the rest," Hank said, bending to investigate another shell.

≈

After they had picked scallops for an hour, the wind began to pick up. They were a quarter mile from shore. The water was up to their knees and thighs in places. They each had filled one bucket and began to work on their second buckets.

"Maybe we should start heading back. The wind can whip up this water pretty quickly," Hank said, looking at the little whitecaps forming on the water between them and Springer's Point.

It was harder coming back than it was going out. The water had risen a bit and walking through it was a workout. Luke could feel the sun on his face and the cool breeze from the land. He could smell the salt air. He could also feel the soreness in his thighs as he pushed through the water. The temperature was in the sixties but pleasant. His waders stayed dry so he did not feel the cold water. Hank pulled the boat carrying the scallop buckets behind him. When they finally got to the shore, they were all exhausted. Hank pulled the boat through the creek to the berm, and Cora and Luke walked the sandy trail back. They all hauled the boat out and into the back of the truck.

When they got back to the house, they laid the scallops out on the deck and waited for them to open up. When one opened, Hank stuck a flat kitchen knife in the slit between the two shells and pried it open further. He then carved around the white muscle, put it in a plastic tub, and moved on to the next one. Soon Luke got the hang of it, and before long, they had shucked all the scallops and brought them to Cora to cook for supper. She bagged what she did not use and put them in the refrigerator. She made some mayonnaise-based slaw and hushpuppies to go with the scallops, which she sautéed in a butter and lemon sauce.

As the sun set, the sky turned pastel red, orange, and yellow. When they sat down to eat, the sun began to set past the marsh and the sound beyond.

After tasting his first scallop, Hank asked, "Luke, I have a job that I need some help with tomorrow. Do you think you can join me?"

"Yes, sir. What time in the morning?"

"Be down at 6:00 in the morning. We can eat breakfast, then head out about 6:30."

≈

Luke went to bed about 10:00 that night. Hank stayed up a bit longer, then headed to bed himself. Cora said she liked to stay up and watch the late night news at 11:00.

The next morning at 6:00, Luke was dressed and ready to go. Hank slid some toast into the oven, and they both ate a bowl of cereal before heading out to the job.

"You know how to swing a hammer?" Hank asked as he backed out of the driveway.

"Yes, sir, I worked as a carpenter in Kannapolis and had my own cabinet shop. People like my work. I love working with my hands. Not much for book learning, I did graduate from high school and got my two-year associate degree from Rowan Cabarrus Community College."

"Well, we just finished putting in the pilings for a house I'm building in Oyster Creek, and we're getting ready to start framing it. The homeowner and I are working on the design of the kitchen, and I'd like to see what you think about the layout and design of the cabinets. You may have some ideas that I haven't thought of. The homeowners are real nice people, a retired couple from Little Washington planning to move to Ocracoke when they finish the house."

Luke and Hank worked on preparing the pilings for the framing.

"Looks like you've done this before," Hank said.

"Yes, sir. I've worked with contractors since I was eighteen years old. I reckon I have done about everything there is to be done on a construction site. I mainly work residential but also some commercial. I've only been doing cabinetwork for a couple of years," Luke said.

After they ate lunch at the job site, Hank pulled out his design for the cabinets.

"The homeowners told me what they wanted, and I came up with this. They haven't seen it yet, though. What do you think?"

Luke suggested raising the height of the countertops in the bathrooms; most homes make them higher now, he said. He also recommended arranging the kitchen cabinets in a way that made a more efficient use of the space.

"Great ideas," Hank said. "I want you to work on them in my workshop when the time comes. Can you do that for me?"

"Sure. I'll be happy to, but I usually make twenty dollars an hour."

"Wages are a little less on Ocracoke. I can offer you eighteen dollars an hour, plus you can stay with us until you find something else."

Hank waited while Luke thought it over. "It's a deal," Luke said and shook Hank's hand.

∾Chapter Two∾

The visitation was at Whitley's Funeral Home in Kannapolis, North Carolina. Luke was in shock; it was like he was sleepwalking. He couldn't believe what had happened. Samuel Coltraine quickly took charge. He had lost his wife five years earlier to breast cancer. He was grieving just like Luke, but Samuel was older and more experienced in matters like this. As he had done when his wife passed away, Samuel steeled himself and knew arrangements must be made. He could mourn privately later.

"We have to make arrangements," Samuel told Luke. "People want to pay their respects, and Karen had lots of friends. We need to meet with our minister and have the funeral at First Baptist in Concord."

Luke had never been through anything like this before. He was so devastated, he didn't even think about a funeral or making arrangements at the funeral home. His father-in-law did not like him, but at this time, they had to work together. Luke had to depend on him for everything. He was incapable of acting on his own.

The visitation was a blur. It seemed like hundreds of people came, mainly family friends of the Coltraines, a prominent family in Concord and Kannapolis. Also people came from the bank, and, of course, there were friends from high school and college. It seemed to Luke that most people came to speak to Mr. Coltraine, not to him. They looked at Luke with pity and didn't really know what to say to him. Karen's brother and his wife and two children were there as were her sister and her sister's husband. One person who came through the line was Luke's mother.

"I read about it in the paper," she said, taking Luke's hand. Luke could see Mr. Coltraine look down his nose when he saw her.

"I am sorry for your loss, Luke," Mary Harrison said. "I think about you a lot. I'm sorry I gave you up, Luke, but that was the best I could do. It doesn't mean I don't think about you and love you." She looked older than her fifty years. Her skin was leathered, her hair had gray streaks, and she looked like she had lived a hard life.

"Thank you for coming," Luke said. From time to time, his mother had tried to contact him. Occasionally, she would call him at Christmas and want to see him. His foster parents were wary of the contact but did not prevent it. He had not seen his mother in several years.

"What is she doing here?" Samuel Coltraine asked between visitors. He was well aware of Mary's story. He had been her boss at the mill when she went to prison.

Luke simply said, "I guess she wanted to pay her respects."

Another couple who came through the line brought a smile to Luke's face. They were the Andersons, the couple with whom he had lived during his high school years. They were good people, and he liked them. They knew Karen and were there when they were married. They stayed in touch with Luke and treated him like a son.

"Luke, I am so sorry for your loss," Lucinda Anderson said, with tears in her eyes. "Karen was the kindest, sweetest girl. She was always good to us, and I know she loved you. I can't believe she's gone."

"I am sorry, son," Gary Anderson said, he was choked up and could barely speak he was so upset. "She will be missed. You take care of yourself."

"Thank you," Luke said, taking both their hands. "I have thought a lot about y'all recently. You know Karen thought a lot of you. You were the closest I ever had to a real family, and I thank you for that."

The casket was closed during the visitation, but before the guests came they opened it for the family. She looked so alive, Luke thought, her dark brown hair all coifed as if for church. She was made up; her cheeks were rosy, and her lips red with lipstick. She wore a light blue church dress that matched her eyes when she was alive. She also wore a white gold stick pendant with three little diamonds on it that he had given to her on their fourth anniversary last June. It was her favorite piece of jewelry, and he wanted her to wear it even in death. It needed to be with her, he'd told the funeral director. He bent down to kiss her; her lips were cold. He shuddered and started to cry uncontrollably.

Karen's sister put her arms around him. She was kind and liked him, not like Samuel Coltraine or her brother. Samuel paid for the casket and the funeral. Luke did not have the money. Samuel had tried to get Karen to force Luke into signing a prenuptial agreement before they were married, but she would have nothing to do with it. The Coltraines had money, and Karen had inherited money from her grandmother. Still, Samuel Coltraine had made sure his daughter's money was tied up in trust, so Luke couldn't get it.

The church was full. It was such a tragedy that such a promising young woman would be taken before her time. The preacher waxed on too long, Luke thought. He mainly talked about Karen's family, her father and brother and sister. They were prominent benefactors of the church. The minister did not know Luke and didn't have much to say about him or Karen's marriage to him.

At the graveside, Luke solemnly stared at the casket. It was so final. When the preacher said, "Ashes to ashes, dust to dust," and sprinkled ashes on the casket, Luke lost it. Grief is contagious. Karen's sister began to sob, and her brother had to wipe tears from his eyes. Samuel was stoic, solemn, and showed no emotion.

Before the funeral, Karen's sister had given Luke a "chill pill." "

Here, take this, it will help," she said.

The rest of the day was a blur. Luke couldn't remember much about it. But in that moment at the graveside, no drug could dull his pain.

As soon as Luke could get away, he went home and went to bed, crying himself to sleep. He kept blaming himself. "If only I had gone with her. If I was driving, maybe I could have avoided that truck."

For the first week, he couldn't work, but then he knew he had to work. He needed something to take his mind off of the tragedy.

Samuel came by to see Luke a week after the funeral.

"Luke, we are going to have to go to the courthouse and file papers for her estate."

Luke was twenty-six, and Karen was twenty-five. They had been married for four and a half years and had talked about starting a family, but they were both working so hard, that they had decided to put it off. Luke had no family and no money. Karen made car payments on her car, a late model Nissan. Luke's Jeep was so old that it was paid for. He had tools in his workshop, but he had paid for them as he brought money in. They almost had the furniture paid off.

Karen had not worked long enough to accrue any money in retirement. She had a small twenty-five-thousand-dollar life insurance policy. Luke used this money to pay off her car and their credit cards and make the final payments on the furniture. The money she had inherited from her grandmother was part of a family trust. Since it was not part of the estate, Luke had no claim to it.

The highway patrol determined that the accident was no one's fault. The truck driver had swerved to avoid hitting another car that was dodging a blown out tire in the road. When he did that, he sideswiped Karen's car and she lost control, running down an embankment into a tree. There didn't seem to be a legitimate wrongful death claim, and the truck driver was devastated. Luke didn't want to sue. He didn't have the stomach for it, but he got calls from several lawyers trying to talk him into it.

The only real issue that was unresolved was the house. In Luke's mind, it didn't belong to him. The only reason he owned it was because Samuel Coltraine had lent Karen thirty thousand dollars for the down payment. There was nothing said about repaying that loan. As long as Luke kept working, he could make his house payment, but he could not afford to pay his father-in-law back.

Luke didn't want the house; he couldn't live there. It was *their* house. He couldn't walk into it without thinking of Karen. Her influence was everywhere.

Luke had no real family in Kannapolis. There was little to hold him there. With the decline of the local housing market and the economy, work had dropped off dramatically. Luke decided to deed the house over to Samuel. He sold the furniture but kept the shop equipment and his tools. Karen's car was totaled, but he got some money from the insurance company.

Luke knew that Samuel was thinking about the house and the money Luke owed him on it.

"Mr. Coltraine, I know what you are thinking, and I'm going to save you the trouble. I want to deed this house over to you. You can do what you want with it. All I ask is that you allow me to keep my shop equipment and a few boxes of personal items in the shop until I am ready to pick them up. Is that a deal?"

"That's fine, Luke," Samuel said, visibly relieved. "The real-estate market has taken a downturn so there is no need to sell it right away. I figure I can rent it. That should cover the house payment and upkeep. You can keep your stuff here. No renters need to use that shop. But I can't keep it forever. You will need to find other arrangements after a year. Is that understood?"

Within three weeks, Samuel Coltraine's lawyer had the paperwork done. Luke signed on the dotted line and was free to go, no strings attached.

He loaded up the Jeep with his clothes and as many hand tools as he could carry and headed for the Outer Banks. With the insurance money, he bought fishing gear and put a bumper on the front of his Jeep with metal pipes to hold the fishing rods. He put the rest of the money in a savings account.

≈ CHAPTER THREE ≈

Luke tossed and turned as he slept in the upstairs bedroom in the Kilgos' house. Over and over again, he kept seeing Karen on that last day, how she stood in the doorway, waving good-bye, then driving off in her car. He saw himself going back into his shop to work on the kitchen-cabinet job. He liked to play the music loud in his workshop; it helped him concentrate. He heard loud music now and what sounded like angelic voices. Was he awake or was he dreaming? He opened his eyes, and he still heard it. It was opera, and it was coming from downstairs. He walked out of his room and looked down at the open living room with the large window that went to the vaulted ceiling. There was Hank, stretched out on the sofa, his eyes closed, completely engrossed.

"What is that?" Luke asked, wearing cotton gym shorts and no shirt.

"What do you think it is? It's opera," Hank said. "In fact, it is an aria from *Madame Butterfly*. Do you like it?"

"I hadn't really thought about it. I haven't heard much opera. It sounds nice, but it's not really my taste," Luke said, kind of puzzled.

"I am an opera nut. Cora doesn't like it as much as I do, so when she is out, I like to play it, really loud." It was Saturday, and obviously Hank enjoyed relaxing to the sound of opera.

Then there was a loud knock on the back door. Hank got up from the sofa and answered the door. As Luke pulled on a white T-shirt, he heard laughter, followed by Hank calling him, "Luke, come on down. I want you to meet someone."

When Luke entered the kitchen, he saw a tall, lanky guy who looked to be about Luke's age with spiky unkempt black hair and a scruffy goatee. He was wearing black horn-rimmed sunglasses, a white T-shirt, and long gray trunks with a red stripe down the side. He had a wide grin and had slung his arm around Hank's shoulder.

"Luke, this is TMJ. He worked for me last summer. He's back from Florida, where he spent the winter. He's going to help me work on the house in Oyster Creek this summer."

"Back in Ocracoke, ready to work, man. Who is this dude?" TMJ asked, looking Luke over. Luke was suddenly aware of how he looked—barefoot in gray gym shorts and T-shirt, his hair uncombed and messy.

"This is Luke Harrison," Hank said. "He will be working with us this summer, too. Pull up a chair. Do you want some coffee?" Hank pulled a couple of mugs from the kitchen cabinet and poured TMJ a cup of coffee. "How about you, Luke? Coffee?"

"Sure," Luke said, sitting in a chair at the kitchen table.

"Tell us about Florida. Where did you end up? Last I heard you were headed to the Keys."

"Yeah, man, I tried to find work in Miami, but if you can't speak Spanish, you may as well forget it, so I wandered down the coast until I ended up in Key West. I met this woman who let me stay with her, then I got a job at a shop on Duval Street."

"What kind of shop?" Hank asked.

"Well, it was sort of a—a sex shop."

"A sex shop?" Hank asked, surprised. "How the hell did you end up working in a sex shop?"

"It was the only thing I could find. Anyway, they paid good money, and it was only for the winter," TMJ said, doctoring his coffee with two heaping teaspoons of sugar and enough milk to turn it almost white. "Now I'm back in Ocracoke. Hey, it is really good to see you. How is Cora?"

"She's doing fine," Hank said. "She's in yoga class this morning. So I thought I'd listen to a little opera. You know how she hates opera."

"Yeah, I love it too, man. Don't get to listen to it often though," TMJ said.

TMJ was the kind of guy who filled up a room when he entered it. He had a big smile and a larger-than-life story. And he was physically big, six feet six inches, and long limbed. You couldn't miss him if you wanted to. Luke listened as TMJ told Hank about his adventures in Key West.

"Yeah, I lived with this woman, Angela, who is a few years older than me. She is divorced with two kids. I think her ex has custody because they didn't live with her, which suited me. Not that I don't like kids or anything. I'm just not ready for that, and they get in the way of partying. Anyway we partied a lot, then she up and threw me out one night. We had been up all night screwing. Then we got into this huge fight, and she kicked me out. Threw my stuff on the sidewalk and slammed the door shut in my face. I found a room after that, and that's when I met Lynn. She is eighteen and cute as a button. She said she ran away from home and ended up in Key West. Anyway, she moved in with me, and we had a great time together. She looked older than she was and had a fake ID so she went to the bars with me, but we mostly partied in my room."

"Sounds like you were busy in Key West," Hank said, topping off TMJ's cup.

"Yeah, I was busy, what part of it I can remember."

"What does TMJ stand for?" Luke asked.

"Thomas Michael Joiner, TMJ for short. Do you have a nickname?"

"Just Luke Harrison, no nickname," Luke said, taking a sip from his black coffee. Suddenly, he remembered the first time he met Karen's father and Mr. Coltraine's reaction when he heard Luke's name. He could feel the contempt in Samuel's voice. The Coltraines lived in a big house in Concord. He knew the former millworkers all too well and didn't want his daughter marrying the son of one.

"The only other Harrison I knew was a Mary Harrison. She worked at Cannon but didn't last long with us. Got mixed up with the wrong crowd and started using drugs. We fired her," Samuel Coltraine said. "You any relation?"

~

"Wake up, man, you just, like, zoned out," TMJ said, popping Luke on the shoulder.

"I was just thinking that's all."

Hank put his hand on TMJ's arm and looked long and hard at him. "TMJ, I got something I want to show you in the shop."

"What is it?" TMJ said, shooting up from his chair.

"I want to show you some really nice kitchen cabinets that this woman special ordered from me. She's from Washington, D.C. She bought some stained-glass windows in an antique shop and wanted me to build them into the cabinets. It has been a challenge, but I think they are really going to be beautiful."

"Sure, sounds interesting. I'd like to see them," TMJ said, grabbing his coffee cup and following Hank out the back door to the shop outside.

"Come on out, Luke."

"I need to brush my teeth and wash my face, then I'll be out," Luke said.

⪦Chapter Four⪧

May was a busy month on Ocracoke. The whole island was sprucing up to get ready for the summer. After the summer came, there would be little time for anything but catering to the tourists. The island thrived on tourism. It was the lifeblood of the community, but locals were ambivalent about the influx of tourists. Although they said they preferred the quiet wintertime to the summer, they also depended on the money that came in during the summer.

Luke quickly discovered that Cora and Hank were consummate volunteers in a community of volunteers. Cora volunteered at the Ocracoke Preservation Society Museum's gift shop, which was located near the Cedar Island/Swan Quarter ferry docks on Silver Lake. Both Hank and Cora volunteered for the fire department—Hank was a fireman, and Cora helped run the fire department's many fundraisers, including Bingo Night.

Hank loved the island history and was always dropping in a fact here and a story there. Hank told Luke that Ocracoke started as a community of pilots, who helped guide ocean-going vessels through the inlet. It grew into a village after Blackbeard's quartermaster William Howard bought it in the mid-1700s. It was a thriving port by the time of the American Revolution. Large sailing ships unloaded their cargo onto smaller boats that allowed supplies to make it through the shallow waters of the sound and on to the ports of New Bern and Little Washington on the mainland. On the return trip, supplies came from the mainland, which were loaded onto the ocean-going vessels at Ocracoke and Portsmouth. Portsmouth was located across the inlet from Ocracoke. After hurricanes closed off easy access to Portsmouth, Ocracoke thrived. Portsmouth eventually withered. The last two elderly residents on Portsmouth were forced to leave in the 1970s, because the government, which owned the island at that time, wasn't able to adequately supply them.

Through this long history, Ocracoke never incorporated. It had no local government, except what limited help the islanders got from mainland Hyde County. There was a county property tax but no municipal tax. As a result, there were no municipal services. There was no fire tax, but there was a limited occupancy tax, which helped fund the fire station and other necessities. The fire department did the best it could with old equipment, a fire station that was too small, and an entirely volunteer staff.

On the Saturday of Memorial Day weekend, the whole community prepared for the big event of the pre-tourist season. Held at the community center on Highway 12, which was the only highway traveling the length of the island, the festival began around five o'clock with a pig picking. Local businesses sponsored the event, so plenty of barbecue was served and the beer flowed freely.

The pig picking was followed by an auction, where local businesses, restaurants, and the large group of artists who called Ocracoke home donated their wares. After the auction came the fireman's ball. During the long winter days, there was plenty of time to kill, so music became a favorite pastime on the island. As a result, Ocracoke had a strong tradition of talented musicians. The dance, which featured the Ocracoke Rockers, the Dune Dogs, and the Aaron Caswell Band, started around 8:30.

The day of the event, Cora urged Luke to come with them to the festivities.

"It's lots of fun, and a good place to meet local people," Cora argued.

"No, thank you," Luke said. "I think I'll stay here, go to bed early, and get some rest."

"If you're going to stay here this summer, you need to get to know some local people. There are a lot of nice young people on the island your age, who you ought to meet," she said. "Doesn't do any good to sit around here and mope."

"Cora, don't push him. He needs some space. Give him time," Hank said, putting his hand on her shoulder.

"I don't think it is healthy to sit around here when there are so many nice young people in the village. He needs to get out."

"He will in due time," Hank said.

That night, Cora and Hank went by themselves to the fireman's ball. It was not a dressy affair; nothing was ever dressy on Ocracoke. However, on this occasion, Cora and Hank did dress up more than usual. Hank wore long khaki pants and a colorful shirt, while Cora wore a casual knit dress, which was really dressing up for her. Luke had never seen her in anything but shorts and T-shirts.

When they returned home about eleven o'clock, Cora told Luke about the ball, "I can't get Hank to dance with me. He used to love to dance, but now he is ready to go home about the time the music gets really cranked up."

"Yeah, I used to enjoy staying up late at night, but not anymore. Ten o'clock is my bedtime, so eleven is really late for me," Hank said, walking to his bedroom.

The next morning at breakfast, Cora showed Luke what she had bought at the auction: a plastic glow-in-the-dark Madonna enshrined in an old sewing-machine drawer. It had little baby dolls made of papier-mâché, hanging from fishing line. Made by a local artist, it was called "Working Mother."

"What in the world did you decide to buy that for?" Hank asked. "It's not useful."

"It's just as useful as that signed UNC basketball that you bought at the auction. About the only useful thing we bought was a dinner for two at the Cafe Atlantic restaurant," Cora said, holding her prize Madonna with defiance. "Besides, I think it will look nice on my bedroom dresser."

After Hank retired from the Coast Guard, he took up the remodeling business. Occasionally, he would build a new house, as he was doing
in the Oyster Creek subdivision. It was this Oyster Creek project that
necessitated the hiring of two assistants, thus the hiring of both Luke and
TMJ.

The pilings had been set in April, so they were well into framing the
house by mid-May. Hank did not have another big job lined up after the
Oyster Creek project, but the house job would last for at least six months.
After that, they would stay busy with smaller remodeling jobs, but Hank
warned Luke that he may not be able to keep TMJ and Luke both busy
full time. That meant that the two young men would probably have to
find other work in a few months. TMJ was used to this. He occasionally
went to Florida for the winter or worked on fishing or shrimp boats, or
worked doing just about anything else he could find. He had even worked
occasionally in the restaurants as a waiter or a cook.

Luke was quickly learning that, to live on Ocracoke, you had to be
able to work lots of different jobs. Luke told Hank he didn't know how
long he would stay on Ocracoke. It might be just for the summer, but he
would commit to helping Hank build the house in Oyster Creek. Luke
was content to keep on working, playing it by ear and staying as long as
he liked it.

On the first full weekend in June, the next big event of the season—
the Ocrafolk Festival—took place. The festival was always centered
around music, but there was also a crafts fair set up on School Road. The
festival started with an auction in the school gym on Friday night and
ended on Sunday with an all-star jam finale under the live oak trees near
Deep Water Theater.

During the annual festival, musicians came from all over the state.
Several stages were set up—one on Howard Street, one among the live

oaks off School Road, and one inside at the Deep Water Theater. This year, there were going to be several local bands and musicians, including Molasses Creek, Coyote, Martin Garrish, and Noah Paley. During the week, local musicians played at the Deep Water Theater, a small indoor gathering place. On one night before the festival, several local musicians jammed and played together in what was an Ocracoke version of the Grand Ole Opry.

Cora had volunteered to work at the main booth of the festival, selling T-shirts, CDs, and raffle tickets for a beautiful quilt made by local women in the quilting guild. Hank had helped set up the stages and had been working with the sound engineer.

The entire community was basically transformed by this official kick-off for the summer. This time, Luke decided he'd borrow a bike from Hank and ride down to see what was going on.

Luke soon found himself enjoying sitting under the live oak trees and listening to the continuous music on the main stage. Although it was hot, the music more than made up for any discomfort. He heard bluegrass, folk music, and local ballads as well as funky fun stuff and fusion bands. One of the highlights was listening to famous storyteller Donald Davis tell his traditional stories about growing up in the North Carolina mountains.

Luke also enjoyed watching the people—there were lots of old hippies, some balding, some with long gray beards, and ponytails. There were also plenty of single people as well as young couples with babies and strollers—all swaying back and forth to the music. One guy almost fell off the low branch of an oak tree, where he had fallen asleep. Most people just sat in lawn chairs and watched the activities. Plenty of food was provided in booths along School Road that were staffed by volunteers from the local school and area restaurants.

Luke eventually wandered over to the Howard Street stage, which was located on a dirt road that wound through live oak trees, ancient cedars, and old houses with white picket fences in front. Luke imagined this was what "Old Ocracoke" looked like before paved roads and modernization. As he strolled toward the stage, Luke noticed several small family cemeteries. He had learned that there were small cemeteries scattered all around the island. They could be located behind homes or beside the road; some even dated as far back as the eighteenth and nineteenth centuries.

When TMJ ran into Luke, he asked Luke to join his friends who were on their way to SmacNally's, a bar on Silver Lake. Sitting at the outdoor bar at SmacNally's, Luke looked over the harbor filled with sailboats as he drank his beer. Docked at the pier at SmacNally's were several charter fishing boats. As they drank their beer, TMJ told Luke that he knew most of the captains and their mates, because he had mated on some of the boats himself. He had also bartended at SmacNally's. TMJ introduced Luke to their bartender, who was the high school physical education teacher during the off-season. Luke learned that it was common for teachers to make extra money by working in the restaurants and bars during the summer. Finding affordable housing on the island during the summer wasn't easy, as real-estate prices soared to accommodate the influx of tourists. As a result, the year-round residents did whatever they could to make ends meet.

"Sure a lot of people," Luke said, watching the crowd build at Smac-Nally's.

TMJ nodded. "There are only about eight hundred permanent residents but during the summer, this place explodes with thousands of visitors."

Luke asked about the scene in front of them. The harbor was surrounded by houses, restaurants, businesses, the fish house, docks, boats, and lots of trees. TMJ pointed out the outlet from Silver Lake harbor to Pamlico Sound and told Luke the locals called it "the ditch." "For a few days in August, the sun sets directly over the ditch," TMJ said. "Man, it's beautiful."

TMJ pointed out the various landmarks around the harbor. To the right were two large ferries. Behind them was the former Coast Guard station, which was recently bought and renovated by the state as a teacher-enrichment center. Across the harbor to the far left was the Ocracoke Lighthouse.

Luke was impressed by the physical beauty of the island and how the people worked together to create a real community. He imagined that in most resort communities, people drifted through, finding jobs and moving on, but this was different. This was a real community where people lived, worked together, and stayed. It wasn't just about the tourists. It was about making their community a better place. He liked it. He was beginning to feel at home here. He had never felt that way in Kannapolis. He thought, this is a place I could really enjoy calling home.

≈

After night fell, Luke and TMJ rode bicycles to Dajios, a nearby bar where one of the festival bands was playing. Nothing was very far away on Ocracoke; everything could be reached by bicycle or on foot. During the summer, the narrow streets were filled with people on bicycles or with tourists walking along the sidewalks. During the summer, the locals were resigned to the fact that you never got anywhere fast in the village because of all the tourists.

Dajios had a nice screened-in bar, with ceiling fans overhead. TMJ told Luke it was a popular late-night spot, even though there was no air conditioning, which meant it could get hot. In addition to listening to the live music and enjoying the beer, Luke noticed patrons were playing darts and ring toss. The place was packed with young people, locals, and tourists. It was evident that Dajios was considered the late-night place to be on the island.

≈

"Did you enjoy the festival?" Cora asked Luke on Sunday morning.

"Yeah, I did. TMJ and I went to SmacNally's and Dajios to listen to music."

"Did you meet any girls?" Cora asked.

"I met a lot of people," Luke said, evasively.

"That's nice," she said, with a smile.

"You are not his keeper," Hank said to Cora.

"Once a mother always a mother," she said with satisfaction.

That afternoon, Luke returned to the festival to hear more live music and stayed until the festival wound down about 5:00.

He was inclined to pull back and not meet people, but he couldn't help but be drawn into the music, the fun, and vitality surrounding him. He was still in mourning. He was an observer for now, but perhaps he would once again choose to be a participant.

⁓Chapter Five⁓

One morning in mid-June, TMJ's truck was in the shop, so Hank sent Luke to pick him up. TMJ lived at the back of the island near the marshes behind the Upper Trent neighborhood. His home was a rented, old, beat-up, white-and-blue mobile home set up on concrete blocks. Luke knocked on the door, but no one answered. When Luke looked in a window, he saw TMJ sitting in front of a computer. He couldn't see what was on the screen, but TMJ was totally engrossed. When Luke knocked on the window, TMJ looked up and motioned him to the front door. Standing on the first step at the front door, Luke looked up as TMJ opened the door, stark naked. Luke was embarrassed, but TMJ was oblivious.

"Come in. I need to get dressed," TMJ said.

"Yes, you do," Luke said, as he sat on a sofa in the "living room," which was piled high with magazines.

"I don't wear clothes at home. It's too hot, and they get in the way," TMJ said from the bedroom. "If I had my way, I'd never wear clothes."

"What happens if someone like Hank comes over?"

"He doesn't mind. He's used to it."

"How about Cora?"

"I usually know when she's coming."

≈

"I forgot to tell you that TMJ is a nudist," Hank said, laughing when Luke and TMJ got out of Luke's Jeep at the work site.

"I found out soon enough."

"You ought to go with him to the so called 'nude beach;' that's where he hangs out with his friends."

"Why don't you join us this Saturday?" TMJ asked. "A bunch of us are getting together on the beach for a cookout. Some guys are bringing their kite boards, surfboards, and sea kayaks. It should be fun. It's down a remote access ramp to the beach in the middle of the island. It is away from the tourists and is a lot more private," he said with a wink.

Luke didn't say anything.

"You ought to join them," Hank said. "It will be fun. TMJ has a great group of friends."

"Thanks, Hank. I think they are great, too," TMJ said. "Lots of good-looking women, and the guys are always ready to have a good time."

"Good, clean fun, you would enjoy it," Hank said to Luke with a big smile.

≈

Dinner that night was fried chicken.

"Fried chicken, that is a treat. We usually have fish," Hank said.

"They had some good-looking chicken at the Variety Store, and we've been eating fish most every day, so I thought we would try something different," Cora said.

"It sure is good," Luke said, taking a bite of crispy chicken breast before picking up a buttered ear of corn.

"Luke's going out with TMJ and his buddies to the beach this weekend. They're having a big shindig out there," Hank said, with a devilish look.

"No! Here the boy hasn't even been with us for two months, and you are sending him out to party with that crazy bunch of kids on the beach. Does he know they run around naked out there?"

"I found out yesterday that TMJ likes to hang out naked, when I stopped by his house to pick him up," Luke said.

"Hank Kilgo. You are a devil, corrupting this nice young man. What would his family think?"

"I don't have a family," Luke said. "Remember, I was a foster child."

Momentarily embarrassed, Cora recovered quickly. "Well, it is our responsibility to look after his moral upbringing while he's living under our roof."

"Get off your high horse, Cora. He is not our son. He is working for me and staying with us until he can find a place of his own. What he does with his private time is his business."

Cora was usually not at a loss for words, but Hank was right and she knew it. Luke was twenty-six years old, living on his own, and it was not her place to mother him.

Luke hoped he would be able to find an excuse to get out of joining TMJ and his friends on the beach. He wasn't really much in the mood to party with a bunch of people after losing his wife. But after Hank had made such a valiant defense of his right to join TMJ and the others on the beach, he didn't have the heart to disappoint him and not go. Luke had worked all of his life. Other than Gary Anderson taking him fishing on the Outer Banks when he was a boy, he had never been on vacation, never really been able to just relax and enjoy himself on the water or on a beach. He wasn't sure he would know how to act.

~

Friday night came, and TMJ stopped by Hank and Cora's to talk to Luke.

"You can swim, can't you?" TMJ asked Luke.

"Yes, I learned how to swim at the YMCA in Kannapolis."

"Do you have a bathing suit?" he asked.

"No."

"You can borrow one from me," TMJ said. "You'll need one when the park rangers drive up, but they are used to us and usually don't harass us. They just drive by once or twice a day. It isn't officially a nude beach, but it is unofficially. You will also need lots of sunscreen and bring a cooler with water. I will have enough beer for both of us, and the women are bringing food. I can either pick you up in the morning, or you can meet us out there, if you want to have your own vehicle."

"I think I'll bring my Jeep. That way I can leave when I want to," Luke said.

"Understand."

≈

The next morning, Luke got up about 7:00 and ate the breakfast Cora had left him—bagels and cereal. She liked to sleep in on Saturday, so he was off before she and Hank got up.

It was a beautiful sunny day in early June. There was a nice breeze and not a cloud in the sky. When the breeze came from the ocean, it kept the bugs away. If it came from the sound, it carried mosquitoes and green heads—biting flies—with it. The wind blew from the northeast. The water was still a little cool, but it had warmed up a lot in the past few weeks and was warm enough for swimming.

When Luke drove up on the beach, there were already several trucks there and a few brightly colored kites lay on the beach for the kite boarders. Surfboards, beach chairs, and coolers littered the beach.

TMJ walked up with his arm around a girl in her mid-twenties, who had a colorful tattoo of a mermaid on her left arm. Both of them were naked and had all-over tans.

"Luke, this is my good friend Mary Ann Johnson." She extended her hand to him. She wore several silver rings on her fingers, large silver loop earrings, large black-rimmed sunglasses, and a wide-brimmed straw hat. TMJ had a few tattoos, too: a tribal tattoo on his upper arm, one on his back, and one on the calf of his right leg.

"Pleased to meet you, Luke. TMJ told me about you. I hope you have a good time today."

Luke got out of the Jeep wearing a white T-shirt and the orange nylon bathing suit TMJ had loaned him. His face, arms, and neck were tanned, but the rest of his body was white as a lily. He noticed that some of the people were naked but most wore bathing suits. The crowd was mostly folks in their twenties, but some were in their thirties, and a handful looked to be in their forties and fifties.

"The older folks are from Virginia," TMJ explained. "They are nudists and come down here just to hang out. They asked if they could join us, and we said, sure. I don't mind. Do you, Mary Ann?"

"Hell, no. I say the more the merrier," Mary Ann said, as she took a swig of bottled water.

Luke pulled up a beach chair in the circle that surrounded TMJ, who was popular with the women.

The waves were good, so some guys picked up their surfboards and ran into the water. They wore bathing suits and tight surfing shirts to keep from rubbing their skin raw on the boards. Luke watched the kiteboarding guys strap into harnesses and hook up to the rainbow-colored gigantic kites that took them out into the water. Their feet were strapped into boards that looked like snowboards or glorified skateboards. Luke watched as the wind picked up their kites and blew them into the surf. They soared above the waves, did flips in the air, and seemed to skip from wave to wave as the wind drove them down the beach.

"Now that looks like fun," Luke said.

He struck up a conversation with Anita Lorrance, who was from Rocky Mount. She had spent the last few summers working as a waitress at Howard's Pub. She wore a bathing suit. She didn't have much of a tan either, so she wore a white cover-up.

"I guess we are going to have to get a tan some time," she said, taking off her cover-up and asking Luke to put sunscreen on her back.

"Yeah, I guess I do too if I am going to be working outdoors all summer," Luke said, removing his white T-shirt and letting Anita put sunscreen on his back. He admired Anita's body as he rubbed sunscreen on her. Her body was slim, firm, and well formed. She had short dark hair and brown eyes.

As more people drove up, more coolers, filled with water, soft drinks, and beer, appeared on the beach. A few of the guys broke out the beer before noon, but most waited until after they ate lunch to start drinking. Some of the girls put out sandwich stuff and chips on a folding table on the sand. Several guys started to play corn hole, a beach game where they threw small sand bags into a hole in a large sheet of plywood propped up at an angle. About this time, a park ranger drove up. All the nudists either pulled on their bathing suits or wrapped towels around themselves. The ranger, who knew TMJ, tipped his hat and drove on down the beach to check on the turtle nests. It was not illegal to have beer on the beach, but they could not have the hard stuff.

After they ate lunch, almost all the guys decided to get into the beer. Some of the women opened wine coolers; some drank beer with the guys. Anita left after lunch to get ready for work at Howard's Pub.

Luke and TMJ joined some of the others in the water. The waves rolled in well-formed curls over a sandbar under the water a hundred yards from the beach. The surf was perfect for body surfing and surfboards, and the water was crystal clear. They swam out to the bar where they could stand and catch waves to ride in. They spent a lot of time in the water and tried their hand at surfing as well as body surfing. Luke had never been on a surfboard before and did fairly well, getting better the more he practiced. Someone also brought a sea kayak.

When they got back to shore, TMJ opened a Miller. "It is time," he said, handing Luke a can of beer.

TMJ looked at Luke's bathing suit. Some of the guys were starting to take off their bathing suits, as the day wore on, and the beer relaxed the mood. "It's time to lose that," he said, pointing to Luke's bathing suit.

Reluctantly, Luke shed the suit, exposing more snow-white flesh to the sun. He didn't realize it, but the sunscreen he put on earlier was pretty much gone after his time in the water. Nothing protected his skin from the full rays of the afternoon sun.

After they downed a beer, TMJ ran back in the water, and Luke followed him. They body surfed before they walked back up the beach for another beer. TMJ spread out a beach towel and threw one to Luke. They both sat on the towels with knees pulled up. Two girls lay face down on their towels beside them.

"Where's the fire?" one of the girls asked. She was large, with big legs, huge breasts, and a big midsection.

"What fire?" TMJ asked.

"I don't know, but I see you brought a fire hose," she said, with a big smile, staring at TMJ's sex.

"Looks like all your friend could bring to the fire is a garden hose," she said, looking at Luke.

"Luke, this is Thelma Garrish," TMJ said, introducing the woman who had made the comments.

They all drank another beer. Finally Thelma stood up, and Luke realized, that despite her size, she had a beautiful face and lovely dark brown hair. She asked TMJ to join her in the dunes. They both picked up their towels and walked into the dunes behind the beach. With TMJ occupied with Thelma, Luke laid face down on his towel to get some sun. He quickly succumbed to the beer and the sun and fell asleep.

Luke woke an hour later with TMJ shaking him. "Wake up, buddy, you are red as a beet. You need to get covered up or out of the sun." Luke looked up and saw TMJ and Thelma standing over him looking concerned. Some people were asleep on towels, while others played in the water. When Luke propped himself on his elbow, he felt the pain of sunburn on his backside.

"Here, stand up, and I'll put sunscreen all over you, then you can cover up with the towel and sit on a beach chair. This should feel better," Thelma said. Luke stood up, and Thelma spread sunscreen over his body, especially where he had burned.

"I think you are enjoying that a little too much," TMJ said, as Thelma spread the SPF 30 sunscreen over Luke's butt and back. Luke turned to face TMJ and Thelma, blushing. He didn't object to Thelma's attentions at all. When she finished, she wrapped a big beach towel around his waist covering his thighs and legs, then she directed him to a canvas beach chair low to the ground. She draped another big towel around his shoulders and put a wide-brimmed hat on his head. Sitting beside him was a very skinny girl, almost anorexic. She wore a red bikini.

"Get sunburned?" she asked Luke.

"Yeah, I fell asleep in the sun. Thelma slathered me with sunscreen and covered me up."

"I see. My name is Luane Dobbins. What's your name?"

"Luke. I work with TMJ."

"I work at the Texaco three days a week and Jason's Restaurant four nights a week. You do what you can. I've come here summers for the past several years and live in Greenville the rest of the year—mainly waitress there." Luke could see that she was nice and pretty good-looking, but her skin was leathered by the sun, and she was impossibly thin. Her belly button had a silver ring through it, and she had a small tattoo of a rose just above her bathing-suit bottom.

TMJ brought Luke a cold can of Miller. "Here, man, maybe this will cool you down!" TMJ and Thelma then ran into the water. Thelma was a big woman, but she was not self-conscious about it. She seemed almost proud of it. Compared to her, TMJ looked downright skinny. He was six foot six but weighed about 180. His chest was almost concave. He was lean and wiry, with veins showing in his arms, and neck, and a washboard stomach.

After Luke cooled down a bit, he put his bathing suit on and decided to jump in the water again. Luane joined him. TMJ and Luke body-surfed the waves, and he and Luane tried to get on the sea kayak but kept flipping it over. Luane didn't even try to get on a surfboard. She did not have the body strength to surf, but she loved the water.

The nudists from Virginia stayed together. The guys fished in the surf, and the women sunbathed. As the afternoon passed, several people left and came back. Most put their clothes back on as the day wore on. Luke and TMJ dug a pit to build a fire. Someone brought hot dogs, chips, slaw, and condiments for the hot dogs. About 6:30, people put hot dogs on sharpened sticks and roasted them over the roaring fire. They drank more beer and wine, then someone passed around a joint. Around 8:30, people began to gather everything up and load it into the cars and trucks, because the beach closed to vehicles at 9:00. Before leaving, they poured water over the fire and covered the fire pit with sand.

Luke decided to crash on the sofa at TMJ's mobile home. He had been drinking a lot throughout the day and didn't want Cora to see him that way. By 10:00, Luke was sound asleep on the sofa, wearing TMJ's bathing suit and covered by a blanket. The last thing he remembered was TMJ sitting at his computer, surfing the Internet.

≈Chapter Six≈

The following Tuesday night, Luke and TMJ went to SmacNally's to see the female arm-wrestling contest, which raised money for the Ocracoke radio station, WOVV. The place was packed with more women than men. The contestants all dressed up and took on assumed names for the contest. Even though several women tried, the same woman who had won the year before won again, hands down.

Luke stood beside a particularly attractive young woman with short dark hair and clear, intelligent, gray eyes. She had a shapely body and wore a well-fitting T-shirt and khaki shorts.

"Is this your first female arm-wrestling contest?" she asked.

"Why? Do I look like a newbie?" he smiled at her.

"I just haven't seen you before," she said, with an interested smile. "This is the second year they've done it. I tried it last year but got beat. At least the Park Service is well represented, since the winner works with us." She extended her hand. "My name is Anna Thomas. I'm a seasonal worker for the Park Service, a biologist working with the turtle and bird programs."

"My name is Luke, and, yes, this is my first year here." He was also interested. He saw her bottle of Corona was almost empty. "Can I get you another beer?"

"Sure."

Luke learned Anna was from Ohio, where she had gone to school, and that she had worked for the Park Service for the past two summers on Ocracoke.

"I'm driving the beach this week with the bird and turtle programs. Do you want to join me one morning?"

"Sure," Luke said. He was fascinated. "I work during the week, but I have Saturday off. Can we do it Saturday morning? What time do you go out?"

"Meet me at the Park Service visitor center by the ferry dock at 5:00 Saturday morning."

"Do I need to bring anything?"

"Maybe some water, sunscreen, and bug spray." They talked for a while longer, but after the prize was awarded, Anna said she had to leave. She had an early start the next day and wanted to get plenty of sleep.

≈

Luke drove to the visitor center early on Saturday morning. Anna was waiting for him in her white National Park Service truck, which had turtle signs and stakes in the back. She was supposed to be on the beach by 5:30.

"Did you get anything to eat?"

"Yeah, I ate a toasted bagel with cream cheese and some juice." He held a coffee cup filled with black coffee.

After she drove to the end of the south point road and came onto the beach at Ramp 72, Anna turned right and followed it to the southern tip of the island. The south point, where Hank had found Luke in the water, was now closed to foot and vehicular traffic due to the nests of piping plovers and American oyster catchers. Anna told Luke the closing of the beach because of the birds was very controversial. Islanders, fishermen, and particularly folks on Hatteras Island were upset that the beach was closed to vehicular traffic to protect the birds. For generations, men and women had fished these waters. When the park was created in the 1950s, the local fishermen were told that they would always have access to the beach. About ninety percent of the fourteen-mile-long island was now part of the national seashore. Only the area around the village at Silver Lake, which faced the sound, was still privately owned. All of the beach fronting the ocean was in the national seashore.

Anna told Luke that a few years back, a group of environmentalists and birders sued the federal government and said the government had no off-road vehicle plan that would protect the rare and endangered bird species in the park or the sea turtles that nested on the islands. As a result, an interim court order was in effect until the Park Service could come up with a set of rules and regulations to govern off-road vehicle use in the park. According to the service's own guidelines, such rules were supposed to have been put into effect years ago, but they were not.

The court ruling perhaps went further than the Park Service would have gone but the rules were drawn up by a group of environmental lawyers in Chapel Hill. That was the state of things until more permanent regulations could be put in place. Thus, there was a lot of local hostility against the birds, the turtles, and the environmentalists—more on Hatteras than Ocracoke. The Park Service took the brunt of it because its rangers had to enforce the rules.

"I don't remember seeing this part of the beach blocked off the last time I was out here," Luke asked, looking toward the south point and Ocracoke Inlet.

"It's seasonal. Until the birds hatch and remain unfledged, this part of the beach is off limits to vehicles and pedestrians."

"You mean people can't even walk on the beach because of the birds?"

"That's right. Those are the rules. I didn't make them, but I have to enforce them," she said. "Some environmentalists showed a picture of a baby bird stuck in a tire track and all hell broke loose. It is true that the birds are small, and drivers of pick-up trucks can't see them sometimes, but I think they might have gone overboard a little about the birds. There are only a handful of piping plovers out here at any given time, but there are hundreds of turtles, thousands including the hatchlings. No regulation is too strong to protect the turtles in my opinion, but then again I am a turtle biologist."

One of Anna's jobs was to check to see if there had been any incursions into the protected area, but there didn't appear to be any. Under the court order, if there was an incursion, Park Service personnel had to move the signs and string barriers out fifty meters for the first violation, one hundred meters for the second, and five hundred meters for the third, further restricting where fishermen and people could enjoy the beach.

Anna turned around and started driving north looking for turtle landings. She stopped and got out of the truck just north of the lifeguard beach. The beach was open for off-road vehicle use for about 1.8 miles between Ramp 72 and Ramp 70.

"Why did you stop? I don't see any turtles," Luke asked, getting out of the truck.

"See those hatch marks in the sand, heading to the dune line," she said, pointing to what looked like twenty-four-inch-wide tractor tracks going into the beach at an angle.

"Yeah," Luke said, walking over to take a closer look.

"These are the marks that the loggerhead turtles' flippers make in the sand as they climb out of the water. They usually climb onto the beach at an angle, then lay their eggs and go back to the ocean at another angle, creating a large V in the sand," she said.

Anna walked to the intersection of the V, a dozen yards from the high tide mark, and dug in the sand briefly before declaring, "It's a false landing. She probably came ashore and changed her mind about where to lay her eggs. They do that a lot."

They got back in the truck and drove up to a barrier made of signs stapled to three-foot-tall wooden stakes. There was twine strung between the stakes that ran from the dunes to the water, north of the beach area where lifeguards were on duty during the summer. This marked another bird-nesting area where not even pedestrians could walk. Vehicles were already prohibited in the lifeguard-beach area. Visitors could access this beach by parking in a large paved parking lot near the beach, then crossing a boardwalk over the dunes. Adjoining the parking lot were bathrooms, changing rooms, and an outdoor shower.

After they passed the "resource protection area," where the birds nested, they passed over the beach in front of the National Park Service campground. They then drove to another area where off-road vehicles could drive on the beach for approximately 1.6 miles. Luke recognized this stretch of beach as part of the so-called "nude beach" where Luke, TMJ, and the others had partied the week before.

Then she pointed up ahead and said, "A turtle landing."

She pulled up beside the tracks in the sand and saw that they went up to the dune line, then came back down. "I think this is a nest. Probably the same turtle that had the false landing a ways back."

They both got out of the truck, and Anna pulled a shovel out of the back of the truck.

She walked up to the side of the dune line. After digging the top layer of sand off with the shovel, Anna pulled on thin plastic gloves, and started digging with her hands. "I like to feel the sand. If it is soft, I know that is where she has been digging, like here," Anna said, taking Luke's hand to show him how soft the sand was in the spot where she dug, as opposed to the area around it.

"I can really tell the difference," he said.

"She digs a hole in the sand that is like an upside-down light bulb—it is long and narrow to begin with but then opens out into a bulb that holds the eggs. Then she shoots her eggs into the hole and covers them up with her flippers. She lays between a hundred and a hundred and twenty eggs."

"Why do you dig them up? I thought you wanted to protect the eggs and make sure they hatched," he asked.

"We don't dig them up," Anna said. "We just dig until we find the top of the nest, to make sure it is not a false nest, then we put a transponder close to the nest so we can locate it if something happens to it. After we do that, we mark the site with PVC pipe and surround the nest with signs and twine to keep people out. When it gets closer to the time for the eggs to hatch, we expand the protection area and add black erosion-control plastic fencing to funnel the babies out to the sea in a protected pathway. That is another thing the ORV people don't like—we rope off the area between the nest and the water, so no one can drive or walk there. This sometimes blocks the beach so vehicles can't drive. The nests hatch in August and September anywhere from sixty to ninety days from the time they are laid. So far there are thirty-eight nests within the national seashore this year. Last year, we had over 104 nests in the seashore. This year we have over twenty nests on Ocracoke alone and are finding about one every day."

Anna leaned over the hole she had dug in the sand, and continued digging into the soft sand with her hands. Sand covered her shirt and pants. Luke began to help, also lying on top of the sand, getting his T-shirt and shorts sandy. When they finally found the leathery white eggs, which were shaped like ping-pong balls, Anna buried a transponder not far away. She then took one of the eggs and gave it to Luke to hold.

"We are doing this experiment where we take one egg from the nest, sacrifice it, and keep a DNA sample. That will enable us to see where the turtle goes and whether it comes back here to lay eggs in the future." Luke held it while she put on rubber gloves and got a Baggie out of the truck.

"I hate to do this," she said, taking the egg from Luke. "But we have to." Then she broke the egg and poured the yoke in the sand, where she buried it. She then put the leathery eggshell in the Baggie and labeled it.

When that was done, Anna and Luke built a twenty-foot, rectangular perimeter around the nest with wooden stakes and signs attached, warning people to keep out. After Anna entered all the information in her log and pounded the wooden stakes in the ground with Luke's help, she strung white twine between the four signs and drove off, calling in the location of the new nest to the office in Ocracoke.

They didn't find any more turtle nests that day. It had taken a while to dig up the nest and put the signs out so, it was late morning and time to drive back to Ocracoke village when they came to the north end of the island.

"I enjoyed that. Thanks for taking me along," Luke said. "Can I go out with you another time?"

"I'm afraid not. They used to let volunteers ride along with us, but they changed the rules this year because of liability questions. This is the last time I can take anyone along," she said.

Luke loved watching how intense and serious Anna was about her work. She was truly dedicated. He wished he could care as passionately about something as she did. He also was taken by her beauty—so natural, no make-up. Even when her hair was messed up or pulled back, she was sexy and beautiful. He loved to just be with her and watch her at work.

After leaving the beach, he went back to the house where he found Cora was busy cleaning.

"What's with all the activity?" Luke asked Hank.

"We just heard that Hank Junior and his family are coming for the Fourth of July. We haven't seen them since Christmas," Hank said.

"How old are your grandchildren?" Luke asked. He loved children.

"Jamie is four, and Sue Ellen is five," Hank said, beaming. "They are as cute as they can be. We can't wait to see them. We don't get to see them much, so when they come, it is a special event."

Cora bustled into the room and said to Hank, "Have you said anything to Luke yet?"

"No, I haven't yet, honey," Hank said.

"Luke, would you mind staying with TMJ over the Fourth while Hank Junior and his family are here? We just don't have enough bedrooms for the whole family and you," Cora said, looking concerned.

"Of course, I don't mind," Luke said. He wouldn't want to interfere with their family time anyway.

"It will only be while they are here. When they leave, you can come back," she said, relieved that he was not upset. "They are flying into Norfolk the Saturday before the Fourth, and we will pick them up at the airport. I am thinking of having a potluck on Sunday, the night of the Fourth, so we can invite all Hank Junior's old friends over to see him. We want you to come, too, Luke. We want you to meet Hank and his family."

"I would love to meet them."

⁓Chapter Seven⁓

A few days later, TMJ called to ask if Luke wanted to go to the beach with him.

"Sure," Luke said.

"I'll be by in about an hour," TMJ said.

Luke ate lunch with the Kilgos then put on a T-shirt and a bathing suit he had just bought at the surf shop. He grabbed a towel, sunscreen, and water.

TMJ picked up Luke in his old Chevrolet pick-up truck. Driving past Howard's Pub, TMJ turned to go down the south point road.

"I like to check out the beach and see what's going on," he said, driving out onto the beach at Ramp 72, heading north toward Ramp 70. It was just past one o'clock, so it was the hottest time of the day, especially with no clouds in the sky. The beach was lined with SUVs and pickup trucks. Some people fished, but most people were enjoying the sun and water. Some sat under cabana-like tents; most had beach chairs and coolers. People were playing corn hole or other beach games. All ages were represented. Even though there were various stages of dress and undress on display, there was no nudity on this part of the beach. They passed one turtle protection enclosure close to the beach. The sand was dry and deep there. TMJ then turned up Ramp 70 and drove past the small Ocracoke airport before coming out to Highway 12. He parked in the busy parking lot at the lifeguard beach.

Luke followed TMJ over the boardwalk and out to the beach. The lifeguard beach was packed with families and tourists taking in the sun and water. The water was almost crystal clear. Although the dry, white sand was hot to walk on with bare feet, it got cooler as they neared the water.

When TMJ walked into the water in front of a group of teenage girls, they started giggling. He just looked back at them and smiled.

"TMJ, you are going to get into trouble," Luke said. "Don't you know jailbait when you see it?" Luke joined TMJ in the cool, refreshing water, and they both swam out far enough to body surf as the waves rolled in.

When they got out of the water, they decided to walk down the beach, drying off quickly in the hot mid-day sun.

"I thought you liked your other beach better," Luke teased.

"I do, but I like to check out the women at the tourist beach, too," TMJ said. "The best part about the tourists is that they are here today and gone tomorrow—no commitments, just a week's romance, and then they are gone."

"That is all well and good," Luke said, "as long as they are of legal age!"

After they had a good leisurely walk, they spread their towels on the sand and lay back in the sun. Luke was not one for sunbathing all day, so he went repeatedly back into the surf.

That night, they went to SmacNally's and then to Howard's Pub. They ended up with the late-night crowd at the bar at Dajio's. They ran into Thelma and Luane, the women Luke had met on the nude beach the week before.

"Hey, Mr. Fireman," Thelma said, "how's it hanging?"

"It's hanging," TMJ said.

"Can I do anything to perk it up?" she asked.

"Sure."

Luke could see where this was heading. He was not interested in Luane, so after light conversation, he joined some guys at the ring toss. He saw Anita, the girl he met on the beach who worked at Howard's Pub. He waved to her, and she came over.

"Do you play darts?" she asked.

"Sure," Luke said, throwing a dart that almost hit the bull's eye.

"Nice shot," she said, aiming for the board but almost missing it.

They made small talk, played more darts, and ordered another round of beer.

"Do you want to drive out to the beach?" Anita asked.

He looked around for TMJ, who apparently had left with Thelma. It was no big deal; he could walk home if he had to.

"Sure," Luke said. Since no driving was allowed on the beach after nine at night or before nine in the morning, Anita drove to the lifeguard beach and they walked over the boardwalk. There were other people on the beach. A few sat around a bonfire. She carried two beach towels from her car. They walked to the water's edge and looked out over the water.

"I take it you are here for the whole summer?" she asked, as Luke lay down on one of the towels and gazed up at the stars.

"Yeah, I started working with Hank Kilgo in April. I don't know how long I'll stay. As long as I have steady work I guess. How about you?"

"I've worked at Howard's for the past four summers. The tips are great. I guess I'll keep coming back as long they'll have me. I come down the week before Memorial Day weekend and leave in November. The owner used to stay open all year long, but starting two years ago, she closed for the winter after Christmas. Her husband was proud of keeping it open 365 days a year, but after he died in an accident on a boat, she decided to close it when business fell off during the winter. No need to stay open in the winter and pay staff when no one is here."

"Are there many tourists here after the summer season ends?" Luke asked, sitting up.

"After Labor Day the crowd changes, more retired people and fishermen. Work is steady, just not as hectic as during the summer. I like it a lot better in the spring and fall."

"What do you do in the winter?"

"I go to Greenville and find a waitress job. It's a college town, so there are lots of restaurants. Usually I work in steak houses or whatever I can find," she said, lying down and looking up at the night sky. "But the real money is down here at Howard's during the summer and fall. I make $500 in tips some nights."

Luke looked up at the stars. "I've never seen so many stars in the sky before. What is that big smudge of stars just over us?"

"That's the Milky Way," Anita said.

"I don't believe I have ever seen it before." He began picking out constellations clearly visible in the Ocracoke night sky.

"Yeah, the sky is real pretty out here. No light pollution," she said. "It makes the stars much brighter and clear."

"Sure is beautiful," he said, staring into the night sky.

"Would you like to come to my place tonight?" Anita asked, sitting up on her elbow.

He did not say anything right away.

"Well? Cat got your tongue?"

"My wife was killed in a car wreck in January. It is still really hard for me. I don't know. I like you, and I thank you for asking. I just don't think I'm ready yet. That's all. I hope you understand."

"That's all right. I have never lost someone I loved, never lost a close friend to an accident. I don't know how I would feel. It must be terrible."

"It *is* terrible."

There was a sudden light along the horizon over the water. It got brighter, until gradually the full moon began to appear—big, bright, and red.

"It's the moon rise," Anita said.

"It's beautiful," he said, looking in wonder.

As the moon quickly rose in the sky, it gradually turned from red to white. The moon's rays spread across the ocean, lighting a path that seemed to be filled with diamonds as the moonbeam lit the tips of waves in the rough water.

After a while they got up and walked to the car. When she dropped him off at Hank's house, he kissed her. "Thank you for tonight. I really enjoyed our time on the beach," he said.

"I did, too," she said. "Will I see you again?"

"Sure."

Luke felt stupid that he didn't go home with Anita. She was a nice, good-looking girl, who wanted him to spend the night, and he blew it. What a dumb ass, he thought.

That night, as he slept, he saw Karen in a dream. They were lying in bed together. The moon shone in their bedroom window and lit their bed with a soft light. She lifted her head and bent down to kiss him. She was naked, and her breasts brushed against his chest.

"I love you," she said.

"I love you, too," he said as he kissed her.

≈Chapter Eight≈

TMJ called him the next morning.

"Hey, man, a bunch of us are going out in boats to a sandbar in the inlet. It should be fun. Do you want to join us?"

"Sure, what should I bring, the usual—water, sunscreen?"

"Yeah, we can stop on the way and fill a cooler with beer. I'll pick you up in about twenty minutes."

TMJ and Luke drove to the Community Store, where they filled their cooler with beer, leaving some room for food. TMJ also bought chips, ready-made sandwiches, a few packs of cheese crackers, beef patties, and buns. They would be out most of the day.

Then they parked at the Community Store parking lot and carried their stuff to a small, white fiberglass center-console Carolina Skiff with a wide, flat bottom. TMJ explained this kind of boat was best for boating in the shallow waters of the Pamlico Sound. It was moored at the end of a dock that belonged to one of TMJ's local friends.

"Who's your friend?" a stocky young man with short, blond hair asked.

"Luke Harrison. He's working with Hank and me on that house in

Oyster Creek." TMJ said. "Luke, this is Sammy Cooper. This is his boat."

"Welcome aboard, Luke. Good to meet you."

"This is the first time I've been on a boat since I got to Ocracoke," Luke said. "I'm looking forward to it. Thanks for including me."

"Sure thing, bud," Sammy said, extending his hand to help Luke on board.

Luke, TMJ, Sammy, and another local guy, Tommy Howard, took off through Silver Lake, heading toward the ditch. Tommy, who had close-cropped brown hair, a good tan, and slim athletic build was friendly but quiet. From the ditch, Sammy headed south toward the inlet. There were several shallow shoals and channels that only an experienced boater would know. Luke was glad Sammy was at the helm. If he and TMJ had been on their own, they would not have been able to find their way around the shoals. As they rode through the water, they could see the village on their left, the inlet and the beach straight ahead, and Portsmouth Island to the right. The inlet, where the waters from the sound met the waters from the ocean, was rough. As they approached the middle of the inlet, between Portsmouth and Ocracoke, they could see a flat sandy island. TMJ told Luke that this plot of land would just appear from time to time. The locals named it Vera Cruz, after a ship that sunk there some time ago.

Several boats were already there. Luke recognized some of the people from the day at the nude beach. He saw Thelma Garrish, Luane Dobbins, Mary Ann Johnson, and Anita Lorrance. There were more local folks than tourists on this beach because they were the ones with the boats. Luke hadn't met many of the local men, so he enjoyed getting to know Sammy and Tommy.

They hung out on Vera Cruz, which was like their own private island, but it was within sight of the fishermen and families in trucks and SUVs on the beach at south point and the boats going in and out of the inlet. Some of them swam in the shallow water. Some of the girls sunbathed, and some of the guys drank beer and played corn hole. At lunchtime, they brought out sandwiches and chips.

Sam Cooper asked TMJ and Luke if they wanted a ride over to the beach at Portsmouth Island.

"Sure," TMJ said.

"Would you like to join us?" Luke asked Anita Lorrance.

"Sure," she said, getting in the boat.

"You need to bring water," Sam said.

They gathered up their things and rode the short distance to the beach at Portsmouth. Sam turned the boat into a creek that ran up to the back of the beach.

"You can go into the deserted village, but it is real buggy. There are several old houses and the old Coast Guard station. The fun part is the beach. There are tons of shells. No one out here to see you," Sam said, pulling the boat up close to the beach in shallow water. "I'll be back in a couple of hours, same place. Don't be late. I don't want to get caught by the tide." Luke, TMJ, and Anita got out of the boat and into the water, which came up to their knees.

TMJ took off down the beach, looking like a man on a mission. Luke and Anita walked along the shore. Anita wanted to hunt for shells. Soon, they saw TMJ drop his bathing suit. He wanted to swim and lay out on the beach naked. Luke didn't know how Anita would feel about it, so he did not join TMJ.

Anita and Luke found beautiful shells—large whelks, conches, sand dollars, coral, and a special shell—the North Carolina state shell, the Scotch Bonnet. The Scotch Bonnet was like finding gold on the beach; it was easy to find broken bonnets but not whole ones. They were delicate, fat, rounded shells that fit in the palm of your hand. Luke and Anita found yellow ones, some the color of tabby cats, some white, and some black. There was a treasure trove of them on the beach that afternoon.

"I would like to go into the village sometime. Everyone tells me it is really cool—the old Coast Guard station, the Methodist church, and all the old houses sitting empty," Anita said. "It's a ghost town. The Park Service bought the whole town when the last residents moved out in the 1970s. The problem is that it's full of mosquitoes that swarm you. You need to wear long pants, long-sleeve shirts, and some people even wear a hat with mosquito netting hanging from it. You also have to cover yourself in bug spray."

"I'd like to see it, too. Maybe another time," Luke said. All they had were bathing suits and T-shirts. They would need to come prepared next time. A tour boat ran regularly from Ocracoke every day taking people to Portsmouth Island for a fee.

"Luke, how did you and your wife first meet, if you don't mind my asking?" Anita asked.

"Are you sure you want to hear about her?" Luke said.

"Yes, as long as you are comfortable talking about her."

"We met in high school. I guess you could say it was love at first sight. The first time I laid eyes on Karen, I knew that I wanted her. I didn't think she would want to have anything to do with me. She was so beautiful and popular and smart. I played football, and I guess that is why she noticed me. She was from a prominent family; I grew up in foster homes. I became a quarterback my junior year. I guess I was pretty good. We had a good run at the state championship my senior year, lost to Charlotte Catholic in the playoffs. Sports were a big deal in high school. Anyway, when I asked her out, she said yes. That was it. I never went out with another girl after that, and she never dated another guy.

"Her father never liked me, but her mother was nice to me. Her mother died of breast cancer just before we were married. After high school, Karen attended Catawba College, and I got a job working as a carpenter. She wanted to get married right away, but I said no. I wanted her to finish college first, so we waited. Salisbury was close to Concord and Kannapolis, so it was easy to date. I went to school too and got my two-year associate's degree at Rowan Cabarrus Community College. After she graduated from Catawba, we got married. She got a job at a local bank, and we bought an old mill house in Kannapolis with her father's help. We had planned to fix it up ourselves," he paused, put his hand to face. Tears welled up. Anita touched his shoulder.

"We were married for four years, but we didn't have children. She wanted to become established at work and enjoyed working at the bank," he said haltingly. He looked off in the distance. "She left the house one Saturday morning, going to the mall. I stayed at home to work in my workshop. If I had gone with her, I might have saved her. Things might have been different." He grew quiet. "But I didn't. I stayed home and worked in the shop. A truck swerved to miss a car and ran her off the road. Her car hit a tree, and she died instantly."

He paused. "A day doesn't go by that I don't wish I had been in that car with her."

"I'm glad you weren't in that car," Anita said. "I guess it wasn't your time. Maybe God has other plans for you."

"If he does, I don't know what they are."

"Maybe you will in good time."

They saw TMJ running toward them stark naked, holding his bathing suit.

"I went in the water to go swimming and ran into a bunch of jellyfish. One of them stung me on my butt, and it hurts like hell. Do you know what to do about it?" TMJ asked, looking very uncomfortable, twisting around and pointing to a large red welt across his left butt cheek.

"You are lucky it stung you on your back side and not in front," Luke said. "It is damn close."

"Sam won't be here for a while, and I don't know if he has anything for this anyway. Man, it hurts like hell."

They both looked at Anita. "I know what will kill the sting," Anita said, as a devilish smile crept across her face. "Trouble is, you're not going to like it."

"What is it? I don't care. I'll try anything if it stops the stinging," TMJ said.

"I've always heard that the best way to neutralize the sting of a jellyfish is with urine."

"What?" TMJ said, shocked.

"Urine. Luke is better equipped to handle that than me," she smirked. "Luke, you know what you have to do, don't you?"

"Do you mean I need to pee on TMJ's backside?" Luke asked. He had to suppress a laugh.

"It will be easier for you to do it than me," Anita said. "I'll turn the other way if you want me to."

"Do it, man. I can't stand this any longer. Pee on me!" TMJ said, pointing his butt in the air in front of Luke.

"Well, okay, if you insist," Luke said, pulling his bathing suit down. Then he let a stream of urine splash off of TMJ's backside and trickle down his legs.

"Oh my God, oh my God," TMJ said, with a huge smile of relief. "It is actually working. Pee on me some more; I love it. It is working. I love you, man!"

Luke continued to pee on TMJ's backside until he didn't have any more to give.

TMJ swung around and hugged Luke.

"Let me at least get my dick back in my pants," Luke said, struggling with his bathing suit.

"I love you, man. You saved me," TMJ said. "Thank you, Anita. You are a genius!"

They walked to the back of the beach where they met Sammy. TMJ told Sammy about the jellyfish sting and the treatment.

"The best way to stop the sting from a jellyfish is to rinse it well, which you apparently just did. But then you need to wash it with vinegar," Sammy said. "The acid neutralizes the alkaline toxin from the sting. I happen to have some here. I brought it for the cookout. You're welcome to use it."

TMJ pulled down his pants and showed Sammy the welts. Sammy poured the white vinegar on the welts, and the pain was gone.

By the time they got back to Vera Cruz, some of the guys had set up a couple of grills and were grilling hot dogs and hamburgers, fish and steaks. The sun hung big and orange over Pamlico Sound to the west. They ate the food off the grill as the sun set over the sound, disappearing into the water and turning it the color of the sky—a tangerine red.

When they finished eating, it got dark quickly. They loaded up the boats and rode the choppy water back to Silver Lake.

Luke and TMJ were tired. The sun had taken the energy out of them.

When they got back to the dock, Anita gathered her things and put them in her Jeep. "I think I'm going to bed early tonight," she said. "Too much excitement on the beach and too much sun." She put a canvas bag full of shells in the back seat of her Jeep.

"Time for me to go to bed, too. I have to get up early tomorrow morning and work," Luke said, looking tired. "Will I see you again?"

"Sure," she said. "Let me get through the week and see how it goes. Maybe some time this coming weekend."

"Okay, I'll give you a call Thursday and see what's up."

She put her hand around his neck and kissed him.

≈

Luke got in the car with TMJ, who didn't take him directly home. He first drove out to the lifeguard beach and stopped in the parking lot. TMJ got out and walked around the dressing rooms, bathrooms, and shower. Luke got out with him. It was dark and lit only by a few streetlights. TMJ picked up a bathing suit and a T-shirt that had been left in the dressing room.

"Size thirty-two, perfect!" TMJ said, looking at the label in the bathing suit. Then he found an abandoned beach chair in the garbage can. He pulled it out to see if it still worked. It did, so he put it and the clothes in the back of his Jeep.

"What are you doing?" Luke asked, as they got back in the car.

"People leave random stuff around here. If I can wear the clothes, I keep them. If not, I give them to someone else. Hey, if I don't find them, someone else will, right?"

Then TMJ drove out on the beach. It was dark, but they still had an hour before the beach was closed to traffic. TMJ drove close to the water where the sand was harder. He saw a pile of clothes on the beach and stopped.

"What if they belong to someone?" Luke said, watching TMJ hold the camouflage shorts and dark red underwear up to the lights of the Jeep.

"They are wet. If they belonged to someone who is in the water, they would be dry and not half-covered with sand. Besides there isn't a truck or SUV out here. I think these have been here for a while—fair game in my book," he said, dropping the underwear but tossing the pants on the floor of the backseat.

"What if they belong to someone who went swimming and drowned or didn't come back?"

"Not my problem," TMJ said, putting the shift in gear and driving off down the beach. As they made the loop between Ramp 70 and Ramp 72, they could see a group of people sitting around a bonfire to the south. "Do you want to see what's going on?" TMJ asked

"Not now, I'm tired. Maybe another time," Luke said. Besides, they couldn't stay out on the beach for long with the Jeep, so they took Ramp 72 onto the south point road and went back into the village.

≈Chapter Nine≈

On Thursday, Anna drove up to the house in Oyster Creek, where Luke and TMJ were working.

"Luke, can you come with me to the beach, right now?"

"What is it?" he asked, climbing down from a ladder where he was working on siding the house.

"There is a dead turtle on the beach. Someone ran over it."

"No!" Luke said, shocked.

"How in the world did that happen?" Hank said. "I mean it's not like they aren't easy to see."

"We don't know what happened," Anna said, visibly shaken. "All I know is that there is a dead turtle on the beach with tire tracks running through her back."

"I'm coming," Luke said, loosening his gear. Anna looked devastated.

"Why did you come to me, Anna?" Luke asked.

"Because I just heard about it, and I didn't want to be alone when I saw it. You know people and might be able to help us find out who did this. I don't know. You were the first person I thought of. I just couldn't bear to see it by myself," she said, practically in tears. The turtles were her whole life. She knew every detail of their life cycle and considered herself to be their protector. To find one dead weighed heavily on her.

"This is the first time I have ever heard of someone actually running over a turtle," Anna said, still in shock. "I know the commercial fishermen get mad because they have to put turtle extruders on their nets, and people who like to drive on the beach get mad when we mark off the nests and they can't drive around them. But I have never heard of someone actually running over a turtle and killing it before."

Anna was the first official on the scene. It was called in by someone on the beach. A small group of people who had been driving on the beach stopped to look.

The large black loggerhead turtle, about thirty inches long and wide, had clearly been run over as she crawled in from the water to lay her eggs. Her shell was crushed, and dozens of eggs had been pushed out of her body when she was killed. Only females land on the beach. Once the males swim out to sea after they are born, they never touch land again unless they are stunned by cold in the winter and strand on the beach.

"The incident must have happened after nine o'clock, when vehicles are banned from driving on the beach and after the Park Service's last patrol to make sure no one is left on the beach in a vehicle," said Anna. "The beach doesn't open to vehicles until 7:00 A.M., and the turtles come in when it is dark."

From the tire tracks, it looked like the turtle had been dragged about twelve feet. It must have gotten stuck under the vehicle because it was apparent that the vehicle backed up to get the turtle loose, and then took off in the night.

Soon several Park Service vehicles were on the scene. One of the older rangers, a native of Ocracoke, said, "I have been patrolling these beaches for thirty-five years, and I have never seen anything like this before."

"Let's try to save the eggs," Anna said, pulling on latex gloves and getting a cooler out of her truck. She picked up about seventy-five eggs, one by one, being careful not to tip them, and placed them in the cooler surrounded by towels. She made sure to place them just as she had found them on the ground. "If you turn them," she told Luke, "the tissue that connects the yolk to the shell can break and kill its occupant."

When Anna had salvaged all the eggs she could, she and another ranger then drove off and buried them close to the dunes, marking the spot.

Luke looked at the tracks and noticed that they were wide and made with knobby tires. There were also footprints in the sand where the occupants had gotten out to look at the turtle, after they ran over it. Luke followed the tire tracks. They veered wildly all over the place, and there was evidence of sand spray as if the vehicle had spun out to get out of there fast and maybe cover up some evidence.

"I don't want to believe that someone did this on purpose," Anna said, upon her return.

"It looks like some kids were out driving on the beach when they weren't supposed to be, had their lights out so they wouldn't be detected, and ran over the turtle. Once it happened, they figured they had screwed up and decided to get the hell out of dodge," the older ranger observed. "I wonder if anyone has shown up at the Jimmy's Garage with damage to their undercarriage."

"You think it damaged their vehicle?" Luke asked.

"A turtle this size? Yeah, it can do some damage," the older ranger said.

One of the turtle biologists stayed behind to do a necropsy. As Luke and Anna left, the older ranger headed in the direction of Jimmy's Garage to ask questions.

Immediately, postings went up on the Internet, and the media was notified. Rewards were offered for information. Loggerhead turtles were not endangered on the North Carolina coast, but they were a protected species.

"It takes thirty-five years for a female loggerhead to come to full sexual maturity, so she was at least thirty-five years old. She returned to the place of her birth, where generations of her family had come for hundreds or maybe thousands of years before," Anna said, visibly shaken. "She could have lived to be over a hundred years old. If this was her first laying, she would have laid at least two or three more times this season. I just can't believe it. Maybe we can at least save the eggs that we salvaged from her."

Later they found from the necropsy that she had the beginnings of yokes of another set of eggs and the tiny buds of yet another set of eggs. This was her first laying of the season.

⁓

That night Anna asked Luke to join her on the beach. A group of musicians from Chapel Hill called Mandolin Orange had been invited to play at a bonfire gathering.

It was after vehicles were banned from the beach, so they parked at the lifeguard-beach parking lot and walked over the boardwalk down to the water, where a bonfire was roaring. A young man played the fiddle as a girl sang. The music was bluegrass with a modern twist. The fiddle player was excellent, and the girl sang like an angel. It was a beautiful, romantic night. The moon, almost full and very bright, hung over the ocean, creating a silver path across the water, as Anna and Luke walked down the beach.

Anna was still thinking about the loggerhead turtle. "I can't believe that she swam all those many miles back to the place that she was born, over thirty-five years ago, finally able to unload her sac of eggs and some drunk redneck idiot drove over her and crushed her shell. It is incredible," Anna said. "And it happened last night. If I had only been out here. If someone had only seen it happen or seen the truck come off the beach." They stopped, and Anna put her arm around Luke's waist. "We'll probably never find out who did it. They are probably long gone by now."

"I will keep my ears to the road," Luke promised. "If it is anyone local, eventually they will have to say something. But if it was someone just here for the night or for a few days, I'm afraid they'll be gone."

"But if they are still here, they may say something."

"Yeah, they might," Luke said.

⁓

The next morning Hank walked into Luke's bedroom at 6:30 and tapped on the covers. "Get up."

"It's Saturday, we aren't working today. What are you getting up so early for?" Luke rubbed his sleepy eyes.

"Tommy Howard called and said he's going clamming. Wanted to know if we would join him," Hank said. "You want to go?"

"Sure," Luke mumbled. "But get out of here so I can get out of bed."

Luke had told Hank that he wanted to experience all that Ocracoke had to offer: fishing, clamming, scalloping, flounder gigging, shrimping. He also wanted to go out with the guys at the pound nets and help them with the crab pots.

They drove to the Community Store dock where they met Tommy. He had an older wooden boat, three clam rakes, and two plastic laundry baskets with floats roped to them.

"These clam rakes are cool," Luke said. "Where did you get them?"

"They come from Wilmington," Tommy said. Kitchen knives were welded onto the frame of a clam rake. "They are spaced apart just far enough to catch the legal-sized clams, anything too small goes through. The knives cut through the soft sand like butter. Old rakes are a pain in the ass; takes too much energy to pull them through the sand. Some guy came up with this idea, and it stuck. This is the only kind of clam rake anybody uses around here anymore. They cost about three hundred dollars at the bait-and-tackle shop."

"Cool," Luke said, examining the sharp knives welded to the end of the rake.

"Be careful not to cut yourself," Tommy said.

They all got in the boat, and Tommy headed to the ditch that led from Silver Lake into Pamlico Sound.

Tommy told Luke that the sound was a vast inland sea, but it was shallow—two- and three-feet deep in many places but rarely more than ten- to twenty-feet deep. "Channels run through it, and you need to know where those channels are," said Tommy. "They are constantly changing. Even if you follow the buoys, you might get in trouble. The locals know the water better than anyone, of course."

Tommy steered the boat close to shore past several houses facing the sound and the Ocracoke Lighthouse.

≈

Tommy continued on toward Springer's Point. Hank pointed out that this nature preserve was saved by the North Carolina Coastal Land Trust. "It is known for its large live oak trees," Hank said.

They motored past Springer's Point through Teach's Hole, the channel where Lieutenant Maynard beheaded Blackbeard, whose real name was Edward Teach, thus the name. Maynard took his grisly trophy back to Williamsburg as proof to Governor Spotswood of Virginia that the pirate had been killed.

"Some say Blackbeard was in cahoots with the governor of North Carolina, Charles Eden, based in Bath, just across the sound from Ocracoke," Hank continued the history lesson. "When Governor Spotswood couldn't get Governor Eden to help him take out Blackbeard, Governor Spotswood took matters into his own hands and sent a crew to destroy the pirate menace. After they killed Blackbeard and several of his men, they imprisoned those who survived the fight and went to Bath Town to capture some more, including William Howard, Blackbeard's young quartermaster. They took Blackbeard's captured men and put them on trial for piracy, but just before they were to be hanged, the men got word by ship from England that they had received the king's pardon and were considered to be privateers in the service of the king against his enemy, Spain. Never mind that they were also accused of preying on local shipping. William Howard came back years later, some say, with his share of Blackbeard's booty and bought the island of Ocracoke, where many of his descendants live today. I believe William Howard is your ancestor, Tommy. Am I right?"

"Yep, all the Howards on Ocracoke are related," Tommy said laconically.

As Tommy powered his boat through Teach's Hole, Luke asked about its distinctive style. The wooden boat had a flat bottom and high gunnels built in the traditional Ocracoke style. According to Tommy, boats built on Ocracoke are somewhat different from the boats built "Down East" in Carteret County and on Harker's Island across the sound and to the southwest of Ocracoke.

When they had come several hundred yards from the sound side of the beach, Tommy pulled up his outboard motor. The water here was very shallow. Hank jumped overboard and took the anchor and set it in the sand.

"Go on over, and I'll hand you the rakes and the baskets," Tommy said to Luke.

Luke went over the side into the water and handed a rake and basket to Hank. Hank tied the basket to his waist with a rope. Tommy followed them, tying the other basket to his waist and taking the other rake. They walked over the shallow sandy bottom, barefoot, wearing bathing suits, white T-shirts, and ball caps.

"What are you supposed to do?" Luke asked.

"Lightly drag the rake across the sand, letting the blades of the knives pass through the sand. The clams usually aren't very deep. When you feel it hit something, push the rake a little bit forward, then dig down and scoop it up like this," Tommy said, demonstrating. His rake pulled up black muddy sand. Luke tried it a few times until he got the hang of it.

"Where do we go?"

"Wherever you find clams," Tommy said, taking off across the water with his floating basket following behind. Luke stayed close to Hank. Hank soon began to find clams. They could see Tommy some ways off, and he too appeared to be raking in clams. Luke didn't have as much luck. He pulled in one or two, while the others seemed to have taken in a dozen or more. They saw Tommy waving them over to a spot where he seemed to be having some luck. They followed him to a patch of seagrass in the sand.

"They are right along the edges of the seagrass," Tommy said, pulling a rake full of three healthy clams.

Hank pulled in some, but Luke was still not having much luck.

"I guess you all heard about the sea turtle," Luke asked.

"Yeah, I heard," Tommy said. "They'll never find who did it."

"Why do you say that?" Luke asked.

"There's lots of hostility about the turtles and birds. Locals say the government cares more about the birds and turtles than it does about people. They say when the park was created, it was created for recreation. Now it is being used for preservation of the animals, and the people be damned."

"Do you think it was an accident or intentional?" Luke asked.

"It was no accident."

"They could have had their lights out and didn't see it," Luke said.

"It was an almost full moon Thursday night. It was clear as a bell," Tommy said. "Even if they didn't have their lights on, they would have seen it."

"Why do you say they'll never find who did it."

"No one will tell, certainly not if it was a local person, but even if it was a tourist. No one should go to jail for that. The Park Service people are outsiders. We look after our own."

Luke hadn't thought about the full moon. He liked Anna and appreciated her passion for the turtles, and he did not like the fact that someone ran over and killed such an innocent creature, but he realized that there were local politics involved. He didn't want to argue with Tommy and say that at least one of the rangers was local, but he was surprised by Tommy's reaction. He saw that he had a lot to learn about this island.

"Looky here," Hank said. "I just pulled up three clams in one try," Hank said with a wink to Luke, obviously was trying to change the subject.

"Looks like this is where they are hiding," Hank grinned, pulling up some more. Tommy and Luke moved behind him and began to rake in circles around Hank. Tommy pulled up several, but Luke was still having a hard time pulling them in.

"I'm not getting anything," Luke said. "Should I be going deeper in the sand?"

"With the high pressure, they sometimes go deeper," Hank said. "I am digging deeper. I have even dug in one place and come back and dug again only to find clams. They are good at hiding."

Luke tried digging deeper, putting his weight behind it at he pushed the rake through the sand. It was hard work, but it did pay off. He found more clams but still not as many as Tommy and Hank, who were old hands at it.

They saw some other men working the beds a few hundred yards away, closer to shore.

"Think they are finding any?" Hank asked Tommy.

"Don't know. Looks like they are dumping some in their baskets. I'm going to stay right here where I know we are finding them," Tommy said, pushing his clam rake through the sand and pulling up two clams. He washed them off and dropped them in his floating basket.

"This is fun," Luke said.

"It's hard work. Remind me not to go clamming again when someone asks me," Tommy said, being the contrarian.

Luke couldn't figure Tommy out. He was a nice enough guy, and he was their "host" and guide, letting them use his clam rakes and his boat, but he could also be contrary and negative, like about the turtles. It wasn't like they had begged him to take them out. He was the one who had called and invited them. Maybe it was Tommy's personality. Could he know more about the turtle killing than he was letting on?

Luke felt loyal to Anna and had promised to help her find the perpetrator, but he also felt a loyalty to his new island friends and didn't want to get anyone in trouble. He was just beginning to get to know the island and its people. He hardly wanted to become known as a snitch. Plus the penalties for killing the loggerhead turtle were pretty severe. He didn't want to say anything until he knew damn well what he was talking about.

"I don't know about you guys, but I am about ready to go in. My back is beginning to kill me," Hank said. Luke was beginning to feel it in his back, too, but didn't say anything. He was glad Hank spoke up.

"How many you reckon we have?" Hank said, looking at his basket and Tommy's.

"I think there is about sixty in mine and sixty in yours," he said. "I've done this enough to figure it out pretty close."

They slogged back to the boat through the knee-deep water, dragging the floating baskets behind them. At the boat, they pulled the heavy baskets into the boat and helped each other over the side.

Tommy began to count the clams in his basket. "Sixty-eight," he said, then he counted the clams in Hank's basket. "Fifty-five. Total of 123, pretty darn close, I'd say. How many do you want, Hank?"

"I'll take half of them. You want the rest?" Hank said.

"Sure," Tommy said.

"Sounds good."

When they got back to the dock, Hank took a basket and Tommy took a basket.

"Cora makes a great clams casino. You want to come by and eat some with us?" Hank asked Tommy.

"Sure, I'll fix mine later," Tommy said.

"Fine, come on by about four, and we'll open them and prepare them for cooking then we can eat about five," Hank said.

"Sounds good," Tommy said.

≈

"Best to stay out of local politics, Luke," Hank said on the way back to the house.

"But killing a turtle?" Luke asked.

"It isn't right, but there is a lot of resentment against the Park Service. The state bought up all the land in the park after the war, then gave it to the federal government for the park. Some say they were cheated. Some say they would be better off without the park. Now there is this thing about the turtles and the birds being treated as more important than the people," Hank said.

"I can see the resentment, but this island wouldn't be what it is without the park. It is what makes it so special."

"I think most people would agree with you, but there are some who don't."

≈

It was lunchtime so they took the clams back to the house and fixed some sandwiches. About four o'clock, Tommy came by and they began to open the clams, which were very tight and hard to open.

The three men pulled chairs up to an old wooden table behind the house. The clams were in a bucket full of water beside the table. "There are two ways to do it, the traditional way like this," Hank said, pulling a sharp knife through the tight space between the two shells, which was not easy and was dangerous. "Or you can do this." He pulled out a little hand-made wooden contraption that held the clam in place with a metal plate attached to it. The plate had a slit in it where he could fit the knife and pull down through the thin line between the shells.

Luke tried to do it without the contraption and almost cut himself. "No, you need to use this," Hank said, pushing the tool across the table for Luke to use.

With the contraption, Luke easily opened the shells.

"Use your knife to cut the muscle free like this, and discard the top shell. Then loosen the meat from the bottom shell like this." Hank placed the half shell on a cookie sheet.

Soon the three of them had opened thirty shells and placed them on two cookie sheets.

Cora brought out a bottle of wine, some sliced pieces of bacon, and grated Parmesan cheese.

"Pour a little wine on each one, then put a little piece of bacon on each one, like this," Cora said, demonstrating. "Then sprinkle some Parmesan on it like so." When they finished, she took the cookie sheets in the house and baked them in the oven.

"This is really good," Luke said later, eating one of the clams. "I can't believe we caught them today and are eating them the same day."

"That's Ocracoke, fresh seafood every day. The catch of the day means literally that—fish, clams, oysters, crabs—caught and eaten the same day," Cora said.

"Ain't life grand," Hank said, smiling.

They asked Tommy to stay for supper that night. Cora had picked up some Spanish mackerel fillets that she breaded and fried and some fresh sweet corn from the mainland. She added a squash casserole. They all ate well that night and went to bed early.

≈Chapter Ten≈

It had been hot in June, with no rain. Usually June was cool and July and August were hot, but this year the week before the Fourth was cool and nice—in the 70s and 80s during the day and in the 60s and 70s at night. It was a pleasure to go to work. Since it usually got hot after lunchtime, the crew started early and got off around three o'clock, but this week, it was so pleasant they worked all day long through Wednesday. On Thursday, July 1, Luke moved in with TMJ, and Hank got up early and drove to the airport to pick up his son and his family in Norfolk, Virginia.

Fourth of July is a major holiday in Ocracoke. It is a time of homecoming when families get together, and it is time for celebration. For many years, there was a Fourth of July parade and a beautiful fireworks display over Silver Lake at night. But the year before, TMJ told Luke, there was a terrible accident. Four people were killed when the truck holding the fireworks exploded as the handlers were preparing for the show that night. The people who were killed were all from the same church near Goldsboro. They worked for the fireworks company to make extra money. Only one person survived. There were no local people killed in the explosion that rocked the island, but the islanders were shaken. They canceled the parade and the fireworks display. The event committee decided not to do a fireworks show in the future. It was expensive and dangerous.

Cora was planning a big potluck at her house after the parade. She was so excited to have her son and grandchildren at home on Ocracoke that she could hardly contain herself. She had invited all of their friends and Hank Junior's old friends. She invited Luke to join the family for breakfast on Sunday the Fourth. She cooked stacks of pancakes, platters of bacon and sausage, fresh biscuits, juice, and coffee.

"Sue Ellen and Jamie, y'all eat up because we have to go see the sand sculpture contest on the beach. If you want, you can enter, and you might win a prize," Cora said to Jamie, her fair-skinned, towheaded four-year-old grandson. Five-year-old Sue Ellen, with long brown hair that hung in curls to her shoulders, looked just like her mother, while Jamie took after his father.

"I want to build a sand castle," Jamie said.

After they had eaten and cleaned up the kitchen, Hank Junior said, "Let's put on our bathing suits and go to the beach." Hank Junior was about five ten, with a sturdy build; a big-chested man, stocky and firm, like his dad. He now wore his hair in a crew cut. According to his mother, when he was Jamie's age, he also had white blond hair.

Hank Junior loaded a canvas bag with sunscreen, boxes of juice and treats, and water for Susan and himself. They brought towels and an umbrella. Cora and Hank put on their bathing suits.

"Are you going to join us on the beach, Luke?" Cora asked.

"Sure, I'll get my bathing suit and meet you at the lifeguard beach."

The parking lot at the lifeguard beach was full. The beach was swarming with families enjoying the sun, the water, and the holiday. Hank signed up the grandchildren for sand sculpture. After they were assigned a space, they started to work in the sand.

"Why don't we make a turtle?" Cora suggested.

"Cool, that would be neat," Jamie said.

Cora and Hank started digging in the sand to mound it up. The children had to make the sculpture. Although technically the adults could only help, they all figured they would do the heavy lifting. The kids could put the finishing touches on it, with helpful suggestions, of course.

The children molded the legs and the head and formed the back of the mound of sand to look like a turtle shell. There was a lot of seaweed on the beach.

"Why don't we put the seaweed around the turtle to make it look like it is swimming in the water?" Hank suggested. Susan and Hank Junior gathered seaweed, and the children spread it around the turtle.

"What are we going to name it?" Cora asked.

"Turtle Island," Jamie said.

"I like that," Cora said.

Susan wrote the name in the sand and gave the judges a paper with the children's names, the name of the sculpture, and their space number. Sculptures were judged by category based on age.

Luke loved watching the kids, their parents, and grandparents work together on the turtle project. He knew he wanted to have children someday, and watching the Kilgos made him want them even more.

The judging wasn't until noon, so Hank Junior and Susan took the kids swimming in the surf after they had finished their sand sculpture. Hank Junior held both of Jamie's hands as he jumped the waves. Sue Ellen took off into the water, with her mother following close behind, catching her in her arms and throwing her in the air. She giggled and laughed. Cora and Hank sat beside the sand sculpture under an umbrella to guard it and smiled as they watched their son and his family play in the surf.

When the winners were announced for the sand sculpture contest, the Kilgo grandchildren won first place for their age group. They were almost too excited to go home, eat lunch, and rest up for the parade, which started around three o'clock. The kids took naps, while Cora and Hank found a perfect parade-watching spot that was not too crowded. They set up their chairs and umbrella behind the Styron Store.

Luke joined the family to watch the parade. TMJ and several of his friends were on the parasailing float, which consisted of a bunch of good-looking young people in bathing suits and bikinis dancing on the boat that takes people out parasailing in the sound. It was pulled on its trailer by a pickup truck. A lot of people rode golf carts that were decorated, something that was new to Ocracoke. The Shriners had their big pirate-boat float. Lots of people walked in the parade, including a group of women, who walked beside a Jeep, which bore a sign labeling them the Queens of Ocracoke. All the floats and costumes were amateurish, which added to the fun. Kids squirted the parade participants with water guns, which everyone seemed to welcome because it was a hot sunny day. The parade participants threw candy to the kids.

After the hour-long parade, the family and their friends gathered at Cora and Hank's house for the big potluck. Most of Hank Junior's friends had children now, so the kids played in the yard while the guys drank beer and the women put the food out. Cora and Hank had boiled several pounds of fresh shrimp. Guests brought ham biscuits, fig cake, ice cream, lots of casseroles, macaroni and cheese, barbecue pork, fish tacos, chips and dip—you name it, they brought it and arranged it out on tables on the screened porch. After they ate, a handful of Hank's friends brought out a fiddle, a guitar, and a harmonica.

After the party broke up, Luke, Hank Junior, and several of his friends went to the community square for the Ocracoke square dance. Luke watched some of the older members of the community dancing the traditional dance to the sound of an old-time fiddler. After the square dancing was over, a local group, the Aaron Caswell Band, took to the stage and played more contemporary rock music.

Luke saw Anna Thomas from the Park Service.

"Do you want to dance?" she asked, holding out her hand. She looked really sexy in her Capri pants with top buttons undone on her white blouse.

"I'm not much of a dancer," Luke said shyly. He was dressed in a plain white T-shirt and khaki shorts. Luke dressed for comfort, not for looks.

"I'm not either, but the music is really good. Won't you join me?" she asked.

"Okay," Luke said, taking her hand and dancing to the music, following her lead. They danced for a while, then she reached over and put her hand behind his neck and pulled him to her, kissing him long and hard. He was a little surprised by her forwardness at first, but then he gave into it and went with the moment. It was a long kiss, and, suddenly, he found he couldn't get enough of her. The warm night air, the beer, her beauty, her smell, and her taste drew him in.

"Do you want to go to my place?" she asked.

"Yes," he said, intoxicated with her.

TMJ danced nearby with Luane Dobbins. As Luke and Anna passed them, TMJ said, "Looks like you won't be spending the night at my place, man."

Luke gave him a smile and a wave.

Luke and Anna rode bicycles to the housing provided to Park Service employees. It was located behind the water plant near the ferry docks. Anna lived in a three-bedroom unit that she shared with two other girls from the Park Service. Her roommates were out, so she quickly led him to her bedroom and closed the door for privacy.

They kissed, leaning against the door, then Anna pushed him onto the bed with one hand. She unbuttoned her blouse; he pulled off his T-shirt. The soft light from a streetlight filtered through the curtains to gently light their bodies. She ran her hands over his back, chest, and flat, hard stomach. He felt her breasts and moved down her back under her pants to her firm buttocks. She took off her pants. He rolled around on top of her and pushed her down on the bed, pulling off his shorts. He wore no underwear. She quickly pulled down her panties. He ran his fingers up the sides of her body, then began to kiss her, first her lips, then her eyes and forehead, then he worked his way down to her neck and shoulders. He lingered on her breasts. When she began to moan softly, he worked his way down until he found her sex, where he lingered again. She ran her fingers over his back, digging her nails into his flesh. She squeezed his butt cheeks, hard. He cried out in pleasure. She moaned as he continued to pleasure her sex. She shuddered once, twice, three times.

"Oh, Luke," she cried out.

He knew how to pleasure a woman. His wife had taught him well. They were connoisseurs of love.

After he had Anna literally shaking with tremors of pleasure, he began to tease the entrance to her sex with his fingers.

She clumsily reached over to her nightstand and pulled something out of the drawer.

"Use this," she said, handing him a condom.

Without stopping a beat, he was knocking at her front door with his sex, now properly covered. He loved to tease. He was also good at controlling his own needs, though it had been a long time since he had lain with a woman.

They made love several times through the night, finally falling asleep, exhausted.

He dreamed he was lying beside Karen after they had made love. He woke filled with an incredible happiness. The sun had just begun to lighten the day. He looked at the beautiful woman sleeping beside him.

It was not Karen.

He felt a rush of guilt. It wasn't fair to Anna to sleep with her and think of Karen. He got up, pulled on his shorts and T-shirt, and left. He slipped out without seeing any of Anna's roommates and rode his bike back to TMJ's house. There he fell asleep on the sofa.

A couple of hours later, he was awakened by TMJ and Luane getting coffee in the kitchen. TMJ wore white boxer shorts (a concession to Luane) and no shirt; Luane wore an old bathrobe.

"I thought you spent the night with Anna?" TMJ said.

"I did, but I came back early this morning."

"Was she awake when you left?" Luane asked.

"No."

"You're going to have some explaining to do," Luane said.

"I'm just not ready for a relationship."

"What makes you think she is ready for a relationship? This is the summer. This is the beach. Maybe she just wanted to get laid," Luane said, taking a sip of coffee.

Luke had to think about this. Luane was right, but he wasn't sure he was ready to have any kind of a relationship, even a one-night stand. He had just lost the love of his life in January. It had not even been six months. But he was young, and he had needs. He couldn't help but notice an attractive woman, especially one as beautiful as Anna. Still he was confused and unsure.

"You had better come up with a good explanation why you left when you see her again. That is if you want to see her again," Luane said.

Luke realized Luane was right.

Hank Junior and his family decided to stay the week after the Fourth of July. Cora told Luke that she had some other guests coming the following week.

"Why don't you stay with me for the rest of the summer, or at least for as long as you can stand it?" TMJ said the next morning, sitting in a chair directly across from the sofa where Luke sat. TMJ did not have a stitch of clothing on as he sipped his coffee nonchalantly. This obsession with nudity really bugged Luke, but he was getting more used to it. He wondered what other people thought about it. It didn't seem to bother Hank or the folks on the beach, but it was obnoxious, Luke thought.

"That sounds like a good idea." TMJ had a lot of idiosyncrasies, he stayed up late at night in his bedroom surfing the Internet for God knows what, and he liked to walk around his trailer naked during the day, but he was also a pretty good roommate. He kept the place clean, and he made good coffee. Luke cooked, and TMJ cleaned. Luke had adjusted to the sofa and found it to be pretty comfortable. He could even clean out the other bedroom and make it his own if he wanted. Plus Luke enjoyed going out on the town with TMJ. They were actually getting to be pretty good friends. Despite himself, Luke was beginning to like TMJ. He had his strange ways, but TMJ didn't try to force his ways on anyone else. He just wanted to be left alone to do his own thing. It was probably better that Luke stay with TMJ than with the Kilgos, since their schedules were more in tune with each other. So he decided to tell Cora and Hank that he would stay with TMJ for the summer, or at least for as long as he could stand it.

"Luke, I don't want you to think I am running you out of here or anything," Cora started. "It's just that in the summer, especially July, we get lots of company. We keep telling ourselves that we are not going to do it again this year, then we invite people anyway. I mean how can I turn down my son and grandchildren? How can I turn down my brother and his wife? How can I turn down my best friend from high school or Hank's fishing buddies? I mean somehow every year it gets like this. But you understand that you have a bed here anytime, except when we fill up the house, like this week with Hank Junior and his family, but you can always sleep on the sofa if you need to."

"Cora, I *want* to stay with TMJ," Luke said. "I know this will shock you, but we actually get along pretty well, and since we go out at night sometimes, it seems to work out better anyway."

"Are you sure?" Cora asked, drying her hands on a kitchen towel. "He has some pretty strange habits," she said referring to his nudity, which was well known on the island.

"Yes, ma'am, he does, but I'm okay with that," Luke said. "I can't say I like it a lot, but I can live it."

"Is he a good housekeeper? I can't imagine that he is. I've never been inside TMJ's trailer, but on the outside, it's not much to look at."

"You would be surprised at how neat he keeps it inside," Luke reassured her. "And he likes it when I cook."

"Well, if you ever need a nice home-cooked meal, you know you are always welcome here," she said. "In fact, let's make it a date. We will expect you every Sunday for lunch."

"What about TMJ?" Hank asked.

She hesitated, "You tell him he can come, too."

"It's a deal," Luke said.

So Luke moved his few belongings to TMJ's trailer. He had no idea how long he'd be there.

≈

That night, Luke and TMJ went to Howard's Pub to listen to a local band, the Ocracoke Rockers. Luke and TMJ sat at the bar. Luke ordered a glass of Yuengling.

Anna came up and tapped him on the shoulder. "What happened to you the other night? When I woke up, you were gone."

She surprised him, and he didn't quite know what to say.

"Cat got your tongue?" TMJ asked, with a devilish grin. Luke could have killed him.

Luke stood up, took Anna's hand, and led her outside. He couldn't talk with the music and didn't want to be within earshot of TMJ. Anna was upset.

"I don't just sleep with anyone, you know," Anna said. Her checks were flushed and there was emotion in her voice.

"I'm sorry, Anna, but it is still too soon for me. I just lost my wife."

"I know. But we really had chemistry that night. I really felt that we connected."

"Yes, we did. It was a magical night," Luke said, head down. "But it scared me. I need to slow down." He didn't want to tell her he had dreamt of Karen that night.

"I felt dirty when I got up, like you used me."

"I'm sorry, that's not the way I want you to feel. I'm just dealing with a lot of emotions right now."

"You still love your wife, don't you?"

"Yes."

She pulled away from him and began to walk away. He knew he was being unfair to her, and she was being unfair to him. He had good reason to still have feelings for his dead wife. Still, he didn't want to hurt Anna. She was a beautiful, sensitive girl, and she was also apparently very proud.

"Anna, come back. I'm sorry. Please, I hope you understand."

"I think I understand very well," she said. Then she turned and walked down the steps leading to the parking lot.

How could she be jealous of someone who is dead, he thought? But she was. He knew that as long as his dead wife still occupied his heart, there was no room for anyone else.

≈CHAPTER ELEVEN≈

Hank Junior and his family left on the Saturday after the Fourth. Hank asked Luke and TMJ if they wanted to go crabbing on the mainland at Lake Mattamuskeet on Sunday. Luke had heard of Mattamuskeet, a huge, shallow, elliptical lake located on the mainland in Hyde County. It was one of the lakes and formations in eastern North Carolina called Carolina Bays. It was eighteen miles long and seven miles wide and a swan's neck deep. According to Hank, it was made into a wildlife refuge in 1934 by Franklin Roosevelt and was now home to more than eight hundred species of wildlife and birds.

"There are various theories about how the Carolina Bays were formed. One is that they were created by a shower of meteors that hit the earth; another was that they were created by fires in the peat bogs that lay under the sandy soil, which caused a depression in the earth that filled with water. The fire theory was supported by local Indian legend," Hank told Luke, going into history-professor mode, which showed his love of history.

On Sunday morning, Luke awoke to a shock: TMJ standing over him, naked, his crotch inches from his face. Shaking Luke's shoulder, TMJ said, "Luke, get up; it's 5:00. We need to be at Hank's by 5:30."

Luke recoiled, putting some distance between him and TMJ. TMJ, that's just gross!"

"It's nothing you haven't seen before. Get used to it. This is my place, and you are my roommate."

"Yeah, I know!" Luke said, in mock disgust.

They rode in TMJ's pickup truck to Hank's house.

"I think I have everything we need," Hank said, sorting through the back of his truck. He had two bushel baskets. They were made with wire and had thin wooden slats. In the baskets were several fish heads tied to sticks with twine.

"I got the fish heads from the fish house, and they are good and ripe," Hank said proudly. Luke could smell them. They were definitely ripe.

Hank also had a couple of nets with long poles that had extensions.

"I bought these from a swimming-pool supplier. They extend to about twenty feet, perfect for catching crabs when you are standing on the bank of a canal or a bridge."

He also had a huge cooler filled with ice, water, and beer.

Cora came out of the house with a thermos of hot coffee and a full paper bag with grease stains on the bottom.

"Thought you guys needed some breakfast for the ferry. Sausage biscuits, sausage-and-egg biscuits, plus some nice hot coffee," Cora said. "You will be on your own for lunch. Hank said he didn't want me to make any sandwiches."

"I thought we'd eat at Martelle's. They have a great lunch buffet," Hank said.

"I also brought along some smoked fish and saltine crackers," Hank said. He liked to smoke blue fish. It was his specialty.

"I brought some Lance peanut butter crackers," TMJ said.

Hank clapped his hands. "Let's get going. It's almost 6:00."

There were not many vehicles in line for the 6:30 Swan Quarter ferry. But cars had already starting lining up for the more popular 7:00 Cedar Island ferry, which led to Morehead City, New Bern, and parts west. The Swan Quarter ferry, which was not used as much, took passengers to the mainland of Hyde County and on to Bath, Little Washington, and Greenville.

Luke, in the backseat, was a little tired so he tucked a pillow under his head and took a nap. The ride on the twenty-eight-car ferry took two hours and forty-five minutes. When they got to the other side, they disembarked from the ferry and drove past the three-story, brick Hyde County Courthouse. They passed through town and were soon out in the countryside.

Hyde County was flat and filled with large farms and woodlands. Hank told Luke that physically Hyde County is one of the largest counties in North Carolina, but one of the smallest in terms of population with slightly more than 5,800 full-time residents.

Hank pulled off the road in front of a run-down building that said "Carraway Bait and Tackle Shop, Motel and Cottages."

"I bet you guys don't have inland fishing licenses," Hank said.

"I have my saltwater license, won't that do?" Luke asked.

"Me, too," TMJ said.

"No, you have to have a freshwater license to fish for crabs over here," Hank said.

Hank got out of the truck and tried to open the front door of the business, but it was locked. A note taped to the window said to call for service. So Hank tapped the number on the note into his cell phone. A woman answered with dogs barking in the background. He told her he needed two fishing licenses, and she said she would be there in ten minutes. About twenty minutes later, a woman drove up in a beat-up pickup truck and let them in to buy the fishing licenses. She turned on the computer, which took a while to power up.

"Damn computer is so slow," she said. It also looked old. But she had to access the state wildlife website to get the licenses, which cost fifteen dollars apiece. Finally, she got them, but then the printer didn't work. She was finally able to print their licenses.

When they left the tackle shop, they turned down a dirt road and soon passed signs announcing the Lake Mattamuskeet National Wildlife Refuge.

"What makes Lake Mattamuskeet special?" Luke asked Hank.

"The Carolina Bays are a favorite place for duck hunters, but a little-known fact is that these brackish waters are also home to huge blue crabs, some with a carapace as big as twelve inches. That's about twice as big as the blue crabs found in the ocean and in the Pamlico Sound," Hank said.

"How did they get in the lake?" Luke asked.

"One theory is that the huge crabs were blown into the waters of the lake by storms, and since they faced no predators, they grew to enormous size."

TMJ grinned, "They look like normal blue crabs on steroids."

Hank told Luke that canals were built in the early twentieth century to drain the lake and use its rich soil for farming. Since it was below sea level, pumps were built to pump the water into the canals with locks. These canals carried the water out to Pamlico Sound. The lake was drained three times. A corporation named New Holland Farms took over the operation, and after investing millions in dredging the lake, digging canals, and building pumping stations, the company went bankrupt. Later, the old pumping station was turned into a lodge for hunters, and the lake was allowed to return to its natural state. The old canals still criss-cross the area and are where the biggest crabs are found.

Hank pulled up in front of the old Mattamuskeet lodge with its signature black-and-white-banded lighthouse structure in the middle. There was scaffolding on the building, the windows were boarded up, and the structure was getting a new tiled roof. When Luke asked about it, Hank told him that state funds had been obtained to restore the old structure, so it could be used as a lodge and conference center. Hank led the group to a dam that went across one of the canals with a sluice gate. He put his fish heads in the canal, wrapping the twine around the metal guardrails.

"The limit is twelve crabs a day per person, and the minimum size blue crab is five-inch carapace, point to point. No one is supposed to have more than five lines out," Hank said, putting out his lines. A middle-aged black man and his young son were also crabbing on the low concrete dam.

Luke watched the twine lines that went into the water. One of them began to jiggle. He whispered to Hank to bring the net. Hank put the net in the water, and Luke gradually pulled up the fish head. The water was clear so they could soon see the fish head and the crab attached to it. Hank expertly scooped up the crab, a big one with a nine-inch carapace. He shook it loose into the bushel basket, pulled out the fish head, and put it back in the water.

They continued pulling up the twine with the fish heads until they had about five big crabs.

"I'm ready for a beer," TMJ said.

"While you're up there, get me one, too," Luke said. It was a warm day, but it was overcast so the sun was not too hot. Also the bugs weren't bad. The area was surrounded by pines, cypress swamps, and wetlands. They saw a six-foot-long gar in the water, looking prehistoric with its long, pointed snout. There were supposedly alligators in these waters, but they did not see any. Turtles sometimes surfaced and occasionally took their bait.

"Damn turtles," Hank said, pulling up a line with no fish head on it.

After about an hour, Hank suggested they move to another spot on one of the canals.

They loaded up the truck and drove to an open field that had been farmed but was now planted with grains and other feed for wildlife. Hank drove up to a bridge that crossed the canal. Two men, wearing long pants and long sleeved shirts, were crabbing on the bridge. Hank, Luke, and TMJ wore shorts and T-shirts.

"Where are you guys from?" Hank asked, as he crossed the bridge to the other side on foot.

"I'm from Manteo, and my friend is from Colorado."

"Pleased to meet you," Hank said. "Is this your first time out here?"

"Not for me, but for my friend, yeah. It's his first time to eastern North Carolina."

"Hope you enjoy yourself," Hank said. "This is Luke and TMJ; they work with me on Ocracoke Island. We build houses."

"Not many houses being built this year," the guy from Manteo said.

"Nope, but just enough for me. I'm retired and do a house a year maybe. Working on one in Oyster Creek for now."

"I'm in the wholesale vegetable business," the guy from Manteo said. "And my friend here is a wildlife photographer."

"Cool," TMJ said. "What kind of photography do you do?"

"I do freelance work for wildlife magazines. Doing a shoot now for *North Carolina Wildlife Magazine*," he said.

As the men chatted, Luke quietly put out the lines along the banks of the canal. Hank crossed the bridge with the net and put out some lines on the other side of the canal. He knew all the good spots and immediately began netting some crabs.

The guy from Manteo gave TMJ a ripe melon that he cut open and sliced up for Hank and Luke. Then he and his friend left. After netting a few more crabs, it was getting close to one o'clock.

"I'm getting hungry," TMJ said. "Where's that restaurant with the good lunch buffet?"

"Martelle's?" Hank asked. "Not too far from here. You guys ready to get some lunch?"

"Sure," Luke said since he was getting hungry as well.

They loaded up the truck, and Hank headed to the road that led to Engelhard.

When they walked in the one-story brick, 1950s-style restaurant, they saw the guy from Manteo and the photographer from Colorado, who had just ordered from the menu. After Hank and the boys loaded up on the all-you-can-eat buffet with vegetables, several meats, and salad bar, they joined their new friends.

"Crabbing works up an appetite," TMJ said, looking at the vegetables, pork chops, and barbecue chicken piled on his plate.

The guy from Colorado told them about traveling around the country, taking shots for wildlife magazines. Luke thought that would be a cool way to make a living.

After they ate lunch, Hank and the boys drove to Alligator Farms, a big farming operation located a few miles west of Engelhard. Hank bought a bushel of sweet corn and a bushel of onions. Then they drove back to the old Mattamuskeet lodge and put out some more crab lines. They caught several more crabs, and Luke caught a big catfish that had swallowed a fish head. They also drank a couple more beers. After an hour or so, Hank looked at his watch.

"This has been fun, but I think we need to start back to the ferry. We have to be there thirty minutes in advance, and the ferry leaves at 4:30," he said.

"Let's stop and get some beer on the way," TMJ said.

"Yeah, I'm thirsty," Luke said. "We need it for the ferry ride home."

They pulled up the crab lines, packed the truck, and headed out. They stopped by a little grocery store, and Hank bought a twelve pack of Yuengling, then they drove to the ferry. While waiting for the ferry, Hank took the crabs out of the bushel basket and put a burlap bag over the ice in the cooler. He placed the crabs over the burlap.

"How am I going to get to my beer?" TMJ asked.

"Looks like you're going to have to fight the crabs for it," Luke said, grabbing one before Hank could dump the crabs on the burlap sack. Then he doubled the burlap sack over, covering the crabs, and put the catfish on top.

"It is best to keep them cool for the trip home," Hank said, plucking a beer from under the crabs.

As the ferry left the dock at Swan Quarter, Luke saw low-lying marshy islands near the channel that stretched for miles out into the sound. The water in the sound, which was dead still seamlessly reflected the blue-gray sky with wispy clouds high up. Seagulls followed the boat, hoping that some tourists would feed them. When no one did, they left to follow the shrimp boats in the distance.

Hank's truck was in the back of the ferry. Luke, Hank, and TMJ all drank a cold Yuengling. One of the ferrymen walked by and waved to Hank.

"Thelma Garrish's dad, Jack," Hank said.

TMJ got the smoked fish out of a Tupperware container and pulled out some saltine crackers. "Anyone want some of this? If Cora made it, it must be good," he said.

"I made the smoked fish, not Cora," Hank said.

"Well, I guess I'll try it anyway," TMJ said.

"It sure is beautiful out here," Luke said, looking at where the sky met the water.

"Sure is. It's fun being with friends, too," TMJ said. "Being able to fart and scratch your ass and drink beer and eat smoked fish and not worry about what anyone will say."

"You don't worry what people say anyway," Luke said.

"When we get home, after you all get cleaned up, you guys come over and eat the crabs. I'll boil them and get Cora to fix corn on the cob," Hank said.

"Well, twist my arm," TMJ said, "That sounds like a plan to me."

"I'm all for that," Luke said.

TMJ made another beer run. He took their dead soldiers and replaced them with fresh beers. "I had to fight the crabs for these. I hope you all appreciate what I had to go through to get them," he said.

Luke had had a few beers, and he was feeling sentimental. "You guys have been really good to me since I came to Ocracoke," Luke said. "I just wanted to tell you that. You took me in, a total stranger. Hank, you saved my life on the beach when I didn't know if I wanted it to be saved. TMJ took me in, too, into his trailer. Hank, you gave me a job, and Cora treats me like a son. A few months ago, I had no idea I would be riding a ferry across the Pamlico Sound with some really good friends after crabbing all day on Lake Mattamuskeet."

"It's nothing, Luke. I used to work for the Coast Guard. It's in my blood. I couldn't let you walk in that water and go under," Hank said. "And you are a good worker, a regular clean-cut guy. What's not to like about someone who works as hard as you do and is as good at it as you are. As for Cora, she is always looking for someone to mother. But we do both like you and want you to be happy."

"Damn this is turning into a regular love fest," TMJ said, trying to lighten things up.

"That's all right," Luke said. "You guys have been the best friends I have ever had, and, yes, I do love you for it, even you, TMJ."

"Even when I walk around the house naked."

"Well, I wouldn't go that far," Luke said, taking a sip of beer and laughing.

"No more need be said," TMJ said, then he let out a really loud fart. "Whooee! That felt good. Nothing like being with the guys and letting a good fart rip."

Luke opened the door and started to fan the air. "Damn that stinks," he said, holding his nose.

"Must be those smoked fish Hank made," TMJ said. "I bet those things will clean you out."

≈

When they got to the ferry dock, most of the beer had been drunk, and the three of them were feeling really good. TMJ and Luke returned to TMJ's trailer, each took a shower, and changed clothes then drove over to Hank's to eat. TMJ picked up some beer on the way to the Kilgo house.

"Just how much did you all drink on that boat?" Cora asked, when Luke and TMJ walked in with a twelve pack of beer.

"On the boat, hell, we've been drinking all day," TMJ said.

"Luke, have you been drinking all day?" she asked.

"Yes, ma'am," he said, sheepishly.

"I didn't expect much out of TMJ, but I expected more out of you, Luke," she said, scolding.

"Leave the boys alone, Cora. We had a great time together," Hank said, intervening. "The best thing you can do is get some food in them to soak up all that alcohol." Hank headed out to check the big pot filled with water that was sitting over a propane heater. He wanted to make sure the water was boiling and ready for the crabs.

"You're right about that," Cora said, picking up some corn and shucking it.

"Can I help?" Luke asked.

"Yes, sir. So can you, Thomas," she called as she saw TMJ trying to sneak out to join Hank.

They cut the corn in two pieces, shucked it, and put it in a boiling pot on the stove. Cora covered her dining room table with newspapers and got out plates, butter, and salt and pepper.

Hank brought in the crabs, which had been boiled in spices, and dumped them in the middle of the table. Cora brought out the steaming corn on the cob in a deep dish and put down plates and wooden mallets to crack open the crab legs.

"Dig in," Hank said, taking a huge crab and beginning to rip it open.

Luke had never eaten crab like this before. "How do you do it?" he asked.

Hank turned his crab over and said, "You see this pointy thing in the middle of his belly? You rip that up and out, then you pull the legs off and put them aside. You need to scrape out this yellow stuff, the fat, and then you cut out the gills, this feathery stuff." He demonstrated. "But you can eat the tender meat under it. It is good." He ate a lump of crabmeat from the body of the crab. Then he took a leg and cracked it open and pulled the meat out like a lobster claw.

Luke soon caught on and was eating his fair share of crabmeat. One of the monster crabs was almost enough. But the guys ate at least two crabs each; TMJ ate three. They also finished off the corn on the cob, slathered with butter and salt. Their mouths and cheeks were covered with butter as they ate.

"This is good, real good," TMJ said.

"It sure is," said Luke. "Thank you, Hank and Cora."

After they ate, they sat around, talked, and drank another beer. Luke couldn't even remember what they talked about he was so tired. When he and TMJ got home, he hit the sofa and went straight to sleep.

≈

Luke had gotten used to sleeping on the sofa in TMJ's trailer. That night, Karen came to him in his sleep. He had not seen her since the night with Anna. She was beautiful and radiant. She came to him in a shimmering nightgown and made love to him on the sofa.

"When will you come back to me?" he asked her.

"Whenever you need me, I will be here," she replied.

"I will never not need you," he told her.

"Someday you will no longer need me. Then you will be able to let go," she said.

"I love you, Karen," he said, burying his head in her ephemeral breast.

"I love you, too, Luke, but someday you will have to let go. You are too young and have too much life ahead of you," she said with a sweet smile. He could almost see through her.

"Don't go. I am not ready," he said, as her image began to fade.

"You will be," she said, and then she disappeared.

～Chapter Twelve～

The next day after work, Luke drove the south point road out to the beach, then he drove as far south as he could on the beach. He couldn't quite make it to the inlet because the beach was roped off to protect the bird nests. He pulled his Jeep up facing the water and got out. He looked toward the inlet and the south point, to the place where Hank had found him in April. So much had happened since then. Hank had saved his life, and the island had sustained him. When Hank pulled him out of the water, Luke hadn't cared whether he lived or died. Now he did care. He wanted to live. He wanted to enjoy the beautiful life that he had been given, even if it would be without his beloved Karen.

He did not know how much time he had left. But he decided that life was a gift, and each day should be savored and lived to the fullest. Instead of being bitter about what he had lost, he decided that Karen was a gift, too. He had the extraordinary experience of sharing his life with her during her brief lifetime. Nothing is guaranteed. Sometimes things happen without rhyme or reason. There is no explaining it. But what he did know was that he was alive, and he could enjoy every minute of every day and thank God for it.

On Ocracoke, he was surrounded by nature, sometimes cruel, most of the times beautiful. That natural beauty and the kindness and spirit of the people gave him a new reason to want to live. He was determined to build a new life in this wonderful place. He did not know what lay ahead for him, but he would push on and see what new twists and turns life had to offer. He was falling in love with Ocracoke and was beginning to call it home.

He walked down the beach. There were fishermen casting their rods and sitting in beach chairs watching their lines. There was a group of teenagers, playing corn hole with their cute girlfriends dressed in bikinis. Surfers tackled a distant line of waves. The water was clear and fairly calm, but the waves were big, long, and curled nicely—good surfing waves. He noticed something dark in the waves. He panicked until he realized that the water was filled with porpoises. Then a huge bull porpoise leaped out of the water into the air, playing in the waves. It leaped and rolled in the air, putting on a show.

Luke smiled. He couldn't believe it. It was the first time he had seen porpoises do that. He looked around to see if anyone else had seen it. He pointed to the sea. Others looked. It was a large pod of porpoises, and they were playing and having a great time in the surf. He watched them for a while until they swam up the beach and finally disappeared. Then he got back into his Jeep and headed home.

～

That Friday night, TMJ and Luke went to Howard's Pub to listen to a new band. They sat in a booth and ordered a beer. Anita Lorrance waited on their table.

"Where have you guys been?" she asked. "I haven't seen you around much."

"We were busy over the Fourth, and then we went crabbing on the mainland," Luke said.

"We haven't been on the beach much," TMJ said. "We need to get out there some more."

"Yeah, I've been on the beach a lot," she said. "I love the beach."

"What are you doing after work?" TMJ asked.

"I don't know, some of the waiters were talking about going out to the beach and building a bonfire. They said the band was interested in joining us."

"That sounds like fun," TMJ said. "Let us know if you decide to go out later."

"Sure," she said as she went to get them two Blue Moons in green Howard's Pub cups.

TMJ saw Thelma Garrish and waved her down. "Come join us," he asked as she walked up.

"I've been looking for you guys. I need to ask you to do a favor for me," she said with a big grin. "We are planning another fundraiser for the radio station. Sort of like what we did in June with the female arm wrestling. Only this time we are going to do a bachelor auction."

"What is a bachelor auction?" Luke asked.

"The planning committee must be made up of women," TMJ said, dismissively. Then he took a drink, waiting to hear Thelma's explanation of a bachelor auction. "It isn't like where the biggest studs are auctioned off to service the ladies is it?" He laughed. "If so, I'm in."

"No, you dummy," she said. "However, what happens after we arrange the date is up to you." She gave TMJ a wink. "Anyway, we decided to make it real innocent and straight up. Each guy will come up with an activity for his date. One guy who works at the Back Porch is taking his date out for dinner at the Back Porch. Another guy is taking his date clamming. Another guy is taking his date stargazing on the beach. Someone else is going to teach his date how to salsa. You know, stuff like that. You stand up, the auctioneer says what your date will be, and the girls start bidding. It should be tons of fun. Do you guys want to help us out and volunteer to be auctioned off?"

"I can't think of a date. What could I offer that some girl would want?" Luke asked.

"Well, you could start by taking off your shirt," she said, giving him the once over. "That would raise some interest."

"Take off his clothes? That's my department," TMJ said.

"No nudity allowed on stage! This is a fundraiser! Not a strip tease," Thelma said sternly. She was used to TMJ and his obsessions.

"Yes, ma'am!" he said, as if a teacher had just rapped his knuckles.

"No, seriously. I don't have any money. I couldn't afford to take someone out to the Back Porch Restaurant. What kind of date could I offer?" Luke asked. He wanted to help, but he needed suggestions.

"You or TMJ could take someone crabbing or clamming or fishing. Or you could fix a nice dinner. You could take someone for a drive on the beach or you could build a bonfire on the beach for them at night. You could do a clambake on the beach or have a fish fry. I don't know; think of something. I will see if anyone else is doing it and tell you. We want variety."

"Could Luke and I do a double date and help each other out?" TMJ asked.

"We prefer to have single dates. It is much more romantic and would fetch a better price at the auction," she said, with a sexy smile. "Think about it and get back to me. We would love to have you guys participate. Just about everyone we have asked so far as agreed."

"It sounds like fun. I'd like to help out, but I need to think of a good date," Luke said.

Thelma left and walked up to some other guys. Luke could hear her giving her auction spiel. She was enjoying talking to all the cute guys in the place and planning the event.

"What kind of date could I do?" Luke asked to TMJ.

"How about taking her fishing or clamming?" TMJ suggested.

"I like the idea of a clam bake on the beach," Luke said. "I could rake the clams that afternoon, then dig a pit on the beach and fix them. Serve beer and watch the stars."

"Okay, if you do that, I will do a fish fry at the house with beer," TMJ said.

"Are you going to cook naked?" Luke asked, teasing.

"I don't know. Maybe it should be 'clothing optional,'" TMJ said.

"That works, let the girl decide how she wants you to do it."

"Yeah," TMJ said. "I like that."

They got up and walked over to Thelma and told her their ideas. She signed them up. The bachelor auction was scheduled for August 1, starting with a champagne reception at 5:30, then the auction at 7:00. They had a couple of weeks to think about it, plan, and get ready.

At midnight, the band stopped playing and Anita asked Luke and TMJ to join the group on the beach. They parked at the airport and walked out to the beach. Some of the guys from the pub brought firewood, and others brought a couple of coolers of beer and wine. They dug a pit in the sand near the water, piled up the wood, and started the fire with newspapers. They did not bring chairs; everyone sat on towels. The moon, which was half full, had risen earlier and was high in the sky, reflecting on the water like a shower of diamonds. The stars were bright, so you could see the Milky Way and the Big Dipper, Scorpio and Jupiter. One member of the band brought out his fiddle and started to play a haunting tune that sounded like it came from the Civil War era. It was a folk piece that was simple, plaintive, and lovely. As the fire grew, sparks flew out into the night. Luke and TMJ pulled bottled Yuenglings out of the cooler. Anita sat beside Luke on a big beach towel and put her head on his shoulders.

"Isn't it beautiful out here?" she asked. "I'm glad you were able to join us."

"Thanks for inviting us," Luke said, then paused and looked up at the star-filled sky. "It is beautiful."

TMJ sat with Thelma Garrish, and they talked.

Anita put her hands on Luke's neck and pulled him to her and kissed him. He reciprocated, and soon they were in a heavy embrace on the towel on the beach. Others were doing the same, so it did not look out of place.

"Do you want to come to my place?" Anita asked Luke.

"Sure," he said without hesitation. He had drunk a few beers at the pub and more on the beach. Filled with passion and the spirit of the night, he would have followed her anywhere.

He had ridden with TMJ, so he walked back to Anita's car, which was parked along the road leading out to the beach.

~

Anita drove into the driveway of the small house that she rented with two other girls, but no one else was home. She wasted no time and took Luke into her room.

Sitting on the edge of Anita's bed, Luke suddenly wanted to put the brakes on this. "What are we doing?" Luke asked.

"What do you think we are doing? You are a damn cute guy. I have been wanting to get into your pants since the first time I met you, and I bet you have been wanting to get into my pants, too. So there, we're even," she said, taking off her blouse.

"Well, since you put it like that," Luke said, pulling off his T-shirt. Soon she had her bra off, revealing her firm white breasts that contrasted with her dark tan. He took one of her nipples in his hand and kissed it. She kissed his neck, and he kissed her lips, her eyes, her ears, her neck. She pushed him back on the bed, and they were soon fully engaged. The overhead light was on as well as a light beside her bed. She got up and turned off the overhead, leaving only the soft yellow light from the bed-side lamp. She pulled her shorts down, then her panties. She reached into a drawer beside her bed and took out a condom.

"Here use this," she said, handing it to him. He pulled off his shorts, he wore no underwear, and slipped on the condom. She pulled down the covers, and they crawled under the sheets. Soon they were making love. They continued until just before sunrise, when they fell asleep.

When he woke up, he heard people talking in the living room and smelled coffee perking in the kitchen.

"Oh, shit, I shouldn't have stayed the night," he said. "What are your girlfriends going to say?"

"Don't worry about it. It is nothing new to them," Anita said. "They'll be happy for me."

Anita got dressed and walked into the living room/dining room/

kitchen combination and sat on a bar stool at the counter overlooking the kitchen. Luke stayed behind. Mary Ann Johnson, who was standing in the kitchen wearing a bathrobe, poured some coffee. Her dark hair was pulled up in a bun. The tattoos on her lower arm were visible.

"Where is Luane?" Anita asked.

"I don't know. We were together last night, then she disappeared. I stayed over at Tommy Howard's, but he had to get up early, so I left when he left."

Luke opened the door and came out to sit beside Anita.

"Damn, look what the cat dragged in," Mary Ann said, giving Luke the once over. Luke suspected he had a reputation among the island girls as stand-offish and obsessed with his dead wife. He didn't date anyone, preferring instead to just hang out at the bars with TMJ and his buddies.

"Good morning, Mary Ann," Luke said. His hair was still tussled, and his shirt was wrinkled from lying on the floor in a pile.

"Good morning, Luke. Do you want some coffee?"

"Sure," Luke said. Mary Ann took down another cup and filled it.

After he finished his coffee, Luke told Anita, "I need to go."

"Thank you for last night," she said, throwing her arms around him and kissing him. "I enjoyed it very much."

Mary Ann went to her room to get dressed.

"I enjoyed it, too. Maybe we can see each other again," Luke said.

"I would like that," Anita said.

≈

Luke walked back to TMJ's trailer, which was only a couple of blocks away. When he opened the trailer door, the door to TMJ's room was closed. He jumped in the shower and changed clothes. When he got out of the bathroom, he found Thelma and TMJ sitting at the breakfast-room table. Thelma wore a bathrobe. TMJ again wore boxer shorts.

"Good morning," Thelma said to Luke.

"Good morning, Thelma," Luke said. "Anybody want some bacon and eggs? I'm about to starve."

"Sure, you cooking?" TMJ asked.

"Yep, taking orders," Luke said.

Luke opened up the refrigerator and pulled out a dozen eggs and a package of bacon.

"How about scrambled with some cheese and salsa?" Luke asked Thelma and TMJ.

"Mild or spicy?" Thelma asked.

"Whatever you want," he said, putting the bacon on first.

"I would prefer mild, thank you," Thelma said with a smile.

"Then mild it will be," Luke said. He grated some sharp cheddar cheese into a Tupperware bowl; added several eggs, a little milk, and a dash of salt and pepper; and then whipped the mixture. He took out the cooked bacon, poured the bacon grease out, and wiped the frying pan with a paper towel. Then he poured the egg mixture into the hot frying pan. Soon he had whipped up an omelet-like mound of scrambled eggs, salsa, and cheese. Thelma got some plates out of the cabinet and put them on the table with forks and paper napkins. Luke ladled the eggs out and put the bacon on a plate in the middle of the table.

"You sure are perky today," Thelma said to Luke as she ate her eggs.

"He must have got lucky last night," TMJ observed, putting a fork full of eggs to his mouth.

"You did too, mister," she said, with a big smile. She was perky, too.

≈ CHAPTER THIRTEEN ≈

"Luke, didn't you learn anything about sleeping with two women at the same time?" TMJ said. "Some time, sooner rather than later, they are going to find out about each other, and you are going to be in for a whole boatload of grief."

"I know, I know. I just got carried away. You know the little head ruling the big head," Luke said, as they sat at the kitchen table that night after fixing fried flounder, rice, and green beans for dinner. "Besides Anna blew me off the other night, and last night I guess I just got carried away. But, honestly, I like them both. I just don't know which one I like the best."

"I thought you were an old married man and knew better than that," TMJ said. "This is a small island. It is bound to get out."

"I never dated anyone before I met Karen. She is the only girl I ever went out with and the only woman I have ever loved," Luke said. "Besides you have a lot of room to talk, what about Thelma and Luane?"

"That is another matter altogether. They are friends and friends share, right?"

"Yeah, right."

"Looks like both of us may have gotten ourselves into a whole mess of trouble," TMJ said.

"You're right about that," Luke said.

The next day after work, TMJ and Luke went to SmacNally's for a beer. Luke saw Anna across the open-air bar with her back to Silver Lake.

"Hey, Anna," Luke said, walking over to her. "How have you been?"

"Fine, thank you."

"Can I get you a beer?" Luke asked.

"No, thank you," she said.

"Have you found any more turtle nests?"

"Yes, every day I go out I find more. We are almost up to forty now, and the laying season hasn't ended. We had a total of thirty-two nests last year," she said, her interest perking up.

"I would love to see the turtles hatch," he said, taking a stool beside her. She was really beautiful, he thought as he looked at her. She was beautiful in a natural way. She did not need makeup to enhance her looks. Her skin was perfect, with just enough tan. Her gray-green eyes sparkled, and her dark-brown hair was pulled back to reveal her long sexy neck.

"I'll call you when we find a nest that has hatched, if you would like. It will be early in the morning. You may be working," she said. "In August and September, we do some controlled releases of the baby turtles. We gather them up and release them on the beach for people to see. I will let you know when that happens."

"I would like that," he said. "Did you ever find out who killed the turtle in June?"

Anna shook her head. "No, just some leads, but so far they haven't gotten us anywhere."

Suddenly, Anna leaned toward him and said, "You know, I may take you up on that beer. Things haven't been going so well at work recently." It sounded like she wanted to change the subject. The subject of the turtle was still disturbing to her. Luke suspected they would never find who did it, and he figured she knew that as well.

Luke ordered her a Corona with a slice of lime.

"What's wrong?" he asked.

"The supervisor I really liked was transferred to Colorado and now things have changed. We have a new supervisor, and I don't know how much she likes me. My job is seasonal and ends in September. I am applying for a permanent position in the park. They could easily not rehire me. I don't want to leave. I want to stay on Ocracoke."

Luke tried to reassure her. "No need to borrow trouble. Who knows, it may work out just fine."

"I hope so," she said. "But I'm worried."

"Would you like to go to Dajio's tonight? I hear a really good band is playing."

"Sure," she said, taking a sip of beer.

～

They met that night at Dajio's to listen to an out-of-town band called Whiskey Rebellion. An Asian girl played the fiddle beautifully. Luke was not comfortable dancing, but Anna put him at ease.

"You don't have to impress anyone, just move and enjoy the music," Anna said, as she took his hand and led him to the dance floor. "No one really cares. They are too much into themselves and what they are doing to notice what we are doing."

When they took a break, Luke saw Thelma Garrish, then Luane Dobbins.

"You looked pretty good out there," Thelma said to Luke. "I didn't know that you could dance." She looked at Anna who was at Luke's side. "Who is your friend?"

"This is Anna; she works for the Park Service."

"Hey, Anna, my name is Thelma Garrish. My cousin Mickey Garrish is a park ranger."

"I know Mickey. He's a great guy."

"Thanks, lots of people like him. People come and go at the Park Service, but Mickey stays. He knows everyone."

"He sure does. I think he has worked for the park for a hundred years."

"Thirty-five to be exact. He has been there longer than anyone."

"This is my friend, Luane Dobbins. Luane this is Anna. What did you say your last name was again?" Thelma asked.

"I didn't say. It is Anna Thomas; pleased to meet you," Anna said, taking Luane's hand.

Luke didn't like the look on Thelma's face. He could practically see the wheels turning. He figured she was trying to decide whether she should tell Anita about Anna. He had a feeling Thelma would save this tidbit of information and use it when it was most advantageous for her.

≈

"You didn't tell me you were seeing someone else," Thelma said to Luke, sitting around the breakfast table at TMJ's the next morning. "TMJ, did you know about this girl Anna?"

TMJ squirmed a little. "Yes. I knew about her."

"What is Anita going to think?"

"Anita doesn't need to know," Luke said, defensively.

"This is a small island. Everyone knows what everyone is doing. Eventually, it will get back to her," Thelma said.

"Will you tell her?" Luke asked, pointedly.

She is my friend, but no, I won't. I will let her find out from other sources, which she will, of course."

"We're not going steady. We've only gone out a few times. There is nothing that says I can't date other people," Luke said.

"You slept with her," Thelma said.

TMJ sat and watched the exchange in silence. Luke knew that look. TMJ could have said I told you so, but he didn't.

"Yes, I did. I guess there is no privacy on this island," Luke said.

"You got that right!" Thelma said. "I know people who are divorced and see their ex-husbands every day. You just have to get used to having your business known by everyone. It is an island."

"So it is," Luke said. Where he came from people didn't know everyone's business. A person could have some privacy. But not here, he realized.

There were plusses and minuses to living on Ocracoke. But this was his home for now. He was going to have to learn to live with it. He decided the best thing was just to be open and honest about it.

"What did I tell you, man?" TMJ said after Thelma left. "Everyone knows your business here. This isn't Kannapolis or Concord."

"I thought you were going to say 'I told you so.' Thank you for not saying that," Luke said. "You go out with Luane and Thelma. They are friends. How do you get by with it?"

"I just tell them the truth, and they tell me the truth. It works best that way. There is no way that you are going to get by with telling a lie, not here."

"I don't want to lie, but I would also like to have some privacy," Luke said, trying to take it all in.

"Be honest. Tell them you don't want to get serious, and you want to see other women. There's not much they can do about it. Women out-number men on the island. So if they want to keep going out, they're going to have to take us the way we are. I don't think they want to get serious either, so it doesn't really matter."

"When the rubber hits the road, it will matter. When you are ready to get serious, it will matter," Luke said.

"Yeah, but you're not there yet, so don't borrow trouble."

"You're right. Thank you, bud."

≈

Luke decided he wouldn't go out of his way to tell Anna about Anita or Anita about Anna, but if they asked, he would be honest with them, even about sleeping with them. He was not ready to get serious, and they weren't either. Anita was too much into having fun. Anna may be a different story, though. He had been honest with Anna, telling her he wasn't ready to get serious. He hadn't lied. He just hadn't told her the whole truth. There was a difference.

The next day, Luke and TMJ did not work. Hank and Cora drove into Norfolk for a doctor's appointment and planned on stopping by

Home Depot in Kitty Hawk on the way back to pick up some stuff for the bathrooms at the house they were working on. TMJ wanted to stay in and surf the Internet. Luke decided to go surf fishing on the beach.

He got up about 5:30, drove north of the pony pens, parked, and walked over the dunes. He carried his fishing rod, a beach chair, a cooler, a bucket, some snacks, and extra tackle. He had also borrowed a scoop from Hank, which he would use to catch mole crabs for bait. When he walked over the dunes, the sun had not yet risen. He could barely make out the light from the Hatteras Lighthouse to the north as its light slowly circled. By the time he got all his gear over the dunes and set up on the beach close to the water, the sun had begun to rise. Since Ocracoke ran almost east-west, the sun rose close to where the beach met the water. The sky gradually lit up, the water reflecting the color of the sky, a cool opalescent blue. Then a pinprick of red appeared at the horizon. The pinprick gradually grew until it was a red-hot glowing ball over the ocean, glinting in the tidal wash on the beach.

The beach in the intertidal zone, near the water, looked like it had been shellacked, reflecting the sky and the rising sun. Gradually, the big red ball climbed the sky and became yellow, then white, seeming to get smaller as it rose. There were many shore birds: plovers, sanderlings, and sandpipers. The sanderlings scampered back and forth with the action of the waves on the beach. The waves were relatively calm, and the ocean looked almost like a lake. He saw porpoises surface beyond the waves and gradually move south parallel to the beach. A couple of fishing boats were putting out nets and orange buoys a few hundred yards from the beach.

Luke walked down to the edge of the water and scooped up a few mole crabs for bait. They constantly moved with the water and burrowed in the sand. He stuck the sharp end of a white vinyl tube in the sand. Sticking his rod inside the tube held his rod straight up so he didn't have to hold it. He sat down and turned on the radio to WOVV, the local radio station. It played classical music this time of day, so he changed it to a country-music station that he liked.

Not too far from him was an enclosure of signs and twine that surrounded a turtle nest. He expected to see a park ranger drive by soon, patrolling the beach for turtle landings. About thirty minutes later, a National Park Service truck drove by to check on the turtle nest. It was not Anna. The park ranger, a young man with a dark beard, waved.

Luke didn't catch as many mole crabs as he planned, but he caught enough to catch a small blue fish. Then he used the blue fish as cut bait to try to catch something bigger. He enjoyed sitting on the beach in the sun, listening to the radio, and fishing. The sun began to get hot so he took off his shirt. He caught a pretty good-sized blue fish; at least it was a keeper. It got hotter as the sun rose in the sky, so he decided to take a dip in the water. It was aquamarine blue, cool, and refreshing. When he got out, he dried off with his towel, then pulled out some Nabs and a Coke.

He caught another blue fish, and then an even bigger one. He put the fish in the five-gallon bucket half, which was filled with seawater.

He was so relaxed that he started to fall asleep in the beach chair. He was the only person on the beach, as far as he could see on either side of him. He decided to reel in his rod and walk a little. He walked to the half-mile marker nearest him, jumped in the water for a while, and then walked back. He looked both ways, then shed his bathing suit. He ran into the water naked. It felt great. This was the life, he thought, walking out of the water, drying off, and sitting down in his beach chair. It was a small island, true. But he could find all the privacy he needed right here on the beach.

He didn't want to hurt Anna or Anita. He wasn't ready to get serious with anyone. But he was a young man with sexual needs. He hadn't made love in six months. Nobody could blame him for doing what he did. The women enjoyed it; he used protection. Anyway, he just wasn't going to let himself feel guilty for doing what young men do.

Down the beach he saw a man and a woman walking over the dunes to the beach, heading his way. He pulled on his bathing suit and cast his line. This time he caught a flounder.

The middle-aged couple was picking up shells. He waved, and they waved back.

"Catching anything?" the man asked.

"Three keepers so far."

"That's good," the man said with a smile as he kept walking.

Soon it was lunchtime, and Luke was ready to go in. He packed up everything and hauled it over the dunes in two trips. Back at the trailer, he found TMJ still surfing the Internet.

"What are you looking at?" Luke asked, peering at the computer screen as TMJ closed the window on the computer.

"None of your business," TMJ said.

"Want a sandwich?" Luke asked, changing the subject.

"Sure," TMJ said, standing up with his back to Luke and pulling on his gym shorts.

"Thanks for putting your clothes on," Luke said. "Now I can enjoy my lunch."

≈

Thelma called and asked them to join her and some other folks on the beach to see the full moon that night.

TMJ and Luke drove to the lifeguard beach, parked, and walked over with a cooler of beer and two beach chairs. It was Monday night, and there was a big crowd on the beach—old friends as well as some new-comers. Anita was there, but Anna was not. Anita and Luke spoke, but she hung with a group from Howard's Pub, and Luke hung with TMJ, Thelma, and some of the locals. They drank and partied until about 2:00 then went home to sleep.

≈Chapter Fourteen≈

The bachelor auction was held on Sunday at the Hemp Shop on School Road. The guys were told to meet there at six unless they wanted to take part in the champagne reception before the auction. The auctioneer, who was a friend of Thelma's, wore a sexy black dress, long black gloves, and a black hat with a blue feather. She had large breasts that threatened to tumble out of her dress at any moment.

Several guys wore little blue bowties like those from Chippendales, the famous male strip club. The auctioneer announced who each guy was and what their date would be. There was a DJ, who played music while the guy was auctioned off. The first guys did not go for a lot of money. The crowd was still warming up as the alcohol flowed freely. Admission was only ten dollars, but the real money was made on the auction. With the third guy—a handsome dark-haired man who worked at one of the restaurants—the bidding started to take off. "Sold for $300," the auctioneer announced with a smile. Someone yelled, "Take your shirt off." With a sexy grin, the man did a strip tease, tossing his shirt into the crowd. That got them really going.

Next was a young Hispanic man who worked in the kitchen at Howard's Pub. His date was a salsa lesson. He went for a good price. Then Tommy Howard was up. His date was a sunset cruise to Portsmouth Island with margaritas on the beach. He went for a good price as well. It didn't hurt that he was good looking and well built.

The front yard of the Hemp Shop was full of attractive young women, who were whooping and hollering and having a great time. Lights were strung in the trees surrounding the shop as night fell. The noise from the auction could be heard several blocks away. Even some tourists joined in on the fun.

Soon TMJ was up and his bidding went up over $300 with Thelma and Luane bidding against each other. He took his shirt off and pulled out the waistband of his pants, threatening to take them off, until the auctioneer stopped him. Everyone knew TMJ liked to get naked, so it was no surprise. Finally, Thelma got him for $350.

Luke was up next. He had a good build, and the auctioneer wanted him to show it off, so she asked him to take his shirt off, which he did. His lean, athletic body showed up well under the lights. He was to fix a clambake for two with wine on the beach. Several girls started bidding, girls Luke did not know. But then Anita joined in and bid. She bid $200, but her bid was beaten by someone he could not see who bid $225. He realized that the bidder wasn't there; she was texting the bid. There was a sign with a phone number on it that said, "Don't want your bid public? Silent bids: text or call." Each girl took a number during the bidding; she must have called in a number. Anita bid $250, and another girl bid $275. The silent bidder bid $300. Then Anita bid $325. The silent bidder bid $350. Anita paused. She didn't know who she was bidding against and didn't know how much further to go. Thelma bid $375, Anita bid $400, and the silent bidder bid $425. The auctioneer said, "Going once, going twice, sold to the silent bidder."

That was the highest price paid so far at the auction. Luke was baffled. He didn't know who the silent bidder was, until he stepped down and asked one of the organizers. They looked up her number and said, "Anna Thomas. Do you know her?"

"Yes," Luke said as he buttoned up his shirt.

Luke and TMJ hung around for a while watching the auction and then left. In all, more than twenty-five men were auctioned off. Most were in their twenties, but one or two were in their thirties and forties, and most of them were in great shape. The auction was a resounding success. It raised well over ten thousand dollars.

≈

Luke called Anna, "Congratulations on winning me at the auction. When would you like to schedule your date?"

"Let's see. What about Thursday night?" Anna said.

"That's fine. I'll pick you up at seven then we'll drive to the beach. I'll have everything prepared," Luke said. "See you then."

Luke picked up Anna on Thursday night and drove her out the south point road to the beach close to Ramp 72, where he had already dug a hole and started a fire. He had been clamming the day before and had raked about sixty clams. He asked Hank and Cora for advice about how to cook the clams. Following their instructions, he put the clams in a bucket of salt water, added some corn meal in the water, and let them sit overnight to clean out the sand and make them sweeter. Although he had built a fire on the beach, he also brought a small charcoal grill to grill the clams. At the beach, he pulled out two beach chairs and a cooler with wine and wine glasses.

"Would you like a glass of wine?" he asked Anna, who sat in the beach chair near the fire pit, which was dug close to the ocean.

"Yes," she said, and he pulled a chilled bottle of California chardonnay from the cooler and poured two glasses.

He then set up the grill, put the charcoal in the bottom, and covered the grill top with aluminum foil. He placed two pieces of corn on the cob wrapped in aluminum foil on the grill then started to line up the clams on the grill. He closed the lid. He set up a small folding table and pulled slaw that he had made out of the cooler, hot corn bread that Cora had made, plates and forks, butter, and a tablecloth and napkins. The bag beach chairs fit nicely under the table. He poured some white wine over the clams as they steamed on the grill. As soon as the clams opened, he took them off the grill but left the corn to cook a little longer. He put the first batch of clams on their plates.

Anna pulled up her chair and pulled the clams out of their shells with her fork. He had fixed a butter and lemon sauce to dip them in. Soon the corn on the cob was done, and he used tongs to pick them up and put them on the plate. He served her coleslaw.

"Very nice," she said.

"Would you like some more wine?" he asked.

"Yes," she said, eating the clams out of the shells and buttering her corn.

"This is delightful," Anna said. "Well worth the money."

"I'm glad you like it," Luke said.

They finished eating and drank some more wine before the sun began to set in the west over the sound. It grew big and orange as it drew close to the horizon. Then it disappeared in a bank of clouds before it sank into the water of the sound. Just before it set, the brilliant red sunlight burst forth from under the clouds in a final beautiful moment.

When it started to get dark, Luke packed up his gear, put out the fire with water and buried it, then washed the grill in the ocean. He buried the charcoal in the sand.

"We have to go in before nine, you know," Anna said.

"I know," Luke said and offered to fill her wine glass once more. They both sat in the beach chairs facing the ocean. He refilled his glass of wine as well.

"I love the night sky on the beach," Luke said, looking up. The moon had not yet risen, and the sky was dark and cloudless, perfect for stargazing. The stars were particularly bright, and the Milky Way cut a swath above them like someone had scattered diamonds across the dark sky.

"Next week is the meteor shower, the Perseids. That would be a good time to go out on the beach at night," Anna said.

"Have you heard whether you can keep your job through the winter or not?" Luke asked.

"No, I am still waiting to hear. I like the winter because we get to save the turtles on the beach that have been stunned by the cold."

"What do you mean?"

"When the water temperature drops suddenly, some turtles are stunned. Their vital functions shut down, and they drift to shore where they can die. The rangers pick them up and take them to the North Carolina Aquarium in Manteo, where they are put in baby pools and are gradually warmed up and taken care of until they are ready to be released back to the wild. This past winter thousands were cold stunned in Florida, and hundreds washed up on the beaches in the Cape Hatteras National Seashore."

"Do you think you would like to stay here this the winter?" Luke asked.

"Yes. It is quiet, and you have the beach to yourself. Not so many people. It stays pretty busy through the fall up to Thanksgiving, and there is a burst of activity around Christmas, but after New Year's, the island really shuts down and is dead. Then things don't pick up until April when people start coming back and the restaurants and shops open up again."

"I need to decide if I am going to stay through the winter. I've never been here in the winter. It would be interesting but maybe hard to get used to," Luke said. "I'm not quite sure what I am going to do when we finish this house. We should be finished by the end of October. I haven't talked to Hank about it. I hope we can stay busy with small jobs and remodels, but I'm not sure. Cora says I'm a good cook. Who knows I might get a job in a restaurant this fall. Maybe I can pick up some work with the fishermen, putting out crab pots or hauling in pound nets. Or even go up beach and see if there is any work in Nags Head or Manteo."

"I agree with Cora about your cooking. You did a great job with the clams, slaw, and corn," Anna said.

"I need to go back to Kannapolis the first of the year. I left my entire shop back there. My father-in-law gave me a year to get settled and make other arrangements. I don't know what to do with my shop equipment because I don't have a place to put it. I may have to put it in storage. Hank would probably let me use his shop, but I'll cross that bridge when I come to it."

"Do you stay in touch with your wife's family? Are you close to them?" Anna asked.

"No. They never approved of me. Karen's mother liked me, but she died before we were married. My father-in-law hates me. He helped us buy a house, but it didn't feel right trying to keep it after Karen died. So I gave it back to him. He agreed to let me store my stuff there for a year," Luke said.

"Why does your father-in-law not like you?" Anna asked.

"He didn't think I was good enough for his daughter. I grew up in foster homes and came from nothing. Karen came from a nice family and worked for a bank," Luke said, a little uncomfortable.

"Oh," Anna said, "sorry, I didn't mean to pry."

"Karen and I loved each other since high school. I didn't want her for her money. I wanted her because I loved her. I insisted that she finish college. I didn't want to hold her back. But her father thought she deserved better than me."

Anna was silent. After awhile, she changed the subject and started talking again about the night sky and the stars.

Around 8:30, they decided to go in and drove back along the long south point road back into the village. Along the way, they could hear the loud sounds of frogs and toads in the marsh. It had rained the night before, and the frogs were out in full force that night. On either side of the road, the fireflies danced over the marsh grass for as far as they could see.

"Do you want to come to my place?" Anna asked.

"Yes."

≈

"Where is everyone?" Luke asked, as they entered Anna's house.

"They went to Howard's Pub," she said. "That means we have the place all to ourselves."

"I am not sure the price of your date included this. It was only supposed to cover the dinner on the beach," Luke said, mischievously.

"Are you going to charge me more?"

"I haven't decided," he said teasing her.

She put her hand behind his neck and pulled him to her to kiss him. "Is that better?" she asked.

"Yes, much better."

Soon they had their hands all over each other and couldn't stop kissing. She took his hand and led him to the bedroom. But she stopped at the door.

"I am not going any farther until you promise me that you will not slip out in the middle of the night like you did last time," she said, very seriously.

"I promise," he said. He would have said anything at that point he was so full of passion.

They made love well into the night until they finally fell asleep in each other's arms, exhausted.

He woke at sunrise and watched the sunlight slowly fill the room. He was naked with a sheet half-covering him. She slept soundly beside him face down with one arm draped over his chest. He considered getting up, but thought again and decided to stay and honor his promise to her. He nodded off.

They woke together. "You got a lot of bang for your buck on this date," he said, with a devilish grin.

"Sure did, you didn't do so bad yourself," she said.

"You're right about that," he agreed. "I know you don't want me to leave early, but I don't necessarily want your friends to see me slipping out of here. Do you mind if I leave now, before everyone gets up?"

"No," she said. "I guess you don't want to be seen with me."

"No, silly," he said. "I just don't want people talking about us. I like my privacy."

"Do you honestly think you have any privacy on this island?" she asked, tickling him.

"Well, no," he said.

"Then stick around and have a cup of coffee with me. I don't care if anyone sees us together. I have nothing to hide. Besides you are officially off our date now. Let me fix the coffee," she said, getting out of bed and pulling on a bathrobe.

"Okay, twist my arm," he said, getting up and pulling on his shorts.

She made coffee while Luke sat at the breakfast bar. There was still no sign of her roommates.

"They must have had a really good time last night. I didn't hear them come in. I bet they are going to sleep until noon," Anna said, about her roommates. After he finished his coffee, Luke left and went back to TMJ's trailer where he found TMJ sitting at the breakfast table drinking a cup of coffee.

"Looks like you got as much out of that date as she did," TMJ said.

"I think that would be a fair thing to say," Luke said, pouring cereal in a bowl.

"I'm looking forward to mine next week," TMJ said.

Luke was getting into the rhythm of island life and found it to his liking.

~

That night Luke stayed in and fried flounder and hushpuppies for him and TMJ.

At about 6:30, Anna called.

"I don't want you to think that I am chasing you, but you asked me if I would call you when we release some turtles," Anna said. "Well, we dug a nest that has been hatching for the past two days and found about eight turtles at the bottom. We've put them in a cooler and are going to release them tonight at the lifeguard beach. Be there at 7:30 if you want to see them."

"Cool. I'll be there."

"Do you want to go out to the beach and see the baby turtles released into the water?" Luke asked TMJ.

"Sure, I don't have anything else to do this early. We can go to Howard's afterwards and listen to the band," TMJ said.

They drove to the parking lot at the lifeguard beach then walked over the boardwalk to the beach. There were already several people gathered. The white Park Service pickup truck that Anna drove was on the beach beside the lifeguard stand. Anna stood beside the truck with two others from the Park Service. They were talking to people who asked questions about what they were about to do. Luke saw people of all ages and several families with children.

"We are going to release the turtles into the ocean," Anna told the group. "We dug them up a few hours ago not too far from here."

"They're not still eggs, are they? Have they hatched?" someone asked.

"They are baby loggerhead turtles about the size of a half dollar."

"What do they feel like?" a little girl asked.

"They are very soft and rubbery. They don't have hard shells yet."

"What do you do with them?" the little girl asked.

"We put them on the wet sand a few feet from the ocean, and they start crawling toward the water unless lights shine and distract them. That is why we don't let anyone have flashlights or use flash photography."

"Is it true that the ghost crabs try to get them as they make it to the water?" asked a boy with the little girl. He looked to be her brother.

"Yes, but tonight we won't let the ghost crabs get them, will we?" she said, smiling at the little girl whose eyes lit up.

"No, we aren't going to let the crabs get them," the girl said.

"What happens when they get to the water?" the boy asked.

"They swim really hard and follow the light of the moon. Eventually, if they survive, they find a place in the ocean called the Sargasso Sea, which is filled with floating seaweed. There they grow and develop," Anna said. "The females will return to the place they were born to lay eggs, but they don't do that until they are at least thirty-five years old."

"You mean the mother turtle who laid the eggs was born here on Ocracoke over thirty-five years ago?" The boy was astonished.

"That's what we believe," Anna answered.

"Let's go," one of the other rangers said. The three rangers in full uniform then picked up the white cooler that held the baby turtles and walked to the water's edge. The other female ranger marked off a square around them and asked everyone to respect the line and not cross it. She also asked that no one use flash photography once the turtles were released. Lots of flashes went off before the turtles were released, however.

Anna and the two other rangers pulled on white rubber gloves, opened the cooler, and lifted out the tiny turtles. They placed the baby turtles at intervals across the beach. The children began to squeal when they saw how small the turtles were. The sun had gone down, but the ocean reflected the waning light of the sky. Luke and TMJ could see the half-dollar-sized turtles move rapidly toward the ocean with their flippers pushing them along the sand until they disappeared into the water.

"How do those tiny little buggers make it all the way to the Sargasso Sea?" TMJ was intrigued. "Just think of all the predators out there waiting to eat a tasty morsel of turtle meat. How many of them make it?" TMJ asked Anna after the turtles were released.

"We are not sure, but maybe one in a thousand. This season we have forty-four nests on Ocracoke with an average of one hundred turtles per nest. Do the math."

"Wow," TMJ said.

"Yeah, but we only had thirty-four nests last year. So we are making progress. Once they survive, they can live to be over a hundred years old," Anna said. "In one season, a single female will lay eggs three or four times."

"Cool," TMJ said.

"We are doing an experiment this year, where we take DNA samples from each nest so we can keep track of where the mother came from, where she goes, and where she actually lays her eggs," Anna explained to TMJ.

"That's cool," TMJ said.

As the crowd began to disperse, Luke approached Anna and asked, "What are you doing later?"

"I've got to work tomorrow morning, so I have to be up at five. I had a busy day today. I think I will turn in early tonight," she said.

"We were thinking about going to Howard's to listen to the band, Ventura Highway," Luke said.

"Have fun," she said.

≈

At Howard's, TMJ and Luke took a seat at the bar where they ordered draft beer.

"Two Yuenglings, please," Luke said to the bartender, a guy in his late twenties with a dark-brown ponytail.

"Hey, man, where is everybody?" TMJ asked the bartender, looking around and seeing a few families dining, but none of the usual Friday night local bar crowd.

"Didn't you know, man? Gaffer's, across the street, is having a big grand opening tonight. Half of Ocracoke is over there. It's a new sports bar in town," the bartender said.

"Isn't Howard's Pub a sports bar?" TMJ asked.

"Yeah, but we are also a restaurant. Gaffer's has twenty flat screen TVs. I don't think they will have a full menu like we have, more bar stuff," he said.

"I hope they do well. That location is cursed, though," TMJ said. "It seems like every summer there is a new business over there, and none of them ever do well."

"You know that Howard's started out in that building," the bartender told him.

"Really?" TMJ said.

"Been downhill since," the bartender said. "But I hear the new owners have restaurant and bar experience, maybe this time it will be different."

"Well, we'll have to check it out," TMJ said.

Luke looked around for Anita and did not see her. Maybe it was her night off.

TMJ and Luke finished their beer and walked across Highway 12 to Gaffer's. It had recently been painted and had a bright new sign. The parking lot was full, with more cars parked along the road. There was a line of people waiting to get in. IDs were being checked at the door.

Luke and TMJ got in line. Inside, the place was crowded. The Aaron Caswell Band played rock-and-roll music. Nearly all of Luke and TMJ's friends were there. Luke saw Anita standing near the bar with a handsome guy with sandy blond hair, a good tan, and a colorful floral patterned half-sleeve tattoo that ran from his left shoulder down his arm, stopping midway on his forearm. The man looked like he was a couple of years younger than Anita.

Anita motioned them over. "Hey, guys," she yelled at them.

TMJ and Luke made their way over to her.

"Hey, man," TMJ said, introducing himself to the guy she stood with. "My name is TMJ; this is my friend Luke."

"Good to meet you," he said, coolly. "My name's John."

John looked them over. "Weren't you guys in the bachelor auction?" he asked.

"Yeah, were you there?" TMJ asked.

"Yeah, I came after you guys. Anita won me at the auction," he said, looking at her.

"Yeah, tonight's our date night," Anita said.

"How was your date?" she asked Luke.

"It was good. I fixed clams on the beach. Sorry it wasn't with you," he said with a smile.

"Who was the mystery woman?" she asked.

"Anna Thomas. She works for the Park Service," he said.

"I don't know her. I hope it was worth what she paid for you."

"I don't think she was disappointed."

"Sorry to interrupt, but Anita is my date tonight and I have promised to show her a good time," John said. Then he pulled Anita out onto the dance floor.

Luke and TMJ stayed until about two o'clock, drinking and talking to friends. Luke watched Anita and her date. She seemed to be having a great time with him. They left together about midnight and did not return.

≈

The next day, Luke and TMJ went to the beach and hung out with several friends at Ramp 67. The water was rough, and the waves were really big from Tropical Storm Colin off Bermuda. The riptide was bad, so most everyone stayed out of the water, except the few brave souls who went surfing. At 4:20, Tommy Howard, who was also a volunteer fireman, got a call on his radio. A family was in trouble in the water at the south point.

"Can we come?" Luke asked.

"Sure, we need as much help as we can get."

Tommy put a red light on the top of the cab of his pickup truck, and Luke and TMJ followed Tommy as he sped toward Ramp 72 and the south point.

By the time they got to the south point, three members of the family, the mother and two young kids, were out of the water, but volunteers were still struggling to get the father in. The mother was crying hysterically, and the boys, who looked to be about ten and eleven, were wrapped up in towels standing by the EMS truck. As soon as Tommy got out of the car, two by-standers carried the father, who was blue and looked to be about fifty, out of the water, unconscious. They laid him out on the sand, and one of the EMS guys administered CPR without success. They then brought in other equipment on the blue EMS four-wheel-drive pickup truck but were unable to revive him. The man was pronounced dead. It was the first fatality in the water on the Outer Banks for the season. He was fifty-one years old and from Maryland. He died trying to save his family, who were pulled out of the water by guys on surfboards.

"So sad," TMJ said. "If you don't get here right away, they don't have a chance. Thank goodness for those guys who were surfing nearby or the whole family might have been lost."

"The poor guy died trying to save his family," Luke said.

"I know. Once that riptide gets a hold of you it takes you straight out. They tell people to swim parallel with the beach to get out of it, but when you are in a panic and trying to save your kids, it is hard to think. Then you get in trouble," TMJ said.

≈

On Thursday night, Anna called and invited Luke to join her on the beach.

"Tonight is supposed to be the best night for the Perseid meteor shower," Anna said.

"Sounds cool. I'll pick you up at sundown, about eight o'clock."

When they drove onto the beach, the sun had just set and it was already getting dark. Out to sea they could see tremendous thunderclouds, some looking like the mushroom clouds from an atomic bomb. Anna spread a blanket on the sand. They sat on the blanket and talked as the sky grew dark. Soon, the stars became very visible—the Milky Way, the Big Dipper, Jupiter—all the stars were clear and bright. Then, Anna saw the first meteor.

"There, look," she said, pointing to a place in the sky above them.

"Where? I didn't see it," Luke asked, straining to see.

"There are some more over there," she said, pointing again.

This time he saw it.

"Nice," he said.

They both lay back and looked up. Soon more meteors began to shoot across the sky. One even had a tail. They seemed to come in clusters, then there would be nothing for several moments until another meteor streaked across the sky.

"Look," Anna said, pointing out over the ocean. The sky lit up, and suddenly, a wild tracery of lightning spread across the night sky in the distance.

"Cool, do you think it is heading this way?" Luke asked, a little apprehensive.

"No, I checked the weather before I left. The storms are going to the north of us, and they are well out at sea. But isn't the lightning show beautiful?"

They couldn't hear thunder so the lightning was far off, but it made an incredible light show over the ocean, spreading out like veins on the human body, except these were made of pure light and energy on the black night sky. Anna looked up and saw a cluster of meteors again.

"This is quite a show, isn't it?" she smiled. There was a cool breeze coming off the ocean. Luke leaned over her as she lay on the blanket and pulled a stray strand of hair from her forehead.

"It is really beautiful," he said, looking down at her. She was beautiful too, her face dimly lit from the night sky, he thought as he gazed upon her.

"Yes, it is," she said, looking up at him. He bent down and kissed her. She reached up and pulled him down beside her. They kissed and embraced.

There was no moon. It would have risen over the ocean, but the clouds covered it.

"Do you want to go home with me?" she asked.

"Yes," was his quick reply.

When they left the beach, he drove to her house. Some of her roommates were up watching TV. Luke and Anna went straight to her bedroom where they made love for several hours. The next morning, Luke got up early, said good-bye, and went home to eat some breakfast with TMJ before they met Hank at the work site.

≈Chapter Fifteen≈

On Saturday, TMJ and Luke went to meet their friends at their favorite secluded place on the beach. It was a beautiful sunny day; the surf was calm. They got out to the beach by 10:00, and there were already several SUVs there. People were sitting in beach chairs, lying on towels, and swimming in the surf.

TMJ, as usual, sat naked in his beach chair. He was not alone, but most people were clothed, including Luke. Luane and Thelma drove up soon after TMJ and Luke arrived and kept their bathing suits on.

A new white, Ford four-wheel-drive truck drove up, and Anita got out of the passenger side. She had brought John, her auction date. Wearing a white T-shirt and a long floral print surfer's bathing suit, John retrieved some chairs and a cooler out of the back of his pickup. Anita wore a skimpy bright green bikini.

"Cute guy," Thelma said, watching John get his cooler out of the truck. Anita had already set up her beach chair beside her. "You done good, girl."

"I kind of think so, too," Anita said. She shot a look at Luke. He thought that she must think he was jealous, but he was not. In fact, he was almost relieved Anita had found someone else, because although he liked Anita, he liked Anna even more.

John took off his shirt and threw it in the truck.

"Great tattoo," Thelma said, admiring the colorful oriental pattern on John's arm. "Great body, too." She said eying John's lean, hard, tanned body.

"I like it, too, especially in bed," Anita said, in a whisper to Thelma that Luke could clearly hear.

John set up a chair beside Anita. "Do you want anything to drink?" he asked, opening the cooler.

"Not yet, hon," Anita smiled back at him.

"Where's Anna?" TMJ asked Luke.

"She had to work today," Luke said. "I'd love to get her out here one day."

"Yeah, it would be a good thing for her to meet everybody."

"I know. She hangs out with the park rangers. I don't think she knows many of the locals." The wind was picking up, but not too bad. Sometimes it blew so hard, kicking up the sand, that made it hard to stay out for long. Today the waves curled long and low. The water was almost aquamarine, it was so clear and blue.

"Do you want to go swimming?" John asked Anita.

"Sure," she said. They got up and walked into the water. Soon they were kissing in the water. Anita pulled her top off then her bottom; John took his bathing suit off. They kissed some more until they walked out of the water naked.

"Oh my God," Thelma said. "Do you see what I see?" She was staring at John's naked body. He was well endowed, in addition to being well built.

"Damn, Anita always gets the good ones," Luane said, enjoying her view of John in all his glory.

"What about me?" TMJ said, hearing them talk and seeing them stare. TMJ was very proud of his physical endowment and never hesitated to show it off, whether people wanted to see or not, but he did not have the body that John had. TMJ was tall, lanky, and skinny in comparison.

"We can see you anytime," Luane said, teasing TMJ. "It is nice to see some fresh meat, and I like what I see." Luane stared at John as he dried off and slowly pulled his bathing suit on.

Luke watched and listened. His body was certainly nothing to be ashamed of, but he preferred not to parade around like TMJ did. He was a bit more modest. He chuckled inside as he watched the women salivate over John. He was happy that Anita had found someone, because otherwise he would have had to let her down easy, and that would have been hard to do because he liked her. Now TMJ, on the other hand, seemed to have no problem with openly sleeping with two women who were also good friends. He couldn't figure out how TMJ pulled it off.

~

When Luke got in that afternoon, Anna called and asked him over for dinner.

"You cooked for me. Now let me cook for you," she said. "The girls are planning to go to Howard's tonight to listen to a new band. So it will just be the two of us."

"What time?"

"About seven o'clock?"

"See you then," Luke said, heading to the shower with a smile.

When he arrived, Anna offered him a beer. He sat on the stool at the bar, overlooking the kitchen.

"I have some good news," Anna said.

"What?"

"They offered me a full-time job with the park, so I will be here all winter," she said. "I am so excited."

"That's great," he said. "I am so happy for you. I'm not sure what I'm going to do. The house job in Oyster Creek is going to end this fall, probably in October. I need to find other work. I know a lot of the summer help at the restaurants leave at the end of August so I was thinking about trying to get a job at a restaurant. I love to cook, and I am eager to learn."

"You would make more money waiting tables."

"I might do that, too, but I would really like to work in the kitchen at one of the restaurants."

"The clientele changes in the fall. The summer tourists are gone. It's mostly older couples traveling and men on fishing trips. It is quieter, but it is still busy enough that everything stays open until after Thanksgiving. Some restaurants and businesses stay open until New Year's, but in January and February, everything shuts down and a lot of people leave the island. I don't know what a guy like you would do in the dead of winter. Howard's used to stay open all year-round, but now even it closes after New Year's and doesn't open again until March," Anna said.

"I will need to get back to Kannapolis in January to do something with my shop equipment," Luke said. "After that I don't know, but I am thinking that I would like to stay all year if I can find work."

"I hope you can stay," she said.

"I hope so, too. What are you fixing? It smells good."

"Parmesan fish with fresh red drum. I got the recipe out of the *Cafe Atlantic Cookbook*. It is really good."

"I can't wait to try it," he said, sipping his Yuengling in a green bottle. She drank a glass of white wine. She fixed the Parmesan paste, spooned it on the drum fillets, and put them in the oven. She also steamed some fresh asparagus and prepared a mixed green salad with homemade vinaigrette dressing.

Watching Anna cook, Luke was intrigued by the Parmesan paste. He would like to make it himself. He enjoyed cooking.

"Can I look at the recipe?" he asked.

"Sure, here is the cookbook."

She set the table with candles and opened a bottle of white wine. She turned on the radio to WOVV, which was playing island bluegrass.

After dinner, they stayed up and talked for a while. Then Anna invited Luke to stay the night.

≈

When he got back to TMJ's trailer early the next morning, Luke found both Thelma and Luane sitting at the breakfast table, wearing robes. TMJ fixed coffee in gray gym shorts.

"Good morning," Luke said, looking around. Both girls had spent the night with TMJ.

"Coffee?" TMJ asked, pouring a cup of coffee for himself.

"Sure," Luke said. He didn't want to act like there was anything unusual. He figured he would ask TMJ what had happened after the girls left.

"Where did you spend the night?" Luane asked, sipping her coffee.

"With Anna," he said.

"I don't think I have ever met Anna, though I have heard about her," she said, glancing at Thelma.

"You are going to have to bring her to the beach one day and introduce her to everyone," Thelma said.

"I will," Luke said. "It looks like Anita has found herself a guy."

"John? Yeah, he's cute," Thelma said with a smile. "She says he is great in bed, too. He sure has the equipment for it."

The girls finished their coffee and ate their bagels then went back to the bedroom to get dressed. Thelma was working the lunch shift at Jason's, and Luane worked the checkout counter at the gas station.

≈

"Did you sleep with both of them last night?" Luke asked TMJ after the girls left.

"Yeah, we've been doing that off and on for a few weeks now. I mostly do it at their place, but with you gone, I asked them over here," he said, sitting down on the sofa.

"So that is how you have been sleeping with both of them without causing a ruckus," Luke said, with a chuckle. "I understand now." He paused. "Are they lesbians?"

"No, they are just good friends who like to have sex with me and sex with each other. I guess you could call that bi-sexual. I don't know, and I don't care. I just enjoy it," TMJ said, with a big toothy grin.

"I guess you do."

"They do me, then they do each other, then I do each of them, then I do both of them, you get the routine."

"Yes, I get the picture," Luke said. "Every man's fantasy, right?"

"Yes, it is just about as good as you could imagine it being. As long as they are cool with it, I sure am cool about it."

~

They were working on the interior of the Oyster Creek house. Luke decided he needed to talk to Hank about his future.

"Hank, I have enjoyed working with you on this house, but I am trying to think ahead about what's next for me. Do you have anything else lined up when we finish the Oyster Creek house?" Luke asked.

"I don't really have anything, Luke. I have been thinking about you guys, too. Usually TMJ helps me with some odd jobs and remodels, but I don't think I have enough work for both of you after we finish this house."

"Would you mind if I took a job at a restaurant? I'll still work here, but now is a good time to look for a restaurant job with the summer help leaving," Luke said.

"That's exactly what I was thinking. I may be able to use you a little this winter, but you will need a good backup job if you want to stay on the island. There is usually more work off island to the north, but with the economy and real estate as bad as it is, I don't think anyone is building houses now. If there is any work, it will be small jobs and remodels.

"Most people around here work two or three jobs at the same time. I sure understand. Good luck. I will be happy to give you a good reference," Hank said.

That week Luke applied at the Flying Melon, the Back Porch, Cafe Atlantic, the Ocracoker, and Gaffer's. He landed a part-time job at the Ocracoker, working dinner three nights a week. The Ocracoker was a family-owned restaurant that had been in business for twenty years. It had a good reputation and specialized in local seafood dishes. Luke was excited about his new venture. He looked forward to learning something new. He did not apply at Howard's because Anita worked there, and the aftermath of their relationship was still a little too fresh. He could always try to work there later after things had settled down between them.

≈

"Hey, would you guys like to go flounder gigging one night this week?" Hank asked one day as they took a break at the work site. "I hear they have had some good luck in the sound behind Oyster Creek.

"Sure," TMJ said.

"That would be fun," Luke said. "What do we need to bring?"

"Just yourselves. I have the aluminum skiff, the gigs, and the lights for the front of the boat. We won't use the motor. We'll pole the boat. I'd wear a bathing suit or shorts you don't mind getting dirty and wet, maybe a long-sleeve shirt over your T-shirt, strap sandals or tennis shoes, because we may need to get in the water to push off the boat if we get stuck where it gets shallow. Oh, yeah, bring bug spray and some water bottles."

"When do you want to go?" TMJ asked.

"How about tonight?"

"Suits me, we don't have anything else going on," TMJ said, "being the first of the week."

"Meet me at the boat ramp at the end of the last road in Oyster Creek about 8:30. We'll put the boat in the water and go from there," Hank said.

≈

That night Luke and TMJ ate at home and put on bathing suits, T-shirts, and long-sleeve shirts. They brought a cooler with water and some beer and plenty of bug spray.

"I'm excited about this," Luke said, driving to Oyster Creek. "I have always heard about flounder gigging but never done it."

"It's fun," TMJ said. "And pretty easy as long as you can find the floun-der. They lay on the bottom in the sand, and when you shine the light on them, they freeze. Then you spear them with the gig and bring them in the boat. You gotta be careful about the size limit and the bag limit. I'm not sure what it is, but Hank will know."

"I love flounder. It's mighty good-eating fish," Luke said.

"Yeah, all those fish camps in Kannapolis and Concord serve flounder, don't they? I don't think flounder is as good as drum, tuna, grouper, or Mahi, but I like it," TMJ said.

"Fish snob. We don't get those exotic fish back home. But yeah, I order flounder at the fish camps and love it."

At the boat ramp, Hank backed his trailer with the boat into the water until the boat floated, then he unhooked it and brought the trailer out of the water and parked it. TMJ held the boat in the water, Luke put the cooler in the boat, and they all climbed in.

Hank gave them paddles, and they paddled out through the shallow water of the sound to a spot someone had recommended. The moon was about half-full, and the stars lit the sky. They could hear the sounds of cicadas, tree frogs, and birds over the water, and in the distance, they could hear the waves crashing on the beach. In the bow of the boat was a contraption with two arms made of white PVC pipe that hung out over the water with lights attached. The pipe had wires that ran through it and connected to a car battery, which sat in the front of the boat. When they got to the area where Hank wanted to gig, Hank attached the wires to the car battery, and the two spotlights glared into the water. The water was only about two-feet deep at that spot. They could see the sandy bottom, interspersed with grasses that grew under the water. There were shells on the bottom, little fish, crabs, hermit crabs, and shrimp.

"Flounder lay flat on the bottom and cover themselves with a thin layer of sand," Hank told Luke. "They are brown on top and white on the bottom, and both eyes are on the top. You can see them by the outline they make in the sand. At this point, we need to use poles, not paddles."

"What are the size and bag limits?" TMJ asked.

"On this side of the sound, they have to be at least fifteen inches long. On the other side of the sound in the ocean, they can be fourteen inches, but they grow bigger out here. Each person can catch eight per day," Hank said. "I assume that you guys have your fishing licenses?"

"Yep," Luke said.

"Me, too," said TMJ.

"Did you hear about the boat that caught the biggest fish in the Blue

Marlin Tournament in Morehead City this year?" Hank asked. "It was not only the biggest of the tournament but a record breaker. Well, it turned out that the mate didn't have his fishing license, so the boat was disqualified and they lost the prize—$1.2 million! Can you imagine, losing $1.2 million over not having a fifteen-dollar fishing license?"

"Wow," Luke said.

"I heard about it. The mate's name was all over the TV and Internet. I would be tempted to change my name," TMJ said.

"The point is the cost of a fishing license isn't much, but the penalties for not having one are heavy," said Hank, pausing when something caught his eye in the water.

"Be still," Hank said, picking up a four-foot-long aluminum rod with a sharp metal three-pronged gig on the end. He looked into the water, put his finger to his mouth, and pointed. "Do you see that?" he whispered.

Luke stared at the sand under the water where Hank pointed and could not see anything unusual. In an instant, Hank gigged the flounder and the fish appeared flailing about at the end of the gig. It looked to be the right size.

"You have to be careful to judge the size right and not get one that is too small. Look for the outline of the fish in the water. Did y'all see the outline before I gigged it?" Hank asked.

"I did," TMJ said.

"I'm not so sure I did," Luke said.

"Let TMJ and me catch a few before you try, until you get the feel of it," Hank said to Luke.

"Okay."

They worked that spot for a while. TMJ speared a fairly large one.

"I saw that one!" Luke said.

"Good, now you are getting the hang of it," Hank said. "We'll work this area for a while longer, then I'll turn off the light and we'll paddle a little closer to shore."

Hank caught another one, then he turned off the light. They made their way close to the marsh, then he turned the light back on. The bottom was nice and sandy, perfect for flounder.

"I think I see one," Luke whispered. "Does it look the right size?"

"Yeah," Hank whispered. "Go for it."

Luke held the gig over the two-foot-deep water and soon had a good twenty-inch flounder on the other end. He brought it in the boat and put it in the five-gallon bucket with the other fish.

TMJ broke out the beer to celebrate. "To Luke's first flounder!"

They tapped the beer cans then continued to fish. Before long, TMJ and Hank caught three more fish and Luke caught two fish.

"Let me try one more place," Hank said. "Then we can call it a night. I think we have done pretty good so far. This is almost better than sex."

"Speak for yourself," TMJ said. "This is fun, but I'll take sex anytime over this."

"When you get to be my age, sex doesn't happen very much," Hank said.

"Well, whose fault is that?"

"Listen, after women go through menopause, they lose interest."

"What about those hormones you hear about?" TMJ asked.

"Some doctors say take them, and some say don't," Hank said. "Cora doesn't believe in them."

"What about Viagra?" TMJ said. "I hear that's changed the sex life of every man over fifty."

"Funny you should ask," Hank said. "It's great stuff, but if she isn't interested, it doesn't help."

"I hear you," TMJ said.

"I guess you guys are out having sex two or three times a week," Hank said, with a bit of envy in his voice.

"Sometimes even more than that," TMJ said with a grin.

"Sometimes with more than one girl the same night," Luke said, looking at TMJ with a grin.

"What?" Hank said, looking surprised.

"Yeah, I got these two girlfriends who like to do a threesome."

"Oh, to be young again," Hank said, lifting a can of Miller to his lips.

"Yeah, it is kind of cool, but sometimes I think I am obsessed with sex," TMJ said. "It's all I can think about."

"That sure changes with age," Hank said, philosophically. "In fact, the reason I got a prescription for Viagra was one time my hydraulics didn't work like they were supposed to. Little good it does me now. It takes two willing partners to have sex."

"Not necessarily," TMJ said. "I found this website online dedicated to masturbation."

"Get out of here," Hank said.

"Yeah, he spends all his free time on the Internet. Now I know what he is doing," Luke said, with a laugh before taking a sip of his beer.

"That ain't the half of it," TMJ said, with a knowing smile.

"Well, do me a favor and don't tell us anymore about your Internet surfing, okay?" Luke said. "The less I know about it the better!"

"Okay, if that's the way you want it. I could show you things that would rock your world," TMJ said.

"I'm sure you could," Luke said. "I prefer my blissful ignorance, thank you."

"You can show me," Hank said. "At my age, I can't afford to be picky."

"I thought we were going to check out another spot to catch flounder," Luke said, wanting to change the subject.

Hank looked disappointed, but they did get back to gigging and not gabbing. They poled to another site, a little further out in the sound. Hank turned the lights back on and proceeded to gig another large flounder. Soon TMJ had one on the end of his gig, and Luke had speared one, too.

"I think it's time to call it a night," Hank said. "We have been successful, it is midnight, and we have to work tomorrow morning."

"Sounds good to me," Luke said. "I sure did enjoy it though." He paused. "I learned a lot."

"So did I," Hank said.

They paddled back to the ramp, loaded the boat on the trailer, and pulled it out of the water. Hank dropped Luke and TMJ off at their place with their share of the flounder before he headed home.

TMJ filleted the flounder before he went to bed. He divided up the fillets, two per freezer bag, and stuck them in the freezer. Freezing their catch in separate bags meant they didn't have to thaw and eat it all at once. Now, they had several good meals ahead of them.

≈CHAPTER SIXTEEN≈

On Saturday, TMJ and Luke went shrimping with Tommy Howard and Sam Cooper in the Pamlico Sound. They used Sammy Cooper's flat-bottomed, center-console Carolina Skiff. When they found a good place in shallow water between Ocracoke and Portsmouth Island, they gradually fed a shrimp net into the water that had lead weights attached to a rope that ran around the edges of the net. Plastic streamers attached to the net prevented it from chafing on the bottom. They fed the net out into the water and dragged it slowly behind the boat for about thirty minutes. When they pulled the net in, dumping their catch in the bottom of the boat, the net was filled with small fish, seaweed, some shells, bits of drift-wood, and hundreds of jumping shrimp, anxious to get out of the boat.

The guys threw the small fish back in the water, but grabbed as many of the shrimp as they could get their hands on. They tossed them in a white five-gallon bucket. Then they repeated the process again two more times.

"I think we have enough shrimp now," Sam Cooper said. They had two five-gallon buckets filled halfway with writhing, jumping shrimp.

"Looks like plenty to me," Tommy said, "We need to put them on ice when we get back to the dock. We can buy ice at the fish house."

"Damn! Shrimp and flounder," TMJ said. "We are going to be eating good this week."

"Why don't we invite some of the girls over tonight for dinner?"

"Sounds like a good idea," TMJ said.

When they got back to the dock at the Community Store, they iced down the shrimp and took it home.

TMJ invited Thelma and Luane, Luke asked Anna, and Tommy and Sam brought their girlfriends.

Luke battered and fried the flounder fillets, while TMJ boiled the shrimp. They fixed some hushpuppies and coleslaw as well. The trailer didn't hold a lot of people comfortably so they ate outside on a picnic table. Thelma and Luane brought some wine, and Tommy and Sam contributed the beer. Tommy brought a guitar and played after they ate. They stuck around talking, singing, and listening to music until well past midnight.

"You know, rumor has it that some boys from Hatteras ran over that turtle in June," a tipsy Sam told Anna. "Folks in Hatteras think Ocracoke got off easy with the lawsuit settlement with Audubon. There have been a lot more beach closings up there than here, so they thought they would try to make things harder on Ocracoke and hoped that maybe the Feds would shut down the beach out here all summer. But it didn't work."

"We heard that, too," Anna said. "But it is just a rumor. We don't have any solid evidence. Our investigators are following all leads, but so far they haven't come up with anything solid. But if you hear anything for sure, or hear any names, let us know."

"Sure enough," Sam said, slightly slurring his words. He was more talkative than he had ever been with Luke and TMJ. His girlfriend noticed and took his arm.

"I think we need to leave. You have had too much to drink," she said, tugging on his arm to get him to stand up.

"I'm having a good time. I'm not ready to leave just yet," he said, yanking his arm out of her grip. She was a pretty big woman, an island girl, and didn't take no for an answer.

"I said I am ready to leave. Are you coming with me or not?"

Not happy to leave but not willing to go up against his girlfriend, Sam sulked, "I guess so." When he gave Anna a smile and said, "Nice to meet you," the girlfriend frowned. She hauled him to their vehicle, then came back to pick up their beer cooler.

"Good night, Luke and TMJ," she said. "Thanks for having us over. We enjoyed the meal." She glared at Anna and did not say good-bye to her. It was clear she was not a fan of the Park Service.

Tommy and his girlfriend stayed another thirty or forty minutes but then they left, too. It was about two o'clock when the party broke up.

Anna invited Luke home with her.

Thelma and Luane stayed with TMJ.

≈

The next morning Luke came home to find TMJ in bed with Thelma and Luane. Thelma got up first and put on some coffee.

"Hope you enjoyed yourself last night," Thelma said to Luke as she poured a cup of coffee. "Looks like you and Anna are an item. I think she likes you."

"And I like her."

"That's apparent," Thelma said, taking a sip of coffee and leaning against the counter. "How long is she going to be here? Is she staying all winter or does she have to leave this fall like the other summer help with the Park Service?"

"They told her she can stay for the winter."

"I know you are happy about that," Thelma said, "assuming you are going to stay all winter yourself."

"I plan to stick around until after New Year's, then I'm heading to Kannapolis to take care of some business. After that I don't know."

TMJ wandered in, wearing nothing but boxers. His hair was all mussed up, and he rubbed his eyes.

"Any coffee left?" he asked.

Thelma poured him a cup. "You guys up for some bacon and eggs?"

"You cooking?" TMJ asked.

"Sure," Thelma said. Then Luane came out of the bedroom wearing a bathrobe.

"Coffee, bless you, Thelma," she said, picking up the pot and filling a mug.

Luke volunteered to fix another pot of coffee, while Thelma fried some bacon and scrambled a frying pan full of eggs. They all ate heartily.

≈

On the 26th of August, Hank and Cora invited Luke and TMJ over for dinner to celebrate Luke's twenty-seventh birthday. It had started to cool down, and when Luke and TMJ walked in, they found Hank glued to the Weather Channel.

"Hurricane Danielle is heading toward the other side of Bermuda. It should kick up some waves here, but nothing bad. The one they are worried about is Earle, which is following close behind Danielle. They say it could hit the East Coast," Hank said. "We are supposed to have an active hurricane season this year."

"Hank turn off the TV. The boys are here for dinner," Cora said.

"Can I get you guys a beer?" Hank said, getting out of his recliner and turning the TV off.

"I am a weather fanatic this time of year," Hank admitted, handing Luke and TMJ bottles of Yuengling. "Sometimes I can't take my eyes off the TV screen. I guess it comes from years in the Coast Guard." He laughed. "If Earle comes this way and we don't have to evacuate, you guys are welcome to come stay with us. A mobile home isn't exactly the safest place to ride out a storm."

"We'll see," TMJ said. "I don't want to evacuate, unless it is really bad. I evacuated one time when I didn't need to, and it was a nightmare. I headed north, and they directed us toward Elizabeth City and Edenton. I left that morning and didn't get to Edenton until late that night. Sometimes the traffic didn't move at all, it was so bad. I had to sleep in my car along the road in Edenton. All the motels were full." He shook his head. "Unless it is a category three or four, I am staying."

"I agree. We have the house and the boat. Plus I have ridden out plenty of storms in my day. Again, as long as it is not a direct hit or a serious cat three or four, I ain't leaving," Hank said.

"We have natural gas to cook with, and I have a well-stocked pantry," Cora said. "When Isabel hit north of us, took out Highway 12, and isolated Hatteras, we still had the ferry from Cedar Island and Swan Quarter. We had grocery deliveries and supplies three days after the storm, and that is the worst storm we have had in years."

"I've never been through a storm, so I am going to have to trust y'all," Luke said.

"Don't worry, you're in good hands," Hank said. They then sat down to eat. Cora had cooked fried flounder, fresh coleslaw, hushpuppies, baked beans, and corn on the cob. When they finished, she brought out an Ocracoke Coca-Cola cake. It looked like a carrot cake. During World War II, they couldn't get sugar on the island but they could get Coca-Cola, Cora told Luke, so they used the sugar in the Cokes to make cakes and the name stuck.

"Here's to Luke," Hank said, holding a glass of white wine in the air. Cora picked up her glass, and Luke and TMJ lifted their beers.

"Luke, you have been like a son to us. Happy birthday. May you have many happy returns," Hank said, toasting him.

"Luke," Cora said, holding her glass, "may you find the happiness and joy that you so richly deserve."

"To Luke," TMJ said, raising his glass. "Here's hoping you have lots of fun on Ocracoke."

Cora then cut the cake and put slices on everyone's plate.

"Mighty good, Cora," Luke said. "I couldn't have made it here on Ocracoke without y'all. Thank you for everything." What he said was simple, but heartfelt, and he could tell from Cora's and Hank's expressions that they realized his sincerity. Hank had saved his life and Cora had taken him in—a complete stranger—and treated him like a son.

Luke called Anna the next day to see if she wanted to go to the beach after work. He had heard the waves were starting to get big. Already surfers were in town, drawn by the big waves. He wanted to see them.

They drove out to the beach, where the water was washing up closer to the dunes than normal. The waves were huge and whitecapped way beyond the breakers. There were lots of surfers and kite boarders taking advantage of the surf.

"We are going to be busy this week, pulling up stakes and taking up the black plastic sheeting protecting the turtle nests," Anna said. "The meteorologists are expecting Earle to either brush the coast or come close enough to wash up to the dunes and affect the nests."

"Do you think it is really going to hit us?" Luke asked.

"It doesn't matter if it is a direct hit or not. If it is between here and Bermuda, the waves will wash up to the dunes and could wash out some of the turtle nests, so we have to be prepared," she said.

They drove down the beach past trucks, Jeeps, SUVs, people surfing and playing in the surf, and people sunbathing.

There had been talk on the weekend of doing an end-of-summer party in the inlet on the island of Vera Cruz, but the waves were too rough and the talk of the hurricane consumed everybody. Out at sea, Earle was a monster, category four, with wind speeds from 131 to 155 miles per hour. It was heading toward the Atlantic coast, right toward the Carolinas.

On Monday, Hank, Luke, and TMJ secured the job site, picking up all loose materials and tying down everything that they could. Then they did the same to Hank's house, securing the boat and putting up deck chairs, outdoor furniture, house plants, and other loose items. When they went home that night, Luke and TMJ made sure the mobile home was ready for the storm.

"Should we stock up on canned goods, water, batteries, flashlights, a small radio?" Luke asked.

"I've got most of that, but we could go to the store and stock up on more nonperishable food, batteries, and water," TMJ said.

～

On Tuesday, there was talk about a mandatory evacuation and an official warning went out from the county. The county authorities posted a notice at the Variety Store and at the post office:

Hurricane Earle, a well-developed current category 4 hurricane, is forecast to impact the Outer Banks as it makes a NE turn off the coast. This will affect Hyde County with significant wind, rain, and storm surges that may flood low-lying areas of Hyde County, both on the mainland and Ocracoke.

Local, county, and state Emergency Management representatives are aware and are monitoring this storm closely. They have decided to implement preparedness measures. They will meet this evening to review the latest forecast. Presently, they anticipate a mandatory evacuation for Ocracoke Island on Wednesday, September 1, beginning at 5:00 A.M. for all residents and visitors.

Swell from Earle will begin to arrive late today with seas building to small-craft advisory levels by Wednesday. The large swell will enhance the rip current threat starting today. Based on the current track, seas up to 20 feet are probable in the coastal waters. Even if the track remains offshore, breakers on the Outer Banks could be up to 15 feet. Overwash issues are likely on the Outer Banks ocean side Thursday night after midnight, peaking between midnight and 6:00 A.M. Friday. High tide will be around 2:30 A.M.

Earle was the talk of the island, and everyone was now making preparations for it.

"What do you think they're going to do?" Luke asked the manager of the Variety Store when they went in to buy supplies.

"I think they are going to order an evacuation on Wednesday. All the tourists will have to leave, but the residents can stay."

"But this says residents and tourists," Luke said, reading from the notice.

"That's just to cover their ass. Residents rarely leave unless it is a direct hit and a really strong storm. It doesn't look like this will be a direct hit, but it will come mighty close," he said. "During Hurricane Alex they didn't warn the tourists in time, and a lot of cars were flooded. They are just being extra cautious this time."

"When they say mandatory, doesn't that mean you have to leave?" Luke asked again.

"They can't make the residents leave."

Luke was excited. He had never been through a hurricane before. TMJ hadn't either, but he had been through storms and stayed. He wasn't as concerned as Luke was.

"We'll be fine," TMJ said, putting some batteries in the grocery cart.

"Are you going to stay?" Luke asked.

"Sure. You are too, aren't you?"

"I guess so. As long as everyone else I know does," Luke said.

Luke called Anna. "Are you staying? They say there is going to be a mandatory evacuation tomorrow morning."

"I have to stay. We are busy getting the beach ready for the storm surge. We have to be here to monitor the turtle nests. We'll be fine. It doesn't look like a direct hit, just high seas and high winds. Maybe the electricity will be out for a few days, but we have plenty of supplies at Park Service housing, and there is the generator."

"What generator?" Luke asked.

"The island has a generator. If the electricity goes out on the island, they turn on the generator, which provides just enough power to supply the residents. Sometimes they turn it off on a rotating basis to save power, but it is enough to keep your refrigerator cold and to cook and see at night," Anna said.

"Cool. I didn't know about that."

"This island is well prepared. Everything changes when the tourists leave, then you get to see the real Ocracoke," Anna said.

Hank drove up to TMJ's trailer later that night.

"Pack your bags tomorrow. Y'all need to move in with Cora and me until the storm passes. They had a meeting tonight, and they are going to order the evacuation tomorrow morning. We are staying, of course, as you all should," Hank said. He held a copy of the second advisory from the county declaring a state of emergency and ordering the mandatory evacuation. Hank read aloud, "Only emergency services, government agencies, commercial vendors delivering essential groceries and supplies, and permanent residential traffic with appropriate identifying stickers will be allowed on the island."

The weather was very calm the next day. It was a bit overcast, but there was little wind. The surf was high, however. The roads were active with people moving their boats, taking the smaller ones out of the water and tying down the bigger ones. People were cleaning up their yards and porches, and getting final supplies. The ferries were packed as visitors crowded on them to leave the island. The route north was packed, too. Ocracoke was the first island to order an evacuation. Hatteras and the others had not ordered one yet, but it was coming. This gave time for the tourists to leave Ocracoke, but people were already leaving the other islands as well.

One man and his daughter who were in line Wednesday morning at the Hatteras ferry taped a video about the evacuation and put it on You-Tube. They were one of the few cars at the ferry terminal that morning and watched as the ferry unloaded "essential supplies" for the island. They taped a Budweiser truck coming off the ferry heading to Ocracoke village.

Soon another advisory was posted: "We are expecting 60-70 miles per hour sustained winds in the Ocracoke area and tropical storm force winds on the mainland. There is a potential 1- to 3-foot storm surge for Swan Quarter and Engelhard," Hank said.

Luke and TMJ packed some bags that morning and moved to Hank's and Cora's house, which was on stilts. TMJ brought flashlights and his battery-operated radio. That night Cora grilled fresh drum and fixed corn on the cob, baked beans, and a big salad. The weather was calm, warm, and humid. There were clouds in the sky, and they could not see the stars or the moon.

The next morning, Thursday, September 2, Luke could not stay in bed so he got up at 6:00 and got on his bike to ride down to see what was going on at the ferry. Several residents that he knew were boarding the 6:30 ferry to Swan Quarter—one family that owned a restaurant had a car filled with their pets. There were several Hispanic families. Most of them lived in mobile homes that could be easily damaged by high winds. They had cars filled with young children. Then there were the two EMS vehicles and the nurses from the island clinic.

"Why are you guys leaving?" Luke asked one of the ambulance drivers.

"Because we don't want this expensive equipment to be flooded or damaged, if there is flooding."

"Oh," Luke said. But it was not very encouraging to see the island emergency services leave!

He also saw Luane and Thelma.

"Where are y'all going?"

"We're staying with a friend in Greenville. When I saw Jim Cantori on the Weather Channel say it was a category 4 storm and it could hit Ocracoke, I called my friend and she said come to Greenville," Luane said, looking sleepy. Their car was filled with suitcases, clothes, and boxes.

"Looks like you are going to stay for weeks," Luke said.

"You never know," Luane said.

"I didn't want to leave," Thelma said, "but Luane freaked."

"I did not," Luane said.

"Yes, you did."

"Does TMJ know?" Luke asked.

"No, be a sweetie and tell him for me, will you?" Thelma asked.

"Sure," Luke said. "I'm not sure why I'm staying. This is my first storm. But everyone seems to think we should stay, so we'll see."

He saw Tommy Howard talking to some friends as he stood beside his bike, which leaned on the white plank fence that surrounded the Park Service information center in the middle of the parking area. He wore a pair of ragged khaki shorts and no shirt, which was unusual for Tommy; he always wore at least a T-shirt.

"I guess you're staying," Luke said to Tommy.

"Yep, no place to go. That question was answered three hundred years ago when my ancestors decided to make their home on a deserted sand-bar way out in the ocean. It is our way of life. This is our home." He looked stoic but also somehow heroic. He and the islanders had endured storms and hardship in the past, and they would endure as long as there was an island. The only way they would leave would be if somehow the island was obliterated or covered up by the sea, then they would have to move, but not until then.

The winds picked up. When the winds reached 40 miles per hour, the ferries stopped running. The final ferry left at 7:00. The last two runs were packed, mostly with residents.

As Luke rode back to Hank's, the wind was blowing in gusts. Dark clouds began to form in the sky in a huge circular pattern, clearly part of a much larger system.

≈

Cora cooked bacon and eggs for breakfast. Then Hank, Luke, and TMJ drove out to check out the island. There were practically no boats in the harbor, only larger ones that were tied up at the secure National Park Service docks near the ferry. Other than the occasional resident making last-minute preparations, the village looked deserted. Some residents had boarded up windows, but most had not. The village was not on the ocean front, the only issue would be flooding from the sound, not wind and water from the ocean.

Hank drove out to the beach with Luke and TMJ and parked at the top of the dune line at Ramp 70 beside the airport. They looked out at the angry sea. The waves were washing up to the dunes. Normally, the waves were a couple hundred yards from the dunes, but not today. Today they washed right up to the dune line, leaving lots of foam. They drove north on Highway 12 beyond the pony pens, and the road was flooded in several places where the waves had broken through the dunes and washed over the pavement. The wind was rising. After riding around and checking the work site, they drove back to the house and turned on the television.

To hear the national news, like the Weather Channel, you would have thought the Outer Banks were going to be wiped off the map by a huge storm, but the local newsmen were more familiar and not nearly as sensational. They had seen worse. It would be a blow—high winds, some flooding—but not a major event as others had been in the past.

Another advisory from the county said Earle was a strong category 4 storm with 145 mile-per-hour winds, but it would not be a direct hit. It would be a fly by. They were expecting 74 mile-per-hour sustained winds with gusts of up to 90 miles per hour in Ocracoke Thursday evening, extending into the night and Friday morning. Winds would begin to become a serious threat to Ocracoke by 4:00 P.M. Thursday. Seas could peak at thirty feet, with storm surge of four to six feet at the backside of Ocracoke and rainfall of three to five inches. The closest path would be at 2:00 to 3:00 A.M. Friday morning, which was also high tide, with hurricane force winds on Ocracoke by 10:00 P.M. Thursday.

Luke texted Anna on the new smartphone he ordered online, "R U OK?"

"Yes," she replied. She called him.

"Where are you?" she asked.

"TMJ and I are staying with Cora and Hank until the storm passes. TMJ's trailer is on low ground, and if the winds get up, it may be a problem, so we thought we'd be safer here. Are you okay?"

"Yeah, all the Park Service employees are here, and we are well stocked. We are hunkered down and ready to get out as soon as the storm passes to survey the damage. There were forty-seven turtle nests on the island this year. I hope we don't lose many. Most of them are up high on the dunes, but we had to move a few that were really close to the water. We lost three last week to the storm surge at high tide from Danielle. I hope we don't lose many more," she said. "Be safe and stay in touch."

Hank, Luke, and TMJ left their cars at the Park Service parking lot, which was on high ground, and rode bikes back to the house. Everyone on the island had identified some point of high ground where they parked their cars to keep from flooding.

At 5:00 P.M. with the winds rising, a few couples from the neighborhood came over and drank gin and tonics.

"A hurricane party," Cora said. "We may as well enjoy it while we can, no telling what it will be like tomorrow or when the electricity goes out." She cut up fresh limes as Hank poured gin and tonic into the glasses of a retired Methodist minister and his wife. The guests didn't stay for more than an hour.

They ate light that night, boiled shrimp and potato salad. The adrenaline was high, and it was hard to hold down a lot of heavy food. They stayed glued to the television and the weather radio. The wind began to rise and hit the house in big, rain-filled gusts. They could hear the wind howl outside and whistle through the screens on the porch. They lost the satellite reception for the TV off and on.

Luke went out on the porch and was soaked by the rain. He could see the tops of the trees dance in the wind. They tried to go to sleep about 11:00, but it was hard to sleep. One time Luke got up about 1:00. The electricity was still on. He heard water and shined a flashlight on the road in front of the house. The dirt road was covered with water that had come in from the marsh creeks. He shined the light under the house. There was water under the house. They were surrounded by water. It looked to be a foot or two deep and rising.

Cora came to the sliding glass door in her rain coat and signaled to Luke.

"Is the water rising?" she asked.

"Yes, the road is covered, and water is under the house," Luke said.

"Last storm we had three feet under the house, but it rarely gets much higher than that," she said, stepping out on the porch to look. She took Luke's flashlight and shined it into the surging water. There were piles of reeds and grass in the water mixed with other debris.

"Looks like we're going to have a mess to clean up tomorrow," she said, as the electricity flickered and went out. "Let's go back to bed and save our energy for tomorrow." She took Luke's hand and led him inside.

"See you tomorrow morning," Luke said.

"Bright and early," she said.

Luke still couldn't sleep, with the wind howling outside and his heart racing. The house rocked with the wind as the gusts hit it hard. He had never been through a storm like this and didn't know what to expect. He heard TMJ snoring in the other bed, sleeping through the whole thing.

When it began to get light outside, Luke got up and looked out the window. The electricity was still out, but the water had receded somewhat. There were clumps of marsh grass and reeds in the yard and still standing water, but the water was not as deep as it had been last night. The wind was still blowing, and it was raining in sheets as wind gusts blew into the house. He could see no trees down, only a few limbs. The sky was dark and threatening. He pulled on some shorts and a white T-shirt, and walked out on the screen porch. It was very warm and humid. The rain blew onto the porch, and the wind whistled through the screens. But it did not seem as bad as earlier. It seemed to be calming down, and the rain was reduced to a misty drizzle.

Hank got up, then Cora. Hank turned on the radio. The storm had passed Ocracoke and was moving along the coast off Hatteras and heading north. The worst was over, and that was not too bad. Water covered the road and the yard so they couldn't get out and see the damage very well. Hank pulled on boots that came up to his knees. Luke did the same, and they walked down the steps under the house. The water was quickly receding. TMJ was still in bed. Cora stood on the steps looking down at them. They couldn't ride a bike and didn't have their cars, but they wanted to get out and see what damage had been done. They walked around the neighborhood, slogging through the water. They saw limbs down and debris blown about, but no trees down, no roofs damaged or windows broken. Soon others joined them as they inspected the neighborhood.

They then walked out to Lighthouse Road and saw little damage, mainly debris and limbs littering the road. The water receded quickly. They walked to the harbor, which was very full, flooding the roads and docks around it. It looked like the end of the pier at the Ocracoke Harbor Inn had collapsed. It was overcast. Hank told Luke that usually when a hurricane passed, the sky was clear as a bell, but the sky today was overcast with clouds in a circular pattern as the storm passed to the north. There was some standing water on the roads, but they were mostly clear. Only grass, pine needles, branches, and reeds that had been washed up during the night littered the road. Apparently water had come up about three feet in a lot of places. According to the county advisory posted that morning, Ocracoke had sustained winds of 73 miles per hour with flooding of three feet. Highway 12 to the Hatteras ferry was clear for four-wheel-drive vehicles. There had been overwash of the road, but it did not wash out the asphalt as it did in Hurricane Isabel. Authorities were assessing the damage. Tideland Electric trucks were surveying damage to power lines.

The water quickly receded, and Luke and Hank continued to walk through the village. Many property owners appeared and began to pick up debris in their yards and put things back in order. They saw a large tree had fallen on the Ocracoke Restoration Antique Store on Highway 12 at Howard Street. The owner and a friend were already cutting it up with chain saws. Other than some damage to the eaves, the tree did not appear to have pierced the roof or done more damage. All in all, the village had survived the storm very well, which was cause to celebrate.

Luke texted Anna, "R U OK?"

She replied, "Yes, I am fine."

They continued walking until they came to their cars in the Park Service parking lot.

"I want to check out the trailer," said Luke, getting into his Jeep and driving to the back of the island where TMJ's trailer was. There was standing water on Sunset Drive, but when he got to the trailer, just off Trent, there was little water. It was apparent that the water had risen about three feet in the night, but the trailer was up on concrete blocks, which kept the water out of it. The picnic table had dead grass and debris on it, but Luke quickly cleaned up around the place and drove back to Hank's house.

They listened to the radio and heard the storm had moved up the East Coast heading toward Long Island and New England. Shortly after noon, the electricity came on, and the sky began to clear up. Luke and TMJ helped Hank clean up the yard, clearing debris from the marsh that had washed under the house and into the yard while Cora fixed lunch.

"Looks like I won't even be able to use my grill," Hank said. "I can't believe how soon the electricity came back on. After Isabel it was out for weeks. We had to depend on the island generator, but then the road was cut in Hatteras and washed out on the north end of Ocracoke as well. The power lines follow the road down from Virginia, so any cut along the way affects us since we are the last on the line."

"Let's drive up to the pony pens and the Hatteras ferry landing to see how bad the road is," TMJ said.

They all got into Hank's truck, including Cora, and drove north on Highway 12. North of the pony pens the ocean had breached the dunes at several places and deposited sand on the road, but the asphalt roadway was intact and had not been damaged. Already the North Carolina Department of Transportation trucks and front-end loaders were hard at work, clearing the road of sand and piling it back on the beach side to build up the dunes. Near the Hatteras ferry terminal there was hardly any overwash at all. The ferries weren't there, but the guys at the terminal said they would soon be running.

There was another announcement from the county at 2:00 p.m. that said all power had been restored in Hyde County. The mandatory evacuation order had been lifted, but the county was still under a state of emergency. A ferry was to leave Swan Quarter at 3:00 p.m. and 3:30 p.m. from Cedar Island on Friday. The Hatteras to Ocracoke ferry was not running but would resume running Saturday morning at 5:00 a.m.

Luke texted Anna, "Can I C U ?"

She replied, "2 busy, will get back to U."

He called her. "What's going on?"

"We are loading up the trucks with signs, posts, string, and black plastic sheeting to mark off the turtle nests. I'm going to be snowed under for the next few days until we can get caught up. We only lost three nests and that was last week," she said. He could hear the relief in her voice.

"That's great," he said.

"You better believe it. We thought we'd lose half of them. But I guess Mother Nature takes care of her own," she said. "I have Monday off. Let's try to get together then."

"Sounds good. I'm sure Hank will keep us busy for the next couple of days cleaning up at his house, the work site, and other places," Luke said.

Sure enough, Hank had a steady list of chores cleaning up around the houses and businesses of friends and neighbors. Everyone pitched in. They figured the island would be open for business on Saturday, so they had better get it in shape for the return of the tourists. It was Labor Day weekend, after all, and a lot of people had made plans to come to the island. The Saturday morning bulletin announced that the ferries were running their normal runs, the evacuation order had been lifted, and the state of emergency was ended. The motels and hotels tried to get the word out that they were open. Some tourists came, but not as many as there would have been if there had been no storm. But it was better than nothing. The same thing had happened the year before. A storm blew through and ruined Labor Day weekend.

Thelma and Luane came back on the Swan Quarter ferry at noon on Saturday.

TMJ and Luke decided to help Thelma and Luane get their place cleaned up.

≈

"Greenville was fun, but I was ready to get home," Thelma told them as they worked. "I had to sleep on the sofa, and Terry's dog kept jumping up all night long trying to sleep with me. After two nights, I was ready to come home."

Luane agreed. "It was fun going out at night, but the drinks were expensive, the bars were loud, and the traffic was terrible. I'm happy to be back on Ocracoke."

"I think we need to organize an end-of-summer party this weekend," Thelma said. "We wanted to do it last weekend, but the weather was bad. Looks like the weather is going to be great now that the hurricane has passed."

"A lot of people are busy today and tomorrow, cleaning up, getting their boats back in the water," Luke said, he was also thinking of Anna. "Why don't we do it Monday? It is a holiday, isn't it?"

"Good idea," Luane said. "I'll get on the phone and get it organized."

After Luke and TMJ finished helping the girls pick up their yard, they returned to the trailer. Luke was exhausted and went to bed. TMJ decided to get caught up on his computer surfing.

On Sunday, the harbor came back to life as everyone put their boats back in the water, and the town bustled with tourists—people walking, peddling bikes, and riding in golf carts. Everyone was out to enjoy the beautiful sunny day. Things were back to normal almost as if nothing had happened. Even the ocean had calmed down. The beach was littered with shells, sand dollars, and starfish. By late Sunday, all the turtle nests had been marked off and everything was back to normal on the beach as well.

≈

As promised, Monday was the day to celebrate the end of summer. Luke, TMJ, and the gang decided to do it on Vera Cruz. The beach still had tourists, and they wanted a private place and what better place to have a summer blowout than on Vera Cruz in the inlet between Ocracoke and Portsmouth. By noon, the island had filled with young people, boats, grills, beach chairs, and beach games. Luke, TMJ, and Anna rode out with Tommy Howard. Luane and Thelma caught a ride with Sam Cooper.

"All the turtle nests are roped off and protected," Anna said. "I'm glad I'm over that. We worked our tails off getting them all marked this weekend."

"Time to celebrate," Luke said, handing her a beer.

"Thanks. I agree. It is time to celebrate."

People danced to the radio, played beach games, and sunbathed. A few went in the water, but they had to be careful, being so close to the unpredictable waters of the inlet. Boats were going in and out all the time. Some partiers went to Portsmouth. Others rode around enjoying the day. They grilled hot dogs and hamburgers for lunch, but they wanted to leave before sundown, so by 7:00 most everyone was gone.

Luke spent the night with Anna that night, and Thelma and Luane stayed with TMJ. Everything was back to normal.

≈Chapter Seventeen≈

That Thursday, Anna invited Luke to see the opening of a turtle nest that had already hatched, north of the pony pens. Several people came, mainly tourists—lots of children and young adults. One of the younger guys who worked with Anna dug the nest by hand, while Anna and another older ranger explained the process to the people.

"The nest hatched over the last two days, but we need to dig it up and count the number of shells to see if there are any stragglers or dead turtles in the nest. That is what Dave is doing right now," Anna said to the group.

Dave found the bottom of the nest and started pulling up turtle eggshells. He also found a few whole eggs as well as a few dead turtles, which he handed to the other ranger to show the crowd. Dave found five live turtles, which he put in a large orange water cooler.

The kids gathered close and looked at the dead turtles in the white-nylon-gloved hand of the park ranger.

"When Dave finishes digging the nest, he will count each egg so we will know how many eggs were in the nest," Anna said.

"How many eggs are usually in a nest?" a young boy asked.

"About 120 to 130 eggs."

"Do all of them hatch?" a little girl asked.

"No, not all, but most do."

"This year in the Cape Hatteras National Seashore alone there were 153 nests, all with about 120 eggs in each one. Hundreds more nests are laid up and down the East Coast. Last year there were only ninety-nine nests in the National Seashore. So you see how important our work is."

"Are you going to release the live turtles into the ocean right now?" a young man asked.

"No, we need to wait until just after dusk, when the sun is down," Anna said. "That way they can swim toward the ocean without being distracted."

Luke loved watching the kids, as they hung on Anna's every word. Her work was important, and she was passionate about it. He loved her for that. She also really seemed to connect to the young people and the kids. She was much more comfortable in the public role than she had been the first of the summer.

At dusk they released the live turtles. The children squealed as the tiny baby turtles pushed their way to the ocean with tiny flippers. Anna took special care to answer every question that the children asked. She smiled as she watched the children's reaction to the release of the turtles.

≈

"I was proud of the way you handled yourself with all those people and especially the kids," Luke said in bed that night.

"Is there a subtle message in that?" she asked.

"What do you mean?"

"Are you saying that I would be good with kids someday?"

"No, I'm saying you are good with kids right now," he said, though he knew what he was saying, and she probably did too, but she didn't seem to mind. Luke had told her that he and his wife had wanted to have children. Luke also realized that Anna had a good career, and she wasn't anxious to have children anytime soon.

That morning when Anna went to work, Luke rode his bike back to TMJ's trailer and drank coffee with Thelma, Luane, and TMJ.

"You know, I would like to do another bonfire on the beach. The weather is great. It is cool at night, but the ocean is still warm. I don't know. It just sort of seems like a fall thing to do," Thelma said.

"I agree," Luane said. "I'll bring the fixings for s'mores. You guys bring the beer and wine, beach chairs, and firewood. We can have a party."

"Okay. Whatever you girls want," TMJ said.

That night was blustery so they decided to wait until the wind died down. The perfect night was Sunday night. TMJ and Luke loaded up their trucks with firewood, a shovel, a bucket to put out the fire, beach chairs, and coolers with beer and wine. The girls brought wire hangers for marshmallow roasting, marshmallows, graham crackers, and chocolate bars for s'mores. They drove out on the beach just before dusk so they could see well enough to find a good spot and dig a pit for the fire. Then the others started coming. In all about twenty people joined them.

By dark, there was a big roaring fire in a fire pit that was about four feet in diameter and about two feet deep. The sky was crystal clear, and they tried to identify the stars. The new moon sat over the ocean, illuminating a faint path across the surface of the water. Thelma and Luane made s'mores and passed them around. Others roasted marshmallows in the fire and ate them straight from the wire hanger. Everyone was drinking either beer or wine.

The vehicles had to be off the beach by nine so several people left at 8:30. TMJ and Luke moved their trucks to the parking lot at the airport and walked back out. Soon the only people on the beach were TMJ, Luke, Anna, Thelma, and Luane.

"Let's go skinny dipping," Thelma said.

"Yeah, but what about sharks?" Luane said.

"Sharks mainly feed at dawn and late in the afternoon," Anna said. "They are no more active now than they would be normally during the day. As long as we don't go out very far, we should be okay."

TMJ was the first to shed his clothes.

"I know where a hose is when we need to put out the fire," Thelma said, reaching out to touch TMJ's rear end.

"Oh, your hand is cold," TMJ said, with a start.

"Just starting to warm up," Thelma said, giving him a big kiss.

Luane and Thelma took off her clothes, and the three of them ran into the water.

Luke pulled off his T-shirt and pulled down his bathing suit. Then Anna took off her clothes. She took his hand, and they too ran into the water.

They stood in the shallow waves, about knee high in the water. The water began to glow around Thelma.

"What is that?" Thelma asked, somewhat surprised.

"It's bioluminescence," Anna said. "Tiny organisms in the water that glow when they are disturbed. It is perfectly safe. Sometimes you see it on the beach in the wet sand."

"Well, aren't you a font of knowledge," Thelma said, sarcastically.

"Sorry, it's my job," Anna said, a little embarrassed.

The water began to glow with a soft greenish light around all of them.

"It lights me up," TMJ said.

"The better to see you with," Luane said, eyeing TMJ's naked body, which glowed green in the crystal-clear water.

They played in the water, splashed each other, and jumped the waves. The girls did not want to get their hair wet. Luke and TMJ went under water, however, and swam under the waves. The water was warm, but the air was cool.

Luane ran up to the fire, then Thelma, followed by TMJ, Luke, and Anna.

The girls dried off with towels. TMJ decided to dry off in front of the fire, showing himself off to everyone.

"I love to be naked outdoors," TMJ said, turning around with his arms raised to dry himself.

"We noticed," Thelma said, covered with a towel.

"Nothing shy about TMJ," Anna said.

"If you got it, flaunt it," Luane said, with a teasing smile.

"I better head out. I've got work tomorrow," Anna said. So she and Luke walked back to his car. They looked back at the beach and saw TMJ, Luane, and Thelma standing by the fire warming themselves. The girls had towels wrapped around their shoulders. TMJ was still naked.

≈

Luke's work at the Ocracoker didn't begin in earnest until after Labor Day, when the summer help left. He worked the night shift, from 5:00 until 9:30 P.M. or until closing on Thursday, Friday, and Saturday nights. The Ocracoker was a small family-style restaurant owned by an old Ocracoke family, the Garrishes. They featured fried and broiled seafood, lots of vegetables, homemade desserts, and a great breakfast. They were a favorite with the fishermen, who started to come to the island in the fall, when the water began to cool and surf fishing really got good.

At first, Luke did what needed to be done: busing tables, washing dishes, making salads, or helping to prep food. He told Rick Garrish, the owner, that he wanted to work in the kitchen and would like to cook. But he had to work his way up to that and prove himself.

The older crowd usually came in between 5:00 and 5:30 to eat family style. The fishermen came a little later after a day on the beach. The restaurant was usually pretty empty by 9:00, unless there were some stragglers. Then the staff had to stay to clean up the place and prepare for the next morning's breakfast. Breakfast was at 7:00 and was always busy.

Some nights, when it was slow, Luke liked to listen to Rick and his wife, Sarah, talk about old Ocracoke. Rick was a big man in his mid-fifties, balding, with dark eyes. Sarah was a petite blonde with fierce blue eyes. She was all business. Rick was a businessman, too, but he liked to fish and go out on his boat and talk about the old days with his friends.

"The Navy changed everything here during the war. Before 1942, Ocracoke was a sleepy little fishing village, trying to promote itself as a tourist destination. Stanley Wahab, who owned the Wahab Village Hotel (now Blackbeard's), renamed the harbor originally known as Cockle Creek to

Silver Lake. He built the first electric generator and the ice house to lure tourists, but it was still at the end of the line on the Outer Banks and hard to get to. Silver Lake was a shallow creek, as wide as it is today, but only about three or four feet deep in most places. The Navy dredged it to make it deep enough to handle its ships. In the process, the dredge spoil was distributed throughout the village. The only way to get here then was to ride on the mail boat *Aleta* that left Atlantic, north of Morehead City. The *Aleta* could hold about twenty-five or thirty passengers but no cars," Rick said.

"There were only dirt roads. Everybody was related to everybody. The ponies ran wild. Most houses were built from wood salvaged from ship-wrecks. Almost no one wore shoes," he continued. "But the Navy changed all that. The Navy built the first paved road, brought the first telephones, but most of all it brought in new blood. The island girls married Navy men, and some of the Navy men stayed. After the base closed down, the village scavenged the buildings. Hell, half of Ocracoke was built using what the Navy left behind. Those were the days."

"Why did the Navy locate here?" Luke asked.

"Because of the German submarines. The Navy needed a base to protect our coast. The German subs were sinking merchant ships and tankers right and left all year long in 1942. Over three hundred ships were sunk off the North Carolina coast alone. They had to do something. They set up a listening station at Loop Shack Hill and sent patrol boats out from here. They built a whole Navy base here. Best thing that hap-pened to Ocracoke. Without it, who knows we might have ended up like Portsmouth—a ghost town."

"What happened when the Navy left after the war?"

"People tried to return to normal, but they couldn't. David Stick and his buddies helped establish the Cape Hatteras National Seashore, and Aycock Brown started promoting tourism for the Outer Banks. In the fifties, they built roads and ferries. Then in the sixties, they built the Herbert C. Bonner Bridge to Hatteras Island. That's when tourism really opened up. The state paved Highway 12 all the way down the banks to Ocracoke, and the rest is history."

~

The next night after cleaning up they had some time to kill, so Luke asked Rick some questions.

"You say there wasn't a road to Ocracoke before the 1950s. What did it look like out here, between the village and the beach?"

"It was sandy and flat. There wasn't as much vegetation as there is now near the beach. The ponies and livestock kept it down before the Park Service bought all the land up," Rick said. "In the thirties and forties, the WPA and the government built up the dunes the way they are now. Before, when the storms blew through, there would be overwash. It was more like Portsmouth, you know, where there are dunes in some places but breaches in the dunes where the water washes over during a storm. They say the way it is in Portsmouth is healthier for the beach because it builds back up naturally. The way it is now Ocracoke doesn't get built back up after a storm. The bulldozers build the dunes back, but the island doesn't get more sand."

"Where Howard's Pub and the Variety Store are now was just a sandy flat," Rick continued. "The sand was deep and hot and filled with nests of birds that would dive bomb you if you walked through their nests. It wasn't easy getting out to the beach from the village on foot. Some guys offered to take you out to the beach in their old army Jeeps. But there wasn't a road or anything. The village was oriented toward the sound, not the beach."

"Wasn't there a ferry from Hatteras?"

"Yeah, but it was private and only held a few cars until the state took over in the 1950s."

"How did the cars get from the ferry to the village?"

"They had to drive on the beach."

"Didn't they get stuck?"

"Sure, they did. Not many people came that way, though. Most people came by boat."

"You said the Navy built a road?"

"Yeah, it was a one-lane concrete road that ran from the Navy station,

160

which is where the National Park Service parking lot and visitor center are now, along Back Road, down Sunset to the Trent neighborhood, where they had several ammunition dumps. Sunset was called Ammunition Dump Road back then, but they changed the name so as not to scare the tourists," he gave Luke a smile. "You can still see the concrete road under the asphalt, and off Trent you can still see the little concrete roads that go off the main road to access the old ammo dumps."

"When you say dump, so you mean they dumped old ammo there?"

"No, there were concrete bunkers where the ammo was stored," he said. "There isn't any ammo still out there."

"Happy to hear that, because that is where TMJ's trailer is located!"

⌒ Chapter Eighteen ⌒

It was the middle of September. Luke was busy with work, and Anna was busy with turtles. The turtle nests were hatching, and the rangers had to record all the hatchings and dig the nests. They did not see each other for several days. But Luke's nights were free from Sunday until Wednesday and Anna had the early part of the week off.

"See U tonight?" Luke texted Anna one Sunday night.

She called him. "Would you like to come over for dinner?"

Her roommates had left so she had the place to herself. She bought some shrimp and scallops at the fish house and fixed a seafood gumbo, serving it over rice.

"Do you like working at the restaurant?" Anna asked, drinking a glass of white wine.

"Yes. I really enjoy the people I work with," Luke said. "Every night I hear another interesting story about old Ocracoke. Rick still doesn't let me cook, but he lets me help with food preparation. I like it, something I have never done before."

During the summer, they had to run the air conditioning all the time, but in September, Anna kept the windows open at night.

"Do you want to go to the beach?" Anna asked.

"Sure, let's take a bottle of wine," he said.

They parked at the lifeguard-beach parking lot. There was no one there. It was around ten o'clock. They walked over the boardwalk that crossed the dunes out onto the beach. The moon was not quite full, but it was bright. The moon would be full on Thursday night. They walked along the beach and looked up at the sky, which was littered with stars. The Milky Way was clearly visible. It was cool, and Anna wore a jacket.

"I love it out here at night. The sky is so clear and beautiful. I wish I could identify all the stars," Anna said.

"I do, too. I hear there is an app for smartphones that shows you the names of the stars," he said.

"I'll have to get it. My phone contract just ran out, and I've decided to get a new iPhone," she said.

"Cool, then we'll be able to pick out all the constellations," he said, putting his arm around her waist. He pulled her to him and kissed her.

They walked down the beach a little further. She looked down and saw the bioluminescence in the sand as they walked.

She pointed it out to Luke. "Look."

"What?"

"The bioluminescence. You have to stomp or drag your feet across the wet sand. See!" She made the little specks of greenish light appear beneath her feet.

"Cool. Is that the same stuff that is in the water?" Luke asked.

"Yes, it is the same organism. It makes the same greenish light that glowworms and fireflies make."

They walked back to his car.

"Before we go in, I want to ride out the south point road," she said.

"Okay," he said, pulling onto Highway 12. Just before Howard's Pub, he turned left onto a dirt road that led to the south point.

After a few hundred yards, she said, "Stop. Turn out your lights and roll down the windows."

He stopped. It had rained the day before, so the ground was wet and the marshes were full of water. With the windows down, the sound of singing frogs and toads surrounded them. Some were deep throated, some sonorous, some high pitched.

"I have a CD that identifies the different sounds the frogs make. It is so cool. I love the sound of the frogs at night," Anna said.

"Yes, it is. I haven't heard the frogs this loud at night before," Luke said.

"I love it. I come out here whenever it rains just to hear the frogs," she said, taking his hand. They kissed. Even though it was September, it had been a warm fall, so fireflies still hovered over the marsh grass in the distance, magically lighting the night.

Back at her house, they made love until well into the night. It had been a magical night. Luke loved Anna's connection with nature and her knowledge of it. He loved discovering her world through her eyes. She seemed to love sharing it with him and watching him see her world for the first time.

It was a beautiful fall. The weather was great. The ocean stayed warm through the end of October, and the temperature was in the sixties and seventies, time to open the windows and turn off the air conditioning. There were two storms, Nicole and Igor, that blew up the Atlantic far out to sea. Nicole caused the channel used by the Hatteras ferry to close up at the end of September and stopped ferry service for a few days, but it was quickly reopened, and the channel was dredged. All the shops and restaurants were open. There were tourists, but not as many as during the summer, and, as Anna had said, the visitors in the fall were older retired couples traveling through and fishermen. The village was quiet but busy. The Ocracoker was a favorite with the fishermen and retired folks because of the reasonable prices and the traditional fare.

≈

"Cora and I have decided to go to Washington the weekend before the election to attend the Jon Stewart Rally to Restore Sanity," Hank announced one day in October at the work site.

"Jon Stewart from Comedy Central?" asked Luke.

"Yup. We're going with some friends from Ocracoke, our neighbors, the retired minister and his wife."

"Wow, what made you decide to do that?" Luke asked.

"I think Jon Stewart is great, and I want to see what he has to say. We need to show our support for decency, respect, and courtesy in the political system," he said. "Besides it will be fun and interesting."

Luke and TMJ did not have a television and did not read the newspaper. There were mid-term elections going on, but as far as they were concerned, the elections did not exist. Luke had voted in the presidential election, but with everything going on in his life in 2010, he was not even aware that an election was being held. Hank and Cora, on the other hand, watched TV every night and kept up with current events.

≈

The week before Halloween, the school had a haunted house and a Halloween parade. TMJ volunteered to be the chainsaw murderer in the haunted house, a part he relished.

Anna and Luke watched the Halloween parade in front of the school. Parents walked with their children—mainly young children—around the circle in front of the school for the judging of the costume contest. Some of the costumes were quite inventive, like the group of kids who dressed like jellyfish using umbrellas with plastic strips hanging down. Others dressed up like computers, and one couple and their child wore Flintstones costumes. There were the standard vampires, mummies, the living dead, and ghouls.

As Anna watched, her eyes lit up.

"They are so cute," she said, taking Luke's hand as the jellyfish kids walked by, waving.

"I know, proud parents, cool kids. It is really neat," Luke said. He could see Anna loved being around children. He so wanted to have children. Now, he realized it was probably for the best that he and Karen did not have children because now they would have no mother. He still wanted to have children, though.

That night, a happy TMJ came in from the haunted house still made up to look like a lunatic ghoul in a white lab coat. "I scared the shit out of those kids. When they came around the corner into my room, they screamed bloody murder, and I went after them with the chainsaw."

"I hope you didn't scare them too much," Thelma said, taking a drink of coffee.

"One little girl was so scared she peed in her pants," TMJ said proudly.

"That is terrible. I bet she'll have nightmares tonight about you," Thelma said.

TMJ apparently really got into it. This was his second year at the haunted house, and he was a big hit.

Hank and Cora drove to Washington with their friends the Wednesday before Halloween and returned on Sunday.

"How was it?" Luke asked. He had waited at the house to greet them. He and Anna were going to hand out candy on Lighthouse Road, near Widgeon Woods, where all the kids came Halloween night.

"I'm really tired," Cora said. "I want to go to bed."

"There was a huge crowd there," Hank began. "We didn't get anywhere near the stage, but they had huge TVs set up all over the place so we got to hear what they said. It wasn't easy finding a bathroom, and you had to bring your own food."

"Do you regret going?" Anna asked.

"Hell, no, I wouldn't have missed it for the world. Everyone was really nice, even though it was crowded. It was like a big carnival. It made me feel proud to be an American."

"That is great, Hank. I'm glad y'all went," Luke said. "Do you want to help us give out candy on Lighthouse Road?"

"No, thanks. I am whooped," Hank said.

Luke and Anna joined some friends who had a house on Lighthouse Road to give out candy. The kids were really cute, and the adults dressed up as much as the kids. It was a fun night, much more fun than it had been in Kannapolis.

≈

Election day was Tuesday, November 2. Luke did not vote. He was registered in Kannapolis, and he didn't know the candidates Down East anyway. If he decided to stay for more than a year, he would change his registration. TMJ didn't vote either. Luke didn't know if TMJ had ever voted. Anna voted, of course.

Wednesday after the election, Luke asked Hank if the elections had gone the way he wanted them to. Hank looked tired.

"I was up half the night watching the election returns. Some went my way; most did not." Hank changed the subject and started talking about finishing up the Oyster Creek job. They were expecting to wrap it up before Thanksgiving.

≈

The second week in November a nor'easter blew through, dumping lots of rain on Ocracoke and whipping the island with winds of 30 miles per hour. The road south of the Oregon Inlet Bridge, north of Rodanthe, was washed over by the high tides and high surf. No traffic could get through for several days. Finally on Monday, the road opened to limited traffic. The surf was still high and rough, but it calmed down during the week and temperatures settled down into the fifties and sixties. TMJ was leaving after Thanksgiving for the North Carolina mountains where he had a job at Sugar Mountain ski resort in Banner Elk. He had tried to get a job in Colorado, where several other guys from Ocracoke had worked the year before, but jobs were scarce. When he heard about the job in North Carolina, he jumped on it.

"This is the first time I have worked in the North Carolina mountains," TMJ told Luke. "Last year I worked in Key West, but this year I wanted a change of climate."

"The Ocracoker is staying open through the end of December. I figure it will be real slow after Thanksgiving, then in January I'll go home to Kannapolis to get my stuff. The restaurant is going to open back up in late March or early April."

"Come to the mountains when you are free in January. They say there are plenty of jobs at the ski slopes. We'll have a blast," TMJ said.

Luke thought about Anna. He didn't want to leave, but he had to work.

"Let me think about it."

≈

The Saturday before Thanksgiving a group of pirate re-enactors call-ing themselves Blackbeard's Crew—stayed at Blackbeard's Lodge and marched to Springer's Point to memorialize the twenty-three pirates and British sailors who died at the "Battle of Ocracoke," where Lieutenant Robert Maynard and his men defeated the pirate Blackbeard. Accord-ing to tradition, after Blackbeard and eleven of his men were killed, their bodies were buried at Springer's Point.

This group wanted to conduct a memorial service commemorating the event. The actual day of the encounter was Monday, November 22, but they were only on the island for the weekend. According to an an-nouncement in the *Ocracoke Observer*, the event began with a parade, which started in front of Blackbeard's Lodge then continued up the beach to Springer's Point. Afterwards, the group convened at Howard's Pub to drink beer and watch a film, *The Ghost of Blackbeard*.

"Do you want to join me? I'd like to see the folks dressed up like pi-rates," Luke told Anna. He had read about the event in the newspaper with interest. TMJ said he wanted to go, too.

"Sure. Meet you in front of Blackbeard's. I think I'll take my bike," Anna said.

At Blackbeard's Lodge, TMJ, Anna, and Luke spotted a large group of middle-aged men and women coming out of the lodge carrying the Blackbeard flag with the skeleton holding a wine glass and a spear piercing a red heart that dripped blood. They were dressed in authentic eighteenth-century clothing. Among them was a filmmaker who had recently written a book about Blackbeard. It was chilly but sunny. One man carried a drum; another carried a period British flag. There were several women wearing bonnets and heavy cloaks. A few men dressed in British uniforms. One man was dressed like Blackbeard with a long black wig and little pieces of cloth tied in his hair. The men wore tricorn hats, capes, boots, waistcoats, knee britches, and long, white stockings. Several carried period pistols, guns, swords, and mugs. Long hair and many beards were present.

Once on the beach at Springer's Point, they laid a wreath in the water, sang pirate shanties, and fired a small cannon. After saying a few words about the Battle of Ocracoke, the group broke up, later regrouping at Howard's Pub.

After the reenactment, Luke and Anna drove out to the beach, where there were a few fishermen a lot of birds. The beach was covered with shells. A pod of porpoises played in the water just beyond the waves. They drove as far as they could go towards the inlet before rope blocked their passage. They passed by the place where Luke had walked into the water in April when he first came to Ocracoke. They saw a small boat at Vera Cruz, and three people walking along the shore.

~

Hank and Cora invited Anna, Luke, and TMJ to join them for Thanksgiving dinner. Cora served up a noontime feast of turkey, sweet-potato casserole covered with melted marshmallows, oyster casserole, green-bean casserole, fresh rolls, and cranberry sauce. For dessert, she made an Ocracoke fig cake and a pumpkin pie.

"Thank you, Lord, for bringing us all together today, especially Luke and Anna and TMJ. Bless Hank Junior and his beautiful family in Oregon," Hank said, blessing the meal they were about to eat.

"TMJ, when are you leaving for the mountains?" Cora asked as she passed the potatoes.

"As soon as I can get packed, probably Saturday. I'm supposed to start work next week. I have already contacted some of the other guys who are working there, and we are sharing an apartment. I hope that Luke will be able to come up and see me after he goes home in January."

"When do you think you will be back?" she asked.

"When the season ends, but definitely by April. I may do some traveling before I come back. I don't know."

"How about Luane and Thelma? Where are they going this winter?" she asked.

"Back to Greenville, waitressing in a restaurant. They probably won't be back until May," TMJ said. Anita was working until Howard's closed the weekend after Thanksgiving, then she planned to head home to Rocky Mount and get a job. John, her new boyfriend, had left after Labor Day weekend, going back to school in Wilmington.

≈

"I hope I'll have another job lined up in April or May for you guys. Nothing yet, but I have a few leads," Hank said, scooping up some oyster casserole.

"How about you, Anna?" Hank asked. "Are you staying in Ocracoke this winter?"

"Yes, sir. We'll be looking for turtles that have been stunned by the cold. If we find any, we take them to Manteo to the state aquarium to be revived. The park is not as busy in the winter, but there is still a lot to do."

"That sounds interesting," Hank said.

"Luke, how about you? What are your plans?" Cora asked, passing the rolls.

"I plan to stay here through New Year's, working at the Ocracoker, then head home to Kannapolis the first of January to pick up the things in my shop and bring them back here," Luke said. "After that, I may join TMJ in the mountains. He said there is plenty of work on the ski slopes. But I'll be back for sure by April. I hope Hank will have some work lined up by then. If not, I can get my old job back at the Ocracoker."

"We are going to Oregon to see Hank Junior and his family for Christmas," Cora said, with a big smile. "Then in January, Hank and I are taking a Carnival cruise to the Caribbean and South America. I can't wait. We like to travel in the winter and haven't been on a good trip in a couple of years"

"Not much going on around here during the winter. It is a good time to travel," Hank said.

"That's for sure," Luke said. Then he looked at Anna.

"That's all right. I love it here in the winter. A good time to get caught up on my reading, and a great time for solitude," Anna said, cutting a piece of turkey.

"Tommy Howard and Sammy Cooper are working in Colorado this winter. This is the second year they have done that. They have jobs at the ski slopes in Vail," TMJ said. "I tried to get a job there, but I was too late applying. I think I'll enjoy the North Carolina mountains, though. They had great snow last winter, and they are expecting about the same weather this year."

"Not as exciting as Key West?" Hank asked, teasing TMJ.

"I figured I needed to find some cooler weather this year, something different. It will be a new experience," he said.

"Yeah, it will do you some good to cool down a little this winter," Hank said with a grin, thinking of TMJ's job at the sex shop in Key West the winter before.

After they ate their big dinner, Luke and TMJ went back to the trailer. Luke took a nap, and TMJ went online with his computer. That night they asked Anna over to eat turkey sandwiches and leftovers that Cora had insisted they take home. Luke spent the night with Anna.

"I hope you don't mind if I go to the mountains to work with TMJ this winter," Luke said that night in bed.

"I know there isn't any work here in the winter. The restaurant is closed, and there isn't any construction work. You do what you have to do," she said matter-of-factly.

"I'll miss you," Luke said.

"I'll miss you, too, but I'll get along fine by myself. Just don't get in too much trouble with TMJ and all those cute ski bunnies," she said teasing.

"I'll try not to," he said with a smile.

"You had better not," she said, pinching him hard on his arm.

≈

Friday night, they all went to Howard's Pub for dinner to say goodbye to TMJ, Thelma, and Luane. The next morning, Luke and Anna were by themselves. Saturday night they went to the Community Center for a concert with local musicians to raise money for the Ocrafolk Festival to be held in June 2011.

≈CHAPTER NINETEEN≈

After Thanksgiving, things got very quiet on the island. Most of the shops and restaurants stayed open through Thanksgiving weekend, then closed for the season. Only Gaffer's stayed open all year. The Ocracoker stayed open during Christmas, even though it was slow, and closed after New Year's.

It was a cold winter, so Anna was busy on the beach rescuing turtles that had been stunned by the cold. The rangers picked up the turtles, put them in little plastic kid's pools to warm them up, then took them to the state aquarium in Manteo where they stayed until they could be released.

TMJ called Luke from the slopes of Sugar Mountain the first Saturday in December.

"It is snowing like crazy up here. I wish you could come. We have six inches on the ground, and it is still snowing. We're supposed to have wind chills of zero today and ten below Monday night. Time for the hot tub!" TMJ said. "Man, we are really busy. People are here from Atlanta, Washington, Charlotte, Florida, all over—lots of hot babes and lots of work. We really need you."

"Things are slow here. The restaurant is only open Thursday through

Saturday, and we have practically no business," Luke said, a bit jealous.

"Why don't you come up for a few days? I can introduce you to my boss, and we can get you a job starting in January," TMJ said. Luke had planned to wait until January to do his job hunting in the mountains, but TMJ talked him into it.

That night, Luke told Rick that he needed to go to the mountains to line up a job for January.

Rick Garrish understood. "Take the week off, Luke. You can see that we are not exactly swamped with business. You need to look out for yourself this winter."

Luke hadn't left Ocracoke since he had come to the island in March. He told Anna that night about his planned trip to the mountains. It would be the first time they had been apart in a long while.

"I completely understand. I will miss you, but you need to line up a job," Anna said, as they held each other in bed that night.

"Thank you for understanding," Luke said.

"Just stay out of the hot tubs. I hear they are real popular this time of year in the mountains," she said with a smile.

"I'll try to. You know TMJ, he probably has them all scoped out by now."

"I figured."

Luke and Anna had gotten into a routine of being together. He would miss her, but he was still not sure how serious he wanted to get. He often thought about Karen and wasn't sure whether he wanted to get serious with anyone so soon after her death. It had not even been a year, but he would miss Anna. He truly cared for her. He was also not sure about staying in Ocracoke for the winter. It sounded like it got really dull, and there was no work. He would go to the mountains to see what TMJ had to offer.

He decided that on his way back from the mountains he would go through Kannapolis and pick up his shop equipment. He might as well do it now as wait until January. Hank's offer to keep the stuff in his workshop was still open, so Luke had storage until he could find a place for himself.

It took ten hours to drive to Banner Elk. He left early Monday morning and drove all day. He had forgotten what driving through heavy traffic was like until he got to Raleigh. Then it all came back. It was a totally different experience from Ocracoke and the Outer Banks. He didn't like it. He drove through Winston-Salem and up U.S. 421 through North Wilkesboro, where the snow began. By the time he got to Banner Elk, there was over six inches of snow on the ground. It was blowing hard, and the wind chill was almost zero. At 6:00 p.m., he met TMJ at Nick's, a popular bar and restaurant, in the Tynecastle shopping center on N.C. 105 where you turn to go to Banner Elk.

"How was the drive?"

"Long."

"Well, let's get something to eat then you can follow me to my place."

They ate burgers and fries and each drank a beer, then Luke followed TMJ up Sugar Mountain to a three-bedroom octagonal-shaped house built in the 1970s. It had orange shag carpet and a black metal fireplace in the middle of the living room with a vent pipe that ran through the ceiling.

TMJ led Luke onto the deck outside.

"This is the hot tub. They're very popular up here."

"So I've heard."

"My roommates are out. You're going to like them. Bryce and Helen. They both work at Sugar Mountain with me. They room together, so that leaves one room open for you."

"Cool."

"Tomorrow I'll take you to the slopes and introduce you to my boss. I already told him about you."

"Thanks, man, do you have to be able to ski for this job?"

"Well, it helps, but there are plenty of jobs that don't involve skiing. I work renting out ski equipment. I told my boss that you work in a restaurant on Ocracoke. He needs help in the restaurant on the slopes. We'll teach you how to ski, if you would like to learn. Bryce works on the slopes with the ski patrol. He's a first-class skier. Helen is a ski instructor."

TMJ turned to him with a big grin. "Some girls are coming over tonight. I figured you wouldn't mind."

Luke hadn't planned on mixing business with pleasure, but this was TMJ. TMJ was all about pleasure. Anna was at the beach, but he had no intention of being unfaithful to her. Still, he knew that when he was with TMJ, there were going to be women and there was going to be partying, so he just accepted it.

That night, two girls came by who worked with TMJ on the slopes. After drinking a few beers, TMJ had them in the hot tub. "Come on in, Luke."

"No, thanks. I have a girl at the beach, man. I think I'm going to turn in early tonight." Luke heard the threesome well into the night, first in the hot tub, then in the bedroom. Bryce and Helen stayed up with the others, too, but went to bed before TMJ and the girls. The girls didn't leave until the next morning.

"Is it like this every night around here?" Luke asked, after the girls left and he and TMJ were drinking a cup of coffee in the kitchen.

"No, not every night, but it does happen a lot. There are lots of hot babes here, and they all want to party."

"I don't know how long I am going to be able to last here without Anna."

"I'll never tell."

"I figured you wouldn't, but that is not what I'm talking about. I think I am really starting to care about Anna."

"Cool, man. Well, if you stay here with all the temptations, and you still want Anna, you will know it is real," TMJ said.

"You're right about that," Luke said. Not that he wanted to test his relationship with Anna, but he also had not planned to find someone so soon after losing his wife. He told himself he was still not ready for a serious commitment.

Luke met TMJ's boss the next morning, and he promised Luke a job either in the kitchen, at the restaurant, or with equipment rental at Sugar Mountain starting the first of January.

On the way back to Ocracoke, Luke passed through Kannapolis, where he rented a U-Haul trailer.

He met his former father-in-law at his old house.

"Luke, how have you been?" Samuel Coltraine asked as he unlocked the door to the shop behind the house.

"I'm doing better," Luke said simply.

"It has been a difficult year for all of us."

"I know," Luke said.

"We will never get over it. Only time heals."

"I know."

"When you called, I went ahead and boxed up your things. Here let me help you load up the U-Haul."

"That's okay, I can do it myself," Luke said, turning on the light in the small out building.

"No, son, I *want* to help you."

Luke saw that Samuel was sincere and wouldn't take no for an answer so he and Samuel both loaded the U-Haul with boxes of tools and shop equipment. There were also boxes with clothing, photographs, and other personal items.

Luke spent the night in a motel that night. The memory of the wreck and losing Karen all came flooding back. He had almost put it out of his mind, but being in Kannapolis, seeing the old house, talking to her father, it all came back. When he went to bed, he cried.

≈

That night Karen came to him in the hotel room and stood over the bed as he slept. He looked up at her and was unable to move. All he could do was look and listen. "Luke, I am gone and you must make a life of your own. I want you to find someone else. You are young. You deserve to find love again and to have a family of your own. Grief cannot bring me back. You must move on. I love you too much to see you so unhappy. I want you to live the life that you deserve." She then kissed his forehead and disappeared into a column of light. Luke wanted to reach out to her and tell her how much he loved her, but he couldn't. He was frozen in the bed. Tears filled his eyes as he said good-bye. He felt like this might be the last time he saw her. She seemed distant and more like a shadow or a ghost than she had been before.

He got up early, picked up a chicken biscuit at Bojangles, and drove to Ocracoke the next morning. Driving down the Outer Banks and crossing the Herbert C. Bonner Bridge, the wind was high and the temperatures were in the twenties. It was hard to pull the U-Haul with the high winds, and Luke worried about it blowing on the bridge. The ocean was rough with lots of whitecaps, and Highway 12 was threatened with overwash. Sand blew over the highway.

When he drove through Oracoke village to Hank's house, Luke noticed that a lot of Christmas decorations had gone up while he was away. There were lights strung on picket fences, cedar wreaths with bright red ribbons, and the Methodist Church had pretty wreaths on its double front door. Crab-pot Christmas trees stood in the front yards of houses. These triangular-shaped "trees" were made of panels of green-coated chicken wire that were decorated with lights. Crab-pot Christmas trees were made Down East in Carteret County and could be found on the telephone poles in communities such as Davis, Willis, Cedar Island, and Harker's Island.

"This is a cold December," Hank said, when Luke drove up to the house late that afternoon. "I've seen some Decembers that were as warm as summer, but not this year. It started getting cold when you left about the seventh, and it hasn't warmed up yet." Luke discovered that when it is cold on the Outer Banks, it is really cold, especially with the wind.

"I'll let you keep your stuff here for a while, but eventually you will have to find a place of your own," Hank told Luke.

"I know, and I thank you for letting me keep it here. I hope to be able to find shop space when I come back in the spring," Luke said.

"That will be fine," Hank said.

≈

Luke and Anna had a pleasant and quiet December. It was cold and windy. Anna did her beach patrols, and Luke worked at the Ocracoker Restaurant. Luke stayed with Anna at her apartment. They shut down TMJ's trailer, cut off the water, and winterized it. They hung an Ocracoke cedar wreath from Hettie's Garden Center on the door and bought a three-foot crab-pot Christmas tree at the Variety Store for the living room.

There were several Christmas events on the island: the wassail party and community Christmas-tree lighting at the Ocracoke Preservation Society Museum; the Christmas pageant at the school; lessons and carols at the Methodist Church; a Christmas concert at the Community Center; community caroling, and the live nativity in front of the Methodist Church. But one thing that did not occur was the annual Christmas party at Jimmy's Garage. The year before there had been a fight between two guys who had too much to drink, so Jimmy decided to skip it this year.

Several events were planned for New Year's Eve including the Annual Oyster Roast and Shrimp Steam Fundraiser for the Ocracoke Working Waterman's Association; a New Year's Eve party featuring the Mighty Saints of Soul at the Community Center to benefit the volunteer fire department, and a big party planned at Gaffer's. Hank and Cora, of course, went to everything and participated wherever there was singing involved until they left the week before Christmas to visit Hank Junior and his family, where they planned to stay until New Year's. Luke and Anna, not being as closely tied to the community, decided to keep to themselves, but they did plan to go the oyster roast and the New Year's Eve party at Gaffer's, where they could see the young people who were still on the island.

TMJ called and said that the snow and cold weather continued in the mountains—he was definitely having a white Christmas.

This was Luke's first Christmas without Karen. He had always loved Christmas: shopping for Karen's present in the malls and seeing all the excitement at Christmas time, watching the kids looking at toys, and observing the parents getting ready for the big day. He wanted to have a family of his own some day.

He didn't know what to buy for Anna. He wanted to give her something really nice, but they had only been seeing each other for a few months, and he didn't want to be presumptuous. In the end, he bought her a hand-made silver bangle from Island Artworks.

They spent Christmas Eve together on Ocracoke. Anna could not get away to be with her family in Ohio because of work. She cooked a meal of fresh fish and vegetables. They opened a bottle of wine and listened to Christmas carols on the radio.

"I love Christmas," Luke said.

"I do, too," Anna said. "In Ohio, it is usually cold at Christmas, and we have had many white Christmases."

"It is supposed to snow this Christmas in Kannapolis for the first time since the 1940s," Luke said. "I remember we would get so excited if we thought it might snow. Sometimes it would be as warm as summer; other years it was cold as hell. One year we had a terrible ice storm just before Christmas that knocked the electricity out for days. But I would love to see snow at Christmas. TMJ said it's supposed to snow Christmas Day in the mountains."

"I hope you don't mind being stuck here with me."

"No, I love being here with you," Luke said, smiling and taking a sip of wine. "I wouldn't be anywhere else."

"I am glad I am with you, too," she said with a shy smile.

By unspoken agreement, they avoided talking of Luke's last Christmas with Karen. It was still too painful for him.

"Let's open our presents," Anna said.

"You first," Luke said, giving her the small package. She opened it and smiled, put the bracelet on, and then gave him a big hug.

"It is beautiful. Thank you, Luke."

Then he opened his present from her. It was a new fishing rod and reel. He loved it. She knew what he wanted and asked the guy at the bait-and-tackle shop for a recommendation for a good surf-casting rod.

"This is great. I'm still trying to improve my surf-casting skills. My old rod was for freshwater fishing in the lakes back home," Luke said. He gave her a big hug and a kiss.

On the thirty-first, they went to the oyster roast and shrimp boil in the parking lot at the fish house on Silver Lake. Then they stopped by the New Year's Eve party at Gaffer's.

Gaffer's was located in a wooden building originally built in the 1970s to house Howard's Pub. It had hardwood floors, and was laid out on different levels. The dance floor was on the lowest level, with an elevated area for bands. Over twenty flat-screen televisions hung on the walls. The bar was pretty full that night, mostly with local young people. The Ocracoke Rockers played until just before midnight, then they turned on the televisions to show Times Square in New York where the crystal ball dropped at midnight. Luke grabbed Anna. They melted together into a nice, long, slow kiss. Then the band started up again, and they all danced. Luke and Anna rolled into bed about two that night.

New Year's Eve was on a Friday night. Luke spent New Year's Day packing and relaxing with Anna. He planned to leave early Sunday morning for the drive across the state. His first day of work in the mountains would be Tuesday.

"I wish you could come visit me in the mountains," Luke said to Anna as they lay in bed Saturday night.

"It will be hard to get time off, and then there is the ten-hour drive, but I will try," Anna said.

"I'm going to miss you, Anna," Luke said. "I have had a wonderful time with you this fall."

"I have, too. Try not to spend too much time in the hot tubs," she said teasing, but she was also serious. "But if you do, think of me back here all alone, with nothing to do but battle the cold wind and drive cold-stunned turtles to Manteo."

"At least I don't have to worry about you hanging out with a bunch of good-looking surfer dudes back here," he said.

"I wish I didn't have to worry about you either," she said. "I will try to get up to see you sometime, but if not, I guess the next time we will see each other will be in March or April."

"That's right," Luke said. He really cared about Anna, but he knew he would be faced with temptations in the mountains. They were not a couple, and he was not ready to get serious, so he left it at that.

2011

≈Chapter Twenty≈

When Luke got to North Wilkesboro on Sunday, there was snow on the ground. It started snowing when he hit U.S. 421 as it crossed under the Blue Ridge Parkway. Within a twenty-mile stretch, the temperature dropped ten degrees. It was snowing in Banner Elk when Luke met TMJ in the parking lot at the Tynecastle shopping center.

"It was seven degrees last night with wind-blown snow. The wind chill was below zero. The snow base at Sugar is fantastic, man," TMJ said, greeting Luke with a smile and a handshake. "We've had so much snow in December the kids only had school for about a week. They are expecting the same for January and February. My boss said this may be the best year ever at Sugar Mountain."

Luke was glad he had a four-wheel-drive Jeep to tackle the icy and snow-packed roads. When they got to the house, Bryce and Helen had fixed a nice meal for Luke and TMJ.

"Fresh mountain trout with rice and broccoli," TMJ said. "It is great having roommates who can cook."

"We wanted to welcome Luke to the mountains in style," Helen said.

She was an attractive petite blonde in her mid-twenties. Bryce looked like a ski instructor. He was six foot six inches tall, lean, and Nordic-looking with dirty blond hair, blue eyes, square-jawed good looks, and wide, athletic shoulders. He was more reserved than Helen. Helen was friendly and welcoming to Luke. Both of them had graduated from Appalachian State University a few years ago earlier.

"Luke, TMJ told us you have a girlfriend at the beach. I know you'll miss her, but we'll try to keep you busy," she said with kind eyes.

"Thanks," Luke said.

After they sat down to eat, TMJ said, "I don't think that Luke will be bored or lonely in Banner Elk this winter."

Bryce cut him a look. Luke was well aware of the parade of women TMJ had brought into the house since he had moved in with them. He wondered if this bothered Bryce.

═══

Luke and TMJ went to work early the next day.

"TMJ told me that you have restaurant experience and that you are a carpenter, Luke," said Mr. Haynes, a middle-aged, overweight, balding man. They were in the resort manager's office.

"Yes, sir," Luke answered him.

"That's good. I may need you in the restaurant, and I may need your carpentry skills as well. But, right now, I need you working with TMJ handling ski rentals. They are slammed down there. TMJ can show you around." Mr. Haynes glanced down at the paperwork in front of him. "I assume I can count on you to stay for the season?"

"Yes, sir. I was told the season lasts through March or early April."

"Yeah. We make our money when the snow is on the ground, so we are totally dependent on the weather here. We make the snow, it doesn't have to be natural, but the temperature has to be right," he said. "This year and last year we not only had the right temperatures, but we also had tons of natural snow. We have over a sixty-inch base right now."

"That's great," Luke said. "I hope that I don't disappoint you, sir."

"I hope not, too. If you do, you're out. There are plenty of hungry twentysomethings looking for a job if you don't do yours." Then Mr. Haynes stood and shook Luke's hand. "Welcome aboard."

From there, TMJ took Luke down to the ski equipment check-out area and showed him the ropes before the crowd started to come in. Once they came, it was a steady stream of families, middle-aged people, good-looking twentysomething girls that TMJ loved to flirt with, teenagers, young guys, and small children—all ages, sizes, and temperaments. Some were obviously from the North and some from the South. There were large church groups that came on buses and groups from South America and Florida. Luke's first day was long and busy. Day skiing stretched from 9:00 until 4:30, then night skiing was available on the lighted trails from 6:00 to 10:00.

＝

That week, it snowed even more. By January 8th, there were ten or more inches on the ground with more snow on the way. On Friday night, at the end of Luke's first exhausting week, TMJ invited two girls and a guy who worked with them to the house.

Helen made a couple of batchs of margaritas. TMJ lifted the lid to the hot tub and turned on the water jets. The water from the hot tub bubbled and steamed into the night air. When he turned on the spotlights on the deck, the air lit up with ice crystals that drifted from the trees surrounding the house.

"Anybody want to take a dip?" TMJ said, walking back in the living room, wearing heavy boots, ski pants, a T-shirt, and a ski toboggan.

"I didn't bring my bathing suit," said Lisa, a cute blonde who worked the ski rentals with TMJ.

"Who needs a bathing suit?" TMJ replied with a big grin.

"I set myself up for that, didn't I?"

"Yep."

"I have a bathing suit that should fit you," Helen offered.

TMJ went into the bathroom and emerged with some big bath towels.

"It's much more fun to go naked," he said, pulling his ski pants and T-shirt off. He wore no underwear under his nylon pants. He left his boots on to walk through the snow on the deck. This was Lisa's first introduction to TMJ and his love of nudity. Her eyes opened wide, but she tried not to let it show that she noticed.

"Where is that bathing suit?" she asked, as she followed Helen into her bedroom.

TMJ opened the sliding glass door, walked through the snow, took off his boots, and stepped into the water. "Come on in. It's great!"

The other guy, Josh, stripped to his underwear and followed TMJ to the hot tub. The steam rose around them as they held their drinks in the air. It did look inviting. Finally, Jennifer stripped to her underwear and tiptoed across the snow, using the footprints left by TMJ and Josh, and joined the guys in the hot tub. Lisa and Helen emerged from the bedroom with bathing suits and ran barefoot across the snow and jumped into the steaming water.

"Wow, this is great!" Lisa said. "Luke, why don't you join us?"

Luke had been down this road before with TMJ. He stripped to his boxers and walked across the snowy deck, drink in hand. Bryce was the only hold out.

"Come on, Bryce. It is really cool, I mean, hot!" Helen said, beckoning him to join them.

Slowly Bryce stripped to a black thong then walked through the snow to join them.

"Am I the only one who is man enough to get naked?" TMJ asked, standing up so everyone could see.

"No, TMJ, I'll join you," Jennifer said, taking off her sports bra and panties. Then Josh pulled his boxers out of the water and slung them on the side of the hot tub.

Helen and Lisa decided to join them. Bryce said, "Well, okay," and grudgingly removed his thong. This left only Luke, who decided he didn't want to be the party pooper so he took his boxers off, too. It was cold out but nice and warm in the hot tub. They could see their breath as ice crystals danced in the air around them.

"Drinks anyone?" Helen asked, getting up to fetch another batch of margaritas.

Luke looked at his underwear on the side of the tub. He picked it up, and sure enough, it had begun to freeze. It must have been between ten and twenty degrees out. "Damn, it's cold. My underwear is already freezing," he said holding it up.

"Damn," Josh said, picking his up to look at it. "Mine is, too."

"But it sure is toasty in here," TMJ said.

Helen slipped into TMJ's boots, walked across the snowy deck, and poured some more drinks. "It is cold out here," she said, quickly stepping out of the boots and jumping back into the hot tub. Then it began to snow.

"This is just too cool," TMJ said. They stayed in the hot tub until their skin began to wrinkle, then, one by one, they ran back into the house and TMJ put the cover over the tub. They dried off with towels inside the house. Bryce had already started a fire in the fireplace. Helen mixed another round of drinks.

"With the snow and ice and drinking, we can't let you guys leave tonight," Helen said. "You can spend the night."

"Don't twist my arm," Josh said. They all knew that it was better to spend the night after a party then to brave the icy roads, so they had pretty much expected to stay.

"We have plenty of room and blankets and sofas," Helen said. "Make yourselves at home."

They partied and drank until past two, watching the snow, going back in the hot tub one more time. Gradually, they drifted to bed, Helen and Bryce first, then Josh joined Luke and TMJ in their room, sleeping on a blanket on the floor. The other two girls slept on the sofas in the living room.

They were all up and ready for work at 9:00 the next morning. Helen put out some bagels and peanut butter and made a pot of coffee. At least the house was near the slopes, so they didn't have far to go.

The snow kept coming. Blizzards swept across the Northeast, and snow covered the South from Atlanta to Raleigh. The high-country area of the mountains always got it worse than the Piedmont. Of course, with fresh snow and days of no school, the skiers came and came and came. The biggest weekend was the Martin Luther King holiday. In preparation, Mr. Haynes let some of the help off during the week, so they could get rested up. Luke, TMJ, and some friends were able to take Tuesday and Wednesday off because they would be working the day and night shifts over the long weekend.

Luke called Anna in Ocracoke. They had been texting to each other, but he had not talked to her since he moved to Banner Elk.

"How is it at the beach?" Luke asked.

"Very cold and very windy. Some days you don't even see cars on the road. It is deserted like a ghost town," Anna said. "How is it up there?"

"Cold. We've had lots of snow, over sixty inches so far. It is kind of crazy up here. Sugar Mountain attracts skiers from all over the East Coast. With snow in the Piedmont, Atlanta, and Washington, school is out, so they come here to ski. This coming weekend is supposed to be really big because it is a long weekend with the federal holiday. They have us working double shifts, so some of us took a couple of days off this week to rest up," Luke told her.

"I miss you," she said.

"I miss you, too," he said. "I wish you could be here. It is really cool with all the snow and the activity."

"I'm too busy taking care of turtles."

"I know."

"I may be able to get some time off. It is just so far away. But I'll let you know."

"Take care," he said. He missed her, he really cared for her, but he was having a great time with TMJ and his friends. He tried not to think of the upcoming anniversary, January 16, a year after Karen was killed in the automobile accident. So much had happened since then. He would be busy because of the holiday. That was good. It would help him get through the weekend without becoming depressed.

TMJ asked Lisa and Jennifer to come by on Monday night for drinks and a dip in the hot tub. It had snowed most of the day Monday, but snow was better than ice, and the snowplows were pretty good on Sugar Mountain and in Banner Elk. As long as you had four-wheel drive, it was easy to get around. TMJ invited the girls to spend the night. As long as they enjoyed themselves, they probably would. It was apparent to Luke that TMJ wanted Lisa and Luke to hook up and that he wanted Jennifer for himself.

Helen and Bryce stayed up with them until midnight, everyone drinking Helen's margaritas. After Helen and Bryce went to bed, TMJ suggested they get in the hot tub. Once again he stripped down to his boots, and Luke and the girls stripped down to their underwear.

The steam rose in the cold mountain air as the snow fell around them illuminated by the outdoor spotlights that lit the deck. It was magical.

Finally, TMJ and Jennifer headed for his bedroom, leaving Luke and Lisa in the living room.

"Helen told me that you have a girlfriend on the coast," Lisa said, once they had gotten dressed and sat on the sofa.

"Yes, we've been dating since the summer, but there is no work for me out there during the winter, so I came here. She's a park ranger."

"I bet you miss her," she said, fishing.

"Yeah, but I'm having a great time here," he said, not knowing quite what to say.

"I understand that you have a very sad anniversary coming up this weekend," she said, trying to be sympathetic.

"Yes, I do. How did you know about that?"

"TMJ told us."

He paused. "I'd rather not talk about that right now."

"I'm sorry. I didn't mean to pry."

"That's okay. It's just that it is going to be very hard for me this week-end. It's only been a year, and it is still very raw," he said with emotion.

"Does your girlfriend know about it?"

"Yes. Listen, I'm pretty tired. Do you mind if I go ahead and go to bed? We have blankets for you," Luke said, handing her a blanket. He took a blanket and, after turning out the lights, lay down on one of the sofas.

The giggling and other noises from TMJ's room kept Luke awake. He thought about Karen and Anna. Was he being unfaithful to Karen and her memory by going out with Anna? Was he being unfaithful to Anna by hanging out with the girls in the hot tub? It was all very confusing. He could not bring Karen back. He really cared for Anna but was not ready to commit, though he was getting closer. Lisa's prying made him uncomfortable. It was going to be hard to get through the weekend. He didn't need to be reminded of it. He needed to be distracted to stay busy.

The next morning, as Luke's mind was crawling awake, he heard whispers in the kitchen.

"I really screwed up last night," Lisa said to Helen. "I brought up Luke's girlfriend *and* his wife."

"Not smart," Helen said.

"I was trying to be sympathetic," Lisa said.

"Still not a good idea. He hasn't even talked to us about it. TMJ told me about it, but Luke hasn't said a word. I figured he would tell me when or if he wants to." There was a pause. Luke rolled over on the sofa. "Hey, Luke, do you want some coffee?"

"Sure," he said. He got up, poured some coffee, and ate a bagel.

That weekend, the ski slopes were slammed. It snowed more, which brought even more people. They all worked day and night. By the time they got home after the night-skiing shift, they were exhausted. It was that way through the weekend and on into the next week. Luke didn't have time to think about Karen. But on Sunday, between shifts, he drove to the little bark-covered Episcopal chapel in Linville and prayed for her, depositing money in the cash box and leaving a bouquet of flowers on the altar that he had bought at Lowes Foods.

The church was empty. Kneeling in one of the pews, his head bowed in prayer, Luke whispered, "Karen, I miss you and will always love you. Thank you, Lord, for giving me the time that I had with Karen. She was a blessing to me. I will never forget her as long as I shall live and will always honor and keep her in my memory."

≈

The blizzards continued unabated across the Northeast, New York, New Jersey, and Washington. The following Saturday, January 22, Anna called from Ocracoke.

"You won't believe this, but it is snowing in Ocracoke."

"What?" Luke said.

"Yeah, there are four inches on the ground, and it is still falling." He could hear the smile in her voice.

She sent him photos on her cell phone. It was beautiful. Everything was covered with snow: the bent trees and bushes, the lighthouse, the ground, the beach. It was rare and beautiful. When it stopped snowing that night, the snow measured seven inches. It was a narrow band that just affected Ocracoke, Hatteras, Atlantic Beach, and Morehead City in Carteret County. It shut down four ferries due to visibility and icing on the decks. The snow didn't stay long, but it lasted long enough for all the kids on Ocracoke to have a great time, building snowmen and playing in the snow. By Monday, it was mostly gone, but school was cancelled anyway so that the children could enjoy one of the only snow days that they had ever experienced.

⁓Chapter Twenty-One⁓

One night TMJ asked two gay friends, Jim and Tommy, over to the house. They were a couple of years younger than Luke and TMJ and worked in the equipment-rental section of the ski slope. Luke had not been around gay guys too much, but TMJ had gay friends on the island and in Key West. He was totally comfortable. They were both nice looking in a guy-next-door kind of way, with short conservative hair cuts, and they both dressed very preppy and sharp.

As the night wore on, TMJ said, "Let's get in the hot tub."

"I thought you would never ask," Jim said with a smile. "Your hot tub does have a certain reputation."

"Last one in is a rotten egg," TMJ said, shedding his clothes. It was snowing lightly outside. Luke was not really in the mood, but after TMJ and Helen and Bryce joined Jim and Tommy in the tub he thought it would look like he was a prude if he didn't join them, so he did. They all sat in the hot tub with drinks on the ledge, watching the snow fall lightly. The water was hot, but the air was really cold. It felt great. Then TMJ got up, and Luke saw Jim whisper something to Tommy. It was hard not to miss TMJ's manly parts as he got out of the water in such close quarters.

"TMJ," Jim began. "I could swear that I have seen that before and not in the bathroom at the ski slopes."

"You're good!" TMJ said, his eyes lit up. "It is rather well known in certain circles on the Internet."

"That's where I have seen it," Tommy said. "X-Tube, right?"

"Well, yes, I have a profile on X-Tube as well as some other sites."

Luke exchanged glances with Helen and Bryce. "So that's what you do on the Internet?" Luke asked, shocked.

"Well, yes, it's a business decision and a great source of extra income," TMJ said, obviously proud of himself.

"Additional income?" Luke was incredulous.

"Yes, when people want to download photos or videos of me, they have to pay."

"Oh my God!" Luke said, not believing what he was hearing.

"X-Tube is generally free, but certain people like TMJ can demand a fee for their videos and photos since they are so well known," Jim said with a knowing smile.

TMJ was an Internet porn star? This explained a lot to Luke—why TMJ spent so much time on the computer and why he sat in front of it in the nude. He had expensive computer equipment, the latest Apple computer, video camera equipment, and a laptop.

"It is a side line I learned about when I was in Key West. Apparently, I am quite popular with some women and men—gay, straight, or bi. Hey, it brings in a little extra cash, and it's fun, too, so why not?"

Luke didn't quite know what to say.

"It's all perfectly legal and on the up and up. I had a lawyer check into it. X-Tube collects the money and puts it in my Paypal account. I even pay taxes on it. It's not like I charge a fortune or anything. It doesn't cost much to download a video or still shot, but it adds up," TMJ said, smiling.

"I'm impressed," Bryce said. "Good way to make some extra cash. You don't have to have sex with anyone, do you?"

"No, I just do my thing all by myself. People seem to like it, and it's easy and fun."

"Man, I can't believe I am in a hot tub with a celebrity," Tommy said. "You are famous! Can I take a picture?"

"Sure, man, have at it. I won't even charge you," TMJ said, standing up in the hot tub.

Tommy and Jim splashed out of the hot tub and got their iPhones.

"So I've been living with a celebrity and didn't know it," Luke said.

"Yeah, sort of," TMJ said.

"And I've been working with him for the past month," Jim said. "I heard someone say they had seen him in the bathroom and it was pretty big, but I had no idea. This is way cool."

After Jim and Tommy had taken a few photos and the buzz subsided, they decided to go inside and fix more drinks.

It got late, so Jim and Tommy stayed and slept on the sofa. The more Luke thought about it, the more he accepted it and thought there wasn't anything he could do. Sure, it was weird, and disgusting, but TMJ was just TMJ. He was still his friend, this didn't change that. This was a way he could make some extra money, and it seemed to be legit.

"Hey, Luke, don't say anything about this to Hank or anyone back on Ocracoke," TMJ said the next day. "I don't know how they would take it."

"My lips are sealed. It isn't any of their business anyway," Luke said.

"You looked a little surprised. I wouldn't have told you if Jim hadn't brought it up. Are you cool?"

"Yeah, man. Whatever floats your boat."

"Thank you, man. You're my bud. I'll remember this," TMJ remarked as they shook and buddy-hugged. Luke decided he would be true to his word and not tell anyone on Ocracoke about TMJ's "other" source of income.

≈

It continued to snow, every week through February but less so in March. Luke and Lisa never "hooked up" as TMJ wanted, but TMJ continued to ask girls over to play in the hot tub, and occasionally Jim and Tommy. TMJ ended up in bed with Jennifer at least once or twice a week.

Luke didn't really care what they did behind closed doors, but TMJ was more than happy to tell him every detail.

Anna was not able to get time off to visit Luke in the mountains. By the end of March, the business on the ski slopes began to wind down and people were moving on to other jobs. Jennifer left to get a summer job in Myrtle Beach. Josh and Lisa stayed in Boone, where they waited tables at Casa Rustica. Helen and Bryce took off for Colorado for a few weeks, then made plans to be river-rafting guides in Alaska for Mountain Sobek during the summer. Jim and Tommy moved to Florida to work at a golf course. This left Luke and TMJ.

≈

The last week in March, Hank called. He had work for them: a job building a new house on Ocean View Road.

Luke and TMJ packed up and left for Ocracoke on the first Sunday in April.

Hank had been checking on TMJ's trailer, but when they got there, it was musty, so the first thing they did was open up the doors and windows and air it out. Then they turned on the water. The line going into the trailer from the street had frozen and shattered, so TMJ called a plumber. It had been a cold winter on the Outer Banks. Lots of pipes had frozen. Although Luke had drained the pipes in December before he left, the line going from the street to the house still had water in it, and it froze.

After work, Anna came by the trailer.

When he opened the door, she threw her arms around Luke.

"I missed you," she said, burying her face in his chest.

"I missed you, too," he said, closing his eyes and hugging her. Then he kissed her—long and hard.

She climbed into the trailer, and they sat at the kitchen table. Luke put his hand on her hand where it rested on the table. "I am glad to be back in Ocracoke. I really missed it."

"Did you have a good time in the mountains?" she asked.

"Yes, but it was not the same as here. This is a real community. Up there it is a resort, very transient, people don't care about community like they do here," Luke said. He was finding that home, community, and place mattered to him.

≈

In April, Luke and TMJ helped Hank put in the pilings for the new house and start to frame it up. Most of the restaurants were open by the middle of April, so young people began to return to the island for work.

The weather was in the sixties and seventies and was absolutely beautiful; low humidity, clear skies, cloudless nights with lots of stars.

The big news in the outside world, other than that a schoolteacher from Ocracoke was winning on *Jeopardy*, was that on May 2, 2011, Osama Bin Laden was killed by Navy Seals in Pakistan upon the order of the president.

≈

People gradually began to return to Ocracoke for the summer. Sammy Cooper and Tommy Howard came back after working in Colorado. Thelma Garrish and Luane Dobbins returned in May from working in Greenville.

"I just got a text from Thelma that they are going to the beach this afternoon. You interested?" TMJ told Luke as they were eating lunch. They had started work at 6:00 and would be finished at 3:00.

"Sure, I think I'll be ready for the beach after work. I'll ask Anna if she can come, too."

Luke texted Anna to see if she wanted to meet them on the beach about 4:00. She answered that she was working in the bird area at the south point and couldn't get in until after 5:00. So Luke told her where they would be, at Ramp 67, and to text him later if she wanted to join them.

They finished work, went home, took showers, put on their bathing suits, and drove to Ramp 67, where they found Thelma, Luane, and several others on the beach. It was late May, so the water was still cool, but the sun was perfect and the temperature was in the seventies.

Thelma and Luane lay on beach towels. They were white.

"This is the first time I have had to work on my tan for the summer," Thelma said.

Luke unfolded a beach chair, put it beside the girls, and sat down. He and TMJ had winter tans from working outside the month of May. TMJ pulled off his bathing suit and sat in a beach chair in all his pride and glory.

"There he is, at it again," Thelma said, rolling her eyes.

"Not like it isn't a surprise," Luane said, rolling over on her stomach, ignoring TMJ and his display.

About that time, Tommy Howard and Sammy Cooper drove up in Tommy's Ford pickup.

"I see TMJ hasn't changed since last summer," Sammy said, walking up carrying a beach chair.

"Yeah, he likes to let it all hang out," Thelma said.

After sitting in the hot sun, TMJ stood up and ran into the water.

"Whew! it's cold," he said, quickly running back out of the water and plopping in his chair.

"I bet it was refreshing though," Tommy said. Then he ran into the water and quickly ran back out. "It's cold as hell."

"You guys are crazy," Luane said, propping herself up on her elbow.

"It is so warm in the sun, I thought the water had warmed up a little," TMJ said. "Not yet though."

"Give it another couple of weeks, then it will be tolerable," Tommy said.

They hung out, lying in the sun and occasionally braving the water for brief dips until about 5:30.

"I think I'll text Anna and see where she is."

"R U coming 2 the beach?" he texted.

"No 2 tired," she messaged back. "Call when U get back."

Around six, Luke and TMJ drove back to the house. Thelma, Luane, and Anna joined them. They fixed supper at the trailer for the guys, fresh blue fish, coleslaw, potato salad, and sliced tomatoes.

Thelma and Luane decided to spend the night. Anna stayed until midnight.

After Anna left, Luke went to bed. Luke could hear TMJ, Thelma, and Luane in the bedroom well into the night until he finally fell asleep. The walls of the trailer were paper-thin and hid no sounds.

~

Luke went to see Anna that morning at Park Service housing and drank a cup of coffee.

"I like TMJ, but damn I can't get any sleep. When Thelma and Luane come over, they are at it all night long. I need to get some sleep. I feel like hell the next day when I have to get up at six and go to work. I don't know how he does it," Luke said.

"Youth," Anna said.

"And hormones," Luke added.

"My supervisor told me about a friend who owns a house on the island but doesn't rent it. He likes to come to Ocracoke in the spring and fall, but he hates it in the summer. He moves to his house in the mountains in June. He asked me if I was interested in housesitting for him for the summer. I said sure!

"Park Service housing is nice, but you have to share it with roommates, and you don't have much privacy. I thought it was cool that he asked me and not someone else. Would you like to join me?" Anna asked Luke. "I'm sure he wouldn't mind if someone else moved in, too. There are three bedrooms and one bath. It's a neat old island house with a screened porch on front, sheds in the back, and a nice kitchen. That way maybe you could get some sleep. Are you interested?"

He could see the relationship heading to a whole other level if they shared a house together, but Luke found himself saying, "Sure." He didn't know how much he was ready to commit to Anna, but sharing a house—he could do that. It would beat staying up all night listening to TMJ getting it on with Thelma and Luane.

"He said I could move in the first of June," Anna said. "I'll ask him if we can both stay there and let you know what he says."

≈

The next day, Anna talked to Tony Franklin, the owner of the house. Tony was a retired English professor from Chapel Hill. He had a summer house in Todd, near Boone, but stayed on Ocracoke during the fall and spring and in Chapel Hill during the winter. He had met Anna because he was a big supporter of the national seashore.

Anna asked Tony if he minded if Luke also stayed in the house. She sweetened the deal by adding that Luke was a carpenter and offering Luke's services to fix things when they needed to be fixed. Tony quickly agreed.

≈CHAPTER TWENTY-TWO≈

On Memorial Day weekend, Luke and Anna went to the Annual Fireman's Ball and Auction to benefit the volunteer fire department. Cora had worked hard on the auction committee, and Hank helped cook the barbecue pork. Luke and Anna first ate barbecue at the pig-picking then went to the auction, but they did not bid on the auction items. The beer was flowing freely, so the bidding went high. They stayed for the dance afterward. The Aaron Caswell Band, the Ocracoke Rockers, and Dune Dogs played into the wee hours of the night at the Community Center on Highway 12.

They moved into the Franklin house in the middle of the first week in June, just in time for the Ocrafolk Festival that weekend.

The one-story house on Lighthouse Road was built in the 1940s by one of the island families. A living room was attached to a small kitchen and eating area. Behind that was a hall that connected to three bedrooms and a bathroom. The walls were white, painted bead board. The trim and doors were unpainted, varnished pine. The floors were varnished oak hardwood, but the kitchen floor was linoleum.

There were one large and two smaller outbuildings in the backyard. Tony had updated the house without changing its character. There was a small laundry room and outdoor shower off a deck at the back of the house. Big old cedars grew in the yard as did live oaks. The exterior of the house was painted white with a dark green trim.

It had been a while since Luke had a decent-sized bedroom of his own. Luke and Anna each took one of the medium-sized bedrooms, both of which had iron double beds with quilts for bedspreads. The smaller bedroom had two single beds in it. The furniture was old, mostly oak. The bathroom had a white pedestal sink and a claw-foot tub with a shower fitting and curtain around it. The house's golden oak floors had hand-woven rugs scattered over them. Comfortable overstuffed furniture, most of it well worn, was placed throughout the house.

The weather was perfect for the Ocrafolk Festival. It was sunny and in the seventies during the day with low humidity. Artists and craftsmen lined School Road, most set up under white tents, and there were two outdoor stages—one beside Books to Be Red and one on Howard Street. The stages stayed busy with music all day Saturday and half the day Sunday. A smaller crowd attended the auction Friday night, which was held outside at the Deepwater stage. There were few items but most were pricey. After eating some barbecue, Anna and Luke decided not to stay for the auction. The year before there had been a larger selection of items of different prices, and the auction and potluck were held inside the school gym. This year, the old gym was being replaced with a bigger nicer gym, so it was not available.

Anna and Luke enjoyed the music during the day. The groups were mainly local and from North Carolina, but some were from as far away as Brazil. There was lots of bluegrass, some modern instrumental music, fusion, folk rock, but all original work. Members of the local Molasses Creek band were the organizers of the event, and they had good taste in music and good connections with other like-minded musicians.

≈

June was a great time to go clamming, flounder gigging, and crabbing before the water got too hot. The best fishing was in May and October, but the fishermen still caught plenty of fish during the summer, mainly on boats in the ocean and the sound.

Tommy Howard asked Luke and TMJ if they wanted to go flounder gigging one Monday night. He had some new equipment, a LED light at the end of a PVC pipe powered by a AA battery. This was a lot easier to use than lugging around a car battery to power the lights as they had done the summer before. Tommy also had new single-spear gigs, with twine attached so after they speared the flounder they could pull the fish onto a string with floats attached.

Tommy had a twenty-one-foot Carolina Skiff. He picked them up about 9:00, and they motored out to the shallows off Springer's Point. TMJ threw one anchor off the bow and set it. Then he threw another one off the stern and set it. They climbed down the ladder in the back beside the motor in the water, which came to their knees. Tommy turned on his light first.

"Wow, that is really bright, and it uses a AA battery?" TMJ said. The light lit up the crystal-clear water, revealing the grass on the bottom, shells, and the occasional crab and shrimp.

"Yeah, it is LED, no car battery," Tommy said, scanning the bottom for the telltale outline of the oblong flounder.

Suddenly, Tommy jabbed at the water and pulled up a fish. As it flapped on the long, straight metal gig, he pulled out his tape measure. "Sixteen inches, it's legal and a keeper," he said triumphantly.

TMJ saw a flounder outlined on the bottom, but it did not look big enough so, he passed it up.

"I wish I had brought my seine net. We could catch a bunch of shrimp tonight," Tommy said. "I left it at home. Next time I'll bring it." They saw many shrimp scampering around on the sand as well as small crabs and baitfish.

"Got one," Luke said. Tommy walked over and measured it. It was fourteen inches.

"Almost, but you can't keep that one," Tommy said.

Luke let it slide off the gig and back in the water. He hoped it would live. He did not spear it in its vital parts, so it quickly swam away.

"Got to be careful, just as soon as we catch an undersized one the game warden will catch us and fine us. Remember it has to be fifteen inches or longer, and we can't catch more than six per person a day," Tommy said.

"Damn mosquitoes," TMJ said, swatting a swarm of mosquitoes that was drawn to the light. "Maybe if we put out the light, they will go away."

"We can try," Tommy said, "but they'll be back." They turned out the lights, but the mosquitoes still swarmed. The moon was just a sliver over-head, so they could see the stars, including the Milky Way and the famil-iar constellations like Orion and the Big Dipper, very clearly. The surface of the water was like ink as it moved, reflecting the light from the stars and the moon.

"Damn mosquitoes. I thought they would go away," TMJ said.

"They are drawn to your breath," Tommy said, with a grin, "and the warmth of your body."

"Yeah, your breath stinks," Luke said.

"You shut up," TMJ said, picking up his PVC pipe with the light on the end and swiping it at Luke.

"I think it is time to open a beer," Luke said, ducking the pipe and walking back to the boat.

"That's a good idea," Tommy said. "Let's take a break." They walked back through the water to the boat. Tommy climbed in, put his flounder on ice in a cooler, and pulled out three cans of Miller Lite. He handed cans to Luke and TMJ.

When they finished the beer, Tommy said, "Let's keep fishing." So they continued to walk through the knee-deep water with the lights on, scouring the bottom for fish. Tommy speared four, Luke got two, and TMJ gigged three legal-sized fish. By then the mosquitoes had become so unbearable that they put the fish on ice and headed back to Silver Lake, where Tommy kept his boat at a dock owned by his uncle.

~

"Ya'll want to take a day off and go crabbing at Lake Mattamuskeet?" Hank asked the next day at the job site. "I hear they are catching some big

205

ones. It is better to go during the week when it's not so crowded. What about tomorrow morning?"

"Sure, as long as our boss doesn't mind us taking some time off," TMJ said, teasing.

"I'm waiting for cedar shingles to arrive from Dare Building Supply before we can start shingling the outside. I think this week is as good as any to go crabbing. When those shingles come next week, we will be real busy," Hank said.

They made plans for Hank to pick them up early enough to catch the 6:30 Swan Quarter ferry. Hank would bring the fish heads, twine, baskets, and nets.

TMJ said he'd bring a cooler with ice, beer, and water.

Both Luke and TMJ had bought coastal and inland fishing licenses when they went fishing with Tommy.

≈

The next morning, they took the Swan Quarter ferry over to the mainland and drove to Hank's favorite place to go crabbing, in front of the old pump house with a lighthouse-like structure in the middle of it.

Hank, Luke, and TMJ walked over a low concrete dam that was built to control the water flow through the drainage canals. It was a perfect place to put out crab lines. There were metal railings where they could tie and drop their crab lines and net the crabs. Hank had brought a bunch of old fish carcasses he had gotten from the fish house. They stunk to high heaven.

"This fish is ripe," TMJ said, as he wrapped twine around a flounder carcass and dropped it in the water.

"The riper the better, the crabs like it real stinky," Hank said, dropping a line into the water. The good meat had been stripped off the carcasses. Their bait was the bony part with the spine and ribs and whatever meat was still left on it, the throw-away stuff that Hank got for free at the fish house.

A few cars drove by on the dusty road, but they mostly had the place to themselves. It was sunny and not too humid. They had brought bug spray but did not need it. TMJ took off his shirt, then Luke. They figured they'd get a little sun while they were crabbing. After they had caught about four big crabs, TMJ decided to get a beer. It was about 10 A.M.

"You want one, Hank?"

"No, not now," he said, pulling up a line to check it.

"How about you, Luke?"

"Sure," Luke said, taking a cold Papst from TMJ.

TMJ pulled his dick out of his pants and hung it over the rail. "I wonder if the crabs would like some of this?" he said, teasing.

"Get that thing back in your pants. What if someone sees you?" Hank said, with mock indignation.

"He just likes to show off," Luke said.

"No, I have to pee," TMJ said.

"Well, do it in the bushes. I don't want to eat crabs that have been swimming in your pee," Hank said.

"Okay, old man."

"Don't you old man me," Hank said, with a mock scowl.

≈

When they had caught about five crabs each, it was just after noon.

"Y'all ready to get some lunch?" Hank asked.

"Sure," said TMJ, who had drunk three beers to Luke's two. "I need some food in my belly."

"You sure do. One more beer, and you'll be drunk," Hank said, teasing. He enjoyed giving TMJ a hard time.

≈

They rolled up the twine on sticks and put them, with the stinky fish carcasses still on them, into wooden baskets in the back of the truck. The crabs were in another wooden basket with a lid on it.

There weren't many accommodations on the mainland in Hyde

County, so they returned to Hank's favorite stop—Martell's family restaurant in Engelhard. Just like their previous visit, Hank got the lunch buffet, which had a choice of two meats, several vegetables, and a salad for $10.99.

"Best deal around," Hank said of the buffet. They hit the washroom first to get the fish smell off their hands, then grabbed plates and filled them up. Barbecue chicken, pork chops, cabbage, green beans, sweet potatoes, mashed potatoes, and salad. The waitress brought them iced tea. It was a feast.

"It is always a treat to eat at Martell's," Hank said. "One of the highlights of the trip over here."

After they ate, they returned to the canals and found a group of middle-aged black men standing in the spot where they had crabbed that morning. There was plenty of room for everyone, but after a while, Hank decided to pull up and drive to a bridge over one of the canals and put out lines there. They filled the wooden basket with crabs averaging a six-to eight-inch carapace, very large, much larger than the blue crabs they caught back on Ocracoke. Hank liked to bring people with him so they could each catch their limit. About 3:00, he pulled up the lines, rolled them up, and put them in the truck. On the way to the ferry, they stopped at a grocery. Hank bought chicken feed for his neighbor and some fresh vegetables. TMJ purchased some more beer, potato chips, and pretzels for the ferry ride back to Ocracoke.

As they waited in line with all the other cars and trucks for the ferry, TMJ got three beers out of the cooler before Hank put the crabs on ice. Since their visit the previous summer, drinking on the ferry had been outlawed. However, the rules were not enforced very well. As long as you hid your beer or drank from a cup and not in an open container, the ferry employees usually didn't say anything because it had been allowed in the past and it was such a tradition.

TMJ and Luke opened their beer and poured them into cups.

"If you insist," Hank said, taking a can of Miller from TMJ. He then poured it in a Howard's Pub cup he kept in the truck, and they drove onto the ferry for the two-and-half-hour ride back to Ocracoke.

"Look, porpoises," TMJ said, pointing at the water behind the ferry as it pulled away from the dock. They were miles from the ocean, but a large pod of porpoises played in the water behind the boat in the sound.

TMJ opened a bag of potato chips and settled into the backseat of the truck.

"So you moved in with your girlfriend," he said to Luke. "How is domestic life?"

"I don't know yet, we just moved in together," Luke said, defensively.

"Don't let TMJ give you a hard time about Anna. She is a real sweet girl."

"Yeah, real sweet but does she give good head?" TMJ asked, taking a sip of his beer.

"Not like your girlfriends," Luke said, glaring at him.

"Now, boys, calm down. TMJ, Anna is Luke's girl. You need to be a little more respectful," Hank said.

"Well, if she doesn't give good head, I sure hope she is good in bed," TMJ said, propping his leg up with his sandaled feet sticking out the window of the truck.

"We have a good sex life and that is all I'm going to say. It is none of your business," Luke said.

"You know everything about my sex life. Why can't I ask you about yours?"

"I don't ask, you volunteer it, plus what you don't tell me, I hear at night through those paper-thin walls in your trailer," Luke said. "That is one reason I wanted to move out, so I could have some privacy and get some sleep."

"My life is an open book. I don't have anything to hide," TMJ said, digging his hand into his crotch and giving it a good tug.

"Some people like a little more privacy than others," Hank said, defending Luke.

Enough said, Luke thought, and changed the subject. Luke and TMJ were as different as day and night in so many ways. In fact, TMJ could almost be Luke's alter ego, but they got along. Luke accepted TMJ for who he was. He tried not to judge TMJ, who was a good friend. TMJ liked to push Luke and Hank, but he knew when he had pushed too hard and usually backed off.

They changed the subject and started to talk about the construction site and what they could expect in terms of work for the next couple of weeks. Then Hank brought up the subject of Anna again.

"Luke, are you and Anna getting serious?"

"I don't know, Hank. I really like her, and we get along really well. It will be interesting to see how well we do now that we're living in the same house," Luke said.

"Do you love her?" TMJ asked.

"I'm not ready for that. It's only been a year since I lost Karen. I don't know. If I am ready to fall in love again, though, it would be with Anna," Luke said.

TMJ got out of the truck to use the bathroom, returning with three more beers out of the cooler.

"Damn near got bit by one of those crabs. I don't know why we didn't bring two coolers, one for the crabs and one for the beer," TMJ said.

"Next time we'll do that," Hank said.

≈

On June 16, Luke and Anna went to Gaffer's to see the female arm-wrestling contest sponsored by WOVV. The year before it was held at SmacNally's, but space was limited, so the venue was changed to Gaffer's, which had more room. The sports bar was jam-packed. The female contestants all wore costumes, but Carm the Arm successfully defended her championship title, despite going against the likes of the Mighty Hermaphrodite and the Black Swan. A few managed to give her a bit of a run, but basically she was the hands-down favorite and undefeated champion. They raised four thousand dollars for the radio station that night.

≈

Luke and Anna got into a routine living with each other in the Franklin house. They started out with separate bedrooms, but before long, they were sleeping in the same bed. Anna liked to cook and the kitchen was nice, so Luke would go to the fish house and buy the catch of the day. They bought fresh vegetables from the vegetable stand beside the bank on Highway 12. They purchased other staples from the Variety Store and the Community Store and settled into a routine of eating at home. Occasionally, they ate out with friends.

"Do you want to join us at Gaffer's tonight? They have a really good band," TMJ asked Luke one day as they were packing up after work.

"No. Anna and I are eating in and planning a quiet night together," Luke said.

"Damn, you are getting to be domestic," TMJ said. "I haven't even seen you two on the beach in a couple of weeks."

"Yeah, it's easier to hang out with one girl than to chase women," Luke said.

"Yeah, but not near as much fun," TMJ said. "Besides you two aren't married. Why don't you get out and have some fun?"

"We are having fun—with each other."

≈

"Do you think we are being too domestic?" Luke asked Anna as he grilled fresh tuna for dinner that night.

"No. I like being with you."

"TMJ said we should go out more."

"And spend money at bars?" she asked. "I'd much rather sit on our front porch and drink a beer or a glass of wine together than go out and spend a lot of money on beer at a bar and not be able to talk over the loud music. If we want to have friends over, we can ask them. If we want music, we know plenty of people who play music who would love to play on our front porch, if we gave them some beer or fed them."

"You're right," Luke said. "I think TMJ misses having a running buddy."

"He has Thelma and Luane, doesn't he?"

"Yeah."

"They should keep him occupied."

"You're right about that," Luke said philosophically.

After they ate, they sat on the front porch, looking west at the changing sky as the sun set over the rooftops in the distance.

"Do you miss going out with TMJ?" Anna asked, taking a sip from a glass of white wine.

"Not one bit," Luke said, drinking a bottled Yuengling. "Remember I was married for five years before Karen died. I don't miss the single life one bit. I am tired of going out to bars and making small talk. I would much rather be on this porch right now, watching the sunset with you."

They both sat in weathered rockers looking across the street. He took Anna's hand. "How about you?"

"I feel at home right here and wouldn't want it any other way."

When it got dark, they drove out to the parking lot at the lifeguard beach and took a blanket and a bottle of wine, walked over the dunes, and lay on the blanket looking up at the stars. It was a clear night, the last Saturday in June, and the moon was just a sliver in the sky. The stars were bright and plentiful. The Milky Way was a smudge of stars above them.

"I love you, Luke," Anna said.

Luke was silent. He loved Anna, but it was hard for him to say it. Finally, he said, "I love *you*, Anna." He rolled over and kissed her.

"I don't think I ever want anyone but you," Anna said.

"I don't want anyone but you either," Luke said. Thoughts of Karen flooded him. Could he let go? Was it time? Was it too soon? But he knew that once Anna declared her love for him, he had to declare his love for her. If he didn't, it would hurt her feelings, and he may lose her. It may be too soon, but he knew that he loved her.

Luke stood up and took Anna's hand and walked toward the water, which was still cool in June but pleasant. He waved his hand in the water, and it sparkled with bioluminescence.

"It is like stardust in the water," Anna said.

"I love it," Luke said simply. They continued to walk down the dark beach for a while. Where they stepped, the same pale green light lit their footsteps in the wet sand. They kissed again.

"It is getting late. Do you want go back to the house?" Anna asked.

"Sure," Luke said, his passion stirring.

When they got home, they made love well into the night. The next morning Luke woke up naked on top of the covers. Their clothes littered the floor. Anna slept naked under the covers, her breasts moved gently up and down with her breathing. He kissed her on the forehead, then he got out of bed and got dressed for work.

≈

The next weekend was the start of the Fourth of July holiday, since the actual Fourth was on a Monday. The Fourth was the biggest holiday on Ocracoke with the annual parade in the afternoon and a dance at the community square that night. As with last year, there would be no fireworks this year due to worries about fire. In fact, there was a stubborn forest fire on the mainland in Dare and Hyde counties that had gotten into the peat underground. Without any rain, the fire continued for weeks. When the wind was right, it blew the smoke over Ocracoke, causing a haze and a smoky smell in the air.

≈

Tony Franklin brought his girlfriend, Tammy, from Chapel Hill to the village for a long weekend over the Fourth. Tony was tall and lanky, in his early sixties with longish gray hair and a deep tan. When he arrived, he was wearing a white Ocracoke Volunteer Fireman's T-shirt and frayed khaki shorts. He had recently divorced his wife of twenty-eight years. They had two grown children. Tammy looked to be in her late twenties or early thirties. She wore tight, bright yellow shorts, and a Kelly-green halter-top, tied in the back in a bow. She had blonde hair with dark roots pulled back in a ponytail and always seemed to have gum in her mouth. She wore a lot of eye makeup and had a good tan.

Tony Franklin loved to throw a big outdoor party on the Fourth of

July for parade watchers. He made Bloody Marys, orange blossoms, and served wine and beer. The yard filled with people who brought their own chairs.

Tammy brought a surprise for Anna. As they were unloading the car, Tammy pulled out a small animal carrier.

"Tony told me that you loved animals. My neighbor's cat just had kittens, so I thought I would bring these cute little babies to you." Tammy opened the cat carrier and pulled out a solid black kitten and a black-and-white-tuxedo kitten. "They are brothers."

Anna was taken aback. Yes, she loved animals. She loved the birds in the park and the turtles on the beach, but cats? That was a commitment. Luke wondered how Anna would react.

Tammy handed the kittens to Anna who, from the way her face lit up, instantly fell in love. Tammy smiled sweetly as she watched Anna and the kittens. "See, I told you Anna would love them," Tammy said to Tony, who raised his eyebrows but said nothing.

"I don't know what to say!" Anna said. "Thank you. They are adorable." She rubbed the two kittens in her hand. They were very squirmy and wanted to be let down. She took them into the house and let them run loose.

Luke rolled his eyes, and after Tammy disappeared into the middle bedroom with her luggage, he said. "Another mouth to feed."

"Two mouths," Anna corrected him.

Luke wasn't sure how he felt about the new additions to their household. He had grown up around dogs. Karen had been allergic to dogs and cats, so they had never even considered pets.

～

The Fourth of July parade had floats made by local people, tourists, and anyone who signed up the day of the parade. People rode golf carts and bicycles. They rode in the back of pickup trucks, in antique cars, on horses, and on elaborate floats towed by trucks or cars. Some people just dressed up and walked down the road. It started on Highway 12 in front of the Variety Store, turned at Lighthouse Road, turned right at Albert Styron's Store, right again at Silver Lake Drive then reconnected with Highway 12 until it ended in the Park Service parking lot at the ferry terminal. It was a hot, humid, and sunny day, typical of that time of year. The parade watchers, who gathered in the yard of the Franklin house, enjoyed the cold drinks that flowed freely.

After the party, Luke and Anna fixed a nice dinner of grilled blue fish, corn on the cob, and squash casserole for Tony and Tammy. Anna also made a wonderful Ocracoke fig cake. Luke baked bread with parmesan cheese and black olives.

After they finished supper, they sat on the screened porch drinking red wine, then rode bikes to the community square where Lou Castro performed with the Aaron Caswell Band. The party continued well past midnight with people dancing, talking, and drinking. They saw Thelma, Luane, TMJ, and all their friends. Tony and Tammy turned out to be quite the dancers, growing wilder the more they drank. They stayed much longer at the party than Luke and Anna. They stumbled into the house in the wee hours, banging the screen door, bumping against the furniture, giggling, fixing more drinks in the kitchen. After they went into their room, Luke heard the metal headboard banging against the wall.

Luke had the next day off and slept in. Tony and Tammy woke up about nine and invited Anna and Luke to join them at the Pony Island Restaurant for breakfast. Tony and Tammy were pretty subdued at breakfast, but Tammy would break into a giggle every once in a while for no apparent reason. It was apparent that she was playing footsie with Tony under the table. Anna and Luke tried to ignore it and just kept the conversation rolling. Tony and Tammy left the next day, leaving the cats with Anna and Luke.

⌒ CHAPTER TWENTY-THREE ⌒

The kittens were wild, playing with each other, ignoring Luke and Anna until they were played out. At that point, the kittens crashed in Anna's lap. Luke had gone to the store and bought all the cat paraphernalia: dried kitten food, water bowl, cat litter, and litter pan. Anna put a saucer of milk out occasionally, which the kittens loved.

"Don't we need to get them neutered?" Luke asked.

"We need to wait until they are older. They are too young now," Anna said. "We can wait and have it done when the free clinic comes to town in the fall."

"That's good," Luke said, picking up the black-and-white kitten. It began to purr in his hand. "I've never had cats. Have you decided what to name them?"

"Yes, how about Midnight for the black one and Trouble for the black-and-white one? He is the one that is always getting into mischief."

"Sounds good," he said. "Maybe they'll grow on me."

"We always had cats. We had dogs, too. I love them all," Anna said, picking up Midnight, holding him up in the air and then cuddling him to her chest.

"They sure are wild when they play with each other," Luke said.

"Yeah, but when they conk out, they are so cute," Anna said.

"At least they entertain themselves, and we don't have to walk them. They aren't as high maintenance as dogs," Luke said.

"Yeah, we just leave them in the house when we're gone. They entertain themselves," Anna said. "I don't want to let them outside until they get more used to us, but, eventually, they will be inside and outside cats."

"I would like to get a dog sometime," Luke said.

"That would be fine with me. I love dogs," Anna said.

"Do you think the cats and a dog would get along?"

"Sure, they get used to each other. If you start them off young, they learn to love each other and play together."

"Cool," Luke said.

≈

"We're having a big party on the beach this Saturday," TMJ said, the next day at work. "Why don't you and Anna come? You'll enjoy it."

"I'll ask Anna," Luke said. "I don't see why not."

Anna said sure, and on Saturday they joined TMJ and their other friends for a day on the beach—surfing, swimming, parasailing, drinking, and eating.

TMJ sat naked in his beach chair as usual. Thelma sat on one side of him and Luane on the other. Several guys surfed the crystal-clear waves. Two guys had kite boards and soared over the waves as the wind picked up their brightly colored kites. One of the surfers decided to do it naked, much to the amusement of the women on the beach. Luke and Anna kept their clothes on until they went into the water, then Luke pulled his bathing suit down to moon TMJ on the beach.

≈

The next day Anna got a call from her father, a high-school math teacher from Ohio. He wanted to come see her. He had never been to

Ocracoke and wondered if he could come stay for a few days. She wanted him to meet Luke.

"I can take him out on the beach patrol with me in the mornings and show him around. I hope you like him," she said to Luke. Anna's mother died of breast cancer in 2006, and she had one younger brother. Anna and her father were close, and she was excited that he wanted to come see her in her new home.

Richard Thomas drove from his home in rural southern Ohio, arriving mid-week. He was a short, slender man in his early fifties with a tan and full head of salt-and-pepper hair. He loved the outdoors, as did his daughter and son.

"Good to meet you," he said, getting out of the car and shaking Luke's hand.

"Nice to meet you, Mr. Thomas," Luke said, smiling, a little wary. He had not have a good experience with Karen's father and wasn't sure what to expect from Anna's.

"Anna has told me so many nice things about you, Luke. I look forward to getting to know you better," Richard said. Luke helped him unload the car and take his luggage in the house. They gave him the middle bedroom.

That night during a dinner of steamed shrimp, Anna said to her father, "I want to show you where I work."

"That would be great."

"I get up early—five o'clock—to make my rounds on the beach," Anna warned.

"I can handle that, but I don't want to be a burden to you or get in the way. I can take care of myself. I don't want you to feel like you have to entertain me," Richard said, reaching for another slice of bread Luke had made.

"It isn't a problem." She had gotten permission from her supervisor for her father to accompany her on the beach patrol.

Luke said, "One thing I thought you would enjoy is going clamming."

"I would love that!" Mr. Thomas said. "But I know you are working. I don't want to take you away from that."

"That won't be a problem. We usually get off work about three in the afternoon. We can go after work one day."

"As long as I don't interfere with your daily schedule."

"No problem." Luke liked Mr. Thomas. He seemed to be accepting of Luke, not judgmental like Karen's father had been. Mr. Thomas was a very nice man who truly loved his daughter. He was obviously not concerned with external appearances and status.

The next day, Anna took her father on her rounds on the beach, and he loved it. She showed him the bird nests and the turtle nests that had just been roped off.

That evening as they all sat on the porch watching the sun set, Mr. Thomas said, "What I wouldn't give to be able to work outdoors like you do. I envy you, Anna. Your mother would be so proud." Luke looked over at Mr. Thomas and saw the glint of tears in his eyes.

Anna hugged her father and said, "I miss her so much. So many times I want to pick up the phone and call her, then I stop myself. She isn't there anymore."

"I miss her too, honey. Not a day goes by that I don't think of her. We were together for twenty-five years," he said, pulling a handkerchief from his pocket and dabbing at his eyes. "She was so brave. You remind me so much of her."

≈

The next day, after work, Luke took Mr. Thomas clamming. Anna was busy and decided it would be nice for her father and Luke to have some time together by themselves.

They drove down the south point road and turned down the side road that led to the sound. They took clam rakes; round laundry baskets, for the clams, with floats attached; and long ropes to tie around their waists as they walked through the shallow sound water, digging clams.

"I see why you enjoy living here," Mr. Thomas said, plucking a clam out of his rake and putting it in the laundry basket.

"I love it," Luke said.

"How long have you lived here?"

"For a little over a year."

"Where did you live before?"

"I was a carpenter in Kannapolis, near Charlotte. My wife was killed in an automobile accident, and I wanted to live in another place, make a fresh start," Luke said.

"It takes a long time to move beyond a loss like that. As you know, I lost my wife to cancer five years ago. I have been very lonely without her. I still miss her very much," Mr. Thomas said, pulling his rake through the sand under the water.

"I miss Karen. I don't think you ever really get over it."

"I know," Mr. Thomas said. "But you and Anna seem to like each other."

"Yes, sir."

"She is a wonderful person. I hope that you treat her well. I would hate to see her hurt," Mr. Thomas said, snagging another clam and putting it in the floating basket.

"I never want to hurt her or anyone for that matter, but, yes, I care very much for Anna."

"I have a close friend who lost his wife of twenty-five years to cancer, and he found someone else within a year. They are very happy together. In fact, I find that is the case more often than not, when a spouse dies, the survivor often finds someone else right away. They can't be without someone," Mr. Thomas said.

The men were silent for a while. Then Mr. Thomas asked, "How long were you and your wife married?"

"Four and a half years," Luke said, then hesitated. "Mr. Thomas, with all due respect, could we change the subject? This is still hard for me."

"Certainly, son, I'm sorry if I hit a nerve."

"It is not that you hit a nerve. It's still so close, that's all."

"I understand," he said.

After a few moments, Mr. Thomas changed the subject. "By the way, how many clams do you usually find on a day like this. Is there a limit?"

"One time, I was out here and collected three hundred clams. The limit is one five-gallon bucket per person unless you have a commercial license."

Their conversation had made Luke uncomfortable. He was truly falling in love with Anna, but he still wasn't ready to let go of Karen. He was confused. The closer he got to Anna, the more he didn't want to lose her. He didn't want to hurt her, either. Still, he couldn't let go of Karen. Karen was the love of his life. He had loved her since high school. She had been his whole life. How could he find someone to replace her? He felt guilty falling in love with someone else so soon after he lost Karen.

When they got back, Luke and Anna fixed dinner for her father: Frogmore stew with unpeeled shrimp, clams, smoked sausage, corn on the cob, red potatoes, and Old Bay seasoning. They drank beer with the stew.

"A perfect meal to finish off a perfect day," Mr. Thomas said.

Mr. Thomas stayed for a few more days. One night, they had dinner with Hank and Cora. Anna and Luke continued to show Anna's father the sights: Springer's Point nature preserve, the lighthouse, the Ocracoke Preservation Museum. One day they rode a boat over to Portsmouth Island to see the deserted village and the newly restored Coast Guard station with exhibits of lifeboats and the old life-saving service.

As he was preparing to leave Thursday morning, Richard Thomas kissed Anna and gave her a big hug.

"Oh, I forgot something. I'll be right back," Anna said, and she ran upstairs.

"I enjoyed meeting you, Luke," Mr. Thomas said, while Anna was out of the room. "I wish you well and hope that you resolve the issues you are struggling with. I truly understand. I only ask that you don't hurt my daughter in the process."

"Thank you, sir. I love your daughter and promise to be honest with her and not to hurt her."

"That is all I ask," he said as Anna came downstairs with a wrapped present.

"I wanted to give you this to take back home to remember us by," she said. He opened it, and it was a beautiful handmade wooden bowl from the Village Craftsman.

≈

The bachelor auction to benefit the radio station was held the latter part of July. Luke was asked to be a contestant but, thinking of Anna, decided to decline. TMJ was asked again and agreed. This year, it was held in the yard beside the Books to Be Red. A large crowd filled the yard, which was shaded by cedars and live oaks. Luke and Anna went to see the auction. The highest price paid was $450 for a good-looking blond local surfer who worked at a restaurant. He ripped off his shirt to show his awesome abs, pectoral muscles, and great tan, then he dropped and did pushups on the stage. This sent the girls into a frenzy and the bidding into the stratosphere. His "date" was surfing lessons on the beach.

TMJ didn't fetch the highest price, but he did inspire a bidding war between Thelma, Luane, and one gay tourist who according to Luane couldn't take his eyes off TMJ's bulge, which showed prominently in his white surfer shorts and no underwear. Thelma eventually outbid the tourist, much to TMJ's relief.

Luke was glad that he had declined to participate.

～Chapter Twenty-Four～

In 2011, there were one hundred and forty-seven turtle nests in the whole Cape Hatteras National Seashore, twenty-nine of them on Ocracoke. In August, the park rangers began to rope them off as the first of the nests began to hatch. This was a busy time for Anna. The rangers monitored the nests, so they knew approximately when the nests would hatch.

Luke enjoyed watching Anna's excitement as she talked about the turtles. She loved to drive the beach in the early morning and spot signs that a nest had "boiled." Then she and other rangers would dig out the nest, gather and count the egg shells, and pick up any unhatched eggs and turtles that had not made it out yet. She would put the turtles in a cooler to be released when it got dark.

It was an August night, and Luke was among a small crowd on the beach, listening to Anna talk about the release of the turtles. He never tired of hearing her at these release events. Anna loved to show the kids the turtles in the cooler and watch them squeal when the turtles were released after the sun went down.

"Is that a real turtle or is it a toy one?" asked one little girl, about five years old in a pink bathing suit, staring at the six half-dollar-sized turtles in the white cooler.

"They are real turtles," Anna said.

"They are so little and so cute," the little girl said. "What are you going to do with them?"

"We are going to let them swim out in the ocean."

"But they're so little, won't they get hurt?"

"They are going to join their brothers and sisters in the water. They go to a special place way out in the ocean called the Sargasso Sea, where there is a lot of seaweed and they can eat and play. They love it there."

"I am happy that they are going to swim out to be with their brothers and sisters," the girl said. "I bet they miss each other."

"Most of their brothers and sisters swam out in the ocean a couple of days ago, but these were left behind because they were too little and couldn't get out of the sand. So tonight we are going to let them go so they can find the others," Anna said. The turtles in the cooler were from two different nests.

"So they were the littlest ones?" the girl asked.

"Yes, these turtles in the cooler were the little ones or the ones that didn't make it out in time to join the others. We are helping them out by letting them go tonight. Otherwise, they could have died buried under the deep sand."

"That would be sad."

"I know," Anna said. "Now say good-bye. The sun is down, and it is time to let them go into the water to swim away."

She and the other park rangers then released the turtles, and the little girl watched them waddle across the sand and into the water.

"Bye-bye!" she waved.

"Bye-bye," Anna said, too. She looked up and smiled at Luke.

≈

August was hot but wonderful. The only negative was when smoke blew over the sound from the mainland forest fires that were still burning in Hyde and Dare counties. There was a steady stream of tourists. Usually tourism was heavy until about the third week in August, when children returned to school and the young families stopped coming. The weather also began to cool down toward the end of the month.

August was also the beginning of the storm season. On August 2, Tropical Storm Emily formed in the Caribbean and headed toward the East Coast, but it ended up being no more than a rain event and did not affect the Outer Banks.

August was a hot, lazy month. TMJ and Luke stayed busy working on the house. They occasionally joined their friends on the beach and went fishing with Tommy and the others. Luke and Anna fixed dinner a lot at the house and went to the beach to see the stars at night.

August was also when the Perseid meteor showers appeared. One night, Anna and Luke walked over the dunes at the lifeguard beach and lay on an old bedspread near the water's edge to watch the stars. Occasionally, a shooting star would race across the sky. The sky was very dark, and there was a new moon.

"Aren't the stars beautiful tonight," Anna said, reaching over to take Luke's hand. He rolled over and kissed her.

"Let's go swimming," he said.

So they took off their clothes and walked into the water.

"I don't like to go out too far into the water at night, sharks and God knows what else are in the water," Luke said.

Anna smiled.

They waded up to their knees and held hands as they walked toward the low waves close to the beach. He pulled her close and kissed her. She waved her hand in the water to stir up the bioluminescence. Soon they were surrounded by a greenish glow, which softly lit their bodies. He ran toward the waves and dove in, disappearing for a moment then reappearing beneath her, lifting her up, and throwing her into the water. Anna screamed and laughed. They then began to splash each other. The bioluminescence was stirred up and lit the water around them. He walked out deeper and body surfed a wave almost to the water's edge.

"I'm not afraid of sharks when the water is clear, and it lights up like this," Anna said, as she waved her hand in the water.

"I guess you are right, as long as you don't go out too deep," he said, running his fingers through her wet hair. After they had finished playing in the water, they walked out, grabbed towels, and dried each other off between kisses. Luke looked around and saw no one on the beach. Dare he ask?

"Do you want to make love out here?" he asked.

"Let's wait until we get home. You never know, someone could come over the dunes at anytime, plus it's sandy," she said.

"I guess you're right. It just seems like the right moment. That's all. It may not be when we get home."

"You're right," she said. He kissed her, and it was decided. They lay back on the bedspread and made love, sand and all, even with the danger of someone seeing them. They made love with the Perseids bursting across the sky.

"See, even the meteors agree that this is the right time," Luke said with a smile.

"I can't argue with that," she said, laying her head against his arm, sated and happy.

≈

On August 21, Tropical Storm Irene was heading toward Hispaniola, Cuba, and Florida and could go either way up the Gulf Coast of Florida or up the Atlantic Coast. By August 23, Irene had become a hurricane, heading right toward the Outer Banks. It was predicted to grow into a category three storm before it hit the coast. Once again it looked like Labor Day would be ruined for the island businesses.

Islanders were expecting an evacuation order pretty soon—first voluntary, than mandatory. Luke and TMJ worked with Hank to secure the job site, putting away or tying down anything that could be swept up by the wind. Luke also secured the Franklin house, while TMJ picked up around the trailer. They could see a steady stream of boats winding through the village as people pulled them out of the water. The larger boats had to be tied down or anchored with extra line. Some owners took their boats to the protected canals in the Oyster Creek subdivision. Others moored their boats at the larger, sturdier Park Service docks. The temperature was in the seventies, and there wasn't a cloud in the sky. Anna went out to check on the turtle nests. Most of them had hatched, but there were a few that hadn't yet. The rangers dug the nests that were near the water and reburied them up close to the dunes. Then they gathered the signs and black plastic and left the nests to nature. There was nothing else they could do.

Luke and Anna took a walk on the beach.

"The temperature is perfect, and the sky is gorgeous," Luke said.

"Yeah, it's when it cools down that you need to worry," Anna said. "As long as it's hot and muggy, there is a high-pressure system that will keep the storm away, but when it cools down, it indicates a low-pressure system, which leaves us vulnerable."

"I guess there is no question that we will stay, right?" Luke asked.

"Yes, unless they say it will truly be a category three when it hits Ocracoke, then I might consider leaving. With a category one or two, I will stay, but anything above that I will leave."

"Well, I am going to do whatever you do. I am not going to leave you here alone."

Hyde County ordered a mandatory evacuation of tourists by 5:00 A.M., Wednesday, August 24. The tourists left in a hurry Wednesday morning, then the island became quiet. The weather was still nice, but the streets were empty. The only people left were islanders who continued to prepare for Irene, getting in boats and boarding up windows. There were several gatherings that night. Anna, Luke, and TMJ dined at Hank and Cora's. It was an early birthday dinner for Luke. His birthday was the 26th, the day before the storm was to hit. They sat down to eat boiled shrimp, coleslaw, baked beans, and Ocracoke fig cake for dessert.

"Happy early birthday, Luke. I don't think any of us will be out Friday night. So this is it, buddy," Hank said, raising a glass of wine to toast Luke.

"Thanks, Hank, and thank you for the wonderful meal, Cora. As usual, you have outdone yourself," Luke said.

The dinner conversation soon swung from birthdays to the storm.

"They say the storm is heading straight toward North Carolina, still a category three," Hank said.

"Should we leave?" Cora asked. "I'm okay with a category one or two, but three?"

"The last time we left we went to Greenville, and it took days before they let us back on the island. Usually, these storms get weaker as they approach land. I say we stay."

"I'll do whatever you say," she said to Hank. "We're in this together."

Then they got a call from their son in Oregon who tried to talk them into leaving the island. They politely told him that they had it under control.

"We have a generator on the island. With Isabel, which was a bigger storm, the generator came on, and when the ferries started running again we had supplies and things were pretty much back to normal within days," Hank paused. "We will be fine, son, but thank you for checking on us."

After he hung up, Hank said, "Hank Junior's been watching the Weather Channel and was scared for us. I told him we are fine. We have been through many storms and will go through many more in the future. We will leave if it gets too bad, but I don't think this one is going to be that bad."

Luke saw what Hank and Cora were going through, trying to decide whether to leave. Once the ferries stop running, if you stayed, you were stuck, so it was hard to make a last-minute decision to leave. That is why Ocracoke was the first to be evacuated. People had to plan ahead.

"Are you sure we should stay?" he asked Anna in the kitchen when he went to get a beer for himself and a glass of wine for Anna.

"Luke, I can't leave. I have the birds and turtle nests to look after. As soon as the storm is over, we will need to check on the turtle nests that remain and salvage what we can. We will be working full-time cleaning up and patrolling the beach. This is when I'm especially needed in the park. I am staying," she said, adamantly, "but you can leave if you want. If I leave the island, I don't know when they will let us back on. I can't wait that long. We'll be fine here."

228

"If you stay, I stay," Luke said. He felt relieved. It was settled. They would stay and ride this out together. At least they would be in good company.

"TMJ, are you going to stay with us or with Luke and Anna?" Hank asked.

"I hadn't really thought about it. I guess I'll go where I am welcome," TMJ said.

"You are welcome to stay with us," Anna said.

"You are also welcome to stay with us," said Cora.

"That is a nice dilemma to be wanted by two households," he said. "Who needs me the most?"

"That would be us," Cora said. "Hank needs someone young and strong to help out around the house in case anything happens."

Hank looked at her real hard.

"What are you looking at me like that for? You are no spring chicken. It always helps to have someone young and strong around here. Anna's got Luke."

"Well, I guess it is settled. I will close up the trailer tomorrow and move my stuff over here for the duration of the storm."

"Thank you, TMJ," Cora said. "Hank would thank you too if he would admit he needs help, but he is too proud, so I will thank you for him."

≈

The next day, Luke and Anna went to the Variety Store and stocked up on nonperishable food, ice, beer, wine, propane gas canisters for the camp stove, canned foods, paper plates and towels, and batteries. Then they spent the rest of the day getting ready for the storm.

Anna called Tony to see if he wanted them to board up the windows, but he said no. The windows were small, and he had never done it before, besides he didn't have the plywood, and it was too late to buy any. Many people in the older part of town did not board up, just businesses with large plate-glass windows and people with houses facing the sound. Because there were no structures on the beach, the main fear for the island was water washing into the village from the sound. "High tide from the sound side," as the locals said.

~

Early Thursday, August 25, a public advisory bulletin for Hyde County was posted on the Internet and in the post office and places of business:

Hurricane Irene is a category 3 hurricane with 115 mph on a direct path to coastal North Carolina. A hurricane watch is in effect for Hyde County and the coast of North Carolina. The potential storm surge for this area is life threatening.

*There is a state of emergency declared for Ocracoke and Hyde County mainland effective 5 a.m., Wednesday, August 24, 2011. There will be a mandatory evacuation for **everyone** in Ocracoke and Hyde County mainland beginning at 5 a.m., Thursday, August 25, 2011.*

A mandatory evacuation is issued when projected storm conditions are predicted to cause the interruption of public safety response, loss of utilities, closure of roads from high winds/water, and threats to the safety of the population in the path of the storm. Mandatory evacuations are issued for your safety. You should leave as quickly as possible. Once gale force winds start, county services are dependent on the weather and not guaranteed. EMS Services on Ocracoke will cease Thursday, August 25, at noon. There will be no reentry stickers issued after noon on Thursday, August 25. The current stickers are valid through 2011.

There are no designated safe shelters on Ocracoke or mainland Hyde County.

During the state of emergency, the North Carolina ferry system will be on a first-come, first-serve basis for all vehicles open to Hatteras, Swan Quarter, and Cedar Island pending road conditions in those receiving counties. At this time, the ferries are running on their regular schedule.

Toll collections are suspended during the evacuation order. **Today is the only consistent day for travel off Ocracoke before winds and inclement weather reach this area. Do not plan on leaving on Friday.**

People with medical needs and unique situations are urged to consider their options. The Ocracoke Health Center and the Engelhard Medical Center will close on Thursday, August 25, at noon. Please pick up your prescriptions from Beach Pharmacy at the Ocracoke Health Center before noon.

A special amendment to the state of emergency has been added that will restrict alcohol sales and firearm possession beginning Thursday, August 25, at midnight until further notice.

NPS has closed the beaches. The National Weather Service has issued a rip current statement. Swells from Hurricane Irene will begin to impact area beaches today. These swells will contribute to a high threat of rip currents along area beaches.

There was a steady stream of people leaving the island by ferry on Thursday, mainly non-resident property owners. Most permanent residents stayed. If it was possible, it was best to leave on one of the Pamlico Sound ferries to Swan Quarter or Cedar Island rather than to get into the long traffic jam on Highway 12 to the north. Hatteras Island did not have a mandatory evacuation until Thursday.

≈

Early Friday morning, Luke rode his bicycle to the ferry terminal to see the last ferries leave for Swan Quarter and Cedar Island. There were some residents, families with young children, and several families who lived in mobile homes and temporary housing. The ambulances left too, once again to protect the equipment.

Wind gusts were already whipping through the village. Luke could see the edge of a huge circular cloud formation in advance of the hurricane. It was overcast and the wind gusted off and on all day. Those who stayed behind made their final preparations.

Luke and Anna ate chicken and vegetables that evening. The fish house was closed. The electricity was still on, but they got all their flashlights and a few kerosene lanterns ready.

"Happy birthday," Anna said.

"Thank you," Luke said. "Not much of a night for a birthday celebration, is it?"

"No, but I love you."

"I love you, too," he said, leaning close for a kiss.

As night fell, the gusts became stronger and more sustained. While the television still worked, it looked like the hurricane was taking direct aim at Cape Lookout to the south of them. The concern was where it would come in over the sound, because if it hit just right, it could blow water from the sound into the village. The worst storm in memory for Ocracoke was the storm of 1944, which blew several feet of water into the village from the sound, flooding houses, tearing up docks and waterside buildings, and washing boats ashore. The last report from the weather station on the radio said the storm had decreased in strength and was expected to be a category one when it came ashore at Cape Lookout. Luke and Anna had a battery-powered radio turned to the weather station. Also WOVV was on the air giving local news and updates about the storm.

When they went to bed, the wind was getting stronger. It was hard to sleep.

"Anna, are you awake?" Luke asked. He glanced at the clock on the nightstand. It was 2:00 in the morning, and the wind was howling in strong gusts.

"Yeah, I can't sleep either."

Luke got up and looked out the windows, making sure the doors and windows were shut tight.

The windows shook, and the screened door on the front porch slammed a few of times, so Luke went out to latch it. He was hit by a strong gust of wind when he opened the front door. Struggling, he slowly pulled the screen door shut and latched it. It was pitch black outside, and the electricity was off. He returned to bed but slept fitfully until daylight.

When they got up, there was no electricity, and the wind was still blowing hard. Luke had filled two coolers with ice before the storm, but they left the food in the refrigerator, careful not to open the door any more than they had to. Most things would stay fresh in the refrigerator for at least a day until the generator could start up. They used the camp stove to fix coffee and ate fruit, yogurt, and juice, trying to eat things out of the refrigerator that would spoil first. The wind sounded terrible outside as it lashed the house in strong gusts, but when Luke looked out, he did not see water rising. They turned on the battery-powered radio and heard the storm was moving slowly over the Pamlico Sound with hurricane force winds all the way inland to Greenville. There wasn't much to do but settle in. There was no going outside or checking the neighbors.

They were stuck.

"Where are the cats?" Anna asked. She thought they were in the house, but could one of them have slipped out last night either before they went to bed or when Luke latched the screen door? That would be just like Trouble. They looked all over the house and found Midnight cowering under a bed, but they could not find Trouble. Anna opened the front door and called for him. The wind drove the rain sideways and swallowed her voice. The sound was terrific.

"I've got to go out and see if I can find him," Anna said. She pulled on a dark blue Helly Hansen rain slicker, rain pants, and her white, shin-high rubber boots. Before Luke knew it, she was outside in the hurricane.

"What the hell?" Luke said. "Anna, get back in here. That cat will be fine."

"I've got to find him." She called "Trouble" over and over again through the wind and blowing rain. Luke pulled on a rain parka and boots and joined her.

"You look in the front and side yard, and I'll look in the backyard," Anna shouted, taking off to check the sheds where Trouble liked to hang out. Luke didn't feel comfortable leaving Anna by herself in the wind and rain but did as she said, struggling against the wind to reach the front of the house.

"Trouble!" he yelled.

There was no sign of the cat in the front so he walked around the side of the house to the rear. He rounded the corner of the house just as a large limb from the big cedar tree dropped and hit Anna on the head.

"Anna!" he screamed as she fell to the ground. He rushed toward her. He pushed the limb away, picked her up, and carried her into the house.

She was unconscious.

Luke tried to revive her.

"Anna, wake up!" he cried, as tears poured from his eyes. Suddenly, he realized how much Anna meant to him and how devastated he would be if anything happened to her. He began to gently shake her.

"Wake up, Anna," he said sobbing.

Slowly, she opened her eyes and said, "Luke?"

He gathered her in his arms and never wanted to let go.

He pulled her rain gear off and carried her to their bedroom. Worried that she might have a concussion, he told her to stay quiet.

Running his fingers through her wet hair, he said, "I love you, Anna. Don't talk, just take it easy. Everything will be alright." There was a goose egg–sized bump on her head. He ran to the kitchen, put ice in a plastic bag, and wrapped a washcloth around it. He hurried back to Anna and gently placed the ice bag on the bump to reduce the swelling.

"Where is Trouble?" she asked.

"I don't know, but I will find him."

When he felt it was okay to leave her alone, Luke went back outside and called for Trouble. Trouble ran onto the back porch, soaking wet. He purred and rubbed Luke's leg, wanting to be let inside. Luke picked up the cat, brought him inside, and closed the door. He dried off the cat and took him to Anna. Her worried expression turned into a big smile as she reached up to take him in her arms.

"Trouble, baby. You are safe." Trouble lay on the bed beside her pillow and stayed with her. Luke also stayed with Anna, talking to her until he felt she was okay, then he let her sleep while he sat in an old wooden chair beside the bed, watching her.

What would he do without Anna? He truly loved her. He knew now that he had to let go of Karen. He had to let Anna know how much he loved her. He was finally ready to let go and let love in once again. He was so blessed to have someone as wonderful as Anna. He didn't need to wait any longer. Anything could happen to either of them. He understood how fortunate he was to have Anna. He realized that now was the time.

The wind howled outside all day and into the night. Anna got up at noon, and they ate sandwiches. They stayed in the living room with the cats close by as they read and listened to the radio.

≈

"Anna, I love you," Luke said, once they had eaten and were settled in the living room with the storm battering the house outside.

"I love you, too, Luke," Anna said, with a gentle smile.

"When that tree limb hit you on the head . . ." he choked up. "Anna, I don't know what I would do without you."

He came to her, crouched by her chair, and held her hand.

"I have already lost one person I loved. I don't think I could stand it if I lost you, too. I am so glad you are not hurt," he said, pushing her bangs off her forehead.

"You have been so patient with me about Karen," he continued. "Karen once told me that if anything happened to her she wanted me to find someone else. I haven't been able to do that until now. Now, I know that you are the one, and I don't ever want to lose you."

"I understand, it is hard to let go of someone you love," she said. "I still have a hard time letting go of my mother, but only time heals and after a while you must move on. You are a wonderful, kind, talented, loving man. You can't let your life stop because you lost her. She wouldn't have wanted that, not if she truly loved you. She would want you to start living your life again. I hope that I can be a part of that."

"You have been so good to me, so kind, patient, and understanding. You are also beautiful, talented, and loving. I am so fortunate to have you," he touched her hair and kissed her.

"I am fortunate to have you, too," she said. "I knew that I would fall in love with you the first time I met you."

"Me, too."

They weathered the storm together. They stayed in the house, read, ate some soup for supper, and went to bed. They were both exhausted, mentally and physically. Despite the incessant wind, they both slept well.

Luke had a dream in which he saw Karen. She was barely a shadow, like a wisp of smoke in a billowing dress. She said, "Be happy, Luke. That is the best way you can remember me." Then she disappeared. He somehow knew that this would be the last time he saw her, but he was not sad. He was happy that she had finally found rest. Maybe her job was done.

$$\approx$$

When they got up on Sunday morning, the wind had died down, and the skies were beginning to clear. Apparently, the northern beaches were hit pretty hard. There was a lot of water in downtown Manteo and in the tri-villages of Salvo, Waves, and Rodanthe. But there was still no "tide" in Ocracoke, no flooding from the sound. Everyone was waiting for it. Luke called Hank and Cora. They had spoken to friends, and although not many had ventured out of their houses, no one reported any significant flooding in the village, which was odd with the storm coming in over the sound. Wind gusts of 110 miles per hour were recorded in the village, but when the storm hit at Cape Lookout, it had reduced to a category one. Since the eye of the storm passed to the west of them, there was never a lull in the storm. It continued unabated all day and well into the night.

Luke picked up Hank and TMJ to drive around the village to see the damage. There was no water in the village. They drove around the harbor. Only limbs were down and garbage cans and debris blown around, but no big trees and no major damage to structures, other than shingles and roofing materials. Even the harbor looked fine. The docks were intact, and no boats were sunk. So they drove down Highway 12 toward the pony pens. At the pony pens, there was standing water in the road, and the parking lot was covered with sand where the ocean had breached the dunes and poured onto the highway. They crept north along the highway in Luke's four-wheel drive. The road was covered with water in places, and the dune was gone at the next parking area. The pavement was not visible.

"I'm worried with the water so deep," Hank said. "Maybe we ought to wait until it drops before we go any further."

When they got back, Cora and Anna wanted to go out and view the damage, too, so they all loaded into Hank's truck and rode around the island. The island had begun to awaken, and people were in their yards cleaning up after the storm and talking to each other.

"We were damn lucky," a man at the fish house said to Hank when they pulled up. "I heard the area north of Avon was hit really hard."

≈

On Sunday, August 28, 2011, the county issued another advisory:

Hurricane Irene is a category one hurricane that made landfall near Cape Lookout Saturday morning. Sustained winds were recorded at 90 mph. There are widespread reports of power outages, downed lines, fallen trees, and impassable roads in Hyde County.

Hyde County officials have announced the beginning of a limited reentry procedure to portions of Hyde County. At this time, utilities, government officials, damage assessment teams, requested resources, essential personnel, and residents with proof of residency are allowed back in Hyde County. There is still no reentry to Ocracoke at this time until ferry service is established.

Power is still reported out for the entire county. We expect outages until service crews can respond, evaluate, and restore safely.

There is a restriction on alcohol sales and firearm possession until further notice.

Airspace over Ocracoke Island is closed until further notice.

The water system will remain fully operational on Ocracoke as weather, electricity, and supply allows.

The Ocracoke Health Center and the Engelhard Medical Center are closed until further notice.

NPS has closed the beaches until further notice.

Mainland Hyde County had sustained considerable damage from wind and high water. Hurricane Irene did a lot of damage to the mainland and the Down East area of Carteret County. The courthouse in Swan Quarter was badly damaged and records were ruined by flooding after Hurricane Isabel, so the county had built a new courthouse and a low dike around Swan Quarter to keep the high water out. During the storm, rumors swirled that the dike had not held, but it had, so Swan Quarter was saved from major flooding during Irene.

With power lines cut to the north, the Ocracoke residents had no idea when regular power would be restored to Ocracoke, so the community generator was turned on. After spending most of the day cleaning up their yards, their houses, the job site, and helping neighbors clean up their property, Luke and TMJ went to Hank and Cora's, where they grilled hotdogs and hamburgers and drank beer.

"What a day," Luke said, taking a drink of his iced-down beer.

"What a weekend," Hank said.

"What a week," Cora said.

"At least, we didn't get the tide that our neighbors to the north got. I heard there was six to eight feet of water running down Highway 12 north of Avon and lots of homes and businesses were flooded," Hank said.

"We also heard that Highway 12 was breached in several places at the S curves in Rodanthe and the Pea Island Wildlife Refuge," Cora said.

They all slept well that night. The clean-up continued for the rest of the week. The generator stayed on all week, since there was still no power from the north.

As news from the north filtered back to them, it was grim. The villages of Salvo, Waves, and Rodanthe had a terrible "tide" of six to eight feet in places. Highway 12 was breached in several places, and the ocean had cut through to the sound just above Rodanthe and in two places in the Pea Island Wildlife Preserve. It would take weeks, if not months, to reopen the highway to the north. An emergency ferry had been set up between Stumpy Point and Hatteras Island to get supplies and emergency vehicles back on the island. It looked like things south of Buxton were in pretty good shape, but north of Avon the flooding was terrible. There had been five to six feet of water in downtown Manteo, which flooded most of the businesses. The waterfront in Duck also sustained a lot of damage. There was terrible damage on the mainland, where tornadoes were spawned and several houses were totally destroyed in Columbia.

The hurricane entered the Outer Banks at Cape Lookout as a category one storm and exited to the Atlantic over southeastern Virginia. From there it made landfall in New Jersey and New York. In all, fifty-six deaths were attributed to the storm and more than $15.6 billion of damage, making it the sixth costliest storm in United States history, only behind Katrina, Ike, Wilma, Andrew, and Ivan.

Anna was busy on the beach, which was littered with debris. The turtle nests that were closest to the water were lost, but most that were up in the dunes survived. She and her co-workers worked hard all week, cleaning up and putting up signs to direct vehicles away from the bird and turtle areas. They retrieved the mile markers that had been washed out on the beach and put them back up. Vera Cruz had disappeared with the rush of water from the ocean into the sound and back out again. A dock that had just been built by Park Service personnel on Portsmouth Island near the beach was completely destroyed. There was lots of debris in the sound—trees and bushes that had been torn from the shore and other debris.

Luke wanted to see the beach. No one was allowed to drive on the beach yet, so he drove to the walkway across from the pony pens. The road was blocked beyond that. The lifeguard-beach parking lot was filled with debris from the storm. People had been taking branches, trees, bushes, and other storm debris there to be ground up and disposed of.

The parking lot at the pony pens was covered by a foot of sand. At the end of the walkway, Luke climbed down the steps to the beach. There was a gap from the last step to the sand, so he had to jump down to the beach, which had been scoured by the storm. The beach was flat and littered with debris. A tree was lying on the beach a few hundred yards from where he stood, as were big pieces of wood and clumps of brown seagrass littered with bits of plastic and other debris. There were mounds of sea foam everywhere. He could see that the waves had eaten into the dunes and breached them in several places.

The waves were big, and the ocean was rough with whitecaps as far as he could see. But the surprise was all the shells that he found. Normally Scotch Bonnets were rare, but today they littered the beach. He went back to the Jeep to get plastic bags, then came back and started picking them up. In an hour, he had picked up about ninety Scotch Bonnets, plus olive shells, conches, welks, helmet conches, starfish, and all sorts of exotic shells that he usually didn't see on the beach. Anna wasn't allowed to pick up shells when she was on duty, so she was thrilled when she got home and found that Luke had gathered so many shells. Anna put them on the rail of the screen porch.

The island generator was running, but residents were asked to use electricity sparingly, since it was designed for limited use only. No one used their air conditioners, and residents were told to turn off lights and appliances not in use. The power fluctuated, going down a few hours and cycling through neighborhoods. Still, it kept refrigerators going and food cold. The Variety Store had its own generators and was kept well stocked by trucks using the Cedar Island and Swan Quarter ferries. With Highway 12 out, the route through Hatteras was impassable. Other businesses and restaurants had generators, as did some residents, so the sound of generators could be heard at night. None of the restaurants were open because only residents were on the island. The restaurants would not open until the tourists were allowed back on the island. The mosquitoes were bad and so were the ants.

The residents worked all week to clean up the island. The north end of Ocracoke lost its dunes, but the ocean had not washed out the highway as it did with Isabel, so when the road was cleared, the way to the Hatteras Island ferry terminal was clear. By Saturday, non-resident property owners were allowed on the island, but there was no access to Hatteras Island through Ocracoke, only through Stumpy Point where a special ferry was run. The island was still under generator power until the first of the week. Tourists would not be allowed on the island until regular power was restored. Regular power was restored on Tuesday, September 7, and tourists were allowed back on the island on September 8, the week after Labor Day.

Close on the heels of Irene came Hurricane Katia, which passed out to sea but stirred up the waves on the beach and washed over the unprotected highway north of the pony pens. After that came Tropical Storm Maria, which again passed to the east of the Outer Banks. Finally, nonresident property owners were allowed back on Hatteras Island. It was reported that the debris piled along the highway north of Avon—a mix of campers, boats, carpet, furniture, and parts of houses—was ten feet tall in places. The tourist season was dead for the Outer Banks. The only way tourists could get to Ocracoke was on the Pamlico Sound ferries. There were no day-trippers from Hatteras Island, as it was devastated and still cut off from the world. Dare Building Supply in Buxton had no way of getting supplies to Ocracoke, so once Hank had used up what building materials were on the construction site, work had to stop on the house. A few of the restaurants reopened when the tourists were allowed back on the island, but there were far fewer tourists than there normally would have been this time of year.

By September 14, everyone was allowed back on Hatteras Island, but the only way they could get there was through Ocracoke. So the island actually began to fill up again. The ferries to Ocracoke were booked for a solid week. The waves were perfect for surfing, churned up by Maria far off shore. The weather was perfect, in the seventies during the day and the sixties at night. By September 22, another tropical storm, Ophelia, was heading up the Atlantic between the east coast and Bermuda.

There was talk about building a bridge over the inlet that the storm had cut across Highway 12 in the Pea Island National Wildlife Preserve. When they first talked about replacing the Bonner Bridge over Oregon Inlet, there had been much discussion about how to do it and lawsuits ensued. Some feared the same issues would arise with the new inlet and reopening Highway 12. However, the feds and the state department of transportation worked out a compromise and agreed to build a "temporary" bridge over the new small inlet on Pea Island, so work began immediately with pre-made bridge trusses put in place and metal sheets brought in for the roadbed. It was too important to the livelihood of the people of Hatteras Island to delay construction, and all parties agreed to the temporary solution. Finally, on October 10, the new bridge opened, in record time, which finally restored access to Hatteras Island along Highway 12 to the rest of the world.

≈

As soon as the bridge opened, Hank decided to take a trip to Home Depot in Kitty Hawk to get some building supplies so he could get back to work as soon as possible. Luke and TMJ rode with him in the pickup truck. Everything looked normal on Hatteras Island until they got to the Food Lion grocery store in Avon. Then they saw debris piled up along the road at regular intervals. Many of the businesses had been flooded, so carpet, refrigerators, appliances, boats, and ruined campers were piled along the road. When they got to the tri-villages, it got really bad. Before they came to Salvo, the first of the three villages, a National Park parking lot was filled with a huge pile of debris, probably fifty to sixty feet high. Once in the villages, it was apparent that the water had risen six to eight feet in places, washing clean through houses, motels, gas stations, gift shops, and grocery stores. Debris was everywhere. They did not see many people.

When they got to the north end of Rodanthe, where the ocean had cut through the highway, several big three-story houses stood surrounded by water, porches sagged, and steps went down to water. Some of them leaned or tilted at odd angles. Certainly, some of them would be condemned or torn down. The devastation was terrible.

Also in the National Park areas between the villages, they could tell the water had risen high and killed the vegetation, which had turned brown. The pine trees were dying. Grassy debris, washed up by the high water, stood halfway up the dunes where the water had washed up eight feet or more. Then they came to the temporary bridge, which was cobbled together with metal sheeting and pre-made trusses and beams. It bridged a narrow new inlet created by Irene. A building teetered on the edge of the inlet about to fall into the water. The water was shallow, but it was an inlet nevertheless and so it fell under the Park Service's new policy to let nature take its course. That meant the service had to keep the inlet open and not fill it in as they had done to the inlet that had been cut just north of Hatteras village just after Hurricane Isabel. So the Park Service bridged the new inlet instead. To the north of that was a lot of dead vegetation, but not as much damage to structures, except in Manteo, where the entire downtown area had been flooded with five to six feet of water.

While in Kitty Hawk, Luke asked Hank to stop at a shopping center. He insisted that Hank and TMJ wander around the mall while he stepped into a jewelry store. When he finally rejoined his friends, he was carrying a small plastic bag. He refused to say what he had bought.

⟨CHAPTER TWENTY-FIVE⟩

A few days later, Luke asked Anna to dinner at the Back Porch Restaurant. This was unusual. Luke was not the eating-out kind of guy. He was frugal with his money and hardly ever spent it on things that were not essential. Anna was pleasantly surprised and accepted his invitation. They had been through a lot in the past several weeks. It would be nice to have a relaxing evening at one of Ocracoke's best restaurants.

Luke dressed in a casual but attractive lightweight linen shirt and khaki shorts. This was dressy for him. Anna wore an Indian printed dress that she had bought at Village Diva and the silver bracelet Luke had given her for Christmas. He ordered a bottle of California chardonnay, and they shared an order of Crab Beignets. Then he ordered the horseradish-encrusted salmon, and she had the Chana Marsala, a vegetarian dish.

"What is the special occasion?" she asked with a sexy smile, after they finished their salad.

Oh, I don't know, we've been through a lot recently, and I just wanted to take you out for a special evening," he said, barely able to contain himself.

"Well, thank you," she said, taking his hand in hers.

"There is one more thing," he said with a big smile. He turned to their server, "Emily, I'm ready." The server handed him a small black box with gold trim. He took the box and dropped to one knee on the floor. The wait staff began to gather nearby.

"Anna Thomas, will you marry me?" he asked, as he opened the black box to reveal a lovely diamond-and-white-gold engagement ring.

Anna was flustered. Her face turned red as the wait staff edged closer with big smiles on their faces. She put her hands to her face. She had sensed that something was special about the night, but she really hadn't expected this.

"Well, of course, I will, you big goofball!" She bent down, took his face in her hands, and kissed him. Then he slid the ring on her finger, and the wait staff broke out in applause. One waiter brought a bottle of champagne.

"This is on the house, compliments of all of us," Emily, the waitress, said. Anna and Luke knew all of the twentysomethings working on the island. They all loved Luke and Anna and wanted to celebrate with them.

After the storm, Luke had decided that when the bridge on Pea Island was finished he would go to Kitty Hawk and buy a ring. He had Karen's ring, but he did not want to give it to Anna. Anna deserved her own ring.

As for how and when they would get married, that was up to Anna. He was ready and would do anything she wanted.

"When do you want to get married?" Anna asked, taking a sip of champagne after they had eaten.

"I don't know. That is up to you," he said. "I can't afford anything real fancy, but I have saved up some money so that we can make it respectable."

≈

When Hank and Cora heard about the engagement, they offered to help with the expenses, as did Anna's father, but the real surprise came from TMJ.

"Luke, I want to pay for your honeymoon," TMJ said.

"What!"

245

"Yes, and I want it to be a nice one, like a cruise to the Caribbean, not just another honeymoon to Myrtle Beach."

"How can you afford that?" Luke asked.

"You remember my little side job," he said with a sparkle in his eye. "Well, I saved that money up. You are the best friend I have ever had, and I want to share it with you."

Luke was blown away. He hugged TMJ and said, "Thank you, man. Thank you so much." He knew the source of this extra income—TMJ's Internet venture—and found some irony in it. He had frowned on TMJ for those activities, and now he was benefiting from them!

"I will need to make the arrangements if you don't mind," TMJ said. "I have miles on my credit card that I need to use. I have already been looking around and found some great deals, so we can surf the Internet together and you can choose which one sounds good to you."

They planned the wedding for the weekend after Thanksgiving. That way Anna's family could come from Ohio, and Luke and Anna could leave on their honeymoon early in December, the date of the best deal TMJ found. They decided to take a seven-day cruise of the Caribbean leaving from Charleston. TMJ arranged the whole package plus hotel rooms in Charleston. They arranged for ocean-view rooms on the Carnival Fantasy and made reservations at the Francis Marion for their stay in Charleston, one night going and two days coming back. Once on the ship, all the food was taken care of. All they needed to pay for was the alcohol. TMJ also gave them money for the extras: off-boat excursions and spending money when they went ashore on the islands.

"How in the world could TMJ afford that?" Anna asked Luke when he told her about his present.

"He saves his money, he doesn't spend it, and he wanted to do something really nice for us," Luke said. He still honored his pledge to TMJ to not tell anyone on Ocracoke about the source of TMJ's funds. Besides, Anna might get upset about it so Luke thought it best not to tell her. He would not lie to Anna if she found out and asked him about it, but he would not bring it up either. He felt he owed that to his friend.

"TMJ, thank you," Anna said, when she next saw TMJ. She gave him a big hug.

"I wanted to do something special for two very special people," TMJ said with a smile. "I consider y'all to be two of my best friends in the whole world. I am just happy that I was able to do it."

"I love you, TMJ. You are the greatest. I don't know how we will ever be able to repay you."

"Just be happy, that is what I want."

"We will do our best," she said with a sincere smile.

≈

As the wedding approached, Luke stayed busy working with Hank. As the economy improved, Hank had more work. They were almost finished with the house on Ocean View Road, but Hank had several remodeling jobs lined up as well as the renovation of a new restaurant. Because he had work scheduled through the winter, he needed Luke's help. TMJ made plans to go to Colorado with Tommy Howard and Sammy Cooper to work on the ski slopes, but Luke planned to stay through the winter on Ocracoke after his honeymoon.

Anna's father and brother came down to join them for Thanksgiving dinner at Hank and Cora's house. Some other friends and family came from Ohio that weekend for the wedding. Luke had no family to come to the wedding. Most of the guests were their new friends from Ocracoke.

Hank and Cora invited the family and out-of-town guests to a dinner at the Ocracoker on the Friday night before the wedding.

"I would like to propose a toast to Luke and Anna," Hank said, raising a glass of red wine at the head of the table. "Here is to my dear friends, Anna and Luke. May they find as much happiness together as my dear wife Cora and I have."

There were several "here, here's," and they all drank.

"I would also like to toast Anna and Luke," Anna's father said. "Luke, welcome to the family. Be good to my daughter, and she will be good to you. May you live a long life together and find much happiness."

"I want to toast my big sister," Anna's brother, Jason, said. "Take good care of her, Luke. I hope you know how lucky you are. She is the greatest, and I want her to find all the happiness in the world. If you are not good to her, I will come back and get you!" Everyone laughed.

After the dinner, TMJ, Tommy Howard, Sammy Cooper, and some of the guys, including Anna's brother, took Luke out to Gaffer's for a bachelor's party. They drank and talked trash then went back to TMJ's trailer.

"You better be good to my sister," Anna's brother, Jason, told Luke. He was pretty drunk.

"Don't you worry. I will be real good to her. If I'm not you have my permission to come back here and beat my ass," Luke said. He had also had right much to drink.

"Okay, it's an agreement. I hope I don't have to take you up on that. I hope that when I see you guys again it will be to see my new niece or nephew." Anna's brother was younger than Anna and single. He had played football in college so he was pretty bulked up, not someone you would trifle with. He and TMJ bonded right away. They were both cutups and enjoyed each other's company.

Anna went out with Thelma Garrish, Luane Dobbins, and some of her girlfriends that night as well. They drank and exchanged gifts.

≈

On the Saturday after Thanksgiving, at 5:00, they all met on the beach at the end of the wooden walk across from the pony pens. Everyone was encouraged to go barefoot. The temperature was in the seventies, the sky was cloudless, and the sea was clear and calm. It was a beautiful day for a wedding.

Luke wore an open white shirt, white khaki pants, and no shoes. Anna wore a long white linen dress with a colorful garland of flowers in her hair; she held a bouquet of flowers. She had decided against a veil and a white satin wedding dress. Everyone stood, there were no chairs, as the minister of the Methodist Church presided. One of their friends played the fiddle—happy local folk music—while another friend sang a solo.

Luke and Anna had written their own vows. After the minister said her part, they each pledged their love, their lives, and their fortune to each other in sickness and in health. They each placed rings on the other's fingers, the minister blessed them, and they kissed. Everyone clapped and gathered around to congratulate them. Then Anna threw her bouquet, and Thelma Garrish caught it.

"Better watch out," Luke said to TMJ. "You might be next."

"No way," TMJ said.

As they were getting ready to leave, Anna's brother, Jason, and TMJ—two kindred spirits—took off their clothes and jumped in the ocean, inviting everyone to join them. There were no takers; the water was cold. When they came out, they held big straw hats over their private parts and pranced around showing off for the wedding guests.

Afterwards everyone met under a white tent set up in the front yard of the white clapboard Wahab House on Silver Lake. Little white Christmas lights were strung from the tent ceiling, creating a magical ambiance. There were tables filled with food, wine, and beer. A local band played music, and a dance floor was set up in the grass. Luke and Anna were the first to dance. They cut the cake and shared it with their guests.

"I love you," Luke whispered to Anna during a quiet moment.

"I love you, too," Anna replied, as they kissed.

After the party, they returned to their house and made love. It was hard to sleep with all the excitement of the day. Anna's father and brother stayed with Hank and Cora. Other out-of-town guests stayed in hotels and bed-and-breakfasts on the island. Most of them left on Sunday. Anna's father and brother left on Monday.

Luke and Anna worked the next week, then drove to Charleston on December 8, before leaving for the Carnival cruise.

After spending a night in Charleston they boarded the ship and spent two days at sea—exploring the boat, dining in the restaurants, sitting around the pool, and drinking exotic drinks—before their first port of call, Grand Turk.

At the pool, they met other honeymooners about their age. In particular, they met two couples who invited Luke and Anna to go snorkeling when they got to Grand Turk. They all signed up to snorkel at a coral reef, which was in a maritime national park. They could have gone shopping in Cockburn Town, the capital of Grand Turk, a British overseas territory near the Bahamas, but Luke wanted to explore the natural beauty of the island. They got into port at 7:00 and the boat was to leave at 2:00, so they got an early start.

One honeymooning couple, Tonya and Will, were from northern Virginia. He was a personal trainer and very fit, tanned, and buff. She was a nurse practitioner and was also in good shape. They were both conscious of their bodies and careful about what they ate. Billy and Frances, the other honeymooners, were from East Tennessee and were not as fit as Tonya and Will, but they enjoyed partying and drinking and were a lot of fun to be with. The three couples took a boat to a secluded beach where they could walk into the water, snorkel, and explore the reef. The sand, made from coral, was soft and as white as table salt. Tropical trees came down to the beach. In the distance, limestone cliffs overlooked the little bay where they landed. There were several other couples as well as guides, but Luke and Anna stayed close to their new friends.

The water was crystal clear and very blue. Swimming in it was almost like floating in the air. Anna and Luke could see the reef very well. Anna, especially, was delighted to swim so close to the turtles and fish that they could practically touch them. On the sandy bottom, they saw colorful corals, conks, and starfish.

The couples' swimsuits seemed to fit their personalities, from Will's tight knee-length black spandex bathing suit that showed off his fit body to Billy's colorful and baggy surfing shorts that came down to his knees. Tonya chose a sporty spandex bathing suit, a two-piece number, while Frances wore a pastel cotton two-piece suit. Luke wore a red nylon surfing bathing suit, and Anna wore a revealing bikini. Luke saw Will admiring Anna in the boat on the way to the beach, and Tonya gave Luke several suggestive glances.

"You guys must work out," Will said.

"Naw, I just do construction work," Luke said.

"On Ocracoke, there are no gyms, but being outdoors all the time—

swimming, boating, walking, and eating fresh seafood helps," Anna said. "I also try to run four miles a day."

"I would have thought you guys worked out in a gym on a regular basis," Will said. "I am impressed."

"You must work out," Billy said, admiring Will's weightlifter's body. Billy was soft in the stomach and did not have a tan. He and Frances were pink from the sun even though they had slathered sunscreen all over themselves before going into the water. When Will and Tonya put on sunscreen, it was more like they were oiling up to show off for a competition. Luke and Anna had tans, but it had mostly faded from the summer. Tonya almost looked like a female bodybuilder. Both Tonya and Will had dark tans.

"You must have gotten that tan before you came on the cruise. You haven't had enough time to get a tan that good," Billy said to Will.

"Oh, yeah, we both worked on our tan before the cruise in the tanning salon connected with the gym where I work," Will said, flexing his arms as he put one around Tonya.

"I tan year-round," Tonya said. "It is addictive." Her skin looked dark and was beginning to show signs of premature aging.

After they snorkeled for a couple of hours, their guides prepared lunch for them on the beach: fruit, sandwiches, and chips. They had to pay for the Coronas, but it was hot and beer seemed the right thing.

"When I get back to the boat, I think I'm going to take a nap," Billy said, taking a sip from his second beer.

"That sounds like a great idea. Time for some hanky-panky, right?" Will said, looking at Tonya.

Luke and Anna laughed. They would probably do the same thing. They were on vacation, no schedule, why not?

"Hey, man, let's get together tonight for dinner and eat by the pool. I hear they have a reggae band and are having a big seafood buffet," Billy said.

"Sounds like a good idea," Will said.

"What time?" Luke asked.

"Seven o' clock?" Will suggested.

"Sure," Billy said, and Luke and Anna looked at each other and nodded their heads in agreement.

They left the beach at one o'clock and rode to the cruise ship. The snorkeling, the sun, and the beer made Luke and Anna drowsy, so they spent the afternoon napping and making love.

As they were dressing for dinner, Luke said, "Did you see the way Will was looking at you in the boat?"

"I sure did," Anna said. "I felt like he was undressing me with his eyes. He stared, and when my eyes met his, he just kept staring." She walked up and placed a hand on Luke's chest. "I also saw how Tonya was giving you the eye."

"Weird. I wonder if they knew what the other one was doing?"

"I don't know. They are on their honeymoon after all. Tonya said they have lived together for several years and finally decided to get married, something about Will and her health insurance."

≈

That night the three couples met by the pool. There were tiki lanterns around the deck and fake palm trees. The buffet was a big spread of Alaskan crab legs, lobster tails, shrimp, fish, and seafood kabobs as well as lots of vegetables and fruit. Fruit drinks and punches were on special that night as were Coronas and Jamaican beer.

The band was good. The Jamaican musicians wore their hair in dreadlocks and were dressed in multicolored island-style shirts and khaki pants.

After they had eaten and drunk a few drinks, Will asked Anna to dance. Luke watched as Will held Anna close and whispered into her ear.

"Want to dance?" Tonya asked Luke.

"Sure," Luke said. Tonya in her wrap-around dress and a low revealing tank top with no bra was a suggestive dancer. She rubbed her leg into his crotch and ran her hands all over his body. She looked to see if Will was watching.

After they danced, Luke went to the bar to get a drink and Anna followed him.

"Do you know what Will said to me?" Anna said.

"No. I noticed he was all over you."

"He told me that he and Tonya are really into sex and like to do it with other couples."

"What!" Luke said. He had seen the flirting but hadn't expected this. "What did you say?"

"I just laughed and didn't say anything. What was I supposed to say?" she said.

"They creep me out," Luke said.

"Me, too," Anna said, taking the drink Luke had just bought her.

When they got back to the table, Tonya pulled her chair close to Luke. Anna stood up to go to the bathroom, and Tonya put her hand on Luke's thigh under the table. Will was dancing with Frances while Billy ordered more drinks.

"Luke, you are hot," Tonya said, squeezing his thigh hard with her hand.

"Tonya, I am really not . . ." then she grabbed his crotch and squeezed.

"I'd like to see what you're packing, big boy," Tonya said then with a quick flick of her tongue, she licked his cheek just as Billy walked up with two drinks. Luke didn't know if Billy saw that or not. He took Tonya's hand off of his crotch. Frances and Will returned from the dance floor, and Luke stood up to help Frances with her chair.

The band started up again, just as Anna came back from the bathroom. Tonya quickly stood up, grabbed Luke's hand, and pulled him onto the dance floor.

Once more she pushed her leg between his legs, massaging his crotch with her thigh, then she put her mouth to his ear.

"Luke, Will and I have been admiring you and Anna since we first met. Will is into men *and* women, and so am I. We want ya'll to join us in our room after the band shuts down. We have a lot of experience at this, and I guarantee you, you will not be disappointed. How about it?" she asked, as she turned his back to the table where Anna and Will sat, once again going for his crotch.

"No, thanks, Tonya. Anna and I are into each other, not anyone else," Luke said, knocking her hand away from his crotch and pulling away from her. He walked off the dance floor.

At their table, he took Anna's hand and said, "Let's go."

"Okay," Anna said, looking up, puzzled.

Luke smiled at the others. "Sorry, folks. Time for bed. I'm tired."

"Don't leave so soon," Billy said.

"Thank you, man, but it is past my bedtime," Luke said. "Have a great evening."

"Bye guys, we enjoyed it," Anna said, waving as Luke dragged her away.

"What was that about?" Anna said.

"I'll tell you in the room."

≈

When they got back to their room, Luke told Anna everything that Tonya had done and said.

"Oooh, that is creepy. I thought something was going on. I bet Will would have asked me if I had given him half a chance. And they are on their honeymoon!" Anna said.

"I know. I sure am glad that you and I are old-fashioned," Luke said.

"What do we do if we run into them again?" Anna said.

"Be nice, I guess, but I don't want to go to their room!"

"I like Billy and Frances."

"Me, too. I don't see any problem with hanging out, as long as we don't take them up on their offer."

Anna and Luke went to bed. Anna fell asleep quickly, but Luke did not sleep well. He couldn't get Tonya's proposition out of his mind. It really disturbed him. He came here to enjoy his time with Anna, then this happened. It added a sour note to what was otherwise a beautiful vacation.

The next day they came into port at Half Moon Cay in the Bahamas. This was a private island with no town, just a beach and time to swim, snorkel, and ride horses. They ate on the beach and had tropical fruit drinks. They did not see Will and Tonya or Billy and Frances. Of course, there were more than two thousand guests on the boat and over nine hundred employees, so it was easy to miss someone.

That night, Luke ran into Billy at the bar by the pool before dinner.

"Luke, buddy, you won't believe what Frances and I did after y'all left. We were so exhausted that we didn't even go to the beach this morning. I was too tired and . . ." he paused, "too sore," he said, with a big grin.

Luke was afraid of what Billy was going to tell him.

Billy dropped his voice to a whisper.

"After y'all left, Tonya and Will asked us up to their room for a drink," Billy began. "Well, we sat down in their stateroom, and Tonya poured us some whiskey on the rocks. Then she said she was hot, so she took off her skirt and her top. Man, does she have nice boobs and an all-over tan. Then, she smiled a big old smile and said, 'Don't ya'll want to get more comfortable?' With that Will took off his shirt and shorts down to a black thong. I didn't want to appear unfriendly so I took off my shirt and shorts down to my boxers.

"'Honey, at least you can take off your blouse,' I told Frances when she objected. I didn't want to make Will and Tonya feel uncomfortable. So Frances stripped down to her underwear," Billy continued, breathlessly.

Luke did not say a word. He just listened. He wished Anna were there to hear this.

"Then Tonya sat in Will's lap and pulled down his thong and started to do him right there in front of us. Frances looked at me, and I looked at her. 'Don't you want to join in the fun?' Tonya asked me. So I sat down in front of Frances and pulled down her bra and started to feel her up. Then Tonya kneeled between Will's legs and went down on him. You know, for all Will's muscles, he doesn't have a very big one, must be all those pills he takes for his muscles. Anyway, Tonya then reached for my underwear and pulled them down to my ankles. Now I may not have a great body, but I do have a big Johnson. 'Ooh! Very nice, Billy, you have been holding out on me,' Tonya said, taking me in one hand. Well, before you know it, we were all in the bed doing each other. Will even started to do me, and Tonya did Frances. Tonya got out some sex toys, and we played games and fooled around until sunrise. When we finally finished and went back to our stateroom, we slept all day. I don't know about Tonya and Will, but I bet they slept, too," Billy said, sounding exhausted just telling his tale.

"I didn't see them on the beach today at Half Moon Cay. You must have worn them out, bud," Luke said, putting his hand on Billy's shoulder with a big smile. He couldn't wait to get back to the room and tell Anna.

≈

"You won't believe what Billy just told me at the bar by the pool," Luke said when he got back to the room with a rum punch for Anna. He then proceeded to tell Anna the whole story.

"I guess that is what they had in store for us if we had gone to their room," Anna said.

"I guess so," Luke said, sitting down beside Anna on the bed. "I'm glad that I have you and don't need anyone else to be happy." Luke laughed. "You should have seen Billy. He was like a kid in a candy shop."

"Sounds like he didn't know what hit him," Anna said.

"And what about poor Frances!" Luke laughed and fell back on the bed hugging Anna. "I love you, Anna," Luke said, kissing her.

"I love you, too, Luke." That night they did not go out to eat. They called in room service.

The next port of call was Nassau. This time they got off the boat and went shopping and sightseeing in town. They did not see Billy and Frances or Tonya and Will the entire day.

The shops along Bay Street were expensive. Some were "duty free," but even without the tax, the stuff was pricey, all designer this and designer that. They saw one set of china from Denmark that sold for more than one thousand dollars a plate with serving pieces going for up to twenty thousand dollars. They saw one of the old forts, the parliament building, and the Nassau Pirate Museum. Luke wanted to go in, even though it was geared toward kids, because it talked about Blackbeard who had lived in Nassau before coming to Ocracoke in the early 1700s.

The weather was great, in the seventies during the day and the sixties at night, and the water was still warm. They stopped for lunch at an island place and had a big plantation punch, then went to the straw market where they bought some souvenirs and headed back mid-afternoon to the boat, which left port at five o'clock.

＝

Anna and Luke didn't really want to dress up to eat in the big dining room. They enjoyed the more casual dining at the pasta bar, the pizzeria bar, and the tequila bar. They liked eating poolside.

That night they ate at the Lido Buffet, which gave them the option of eating on the deck or near the pool. They ran into Will and Tonya and Billy and Frances having drinks by the pool. Billy asked them to join them. He looked a lot more confident this time and had his arm around the back of Frances's chair.

"Did y'all enjoy Nassau?" Billy asked.

"Yes, it was nice. The town is pretty but expensive. About the only things we could afford were in the straw market," Luke said.

"There is some fabulous jewelry on Bay Street," Tonya said.

"And really nice china," Frances said.

"We saw all that, but it was too rich for our pocketbooks," Luke said.

"I guess tomorrow is our last full day on the boat," Tonya said.

"Yeah, we plan to take it easy and just mess around the boat," Anna said.

"We do, too," Frances said. "Tonya and I are going to the spa, and Billy and Will are going to get massages and go to the steam room. We're going to the night club to dance, then Tonya and Will asked us to their room later tonight for drinks. Would y'all like to join us?"

Tonya cut Frances a look.

"No, thank you, Frances, we may go dancing, but after that I think we are going to turn in and make it a night," Anna said.

"Anna, why don't you join us tomorrow at the spa, that should be fun?" Frances suggested.

"I'd like that," Anna said. "It isn't often that I get to pamper myself, and it is our last day on the boat." She looked at Luke. "Is that all right with you?"

"Sure, I may join the guys in the fitness center and the steam room."

"We've been getting together with Will and Tonya for the past couple of nights for drinks, and we've really enjoyed it. Haven't we, Billy?" Frances said innocently, not knowing what Luke and Anna knew.

"We sure have," Billy said, looking at Will with a big smile and winking at Tonya.

After they had a drink, they all went to the nightclub and danced to the music of a DJ. After a few dances, Billy and Frances and Tonya and Will left for their stateroom. Luke and Anna danced a few more dances then went back to their room.

"If I didn't know any better, I would say that Billy is liking this swinging thing!" Luke said, as they closed the door to their room.

"It sure does look like it," Anna said. "He has found a new calling."

"Wonder how this new lifestyle will play once they get back to East Tennessee," Luke said.

~

Anna joined the women at the spa the next day, and Luke went to the fitness center and walked on the treadmill and lifted some weights. He had been eating so well on the trip that he needed to work out a little, then he went to the steam room and sauna where he found Billy and Will. He saw firsthand what Billy was talking about regarding the two men's bodies. But they had fun talking sports and stuff. Each to his own, Luke thought. Who was he to judge?

When they landed in Charleston, they said good-bye to their cruise friends; exchanged addresses, phone numbers, and e-mail addresses; and promised to stay in touch. Luke and Anna stayed in Charleston for two nights and enjoyed eating out in some of Charleston's restaurants, seeing the Slave Market, and taking a ghost tour of the city at night. Then they drove back to Ocracoke.

It was cooler in Ocracoke than on the cruise.

~

They had only been back from their honeymoon two days before Anna got a call from Tony Franklin.

"Anna, I heard you guys got married, congratulations! Tammy and I are excited for you," he said. "Tammy and I have been talking, and we have decided to sell the house in Ocracoke. I hardly use it anymore, and Tammy doesn't really like Ocracoke. She likes a beach with a little more going on, like Myrtle Beach. She wants me to find a condo there. Anyway the real-estate market seems to be coming back a little, so I have decided to put the house on the market, but we want to give you and Luke first shot at it."

"Wow, I don't know what to say, Tony," Anna said. "First of all, please give Tammy my love. I love the kittens she gave me. They are such wonderful pets for both of us." She hesitated. "As for the house, you know we can't afford much."

"I talked to a realtor who I trust down there, and she told me to get an appraisal, which I did. It came in at $175,000. That is less than the tax value, but we are willing to sell it to you guys for that price. For you and Luke, I would be willing to finance $150,000 at 3.5 percent for thirty years. You would just need to come up with a down payment of $25,000. The monthly payment for the loan would be less than $700," Tony said. "If you put more down, your payment would be less. Think about it. I know that you two can't afford a lot, but I thought this would be something that you might be able to pull off. It is Christmas, and everybody is busy. I don't plan to put it on the market until after the first of the year. You are the only people who know about it, except my realtor and the appraiser, of course."

"I'll talk to Luke and get back to you, Tony," Anna said. "Thank you for offering it to us first, and thank you for offering to finance it. I don't know how easy it would be get a bank loan these days."

"Not easy at all, especially for first-time homeowners," Tony said.

"Again, thank you and Merry Christmas," Anna said and hung up.

She immediately told Luke.

"You know, I am kind of excited," Luke said. "This is a great opportunity for us. The price is right, and with Tony offering to finance it, we don't have to hassle with a bank. The only issue is the down payment."

"Let me talk to my father," Anna said. "He always told me that when I wanted to settle down and buy a house he would help me out."

"I hate to ask him. Karen's father loaned us the money for the down payment for our house in Kannapolis. When Karen died, it created an uncomfortable situation," Luke explained. He didn't have good memories of that transaction. "I didn't like getting him involved, but it was the only way we could afford a house. I don't know. It is up to you. I would love for us to own our own home. I could set up my workshop in the backyard. We can gradually work on the house, but it is in pretty good shape now. Houses are hard to come by in Ocracoke, especially for folks like us."

"I know," Anna said. "Real-estate prices got crazy around here for a while, but after the economy crashed, they settled down and are pretty reasonable now. They are bound to go up again."

Anna called her father, and he immediately said, yes, he would give her the down payment. He was happy to help her. He wanted her to have a place of her own, and he loved Luke.

"It will be my wedding present to both of you," he said. "I will do the same for Jason when he is ready. That is the least I can do for you all. Are you sure this is the right house for you?"

"Yes, we love it. It is in a good location, just the right size for us, and it has a big lot and an outbuilding that can be a workshop for Luke."

"What if you have children? Is the house big enough?"

"There are three bedrooms, and there is room to add on," she said. "If we outgrow the house, we could sell it and move somewhere else. It is in a good neighborhood and should be a good investment."

"You convinced me," her father said. "Merry Christmas! I am so sorry that I will not be able to join you this Christmas. I just saw y'all at the wedding and Thanksgiving, so I promised my sister that I would be with her this Christmas. She is not in good health, so I want to be there for her. Please know that I love you and will be thinking of you both."

≈

Luke and Anna ate dinner with Cora and Hank on Christmas Eve. TMJ joined them. TMJ was leaving for the ski slopes of Vail, Colorado, after New Year's. The snow was not good in the North Carolina mountains this season, nor was the forecast good for the rest of the winter. Hank still had work, so he needed Luke to stay and help him with a few renovations and small jobs around town.

"I want to propose a toast to Luke and Anna," Hank said, holding up a glass of red wine. "May you live long and happy lives together, and may you be fruitful and multiply." His face was flushed with the red wine, and he was in good spirits.

"Hank, that is their business," Cora said sternly.

"I know that, but an old man can hope, can't he?" he said. "Here's to the newlyweds." They all lifted their glasses. Cora had cooked a glazed ham, sweet-potato casserole, onions, green beans, and homemade rolls. For dessert, she made a red velvet cake with white icing.

"How was your honeymoon?" Hank asked.

"It was great, thanks to TMJ," Luke said, glancing at his friend, then taking a bite of sweet-potato casserole.

"The weather was great, and the islands were beautiful. Thank you, TMJ, again. What a great wedding present," Anna said, taking a sip of water.

"Did you meet any people?" Cora asked, cutting a piece of ham.

Luke and Anna exchanged grins. They hesitated then Anna answered, "We met some nice couples our age and hung around with them some of the time."

"What was that look about?" TMJ asked.

"Well, they wanted to do some things that we weren't too comfortable with," Luke said.

"Were they swingers?" TMJ asked. Luke blushed.

He swallowed a mouth full of sweet potatoes and finally answered, "Yeah, they asked us to join them in their stateroom, and we politely turned them down."

"Damn, I'm going to have to go on one of those cruises," TMJ said. "It sounds like my kind of place."

"Now, TMJ," Cora said, "this is not a subject for the dinner table."

"Maybe not now, but I would like to hear the details later," TMJ said, with a big smile.

"I bet you would," Cora said, with a scowl. Hank didn't say a thing, and Anna kept eating her dinner.

Later at home, Luke and Anna sat around the Christmas tree in their living room: their first one together as a married couple. They talked as they drank a glass of wine before going to bed.

"I can't believe that we are married," Anna said.

"I know, isn't it wonderful?" Luke said, putting his head in her lap as they sat on the sofa.

"Our first Christmas together as a couple," Anna said, running her hand through his hair.

"First of many I hope." He paused. "I love you, Anna." Then he reached up to kiss her.

"I love you, too," she said, kissing him.

≈

It was in the sixties on Christmas Day with cool breezes coming from the ocean. It was a bright, sunny day. They exchanged gifts after breakfast. Anna gave Luke a new power drill that he said he wanted from Ace Hardware in Avon, and Luke gave her a silver-and-pearl necklace from Island Artworks, handmade locally.

They drove out on the beach the next morning. The entire beach was open to driving during the winter; the lifeguard beach was not roped off, nor the area around the campground. They drove up and down the ridges of sand on the beach. In the distance, they saw a vast black patch on the beach. As they got closer, they saw it was a huge flock of black sea birds standing at the water's edge about thirty deep and swimming in the water extending about a quarter mile or so down the beach. There were thousands of them.

"What kind of bird is that?" Luke asked. He figured Anna must know since she knew her birds.

"I think they are cormorants. I've never seen so many on the beach before. I have seen hundreds of them flying in the air, but not like this," Anna said. They drove slowly around the birds, so as not to disturb them.

At one point, they saw what looked like spouts of water just beyond the waves.

"What is that?" Luke asked.

"It may be a whale. They migrate south this time of year," Anna said. Recently, a baby humpback whale had been found beached on the north end of the island. On occasion, they would see seals, and in the marshes, they would spot otters and mink along with the nonnative nutria.

"Stop, I see a Scotch Bonnet," Anna said.

"How can you see a shell from a moving car?" Luke asked, skeptically.

"Easy. I can spot one a few hundred feet away. Their shape is so distinctive. I guess it comes from driving the beach every day working for the Park Service," she said.

He stopped, she got out, and, sure enough, she picked up a perfectly striated Scotch Bonnet.

"I'm impressed," Luke said, examining the flawless brown-and-white shell.

They drove on, and she had him stop a few more times to pick up Scotch Bonnets or conches or whelks, starfish or sand dollars, or just to stop and walk when she saw a large patch of shells. Neither of them had to work that day, so they took their time and enjoyed the sun and the air on the beach. At one time, they saw a pod of dolphins playing just beyond the waves. For miles there were no people or trucks on the beach. They had it all to themselves.

~

The week between Christmas and New Year's, there were parties and gatherings. Luke and Anna went to dinner one night at Hank and Cora's. One night they had TMJ over for dinner. The weather was great. On Friday, December 30, they went to the Sixth Annual Oyster and Shrimp Steam. Hank and Cora were busy volunteering, of course, as they always did. Hank helped cook, and Cora sold desserts. Tables were put up in the parking lot of the fish house, and people ate outdoors.

TMJ, Tommy Howard, and Sammy Cooper were leaving for Colorado in two days, taking two cars.

2012

≈CHAPTER TWENTY-SIX≈

Luke and Anna signed the purchase agreement to buy the house the week between Christmas and New Year's. An attorney, who had a house on Ocracoke but lived in Little Washington, prepared the paperwork and searched the title. He was a friend of Hank's and also knew Tony Franklin, so Tony trusted him to prepare the deed of trust, note, and deed. The lawyer got the title insurance and prepared the purchase contract for Anna and Luke.

Anna's father gave them the money for the down payment the first week in January, and they closed on the 17th of January, taking title to their new home. They signed the closing papers in the realtor's office in Ocracoke. Luke couldn't help but note that the day they closed was the day after the second anniversary of Karen's death.

That January, Luke and Hank worked on remodeling a couple of houses and upfitting a restaurant. In his spare time, Luke worked on getting the shed ready for his workshop. First, he had to clear it out. It was full of old lumber and odds and ends that Tony and the previous owners had left—years of accumulated stuff. Luke kept some of the old wood for future use, stacking it in a smaller outbuilding. He had to do some wiring to bring electricity to the workshop, and he built worktables, peg boards, shelves, and hooks to hold his tools. He brought his tools out of storage, and in a few weeks, he had his workshop all arranged. He decided to use the old wood to make a table, bench, and some stools.

Because the winter was so mild, there were no turtles that were stunned by the cold, so Anna just did her routine patrol of the beach every morning, usually with little action other than monitoring the birds.

While Luke was busy working in his shop, Anna decided to take up quilting. Cora belonged to a group of local women who liked to get together and quilt. She invited Anna to join them. Anna had a good sense of color and found that she really enjoyed it. She researched quilt patterns on the Internet and ordered material online, since the closest fabric stores were in Morehead City and Kitty Hawk.

Ocracoke was quiet during the winter. In January, a local blogger said that tourists ask what the people of Ocracoke do during the winter when the restaurants, shops, and theater are closed and there are no Park Service programs being offered. The blogger noted that there is plenty to do: church socials and bake sales, meetings for nonprofit groups, spaghetti suppers, movie nights, potluck dinners, and poker and bridge nights. Islanders work and go to school and keep busy with all kinds of hobbies: they quilt, write, read, draw, make jewelry, and walk on the beach.

Another pastime in the winter was basketball at the Ocracoke School, which had a new gym. The school also had a little league baseball team in the spring, but there was no place to play ball on Ocracoke, so they had to play on the ballfields in Hatteras, and practice in someone's front yard on Ocracoke.

≈

Luke and Anna went to a high-school basketball game between Ocracoke and Hatteras in late January. The gym was filled with families. Luke noticed Anna eyeing the babies and young children.

"They are so cute, aren't they?" Anna said, watching two toddlers who were playing hide-and-seek under the stands while their mother was trying to find them. She pointed to a young father with a pink baby blanket over his shoulder, holding a baby in one hand and a bottle in the other. He looked to be in his mid-twenties, about Luke's age, with longish blond hair, a goatee, and tattoos on his arms.

"That could be you one day," Anna said.

"Yeah, it could be," he said. Luke had already noticed how good Anna was with kids. He did not have a lot of experience with children, but he loved to play with young children. He loved their energy and curiosity.

～

When they got home that night, he asked Anna, "Do you want to have children?"

"Yes," she said simply.

"I do, too," Luke said.

"Don't you think we should wait?" Anna asked.

"I don't know. Sometimes I think the younger you are, the better parents you are. Young people can keep up with kids and relate to them better."

"With women, it is better to have children when you are in your twenties or early thirties, after that the clock starts ticking," Anna said.

"We have time, but I don't want to wait too long."

There was a pause, then Anna said. "What would you say if I went off birth control?"

"I guess that is your business."

"No, that would be *our* business. If we have children, they will be our children, not just my children. I expect you to be a fully engaged father to our children," she said.

"Well, certainly, I will be. I want to be a father. I want to be a part of their lives. I would never leave you with the responsibility of raising our children. I want to do my fair share."

"Then it is not just my business, is it?"

"No."

"Well, I am back to my original question. What would you say if I went off birth control?"

"I would say, if you are okay with it, I am okay with it."

He couldn't believe they were having this conversation. He couldn't believe what he was saying, but he was being honest. He thought they would wait to have children, but if Anna wanted them now, why not? Karen and he were at the point where they were ready to have children when the accident happened. He was ready then, why not now? He just hadn't realized that Anna was ready, too. She was such an independent woman.

"Are you sure you are okay with it?" he asked. "What about work?"

"That is where we would need to share responsibilities. I want to keep working."

"We certainly need your income with our house payment and other expenses."

"We both have schedules that we could work around, plus there is the Ocracoke day-care center, if we need it," Anna said. "I don't think anyone would be as excited as Hank and Cora if we had children. I think they would treat our children like their grandchildren. Hank said as much at Christmas."

"I know, I think he would understand and be flexible with my schedule," Luke said. "I wouldn't be surprised if Cora would even babysit for us from time to time."

"Well, then it is settled. I will stop taking my birth control pills, and we will see what happens."

"Wow, I can't believe we just made that decision!" Luke said, almost breathless.

"I can't either," Anna said, as she threw her arms around Luke and hugged him. He kissed her long and hard. It would take a few weeks after she went off birth control before she would be fertile. She went to the clinic and connected with a gynecologist in Nags Head who was associated with the Outer Banks Hospital there.

Other than contacting the doctor, they decided to keep their decision to themselves.

On February 1 , Luke cooked a meal for Anna for her birthday, all vegetarian, which she preferred. He also made a fig cake, his first, for her birthday cake.

The weather was unseasonably warm, but there was a cold snap that blew in on February 11. Temperatures got down to near freezing, and the winds rose to thirty-five to forty-five miles per hour. The next morning temperatures were in the twenties. Before that, the winter had been so mild that flowers had started to bloom and people were walking around in shorts and T-shirts, but the cold snap reminded everyone that it was still winter. The cold snap didn't last long, and soon the warm weather came back.

Luke and Anna loved to drive on the beach, but as of the middle of February the Park Service required beach-driving permits that cost $120 for the year or $50 for a week. You had to watch a video at a mobile unit set up behind the Park Service visitor center near the ferry docks. Luke was one of the first to get his beach-driving permit. This was part of a several-year effort by the Audubon Society and the Southern Environmental Law Center to force the Park Service to put rules in place governing off-road vehicle use in the Cape Hatteras National Seashore to protect bird and turtle habitat in the park. Not everyone was happy about it. Folks on Hatteras Island were the most unhappy because of their concerns about its effect on tourism. At the same time, the North Carolina legislature, under new leadership, proposed increasing the ferry toll for the Pamlico Sound ferries and, for the first time, charging a toll to use the Ocracoke-Hatteras ferry. It was seen as a double whammy to tourism on the Outer Banks.

"I knew when the legislature changed in 2010 it would be bad for the Outer Banks. We need Senator Marc Basnight back. He wouldn't put up with this mess," Hank said to Luke one day at work.

"Those damn fools from the Piedmont and the west don't understand the needs of the people of the Outer Banks. Senator Basnight was from Manteo. He looked out for us," Hank continued. "People in Charlotte don't have to pay a toll every time they want to go to work, or to the pharmacy, the doctor, the dentist, or the hardware store, so why should we? They want to charge us $10 each way. Think of the impact on local people and the impact on tourism. The day-trippers who come over from Hatteras during the summer will think twice before paying $20 round-trip just to spend the day on Ocracoke. Then there are the service providers— the supply trucks, UPS trucks, mail trucks, gas tankers, food and beverage trucks, and county employees. They would all have to pay, making it more expensive to do business on the island."

"They just don't understand that we have to take the ferry to get off the island, that we don't have a choice," Luke said.

"They say the ferry service costs money to operate and should 'pay for itself'. Tell me something—does that big new highway around Charlotte 'pay for itself'?" Hank said. "I don't think so. That's why we pay taxes, so we can have good roads and transportation."

≈

Hyde County, the Outer Banks Chamber of Commerce, and the Ocracoke Civic and Business Association hired a lobbyist in Raleigh to defend their interests and work against what they called the ferry tax, but the representatives on the state House transportation and budget committees were from the Piedmont, not from the east.

The leadership of the Democratic legislature had been strong advocates for the Outer Banks, but since the Republicans had taken both the House and Senate for the first time in 150 years in 2010, things had changed. There was new leadership in place, little of it from the east. The governor, a Democrat and an easterner, objected to the new "revenue enhancements" and on February 28 signed an executive order placing a twelve-month moratorium on the new ferry tolls, which took care of the matter, at least temporarily.

"Thank goodness for Governor Perdue," Hank said. "She is about the last Democrat left in Raleigh with any power. She's from New Bern and understands us. Now we've got to get to the legislature and get them to take it out of the budget for good," he paused, then added, "Didn't I see one of those budget committee members was from near where you're from, Concord or Kannapolis?"

"If he is, I don't know him. I am just a little peon. I don't know any big politicos back home," Luke said. "My former father-in-law probably knows him, but I am not about to ask *him* for any favors."

≈

One night, snuggling in bed, Anna asked, "Have you thought about names for a baby?" Her head was on Luke's chest, as they lay in bed. She twirled her fingers in his chest hair.

"If we have a boy, I would like to name him for your father, Richard. I don't have a family name that I would like to use, other than maybe Hank," Luke said, pushing her bangs gently off her forehead.

"I like Richard. I know my father would be honored. But what if we have a girl?" she said.

"Why not name her for your mother?"

"That would be Emily."

"I like the name Emily. I don't think I have ever heard your mother's name before."

"She died when I was twenty, but I can still see her like it was yesterday. It is hard to believe it has been six years. I loved her so much. My father has still not gotten over it. She was a wonderful mother to Jason and me," Anna said.

"Then it will be Emily," Luke said, then paused. "Have you thought about how many children you would like to have—if we are so blessed?"

"I think the right number would be two. I would hate to have just one and she or he would be an only child. Kids need someone to play with their own age. Two is the right thing to do," Anna said.

"I agree, more than one, but no more than two or three," Luke said.

"You never know, we could have one, then have a set of twins. We can't control everything," Anna said.

"It will be fun getting a room ready for the baby," Luke said, smiling.

"We'll need paint, decorations, a baby bed, a car seat, a high chair, toys, and all that," she said.

"But how will we know what color to paint the room?"

"I guess we have to wait, use a neutral color, or have an ultrasound," Anna said.

Luke realized he would need to buy some books about babies and raising children. There was so much to learn.

"It is a lifetime commitment," Anna said. "Once you have a baby, there is no going back."

"I know."

"And it changes your life forever."

"I know that, too."

"Are you still ready to do this?"

"Yes, I am," Luke said with conviction.

"I am, too," Anna said.

As he stroked her arm, Luke imagined their future: raising a baby; watching it grow into a child, a teenager, and a young adult; the agony of childbirth, the joys, the sorrows; the sleepless nights; the inevitable heartbreak; but also the sublime happiness of bringing a life into this world and seeing it grow and develop into a person. It was a perilous journey that they were about to embark upon, filled with uncertainty and many potential pitfalls, but they were both prepared to do it, to take the risk, for the potential reward was so great.

≈

In March, Anna didn't feel quite herself. When she got up in the morning, she threw up. Her stomach was queasy. Certain foods put her off. She had headaches, and she was very tired for no apparent reason. She also urinated frequently, and her breasts were tender. Luke noticed her moods changed quickly, often for little or no reason. Then she missed her period.

"I think I need to go to the clinic and take a pregnancy test," Anna said to Luke one morning. "I could dismiss these other symptoms, but not missing my period."

"Oh my God!" Luke said.

"Don't flip out. Let me go check it out before you get all excited."

Luke drove Anna to the clinic and waited in the lobby. He tried to read an article in *Our State* magazine, but he was too nervous.

Finally, Anna came out, a big smile crept across her face and he knew. He jumped up.

"Well?" he asked.

"I'm pregnant!" she said. He swept her up into his arms.

"I'm so happy," he whispered to her.

"It is too early to celebrate," Anna cautioned. "Things could happen. We could still lose it. I need to go to my gynecologist. The nurse here told me what vitamins I need to take and what diet I need for good prenatal care. There is so much to do."

"I guess I better go to the library and start reading up on all this," Luke said, unable to stop smiling.

"I have to admit that I have been reading about this online already, trying to learn as much as I can." Anna paused. "I don't want to tell anyone yet. Anything could happen. Can you keep it quiet?"

"I will try," Luke said, beaming.

≈

The next night, Hank and Cora asked them over for dinner. Hank offered to pour Luke and Anna a glass of white wine, as always, but Anna turned him down.

"No, thank you, Hank. I think I'll pass tonight," Anna said, following doctor's orders. Hank poured a glass for Luke and Cora, and they sat down to one of Cora's delicious dinners: grilled shrimp and grilled scallops, green beans, salad, and fried okra.

Cora noticed that Anna just picked up the grilled shrimp from the platter, not the scallops. "No scallops tonight?" she asked. "They are great, fresh out of the sound. Frankie Garrish brought them over this morning. He also brought the shrimp."

"No, Cora, I just don't feel like eating scallops tonight, but the shrimp looks great," Anna said.

Halfway through the meal, Anna got up to use the bathroom.

"Is Anna all right?" Cora asked Luke. "She looks kinda pale."

"She's fine. She just hasn't been feeling well lately," Luke said.

"I'm sorry to hear that," Hank said, popping a grilled shrimp into his mouth.

"I'll go check on her," Cora said, getting up and heading for the bathroom.

≈

Luke followed behind Cora. As Cora knocked lightly on the door, she asked, "Anna, honey, are you okay?"

"Sorry, something about the smell of the scallops," Anna said, coming out of the bathroom.

"Honey, you can't hide anything from me. You're pregnant, aren't you?" Cora asked. "Scallops did the same thing to me. I used to love them, but when I was pregnant, I couldn't stand them."

"It's hard to hide anything from you, Cora. Yes, we have been trying since January. I haven't been feeling right, then I missed a period, so I went to the clinic yesterday and took a pregnancy test. It was positive," Anna said. "I think you can appreciate why we didn't say anything. It is still so early."

"I know, honey, but you are like family to us. I have to tell Hank. He'll be so excited."

"Okay," Anna said, and they walked back to the dinner table in the great room.

≈

"Hank, Anna and Luke have something to tell us," Cora said, with a gentle smile. Luke looked at Anna, and she nodded it was okay.

"Hank, I am pregnant," Anna said.

"You are WHAT?" Hank said, barely able to hide his enthusiasm.

"Yes, sir, in January we decided that we were going to try to have a baby. Anna started showing signs of it, so yesterday we went to the clinic and took the test, and it was positive. We are expecting," Luke said, beaming.

"Well, I'll be. I can't believe it. I am so happy for both of you. Luke, you are like a son to me, and, Anna, you are like a daughter. What more can I say. I am profoundly happy for both of you," he said, with tears forming in his eyes.

"Hank, it is still early and things could happen. They want to keep it quiet for now, and we have to respect that," Cora said. "You know, we were the same way."

"I know," Hank said. "But you can't blame me for being happy. It is such a wonderful thing. I am so happy for you all and love you both so much," he said, launching out of his chair and shaking Luke's hand then pulling him into a big hug.

Luke thought, it had been two years since Hank dragged him out of the water of the inlet at the south point and brought him home to Cora. They dried him off, fed him a hot home-cooked meal, and gave him a fresh start and a new life on Ocracoke. Luke felt like a son to them.

Hank whispered in his ear, "You have come a long way, son. I'm proud of you."

<hr/>

On the way home, Anna said, "Now that Hank and Cora know. I guess I need to call my father."

"Yep, I think you do," Luke said simply.

"What great news!" Anna's father said on the phone when they called him. Anna held her phone close to Luke so he could hear.

"We just found out, so it's a little early," Anna said. "But we wanted you to know."

"Thank you. I will try not to tell anyone, but I have to tell your brother, of course, and then there is . . ."

"Dad! Tell Jason, but please hold off on telling the rest of the family. Let's make sure I am going to keep the baby. At this stage there can be complications, as you well know," Anna's mother had a miscarriage before she had Anna.

"Yes, I know, darling. I will try to dampen my enthusiasm at least for a while until we are more certain," he said.

"Dad, I want you to know that Luke and I have talked and decided that, if it is a boy, we want to name him for you, and if it is a girl, we want to name her Emily."

"Darling, darling, sweet child. I don't know what to say." Richard's voice filled with emotion, then there was silence on the line as he obviously tried to regain his composure. "I wish I could kiss you right now. Thank you so much. And thank you, Luke. Are there no family names that you would like to use?"

"No, sir. As you know, I was raised in foster homes and barely knew my mother and never knew my father. Anna and I have decided that this is what we want. You have been like a father to me, and I want to honor you this way just like we want to honor the memory of Anna's mother," Luke said sincerely.

"Well, children, I am deeply touched and honored. Thank you and bless you," Richard said with emotion. Luke and Anna could almost feel his joy.

"Well, you realize we have a big responsibility here," Anna said, after she got off the phone. "You think it is just about us and our child, but it is about a lot more than that. It is about Hank and Cora and my father and my brother and our entire family."

"I know. It is big, really big," Luke said, at a loss for words.

Then the phone rang. It was Jason.

"Big sister, Dad just told me the good news!"

"Dad didn't waste anytime, did he?" Anna said.

"Boy, you all didn't waste any time either. You got right on it, didn't you?" Jason said. "As soon as we left, you got down to business! I'm proud of you both. I guess there are good things to come out of living in a place where there is nothing to do during the winter."

"Jason!" Anna said. "That is enough."

"I am damn proud of you, Anna, and you, too, Luke, you old horn dog."

"Well, I've been called worse. I guess I should consider that a compliment," Luke said with a wry smile.

"Yes, you should," Jason said. "Good luck to you both. You know I love you, sis. I can't wait to see my new niece or nephew. I guess this will be a good excuse for me to visit you guys."

"We will keep you updated on the progress and let you know when we are ready to receive visitors," Anna said.

"Got you, sis. You just let me know. I can paint, hang wallpaper—just let me know how I can help."

"Okay, bro," Luke said.

"I love you both. God bless you and take care of each other, okay?" Jason said.

"We sure will," Luke said.

There was one other person that they needed to tell. Luke had TMJ's cell phone number.

"Anna, I have to tell TMJ," Luke said.

"Won't he tell the world?"

"No, we have this understanding. When we promise not to tell something, we respect that. He does and I do. It is a guy thing, I guess. He is my best friend after all," Luke said sincerely.

"Okay. Call him," Anna said.

TMJ answered the phone in Colorado. "Hey, buddy, what's up?"

"When are you guys coming back?" Luke asked.

"We're leaving in a few weeks. The snow ski season is winding down, but we want to do some traveling on the way back, stop in Las Vegas and New Orleans and take our time. I guess we will be back on Ocracoke toward the end of April," TMJ said.

"I have some good news from Ocracoke," Luke said.

"What's your news?"

"We're going to have a baby," Luke said.

"Damn, you all didn't waste any time, did you? Must be all those quiet winter nights in Ocracoke," TMJ said with a laugh.

"We just found out yesterday, so we aren't telling too many people, just family and close friends like you, so don't say anything to the other guys just yet. It is still early."

"Sure, man. Wow, this really changes things, doesn't it? You're going to be a family man."

"I know. I'm excited."

"You'll make a good dad, Luke, and Anna, a good mom. I wish I could have had parents that were as good as you guys are going to be."

"Thanks, TMJ, we will do our best."

"Hey, tell Anna I said hello and congratulations."

"I will."

"Damn, first comes love, then comes marriage, then comes little Tommy in a baby carriage!" TMJ said.

"Yep, once you make up your mind about something, you might as well get on with it, no reason to put off until tomorrow what you can do today. Life is too short," Luke said.

"You know about that, don't you, bud?" TMJ said sincerely. "Hey listen, I'm proud of you. You've been through a lot and came out with flying colors. I wish you both the best. God bless you and that new baby of yours."

"Thank you, TMJ, that means the world to me coming from you. You are my best buddy, and I will never forget that."

"I guess I'll see you when I see you."

"Yeah, have a good trip home."

~

On the second Sunday in April, Hank and Cora asked Anna and Luke to join them at church for the Easter sunrise service on the beach. It was lovely as the congregation gathered at the lifeguard beach. Everyone was dressed comfortably. There was a gentle breeze and dark clouds in the sky. After lunch, a big downpour drenched the village and flooded the streets. When the rain stopped, Luke decided to ride out to the beach while Anna took a nap. He drove out the south point road as the clouds began to clear. They were still dark, but the sun began to shine through them. Just as he steered out on the beach and headed toward the inlet, a rainbow appeared in the sky. He kept driving down the beach until he came to the place where the inlet met the ocean, stopped his car, and got out to admire the rainbow. The ocean was rough. He looked out over the ocean and up at the sky and saw the sun shining through the dark clouds. The rainbow ran from one end of the beach to the other. It was beautiful and complete, not a partial rainbow.

Then he realized what day it was. This was the same spot where he had stood exactly two years earlier in despair, ready to end his life. Shivers went through his body as he remembered. If it had not been for Hank, he would have ended his life then. Instead he stood today, two years later, happily married and soon to be a father with a life and a wonderful future ahead of him.

Anything could happen in the future. He could lose someone he loved again, there could be complications with the baby, nothing was guaranteed, but he realized that there was hope and joy and that he had been given a second chance. He promised himself that he would use this opportunity and never take it for granted. He was not a religious man, but he thanked God for Anna, Hank, Cora, Richard Thomas, and, yes, even TMJ. He had been so blessed and had so much to be thankful for.